Praise for

Mr
Peacock's
Possessions

'A thrilling story of love and courage, brutality and hope all told
with equal measures of deep humanity, imagination and élan.
Lydia Syson has an amazing gift of bringing history alive through
richness of language, dramatic pace and fabulous visual imagery.
This is better than watching a film!'
Anne Sebba, author of Les Parisiennes

'*Mr Peacock's Possessions* is a wonderful book, full of drama,
courage and aspirations. The language is rich and the
characters so humanely drawn'
Carol Drinkwater, author of The Lost Girl

'With its chorus of vivid voices, Lydia Syson's novel reminds us
why we consumed *The Poisonwood Bible* and *The Underground
Railroad* so avidly, but it has a (literally) breathtaking bravura
and an intensity all of its own'
Michelle Lovric, author of The Book of Human Skin

'This tense, evocative, richly-imagined novel conjures the voices
of a strange time and place, and makes them universal'
Emma Darwin, author of A Secret Alchemy

'Lydia Syson writes very well about the natural world . . . [and] the dark tensions in family life that overwhelm the Peacocks'
Miranda Miller, author of Loving Mephistopheles

'One of those rare novels which keeps you up much later than you'd planned . . . you can't put it down until you discover the truth. *Swallows and Amazons* for grown-ups'
Alex Monroe, author of Two Turtle Doves

'As compelling, mysterious and haunting as the troubled tropical paradise it portrays . . . Syson doesn't just write about the past, she transports us there. A tour de force'
Piers Torday, author of The Death of an Owl

'*The Swiss Family Robinson* meets *Lord of the Flies* in Lydia Syson's superb and engrossing book. This scintillating story evokes an island paradise which descends into a nightmarish hell as *Mr Peacock's Possessions* builds towards a shocking revelation and a thrilling climax'
Wendy Moore, author of The Mesmerist

'What a powerful, rich and fascinating book. Dark historical events are interwoven with the mystery of a missing child on a remote Pacific island in 1879. Highly compelling'
Anna Mazzola, author of The Unseeing

'A gripping yarn with unexpected outcomes . . . Syson writes engagingly and evocatively'
Morning Star

Mr
Peacock's
Possessions

Lydia Syson is the author of three critically acclaimed historical novels for young adults – each drawing on the radical backgrounds of earlier generations of her family – as well as a biography of the notorious eighteenth-century 'Electric Doctor', James Graham. For *Mr Peacock's Possessions*, her adult fiction debut, she took inspiration from the family history of her partner, who was born in New Zealand. Lydia is a Royal Literary Fund Writing Fellow at The Courtauld Institute of Art.

Follow Lydia on Twitter: @LydiaSyson

Mr Peacock's Possessions

Lydia Syson

ZAFFRE

First published in Great Britain in 2018 by
ZAFFRE PUBLISHING
80-81 Wimpole St, London W1G 9RE
www.zaffrebooks.co.uk

A CIP catalogue record for this book is
available from the British Library.

HB ISBN: 978-1-78576-186-7
TPB ISBN: 978-1-78576-488-2

Also available as an ebook

1 3 5 7 9 10 8 6 4 2

Typeset in Adobe Garamond Pro by
Palimpsest Book Production Ltd, Falkirk, Stirlingshire

Printed and bound by Clays Ltd, St Ives Plc

Zaffre Publishing is an imprint of Bonnier Zaffre,
a Bonnier Publishing company
www.bonnierzaffre.co.uk
www.bonnierpublishing.co.uk

To Rufus & Solomon

'This unit of land which fits within the retina of the approaching eye is a token of desire.'

James Hamilton-Paterson,
Seven-Tenths: The Sea and its Thresholds

1

To be sure I am a doubting Thomas. Too much curiosity, too little faith, and that from early days and always. Off-duty, I stand on deck, wave-watching, awash with qualms. I let drift my mind and vex myself alone, afraid to fright my fellows, whispering only to wind and water. All is wind and water here.

I did not choose this path – the path of doubting, that is to say, doubting both myself and higher matters. And now the ocean path we follow here, a path so freely taken, stretches before me unclear, unknown, unproven, and I worry and wonder still if it was wise to take it. What if we find no island, or if there is no master living? Where then will the captain take us? And what if this Yankee has lied to us despite our minister? We have no papers. Proof of nothing. We leapt so fast. Nine days at sea, and we see nothing of our landing place.

My setting-forth desire was like an itch that I must scratch. It made me restless. I could not walk in circles all my days while others winged away. We hear how the world turns, and we want to see its turning with our own eyes. Its riches too. This is natural, says Mr Reverend. We whose fathers have been plucked from us, perhaps we feel most strong the call to venture. But there are calls and callings. I am no Gospel Ploughman, and do not share my brother's thirst for pioneering in that blessed field.

I search again for my voyage-spirit, so strong on parting, so soon sped away. Way beyond our reef, the winds that blew within now skim my words away, quick as quickness, or blow 'em down my throat again, back into hiding. I tell myself it was timely to go, to seek a living beyond the skyline, to better all my family. I tell myself we can never know what is to come. I try to hide my fears – of failing, falling, flailing – but cannot shield all from all.

Because Solomona – holding the rail beside me, knuckle-soft – Solomona sees everything. Older (a little), taller (a little), steadier (always), my brother shake his head. Maybe he sees even into my cauldron-bubbling-mind. All-seeing, all-knowing, you know how it is. Like Him above, or would like to be, I sometimes reckon, before I dam my thinking. When the trader-captain came to our island, asking for men, quick quick – good jobs for good kanakas, working for an Englishman, no big plantation, no guano-gathering – it was not for his strength that Mr Reverend recommend Solomona but for his faith. And other reasons. All psalms, no qualms is my brother, even when grief is greatest. When I think it over more, very possibly, yes, indeed, most probably (I can have no doubt now), Solomona say what he say, despite all things, because he say what he always say, whatever he sees or fails to. Same as ever. Yes, same as ever.

God will provide.

God will provide.

Maybe so. Maybe no. But, I say – to myself alone, you understand, only inside my own head's thinking – faith in the Lord is one matter, faith in men another. Right now, we are here at sea, a handful of Rock fellows ready to work, and days passing bell to bell on this vast vessel. Tar and copra, rope and strangers in our noses, many lands' voices in our ears. Talk I must learn harder to track. Some men call themselves God's Englishmen, but their speech is nothing like the Reverend's. Pig-tailed Celestials (as Yankees call the yellow men), a night-dark fellow whose name is Baltimore, some other Islanders who work with us in the ship's waist: all their words come strange and fast and loud and snaking, and I skip after them, catching two or three and losing four, so I cannot be sure always that I grasp what they may signify. My own words pitch and roll. My English tongue tangles as home twists in me, and a longing for land I had no need to know before.

High and dry we stand on deck on the big palagi ship called *Esperanza*, Auckland-bound, and the two-blooded deckboy from Samoa tell me as he passes, without a smile, that *Esperanza* is a word that signifies hope, in the language of the silver mines. Then on flies my mind, wayfinding without a body, all over and every-where, wandering, wondering. How long will we voyage, in this ever-cooling air, and see no other island? I must try harder to keep faith with Mr Reverend, and Solomona too. These people are good, they tell me. This is no man-stealing ship. No chains. Look how we stand on deck, bound only to God. We will work, and our island master will pay as promised, and we will return with all our bounty, and our families will be raised in all eyes and we will make them proud. I will know a little more of the world and its wisdom. And Solomona's splintered heart will come back whole and healed.

Sunday comes again. Far ahead, clouds gather at the meeting of sea and sky. A brief line, darkening at its base. When I see the moving of another, darker cloud – a cloud of birds – and know that soon I will hear their clacketting calls, this is how I know that Monday Island will also soon be here, and then, like the birds, I will be wide awake indeed.

2

LIZZIE STICKS A KNIFE INTO THE BREAST OF THE nearest mutton-bird: a vicious hiss as a stream of hot oil hits the smouldering log below. It flares up, too high, and she jumps back, shielding her face. It's time to turn the rack, to keep things even, and ward off her mother's chiding. Where's Ada got to, or Billy, come to that? Out of sight and out of hearing. The smokery is built a little distance from the dwelling huts and outhouse, to save them from its powerful odours, and the vegetable gardens, where Ada and Ma were weeding earlier, lie on the other side again, on the flats above the beach. Strong as she is, Lizzie can't shift the weight of sixty spitted chicks on her own, and they will catch if she doesn't. She will have to move the fire instead. So she leans into the heat to spread and shift the embers with the stripped green stick she's using as a poker.

Then Billy's cry puts everything out of mind.

'A sail! A sail! Have you seen?'

She turns instantly, looking out to sea, seeing nothing yet. Billy appears but doesn't stop – and she knows just where he's going.

Abandoning fire and birds without a second thought, Lizzie scrambles down the tree-filled gully after him and up the other side to the higher bluff beyond, the lookout cliff. She moves quickly in her loose tunic, but not as fast as her younger brother, and not as fast as she'd like. At the top first, Billy squints at the ocean, and windmills his arms at her.

'Look!' he shouts. 'Right over there.'

'Where?' A sail is too easy to imagine, never more than when the sky and sea are bright. The sun catches the flat side of a wave at the wrong angle. A crest of foam. A whale's fluke. From far away anything can look like a billow of canvas if you want it hard enough. 'If you're wrong . . . '

'I'm not. Look harder. Look over there.'

Lizzie's brother lines her up behind his back as soon as she reaches him. He'll be catching her up in height before she knows it. His warm brown hair, darkened with fresh sweat, is already at her nostrils. But though his chest is broadening too, a little, she can match him for strength still, and let him know this when she needs to. Which isn't now. Billy pulls Lizzie's arms down around his own shoulders so that her eyes can follow his, and together they trace the line of his arm and pointing finger.

'You must be able to see her now.'

She can.

At last.

Billy pulls away, leaps and prances, as if his energy will speed the ship, but Lizzie resists the urge to join him in his dance. The vessel is a long way off. It's hard to tell its course. This unknown ship could be sailing away from them already, could go on sailing, straight-waked, and never come close, never see them.

'Does Pa know?'

'I don't know. He's not back yet. Nor Albert.'

Lizzie's eyes widen at the thought of Albert, and his joy at this. A vessel on the horizon would please nobody more. Away from Ma and Pa, well away and out of earshot, Albert talks of little else, on and on, relentless speculations, till only Ada can stand to hear him. Billy nods.

'I know. Maybe he'll shut up. If it really comes.'

'What do you think she is?' Lizzie asks, still looking, hope tacking. 'Can you tell?'

'Not yet. Three . . . no, four masts. I think. A windjammer?'

'Never mind. We're wasting time. Quick. Kindling.'

Like a cork from a bottle, Billy's off, sprinting up towards the forest while Lizzie shouts after him: 'Green wood too, remember, and plenty of it!'

The trickles of smoke already rising from the small cluster of huts on the flats and from the nearby smokery are too quickly dispersed, too missable. They need a proper fire, a huge one, a bonfire to darken the clouded autumn sky and roar, a fire that can't be mistaken for anything but a signal. They always keep some heavy fuel here on the bluff, ready and waiting, just in case. If a ship's sighted, they must act quickly, Pa used to warn the children, day after day. But he's said nothing about the fire for months, and the lighter branches are all blown away. There's nothing left here to catch a flame. Once or twice Lizzie's heard Pa remind Ma, quietly, how long it can take for word to spread when a place as remote as this is settled. The whaler that came last year, before they moved this side of the island, the mate who talked of work gangs . . . his ship could have wrecked itself a week later, and their message gone down with all hands. As for the *Good Intent*, which brought the Peacock family here, it's been two years since they waved her off. No hope nor desire of seeing her again.

'I'll run and tell Ma, and Ada!' shouts Lizzie. Her voice trails off, because Billy's out of earshot, and she's talking to herself. Is it too soon, too cruel to raise Ma's fragile hopes? Part of Lizzie wants to hang back, until they are certain this ship will really come, until she's checked with Pa, but she can't risk any delay. An ignorant ship might try to put ashore by chance, if it had to, a ship short of water or meat, a nosy ship, an adventuring ship, but even on this side of the island, landing took skill. Why come close if you could keep yourself well clear of all the rocky islets on this side? Who'd ever guess a family might be here and longing?

Then Lizzie remembers the unturned birds and groans, anticipating ruin – half-charred carcasses; black on one side, bloody on the other – and Ma's silent disappointment, so hard to bear. A scramble back down and up again, as it always goes on this island, into the trees and out the other side. And she finds her mother standing by the smokery, one hand in the small of her back, the other skewering. The birds are perfect.

'Oh, Lizzie,' she says. 'How could you? Running off like that, and telling no one. Lucky for you I noticed.'

'But Billy's seen a ship! He really has! I've seen it too.'

The skewer falls and Mrs Peacock's hands move swiftly to her ever-thickening waist, just for a moment, as if to pass a message to the child inside. Then she's back with the one she birthed fifteen years earlier. 'Then what are you waiting for?' Her voice is sharp and urgent. 'Back up there at once and get the bonfire going. Queenie can help me take these birds off. Ada will go with you – look, here she comes. Where's Billy?'

'Gone for kindling and more wood. But I don't know if Pa and Albert have seen it. They need to know.'

Ma scans the trees that rise at the back of the buildings and climb towards a broken peak, mist-shrouded as many days as not. 'They'll soon see the smoke, with luck, if they've not seen the sail. Depends where they went hunting. Can't wait for 'em though.'

Ada arrives panting.

'What's all the fuss?'

Lizzie stays long enough to have the satisfaction of giving her older sister the news.

'A ship.'

She offers the words like a present, with a faint pop of her lips. Ada closes her eyes for a moment and swallows, swaying slightly. The first visitors since the whalers last winter. The second they've ever had.

'At last.'

Lizzie grabs Ada's upper arms, to hold her still and calm, and then to shake her into action. Unspeakable expectation skips through both pairs of eyes.

'Hurry up girls! And take this to light the fire.' Ma bends, with difficulty, to pull out the thick branch which Lizzie had been slowly feeding into the heart of the smoking fire. 'Tell Billy to bring up the logs Albert cut for seasoning yesterday. For speed. They're good and green.'

'Yes, Ma,' said Lizzie.

'We mustn't count our chickens though.' Cheeks flushed, Mrs Peacock turns back to the mutton-bird racks, but only for a second, and then she's looking again from daughter to daughter. 'We can't imagine . . . It would be foolish. No. Could it really . . . ? Oh, but quickly now, Lizzie! Don't let those embers die.

Get back up there right away. I want to see that bonfire blazing. Blazing, do you hear?'

Lizzie steps back from her mother's heat.

'Ada, you run and get wood too now.' Ma's arms flap her away. 'And send Queenie here. With Gus of course. Quickly now. Go!'

The sisters charge off in opposite directions. Lizzie holds her torch awkwardly away from her, determined not to stumble. Pa and Albert must have seen, she tells herself, what with being higher, and they'll surely be on their way. If they've not seen the sails, they'll soon see the bonfire. She longs to see Pa's face, just at that moment. She aches for this ship to be the one they're all hoping for.

Back on the bluff, Billy takes the glowing log from Lizzie and blows it hot again, then kneels as if he's praying. Through a hollow green stem, he whistles up a flicker from the pile he's made of twigs, dry leaves and broken embers. It falters and retreats a little before the flames take hold. Finally, urged on by both children with all their might, a thick dark column spews angrily from the bonfire and billows into the sky.

They pile on more green branches – and more. Burning leaves take off like fledglings, swirling and dancing above the flames, rising and falling, glowing and dying. Blackened fragments stick to Lizzie's sweaty face as she pokes impatiently at the mass of vegetation, shifting branches here and there to make passageways for the air, then stepping back with outstretched hands when the heat becomes unbearable.

'They've seen us!' shouts Billy, staring out to sea again with red-rimmed eyes, which he wipes with the back of his hand. He blinks a few times to clear his vision. 'Look! She's coming about . . . she surely is.'

He's jumping again, in danger of waving both arms from their sockets. Lizzie's eyes are streaming too. When she squeezes them shut, it's like closing her lids on thorns. She tries to shake away the piercing, forcing herself back into the heat and smoke to heap yet more sticks onto the fire, young ones, leafy ones, mossy ones.

Can't be sure yet.

Billy still might be mistaken. The ship's captain could change his mind and course at any time.

More fire, more smoke. Don't stop. Effort now, reward later. That's her training. She's learned it well.

'Did you see Pa?' Lizzie asks Billy for the second time. 'Are they back?'

'I've not seen him or Albert. I already told you.'

'I do wish Ada would hurry up.'

Ada will be rounding up her smaller sisters, soothing their mother. She'll hardly dare look out to sea for fear of disappointment.

More wood. More smoke.

'Oh, where *are* they?' Lizzie frets. 'Did they say? How long *can* they be?'

Billy doesn't remember either where Pa planned to hunt – just that Ma wanted to smoke and barrel up some meat while the smokery was going.

'If they've struck lucky, they'll still be butchering, and never looking up,' says Billy. 'You know Pa told Albert he had to do it by himself this time? So he'll be watching him. Making sure he doesn't do it wrong.'

'Poor Albert,' says Lizzie. 'How he does provoke Pa.'

She swings on another log. Smouldering branches shift and crash, releasing a new stream of sparks. Satisfied they've both done all they can for the time being, Lizzie plants herself beside her younger brother. Feet apart, they stand and watch the sea.

That's it, she thinks, and her heart contracts. The windjammer is some way off still, but she's surely seen them. Yes, she's changing course. She's drawing closer. No doubting. Again Lizzie regrets she cannot see her father's face.

'Look, Billy! We just need patience now.'

'You'll tell Pa I saw the ship first?' Billy says.

'Maybe I will,' Lizzie teases. 'Maybe I won't.'

Billy aims a sideways kick at her shin. She catches his leg without a thought and traps his muscled calf in the palm of her hand, so that he's left tottering on the other foot.

'What's it worth?' she asks.

He twists away from her, unsuccessfully, for now she's used to catching kicking goats by the hind leg, and she knows how to hold on. His hands go down for balance, his head hangs between them. He doesn't reply, because she knows the answer: praise from Pa means everything to Billy.

'But will you?' he pleads again.

Grinning at the desperation of his desire, Lizzie lifts his leg still higher. She can afford to be amused. She hardly needs a ship-sighting to prove herself. If anyone does, it's Albert, she reflects, and this makes her hope harder he's seen it too by now.

'Yes. I'll tell him. Of course I will.'

Her younger brother escapes without much trouble, and pushes her briefly, not hard.

'A ship!' she shouts, pushing him back.

'A ship!' he replies, crashing back into her. Hysteria erupts with the speed of overboiling milk, a crazy, barking laughter that leaves them quickly still and empty.

'We mustn't stop watching,' says Billy, eyes back on the sea.

Something's changed. Lizzie can't say quite what, but it unsteadies her.

'Are you sure she's seen us?' she asks.

'Yes. No. Yes, I'm sure.' His fingernails dig into her arm with every urgent contradiction.

'I suppose they could be . . . ' Lizzie's other fear is best not spoken. What kind of ship is this? It's hard enough to judge the character of a captain when you've spent weeks as his passenger. From a clifftop, it's impossible. But weren't their fortunes turning now, the scales rebalancing at last? The Peacock family was surely on the up. Pa had said so, just a few weeks ago, looking at the thriving vegetables, and Ma had agreed, and they had looked at each other in such a way Lizzie knew it couldn't be for show. They had earned their change in luck, Ma said. And this ship would be the proof and crown of it.

Holding her elbows, Lizzie moves her weight back and forth from foot to foot, side to side, a slow but deliberate rocking rhythm. Step by step, she is bringing this ship in with willpower, as you might sway a baby into slumber.

Some moments later, she spits hair from her mouth, and thrusts her hands into the pockets of her flapping tunic to hold its skirts down.

'Do you feel the wind rise?' she presses Billy.

'No. Yes. A little, maybe. It's always windy up here.'

It seems windier than before though. The clouds are moving faster. A squall? Now? No. No. No. She refuses to contemplate the possibility.

'Lizzie! Billy!'

It's Queenie, running to join them, slowed by her reluctance to take her eyes off the sea, and the awkwardness of her burden.

'Oh no,' she wails, as she gets closer, letting her logs fall. Her fingers pincer Lizzie's arm. 'It's not going away, is it? It can't leave us now. It can't.' Queenie shouts out, uselessly, waving and jumping as she calls: 'Ahoy! Come back!'

Then Ada and little Gussie climb to meet them, with more wood, and also the young dog, Spy, barking sharply.

'Come and see! Quickly! Ada!' calls Lizzie.

Whirlpooling in the children's flood of desperation, Spy rushes around the fire and leaps and growls and, without Albert there, Queenie and Gussie can do nothing to calm him. Lizzie begins to wave too. She's sure the pitch of the growling surf below is rising. And the ship now seems to be getting smaller instead of bigger.

'Keep waving, Queenie. You too, Gussie, wave harder! Make sure they see us.'

Ada is waving hardest of all of them, her body stretched to snapping.

'Oh look over here! This way! Come on!'

They leap and sweep their arms through the smoky air like nesting terns. Ada stops to fumble in her tunic pocket.

'Wait! I've brought Pa's spyglass. Ma's idea. He won't be angry.' She unscrews the instrument and screws up one eye. But her hands are loose and bony, and the horizon is bucking with her nerves.

'It *is* a windjammer,' says Billy at last, with satisfaction, without the need of magnification.

'Can you see a flag?' The words burst from Lizzie, who balls her fists to stop them snatching the glass from Ada.

'Of course not,' says Ada. 'Not yet.'

In fact Ada can't see a thing. Her eyes are filling with tears – of relief, of hope. She's not even sure herself why she's crying.

3

ESPERANZA ROLL AND PITCH, STILL IN DEEP WATER plenty lengths from land, and beyond her monstrous roaring. On the quarterdeck, our Yankee captain shake his head and flatten his lips. We six Rock fellows stand together, skin to skin, breath hard and quick, all holding tight the foredeck rail, keeping nerve and body steady. Here we are, but this place has yet to show itself. Our hearts little know if they should leap or bottom-sink, and we cannot command them.

We had no imagining of an island so unlike our own, so small from far off and yet so tall before us, rising high, even into cloud, so many trees above and so wild of sea below. Scatter of islets to one side. We stare through spray at breakers hurling on a grey beach of sand and stones, and stare at the green land above, upping here and downing there, dark and light in turn. Most of all we stare at the creatures we spy out where the land rises close and high above the shoreline and no trees grow, human creatures who up and down themselves as quick as quick.

Vilipate questions Solomona. Have we come to work only for children? How will they pay us? My brother's shoulders rise and fall. He hate to say he does not know. He knows as much of this as you, I say, but silently, to shield my brother. What can anyone know from this distance?

'You are certain it will not be like Flint Island?' asks Likatau, who we call Luka. 'The work?' Ten from our village went last year to scrape guano for Mr Arundel. Mr Reverend say he is a proper Christian gentleman, like our Mr Peacock, but still he sent a native teacher with them.

'You know we come to clear the land for planting,' I say, staring at the trees, so many and so tall, trusting I speak true. 'You know our labour here.'

Then up through the hatch comes Cook's scowling face, question-full. Solomona points.

'Little ones . . . Palagi . . . '

Up and down they jump, mouths open, flapping wings, dark little birds waiting to be fed. No colour to 'em. We only see their shouts. The sky sucks up smoke from the bluff, and throws it around.

Cook – a little Englishman who scuttles side to side of his galley kingdom on crayfish legs, all that food and yet so thin – Cook stares too, peg-teeth on show.

'Practising their war dances,' says he, and raise finger-waggling hands and monster his mouth at us. His tongue is short and whitely scummed. Our eyes return to land. 'Only joking,' he says, grinningly, coming to stand with us, his well-cooked smell all about him.

One by one, one, two, three, four – now five I see – one tiny child on another's hip – the bodies fall still. Only the dog dances on. They want to see who we are. If we stay or go. I feel their wanting swell me from inside.

'Poor little blighters,' says Cook. 'Don't they have no parents? Who'd have dreamed it? What could have happened? Nasty landing, all right, but have to make the best of it. Can't leave 'em now, not in this Godforsaken spot.'

No bumboats here to greet us. At home we send out vaka to meet palagi vessels. Pilot boats – canoes, as Mrs Reverend call 'em – to show the way to strangers, or offer goods for sale, though once upon a time we welcomed no one. Before Christ came. Here we see no greeters on wave or shore. Only these little ones up high, waiting and watching back.

Lower, the land flattens but is nowhere flat. Small buildings, three or four rough huts with empty eyes, unglassed, gather under tall trees. Another fire's smoke is whirling there, no, I see two – the darker beyond the buildings. Straight lines of taro and beans grow lush. Near to them, youngster orange trees, too much sapling yet for fruiting but strong of growth. A green meadow where goats are tethered. Not one coconut palm, and strange to say, not one other person.

'Well, there's a relief . . . thought we'd be taking on a party of orphans for a moment,' Cook says.

Pineki shifts my gaze with a pinch. Iakopo's smile is wide. I see the reason. Here comes Mother Bird, smallish herself from this way off. We watch the lady climb the brow, dark skirt full-long and blouse high-button like Mrs Reverend. She lean from side to side, and forward and back, for it is not easy for her to walk so fast. She is with child, and near her time by anybody's reckoning. But where is that child's father? Nowhere visible. Just one boy stands with all the girls, one white shirt alone on the sky's edge.

Esperanza shudders. Our captain nod, and first mate shout order. And down the anchor rattles.

Now the ship fights her ties, and we must hold the tighter.

Sails down, davits out.

Pulley wheels like morning birds as tars begin to down a small boat, ship's gig, but just as quickly stop for fear it smash. Up it come again, still squeaking. No good for landing yet, in gig or longboat. Captain and first mate still looking, talking, disagreeing somewhat it might seem, for we note more shaking heads. Shame. We need vaka, we fellows all agree. We must ride the surf, not fight it, says Pineki, and Vilipate is with him, and I see Solomona's eyes agree. Yet he will not change our words to theirs, and I dare not either. We are cargo once again, no longer crew. Cargo make no choices. Besides, we have no vaka with us. So it is idle thinking. We need another way to reach them.

Loud seas against the ship and shouting orders and wind in rigging all drown the children's calling voices. Their bodies slump, no longer jump. Hope leaks away, shivery. The dog falls out of seeing.

My eye measures rocks, sizes rollers, breath-counts waves. I ready-steady my knees.

'Now?' I say to Solomona.

'Wait, Kalala. Wait!' he say. He always want to wait.

My shirt is over my head already. I cannot wait. One hand on Luka's shoulder, a heave from bold Pineki, and I swing my leg to the topmost rail . . .

4

U P ON THE BLUFF THE WORLD TURNS A LITTLE BUT nobody talks until the windjammer is bucking at anchor. Ada clutches at Lizzie, who grips her back as bruisingly. Still no sign of Pa. Billy has the spyglass.

'They've got Islanders on board.'

'Give me the glass,' says Ma, arriving beside her children, hips creaking and grinding, bones slowly parting. She gathers the air back into her lungs, holds out a swollen hand.

'The ship's called *Esperanza*. These must be our kanakas, come at last,' she says. 'Look at the colour of them.'

'One of them's escaping!' calls Lizzie. 'Look out! He's on the deckrail.'

'He's going to dive!' squeaked Queenie.

'He's in the drink,' says Ma. 'Gone so quick.'

5

IN WATER ONCE MORE, ALL MY LIMBS ARE JOYFUL, AND
my ears too, joyful with bubbling whoosh, all sluice and
surge and flow, a dulled and busy quietness which is never
silence. Eyes open in bluest blue. A slow-winging turtle rises. I
rise myself, for air, and sink again. The sea argues; back and forth,
it tests me sorely – but I know these tricks and tumbles, and I
have power enough in mind and body to work these waves to
my delight.

Head up and out.

The shore approaches.

I am down and under, and now give way and let the water
roller me in – the rocks cry out a warning – I swim sideways
with all my ebbing strength – so fast so fast – and then a mighty
power throws me down, hard, in whiteness. Yet I claw for life
with so much longing that nothing can pull me back. Fiercely I
fight – my enemy, my friend – the suck of it, guzzling and gulping
at my legs. Ploughing and pushing, now in air, gasping, now
under foam, I launch my body and dive for land.

My bellowing back ups and downs, unasked. My chest is first fast and roaring, then slower and slower still. Smallest of stones print my face, embed their heat in all my body. Ears whine and sing. Foam flecks and waves reach, rush, drag at my feet, trying to lure me back into water, over and again, but I resist the sea's entreaties, crawl from its hungry reach. My head hammers and hums and stars whirl brightly in my closed eyes. I wait for all to slow, for glow to dim, for land to cease its tipping.

And then I raise my head and look up and down the beach. Nobody. Spume slides slowly on flat wet sand where sky and clouds lie spread and wrinkled. Some scattered rocks. So much sand. On and on and on all along the shore. Out of the sea's reach, the land dries and lightens, stretches up to a wall of rock, grass at bottom and green bushes tipping from on top. Not so high you could not climb it. There will be holes for fingers and toes in the red-brown lumps and chunks. Or I will find another way to reach the houses and the children. When I can breathe. I hardly can hold my head up yet.

Thud. Thud. Thud. As this thumping lulls in head and heart, I gather strength. Here I am, Monday Island. I have come as commanded. Now it is for you to make good your promise.

6

WITH THE SAME GAZING FORCE THAT DREW IN the *Esperanza*, Lizzie willed the young man's headway through the waves. Once, his head rose in the foam, and twice an arm flashed, but after that, they saw nothing.

This island interrupts the ocean like the head of a loosened nail. The rollers drive in with the force of all the Pacific behind them, as if their one desire is to join the waters on the far side. They come crashing against the rocky shoreline and against the sand, and stagger back to battle with the next incoming wave. Unpredictable whirlpools and eddies of current fight night and day for possession of the waters of the bay. But there was nowhere easier to come ashore than the stretch of beach below this bluff. The stranger had a chance.

'He must know what he's doing,' says Lizzie uncertainly, scrawny hand dropping from her open mouth. Her grey eyes are dried out with stretching them open in this wind. Where *is* Pa?

'I hope he does,' says Ma, chest still heaving. She slips a few fingers down the back of her neck to unstick the linen from her damp back, but does not release a button. She sticks a loose pin back into her hair. Gus, who can walk on her own two feet, clings closer.

'Can you see him now? Can you see him?' Ada can't stop fretting.

'Why is he coming alone? Why doesn't he wait?' Queenie asks what they all want to know.

'We'll find out soon,' says Lizzie. 'I'm going to see if he's made it.'

'You go with her, Billy,' Ma orders. 'Be careful.'

'We'll follow soon – as soon as we know they cannot leave,' says Ada. 'When we see they are sending the boat. Look! It's calmer again now. Sit down and rest, Ma, do, and give me Gus . . . We will look pitiful. Truly pitiful.'

Lizzie is already running, down to the invisible shore.

7

A SAND-FLICKER ON MY SKIN, A DOG'S WET NOSE IN my wet hair, a growl and summoning bark, and then a falling shadow. A smell half known, half not, of fish and feathers and oil and something else. A rotten, eggy, hanging odour, sweet and sour together. The feet that stop so close to my opening eyes are rough and tough and bare and old. Man's feet. Ragged, grey skin, black-lined and splitting, toenails like hihi, unshined, scratched yellow, and broken like empty snail shells too. Thick hair, like a black goat's, creeps down from rolled-up trousers.

'Quiet, Sal!' The man's order is quickly obeyed.

Now the dog lies watching me for movement, pink tongue lapping air.

I raise my head. Paws forward creep, stopped by a pointed finger. Tongue swallowed.

I tilt my neck and look into eyes like sky or sea or glass or light, always moving, never resting. Eyes you long to land on you alone. You seek their favour with your own. Like Mr Reverend's, in that way, and yet not like, for my minister's are soft and brown and steady. I see power of a different nature in the man who marks me now: power of purpose. Strong because he knows he is, he has strength of mind as well as muscle. Our master, then, and a man always to be quickly obeyed. So I urge my limbs to move.

Yet this is also a man gone almost to rags. His shirt is torn. A salt-specked, broad-brimmed hat pushes back from a brow that shines with sweat. His beard is vast and brown like coconut hair, and near as coarse. Some scattered grey. He does not look a wealthy man, which will not please Luka. His hands are empty. But the father of these children lives.

Like me, he cannot still his shoulders. Like me, he tries. Up and down, our backs heave helplessly, and in and out together. In our running and swimming we have both stretched our bags of breath too far. I think of Solomona, and Mr Reverend, and give thanks to God for safe deliverance. I push myself back on my heels. I sit and cross my legs, to show my humbleness. My mind remembers busily what is the something else I must do, and do at once. Shake hands, yes, shake hands, don't forget to show him what kind of fellow you are. Which hand? I look at both, so quickly he cannot see, I hope, and with them both I make the bottom of a square, palms down. One thumbs 'L' for 'Left', and then I know, so I give him the other. The Right hand is the right hand. I do not stand too close. I do not stand at all. I remember that too. I remember everything, and I want to tell my Mission friends so they know that I have minded their wisdom.

The clasp of his hand is like wet mud in sun, and moistens mine. Up and down I move them both, just like Becky show me. Yet calmly too like her mother, Mrs Reverend, tell me. I am

a gentleman like Adam. Mr Reverend has made a gentleman of
me. I am ready.

'How do you do?' Slow, careful, am I. Eye to eye, as bidden.
'Pleased to meet you. Sir.'

Then full-square he looks at me, eyes on every little portion
of my person, so piercing quick I feel his looking on my body
like crawling ants or dripping water. From up to down his sky-eyes
go, and then from down to up, then once again, top to bottom,
bottom to top. Still no movement in his lips, so I am silent,
smileless too. Only our breathing speaking. He folds his arms.

I see what he wants: to poke my flesh . . . test my strength
. . . feel my true weight. Am I the thing he ordered?

'Just one?' he ask at last. 'Only one of you come?'

At first his words make little sense to me. He breaks gaze before
I can. Down then he bends again. Down comes his hand to me
once more, but not for shaking this time. Rope-laddered, rigged
with veins, spotted brown, as hairy as his toes. I take the hand,
and close my fingers, and as I do he pulls me hard, so hard I am
quickly standing. I rock on my feet, head swimmerly, and he lets
my arm fall, and steps back again to see better what has he in me.
He is tall, I find, taller than me, somewhat – and broad too – but
not so tall as Mr Reverend, who is a long, stretched man with a
long, stretched neck and long, stretched fingers.

'*Tally gally fy eh fy ah,*' say he. He quickly sees this too means
nothing to me. 'Ah. So you speak English? Savvy?'

'Yes, sir. Certainly.' I say with pride. But I am fearful, a little,
of releasing from mine this man's visive powers.

'My name is Kalala.'

'Kalala. Well, Kalala, how do you do? I'm Mr Peacock.
Welcome to my island.'

BEFORE

This is a story which began two years earlier, on another South Sea island, larger by far than Monday, and a good way off. Perhaps a thousand miles away.

*

Beyond the blackened window-glass, night had arrived in Apia with the tropical speed that still sometimes took the Peacocks by surprise. There was a new vessel in port and the hotel saloon was beginning to fill up, lamplight and shadows swinging as the first comers passed each other, negotiated positions, and settled or moved on. Whalers and beachcombers, pearl hunters and sandalwood traders, sailors from every nation – all drank here. There was nowhere else to go.

No place for nice girls, Mrs Peacock tutted. Keep away. Her daughters laughed and parroted Ma behind her back. Lizzie took her crossness as a clue, lingering longer in the bar-room for any gleanings that could be picked up and picked over later, in her head, or better still with Ada. Stories of stowaways, tales of castaways and cannibals. Sightings of the new gunboats on patrol. (For what?) Hot arguments: which port was the orifice of Oceania; whether to hard drive or reef down in a

gale's teeth; which island missionaries kept too close a watch
on vice.

When men saw Lizzie listening, their voices thickened and
slowed or stopped. They looked too long and hard at her, so hard
you'd think they saw right through her apron, blouse and shift
too, as if they knew more about the tenderness that newly tingled
beneath the layers of cotton than Lizzie understood herself. With
Ada, their longing was more open. So that night Lizzie listened
out of sight, crouching on the ale-soaked boards behind the bar,
ready to jump up at any moment to ask Pa for the brandy Ma
wanted to dab on the baby's swollen gums. No doubt there'd be
words later about why she'd taken so long, but Lizzie didn't care.
She'd seen again a look in her father's eye – one that meant change
was likely afoot once more. She wasn't moving until she found
out more. Mr Peacock had left the counter and was sitting at the
nearest table, leaning in towards a man who looked familiar.

'You could be king of the Kermadecs,' the speaker assured him.

'So you say.'

'Because it's the truth.'

'And I believe you.'

Did Pa believe him? Lizzie wasn't certain.

'The island's yours for the taking and you'd be a fool to let it lie.'

Mr Peacock didn't rise, as Lizzie had expected; merely asked
another question.

'No nation has claimed it still?'

'Not yet. No nation nor no other man, not of any faith or
hue. Not that I know of. And I've kept my ears open since we
left, believe me. What a place it is . . . '

'So why not go back yourself? What's keeping you, if it's
as good as you say?'

'Isn't that obvious?' A bark of a laugh. A swig and a swallow. Lizzie risked raising her head, and for a moment thought he'd seen her, though he gave nothing away. But then she understood. Robson was blind. She'd seen him before, being led along the seafront, white beard jutting out as he tasted the air ahead, his hand on the shoulder of one of his great crew of children, all native enough for the young Peacocks to be told to keep away from them.

'Fair enough.' Mr Peacock retreated, almost apologetically. 'Fair enough.'

'Anyway,' the blind man continued, 'we'd had some bad luck. Sickness brought by strangers. And my wife missed her family here. But that's the past. *I* may be past my best, but *you're* still young enough, strong enough . . . '

Mr Peacock could see through flattery, so Lizzie wasn't surprised by his silence. Perhaps he also noticed, as she had, a certain caginess in the man's response.

'I've had my eye on you since you arrived,' Robson continued. 'As it were. Yes, I know you're smiling now. I can still watch you, after my own fashion. And there's things I see that other folk miss. It's plain you're wasting yourself on this hotel.'

True enough, thought Lizzie, proudly. Ma had often said as much, these last few months.

Pa grunted. 'Maybe.'

'You're too late getting here for what you're after,' said Robson. 'Far, far too late. But over there . . . seize your chance quick enough, and this island could be another story.'

'The name of the place?'

'On the maps, Monday Island. It was sighted on a Monday, years ago. Some call it Blackbird Island.'

He didn't elaborate.

'Not sure I know of it,' said Pa, uncertainly.

'Well, the climate's heaven itself. Blessed, I'd say, right blessed, and I'm not one to take the Lord's name in vain. I've never seen a place so fertile. Take the right seeds with you and you can't but thrive. Goats galore, too.'

Pa kept his voice down – a sign of interest? – but Robson kept at his theme loudly enough, and his promises made Lizzie's stomach sing: the sweetest, juiciest oranges Mr Peacock had ever tasted; the biggest peaches. Bananas. Figs. Grapes. There was nothing you couldn't grow on this island, it seemed, if you set your mind to it; no sooner a seed met the soil than it began to shoot. Like Jack and the Beanstalk. Fee-fi-fo-fum. And the few plants Robson had had the chance to put in twenty years ago should still be there full-strength, gone native by now. He was beginning to sound homesick.

'Why are you telling me about it now?' asked Pa, suspicious again.

Robson didn't answer immediately.

'It's an opportunity.'

'What makes you think I need one?'

'Doesn't everyone? And you've always struck me as a man who knows how to make the best of an opportunity.' Admiringly. Robson let that thought sink in.

'What's in it for you?' asked Mr Peacock, and then Robson became evasive.

'I'd heard you'd a mind to selling out.'

It was the first Lizzie had heard, but that meant nothing.

'Who told you that?'

'Never mind who. Is it true or not? And do you want my help?

Or do you want someone else to take this island? Are you happy to stick around here, living on other men's scraps for the rest of your days?'

Lizzie sucked in her breath. Pa wouldn't like that. And he didn't. His chair scraped back and his voice dropped to a threatening hiss.

'So we got here too late. Ten years or more. Do you think I came to Upolu looking for scraps? How was I to know the Germans would have snapped up every decent trading station from here to Auckland? Or that the climate wouldn't agree with Mrs P?'

'Calm down. Calm down. Only trying to help.'

'I shouldn't have brought her here. It was never my plan.'

'Then listen to me. I'm offering you a chance to get Mrs Peacock and the little ones out of the tropics. Make a better life for you all. A piece of paradise, all to yourselves. And someone who can take you there. The *Good Intent* docked this morning from San Francisco. They've been unloading all afternoon. And she's Auckland-bound.'

Lizzie knew this already. Her brothers had sidled off to the quay earlier to watch. Of course Pa had been none too pleased to be given the slip when there were crates to be stacked, and bottles washed, and as usual it was Albert hauled over the coals, not Billy. When Pa's wrath flashed in full, Lizzie had retreated. It was Ada who later soothed their brother's stinging back.

'And?'

'There's a fellow coming by tonight who'll have money in his pocket. A buyer for this place, if you want one.'

'What fellow? Do I know him?'

Still a hint of suspicion in Pa's voice.

'Not yet. But I can vouch for him.'

The bar was getting busier, and the two men's voices harder to hear. The last thing Pa said, Lizzie couldn't catch at all. Her thoughts were leapfrogging too loudly anyway. She missed some more. Until Robson hissed indignantly:

'No, of course not. Not to anyone.'

And again her father's voice dropped away.

Then: 'Day after tomorrow. And yes, New Zealand for certain sure. So that'll please your missus. MacHeath'll pass the Kermadecs on the way, and it seems – for the right price, mind you – he'd drop you off to have a look at the place. If you don't like what you see, why, you can just keep going.'

'What? Go back to the North Island with my tail between my legs?'

'No shame in that, and you'll have money in your pocket. I told you, I can get you a good price for the hotel. But trust me, when you see this island, you won't want to keep going, and very likely, Mrs Peacock won't neither.'

'There's really enough passing trade? There aren't the whalers around these parts there were twenty years ago . . .'

'There aren't the whales. Any shore station's a struggle if it's depending only on whalers now. But there's nowhere else for miles, and word will soon get about. Sheep'll thrive once you've cleared the grazing, and wool will never perish while you're waiting. As for the oranges, and other fruit . . .'

How often did a chance like this come along? Nobody to interfere in anything. Not a native in sight, not that Robson wasn't partial to the right kind of native, as was surely plain enough. Truly, a private empire, over which Mr Peacock could rule for the rest of his days on earth. His very own Garden of Eden.

'Make sure your missus knows this island's not in the tropics. That's its beauty.'

Lizzie bit her hands while she waited for her father's response.

'Well, will I bring you the buyer?' Robson prompted.

'Where's the snake?' Pa's voice was loud and clear and a touch sarcastic. Perhaps he'd just remembered that he wasn't born yesterday, and needed to prove it. 'There's always a snake. And who calls it Blackbird Island? I feel I have heard that name before.'

At that moment the double doors to the road outside opened again and the bar filled up with a sudden roar. The crew of the *Good Intent* had been released, and shore leave might be four hours or twenty-four. With no certainty, the sailors treated every passing minute the same. This was what turned Ma's stomach, and had her shooing the girls out of sight and into the back rooms. The swearing and the rolling and the smell and press of men fresh off a ship who hadn't seen land for months. The appetite in their eyes.

Rattling change and tattooed fists and forearms would soon be thumping down all along the countertop above Lizzie: anchors, turtles, Chinese dragons, and from time to time the blue-as-black geometry and intricate swirls of a visiting Islander. The tobacco fug thickened. She'd be trapped if she stayed another moment. Lizzie crawled out through the doorway on hands and knees as fast as she could.

*

In the bedroom above the bar, she slept badly. Long after the last drinker had staggered bellowing into the night, her eyes flicked open with every gecko cluck. When she tried to wake

Ada to tell her about the blind man's promises, her sister batted her away, grunted and rolled over. On Ada's other side, Harriet slept on her stomach, head pillowed on folded arms, quietly dribbling and equally unresponsive. Doubt began to unpick Lizzie's memory.

Just as she thought she'd never sleep again, a low murmuring purr seeped through the wall into her wakeful dreams and she knew what she'd heard was real: Pa was finally trying out the notion on her mother. That meant Ma would be holding it up to the light to check its worth and quality, test its freshness. In her mind she would be rolling and squeezing and pressing the sparse facts like dough, pushing possibilities back and forth until they were worked enough to rise. Hearing only the tone of each question and answer, Lizzie's ears hummed with the effort of listening, and trying to guess which way matters would fall.

Surely Ma understood, as Lizzie did? Pa wasn't right for this place. He deserved so much more, a man like him: so capable, so determined, so strong and brave and clever. She must know that. Lizzie had seen how she sometimes looked at Pa when he came late into the kitchen from the saloon, and she set his supper down before him. Ill luck had brought them to Samoa – Lizzie couldn't entertain the thought it might have been ill judgement – but it didn't mean they had to stay for ever. Nobody could expect a man like her father to spend the rest of his life serving liquor to ne'er-do-wells and broken-down swells, breaking up brawls. Lizzie could see it was time to move on. Pa hadn't the temperament for this. He wore his restless ambition like a medal. Strangers were drawn to him at first, their curiosity pricked just by the way he bore himself. Then they discovered his quick temper. As for Lizzie, she had no desire to see out her own days doing laundry for strangers, nor hiding away in the back rooms of the hotel.

But taking off into the unknown like this? Again? Lizzie prayed Ma would not choose safety over opportunity now. For Lizzie was her father's daughter, a moth to the flame of new hopes and possibilities. Curled up under the sheet, thighs sticky with sweat, she crossed tight her fingers and her ankles. Say yes, Ma. Say yes.

*

She woke late to the muffled triple-throb of fruit doves feasting in the banyan tree outside the window. When her bare foot stretched out across the mattress and found a space, cool and empty where it should have been warm and solid, Lizzie was out of bed in a moment, hammering straight down the wooden stairs and into the kitchen. Unreadable faces turned her way.

'Why didn't you wake me, Ada?' All innocence.

Albert opened his delicate mouth, and closed it again.

'Lizzie! Go and get yourself dressed right away,' said Ma. 'What were you thinking?'

'Let her stay, Mrs P, now she's here,' said Pa, softly. 'We've news that'll please you of all people, my little Lizzie.'

He reached an arm for her, and Albert moved to make space in the chair next to their father.

'An island, Lizzie-Jane!' said Billy. 'We're going to a new island. Not like this place. An island all of our own.'

'What kind of island? Where?'

'A small one. A South Sea island, more or less. Hardly six miles across,' said Pa, playing the table like a piano. 'But a paradise, I'm told.'

He seemed to be waiting for applause.

'We hope,' added Ma, but she could force the corners of her mouth down no longer, and her eyes shone.

'Is it near here?' asked Albert.

'Oh no. Some distance southish,' said Pa. 'Not so far as New Zealand, but more than halfway back that way, I believe. A few weeks' travel.'

'So will we keep a store there?' asked Ada.

'No Germans yet? It won't be like Nuku'alofa?' Albert asked, keeping his voice deliberately flat to stop it squeaking and because he didn't want to suggest criticism. Even before the bloody flux had nearly seen off Albert, The Friendly Islands had been a disappointment to his parents. Nobody could hope to prosper with such well-established competition. Coming to Samoa seemed a greasy slide from frying pan to fire. Albert's exquisite china-blue eyes locked bravely with his father's lighter, sharper ones, their steady focus the only sign of how much the answer mattered.

But Mr Peacock only laughed.

'No,' he said, surprising everyone. 'I told you. There's nobody there at all.'

'Nobody?' said Lizzie, in feigned amazement, still playing the game.

'Not a soul. No store, no church, not even a house. Nothing . . . It will be ours alone, to do what we want with. If we like it and choose to stay. We can grow everything we need to live and plenty to sell too. Orange groves. Timber. Grazing.'

The children could hardly comprehend the idea of an empty island, a place that belonged to no one.

'No savages?' asked Billy. 'No cannibals?'

'No bigwigs?' asked Harriet. She was still called Harriet then.

'Not one. No natives at all,' said Ma. 'You heard your father.'

'We don't have to take the place from *anyone*?' Albert asked, still careful, straight-backed. Just a glance at Ada.

'What did I just tell you?' said Pa. 'It's ours for the taking. If we're quick about it.'

'So that makes *us* the natives,' said Harriet, thoughtfully.

'Certainly not!' her mother snapped.

'Natives are born in a place,' explained Ada. 'We're *going* to this island. We don't *come* from it.'

Albert frowned. There was more to it than that. There was a pause while the children separately reflected on the question, and wondered exactly where they did come from. They'd all – except Gussie – been born in different parts of New Zealand. Would they always be settlers?

'Well, Lizzie?'

Mr Peacock gripped her hands in his as if he'd squeeze out an answer, and she held on dizzily. If Pa let go, there was no telling what might happen; anticipation was glowing like a fever in her bones.

'It's what I've always dreamed of,' she whispered. 'Some-where that's only ours.' Not borrowed, or stolen, or rented. Somewhere they could stay and build and grow. 'For ever.'

She should never have doubted him. Of course he'd persuade Ma. Who could possibly resist Mr Peacock when he had a plan? She smiled at Pa, but he had turned his gaze to Albert.

'And this will be the making of you, my son,' he said. 'You'll see.'

'Yes, Pa.' Albert sat up still straighter.

Ada nodded her encouragement. Albert needed strengthening, after so much sickness. Mrs Peacock was murmuring to the baby, who wriggled and twisted on her lap, having sat still too long.

'Are we going to an island?' Ma rubbed her own well-defined nose against Gussie's small bump like a New Zealander, and even babied her voice. 'Our very own island? Would you like that?'

Gussie shrieked, perhaps with approval.

'She says yes,' said Harriet. 'I'd like it too. Ma, can I be the queen of our island?'

But it was Pa she watched as she spoke.

'You can,' said Pa. 'We'll crown you when we land.'

Ada and Lizzie clapped their hands and Harriet curtseyed.

'We can have a coronation feast,' said Ada. 'We'll invite the goats.'

'Ghosts?' Billy caught Pa's arm.

'Goats,' corrected Lizzie.

'Yes. We won't go hungry on Monday Island, eh Queenie?'

So that was their island's name. And now their sister had a new one.

Albert stared at the remains of his breakfast and crumbled a hunk of uneaten bread into a mass of tiny islands on his plate. His porcelain face shadowed as he sucked in his cheek-flesh, and worried it with his back teeth. Lizzie guessed his thoughts.

'How long's the voyage?' she asked on his behalf, adding, below her breath: 'Stay on deck, in the air. You'll find your sea legs this time.'

At the mention of legs, Ma's hand slid down to her ankles. Tropical fevers and disease were such a worry to her: hadn't they nearly lost Albert? Her greatest horror was the elephant disease – fey-fey, or fee-fee . . . something like that. The limbs you saw in these parts could make a grown man weep. Vast, swollen, deformed. In fact everything here grew a sight too much for Ma's liking. It didn't seem right, all this unearned fecundity. Flowers that unfurled their perfume unbidden, petals and even leaves so brightly coloured they seemed brazen. Vines carelessly floating their seeds any which way and honeyed fruit that flaunted itself, then rotted, reeking where it softly fell. It encouraged indolence, all this lushness, there to pluck or plunder or simply pass by. Reward required toil to make any sense to Ma. She had never thought much of showing off.

'What about Sal?' asked Harriet suddenly, her voice fluting. The terrier lay in a box near the stove, three puppies attached to her teats. A fourth stumbled blindly over its mother's legs, nosing out breakfast.

'Joseph?' Mrs Peacock looked at her husband. 'We're taking Sal, aren't we? She's come so far already.'

'Of course,' said Lizzie. 'We'll need Sal, won't we. Pa?'

Mr Peacock's eyes were on the ceiling; he was making other calculations in his head. It took him a moment to work out what was being asked.

'We will. We'll train her and the pups to hunt. Your job, Albert.'

'Yes, Pa.' Albert nodded, thoughtfully. He was good with animals, but hunting?

'What if she jumps overboard on the way there?' squeaked Harriet.

'Shhh,' said Ada. 'She didn't coming here.'

She could see Pa was losing his patience.

'That's enough nonsense! Now, drink up quickly. We need to pack.' Pa's energy crackled through the air like an approaching storm. 'Come on, Albert.'

'Now?' He pushed back his chair and his mug tottered on the table.

'Yes. We sail tomorrow.'

That stilled the children's tongues. Their mother was already on her feet, clapping her hands to hurry them all. Such a perfect alignment of circumstances – it might never happen again.

'Everything and everyone is to be on the quay by ten-thirty sharp,' said Ma.

'We can't keep Captain MacHeath waiting,' said Pa. 'Albert, you'll be my right-hand man, eh?'

Lizzie watched how Albert swallowed before he nodded to their father, and she sighed inside. She didn't need to be asked a question like that. But Pa would never ask her.

'I'll do my very best.' Her brother's words were eager.

'This island will change everything for the family,' said Pa, firmly, steering Albert from the kitchen. 'Land. That's the important thing. That's what a man needs to survive. To take his place in history. To keep his name. This land will be our future. Your future.'

Not just his, thought Lizzie.

BEFORE

Clearing out and clearing off.

'What else, Ma?' asked Lizzie. Mrs Peacock sat at the table, pencil in hand, eyes distant. 'What shall I do now?'

Already the everyday dishes were washed and dried and packed away, and the beds not made but unmade. The lid of the heaviest trunk hung back on its hinges. Each time Lizzie snapped herself in two to stick her head into its depths – laying down a pile of freshly folded blankets, or the next bundle of linen – she surfaced with the welcome smell of upheaval in her nostrils. The cake tin Harriet was balancing on her head for a crown clattered to the unswept floor as Albert arrived, bearing the huge family Bible and Ma's Shakespeare, and stacked on those another treasure: a pile of old illustrated newspapers, three years old, left a few months earlier by a kindly hotel guest, 'to amuse the children'. They only knew the pictures. Ma had quite lost the habit of reading to them, now they were so many.

'Can we take the papers too, Ma?' he asked.

She looked at him, considering. Albert Peacock kept his eyes fixed hopefully on another Albert: Bertie, Prince of Wales, flanked by oarsmen and raising a bowler hat on a quayside as he embarked on the Royal Tour of India. There were supplements here too, wonderful ones, filled with tiger hunts and men in turbans who rode on elephants. Probably maharajahs, said Ma. Albert had not given up hope yet of making sense of the writing.

'I suppose the girls can wrap the china in them.' Mrs Peacock was regretful. She knew it was a waste, and how much Albert loved them. And a glimpse of the domed building in the header gave her a wistful kind of a pleasure. *Look!* she'd tell the children. *Look at the beautiful spires and the bridges and houses and all those boats. That's the city where I was born.* London hardly seemed real to her now. 'And maybe we can smooth them out for another day.'

'Oh thank you, Ma!' Summoned by another shout from Pa, Albert vanished.

For the first time in their lives, Lizzie and Ada were entrusted with The Tea Set: Copeland Spode, Blue Italian, acquired for Ma by Pa in his short-lived soldiering days in the early months of the Maori wars, when she was still a seamstress not long arrived in the colony – though already running a workshop – and he had recently proposed. He'd rescued the set from an abandoned farmhouse. Quite how and why it had been forsaken the children were never told. It would give them nightmares, Ma once admitted. Lizzie unhooked the cream jug, sticky with dust, tipped out a desiccated spider, and took her place at the draining board. Ada washed clean all the castles and ruins, all the sheep and shepherds, trees and leaves and Chinese swirls, carefully handing each piece to her sister to dry. But she was making heavy weather of it, and one cup nearly slid from her soapy fingers.

'What's the matter?' asked Lizzie, after a sigh so deep it begged a response. She felt her sister's forehead. 'You look a bit all-overish.'

'Stop it.' Ada twisted away from her solicitude, and Lizzie held back her questions. You needed patience for Ada to confide.

Three saucers later the older girl finally whispered: 'Aren't you fed up with moving?'

They had always been a roving family. It was in their blood, Lizzie assumed. Two parents, both from England, who met and married the other side of the world. This was the third time in five years the family had packed up their entire life and moved on. Pa's discontent had surfaced within a few months of buying the Apia hotel.

'Do you like it here?' countered Lizzie.

'No, of course not. And of course I want land that's ours for ever. A place we can make something of. Like Pa says. I'm just not sure . . . '

'Nobody can be sure of anything,' said Lizzie, firmly. 'Even Ma says we won't know till we get there. We have to hope for the best.'

'As usual. But I'm worried about Albert.'

'Because of the voyage? Because you think he's still not better?' Lizzie shared her father's suspicions of her brother's mysterious aches and pains.

'Not just that. Because of Pa. He expects so much of him. More than he does of you and me, I think. That's why he'll never let him be. Another change, a different kind of life entirely . . . it might make everything worse. You know Albert's not like us. You two should have been the other way round. Think what a son you'd have made.'

Only Ada could say this out loud, and only to Lizzie. The two older girls had always been more practical than Albert, slower in thought but quicker in action. More resilient. Less prone to sickness. Less beautiful.

'Maybe if you didn't always try to protect him . . . ' Lizzie began to suggest, but she stopped as soon as she saw her sister's face. She never seemed to say the right thing. So she gave up trying to help and reached up for another cup. Her thoughts turned from sheep to beans, growing before their eyes, pumpkins and melons swelling as they watched, a plump fish leaping on a line. All to themselves. And Albert would surely thrive better in a kinder climate. Lizzie couldn't dismiss Ada's fears, but she refused to encourage them.

'I can't wait to see the island,' she said, happily. 'We'll have to camp to start with, while we build a house. We'll have to build everything. And at least we can't be stuck in a kitchen if we haven't got one.' She tried to enthuse Ada. 'What will it look like, our house?'

'However Pa wants it to,' Ada said, dryly.

'I know he'll make it beautiful. Our own deserted island,' Lizzie continued, dreamily. 'Our very own . . . '

The front door banged, and a moment later Harriet rushed in. 'They're here,' she hissed.

Lizzie went to look. Blind Robson was in the hallway, with a stranger. Mr and Mrs Peacock stood side by side while Robson introduced Herr Heiselbaum, a German adventurer with Pacific ambitions, lean and keen and remarkably whiskerless. He wanted to look round the hotel right away. During the inspection, the children stayed fidgeting in the kitchen. As soon as they heard the visitors step onto the veranda, Albert ran to the window.

'He's shaking his head,' he reported, alarmed.

'Let me see. No. It's just an act,' decided Lizzie. 'He wants to get the price down.'

'You're right. Look. They're shaking hands now.'

*

A few hours later, Mr Robson and Mr Heiselbaum returned with a fat carpet bag, and left without it. When Pa emerged, he locked the back office door behind him.

'That's settled then,' he said. 'Albert! Get the barrow. We're going to see Herr Weber.'

Albert turned a little green, and obeyed reluctantly. It was whispered that Godeffroy & Sohn's Pacific office manager didn't just buy mother-of-pearl, copra and coconut oil. Herr Weber also paid good money for native skulls, and sent them back to Hamburg to sell to scientists, on ships that left under sealed orders. You might as well be eating bones, Lizzie had told Albert the last time he came home crunching on rock sugar. He spat it out, and she fished it from the midden later.

With long, rapid strides, Pa led the way along the palm-lined road that curved round the wide bay. Past the church – built of coral, built on coral, slowly blackening – past the convent school and its garden, past the chuff-and-rattle of the cotton gin, Albert hurried a few steps behind his father, wheeling the empty hand-barrow with effort over the crushed coral sand. On the seaward side, above beached outriggers dragged up from the water's edge, boys hung from trees and slung down fruit. Dotted among lush groves of palm and breadfruit on the other side, native houses, neatly thatched, stood half open to the breezes. Men lolled on mats, neither inside nor out, spitting freely. Mothers and daughters sat pounding arrowroot, tending hair, twisting coconut fibre into string, weaving clouds of the finest pandanus threads into mats as fine as linen. Babies slept or fed. Mr Peacock's speed of movement always attracted attention and some laughter. Perhaps the news that the hotel was changing hands had already begun to spread.

Cool and airy, the store smelled as usual of sacking and flour and grease and metal, with just a hint of sweetness.

'Come in, come in,' called Herr Weber from the back office and, for the first and only time, Albert passed into the inner sanctum to stand before the agent's mahogany desk. But today Herr Weber offered no childish treats, giving father and son an equal portion of his measured, wire-rimmed gaze. He knew everything, already. 'Away on the tide tomorrow? Well, well. And I never managed to convince you. A shame. I've always said you're the man we need to run a depot for us on one of the small islands on the Line. No nonsense with natives, or missionaries either – and in time, perhaps, young Mr Peacock may—'

Albert had barely recognised himself when Pa held up a palm.

'Thank you, again, and most sincerely, Herr Weber, but you know I'll work for no man but myself. And the same applies to Albert.'

Albert closed his mouth, and nodded obediently.

'Well, if you change your mind,' said Herr Weber, affably enough.

'Unlikely. My son has a promising future – land of his own, a climate that will suit us all better than this one. We're well on our way . . . '

When his heavy hand fell unexpectedly on Albert's shoulder, the boy quickly straightened his narrow back to bear against his father's weight, determined to make himself worthy. Fragments of negotiations drifted by, each purchase provoking yet more vivid possibilities in Albert's mind – a whetstone, a saw, a fowling piece, an axe, several hoes and clasp knives and a whole box of fish hooks. A list supplied by Mrs Peacock produced more domestic necessities.

Albert and Pa left with the barrow so heavily loaded they each had to take a handle to push it back to the hotel. When she heard Billy's ahoys, Ma abandoned the sewing machine she was oiling, wiped her hands, and came to inspect the purchases. Some bales of navy workcloth, as hard-wearing as you like, and plenty of cotton drill too. Creamy calico, which she fingered but did not unfold. The children weren't going to stop growing, Ma said. She checked bobbins of thread, counted needles and buttons, ordered the packing of everything, and returned to the Wertheim, locking her darling's lid and wrapping the machine tenderly in oilcloth. When she was small, Lizzie used to listen to its comforting trundle and feel grateful to the little crouching dwarf embossed on its end, hammering helpfully away. Her mother simply seemed to guide the cloth. But one day Lizzie realised her mistake. It was Ma who made the machine work; like her own children, the dwarf was merely obedient to her command.

Lizzie's next task was to heave the camp oven out from the very back of the cupboard. A gigantic cockroach was scrabbling hopelessly up the side. Ma crushed it, then checked the vast cauldron for the ruddy bloom of rust.

'Won't you miss the range, Ma?' asked Ada. Her mother glanced dismissively at the wood-burning stove, and handed her a rag. She would hardly miss the furnace it made of the kitchen. Going back to the open fire and camp oven of the early days of the Peacocks' travelling life held no fears for Ma. While her eldest daughter bent her head over the heavy metal lid and rubbed in coconut oil until it glistened, Ma's own head vanished into the belly of the pot. When she spoke – to remind Lizzie to fetch the dolly-stick from the outhouse – her voice moaned like a ghost's. *What would be bubbling in that pot once they reached the island?* wondered Lizzie. Not once did she imagine it empty.

*

Years ago, Lizzie had asked her father if he ever missed the Yorkshire village where he was born. Would he have left had he known he'd never go back? 'Never say never,' he'd replied. But all the children's unknown grandparents were long dead, while Pa's cherished older brother, with whom he'd taken passage, had been an early victim of the Maori wars. Nothing left to tie either parent to any part of the world, in either hemisphere, Lizzie realised. And then Pa changed his tune, telling them that anyway, a settler has to look forward, not back. In the midst of Queenie's brutally efficient farewells (*goodbye bedstead, goodbye window, goodbye crack in the ceiling, goodbye dented pannikin – you're not coming*) Lizzie firmly reminded her of this.

Albert, waiting in the doorway, raised his eyebrows.

'Doesn't a settler also have to settle?' he asked, brittle-voiced.

'Of course,' said Lizzie, with acid sweetness. 'When the time is right.'

'I hope that's now,' said Ada, wearily. 'It's about time.'

Herr Weber hired out his horse and cart for the short journey to the harbour. Pa's fiddle and music case were carefully wedged on top next to the box of puppies, and the children. Quite the travelling circus, remarked Ma, with more pride than disapproval. The cavalcade scattered chickens across the road, glossy gold and red, and small black pigs scrambled out of ditches with snouts raised. Dogs barked, and Sal replied. The local children followed too, as close as they dared, and from time to time the boys broke into improvised, incomprehensible, and mildly mocking song, which sent the girls into fits of giggles and pointing.

On the long wharf at the waterfront their collection of trunks and crates and sacks looked considerably smaller. The family huddled together uncertainly. Canoes from all the outlying islands clustered around the *Good Intent* like iron filings, eager for metal fish hooks, knives and chisels. Already she lay lower in the water, reeking of coconut, her hold filled with sacks of copra. Ma had trained the children not to stare at all the bare flesh forever on show on these islands. But it was hard when the calls kept coming. Look! Look! This way! Over here! The young men's thighs and knees were engraved with blue as if they wore navy breeches beneath their lava-lava. Women with ambitious hairstyles, piled high with pink hibiscus flowers, lolled enticingly on rafts formed by outriggers, their bare breasts lustrous. Surely the sailors would need a few more coconuts before they left, or how about this lovely comb? Look at this! It had been the same when they'd arrived. It was the same with every ship that came and went.

'When will we go on board?' asked Albert. Constantly and queasily drawn to the movement of the water sloshing below them, partly visible through the gaps in the jetty planks, he steadied himself on Ada.

'Pa?' she prompted.

'Not long now,' said Pa, with satisfaction.

'I'm looking after Sal and the puppies,' said Queenie, who no longer answered to the name of Harriet. 'They're not going in the hold.'

'They might be safer there,' said Ma.

'They'll go in the hold if I say so,' warned Pa fiercely, and Queenie quaked.

At last embarkation orders sang out across the water and Mrs Peacock mustered the children.

'A fine collection of stowaways we've got here!' said Captain MacHeath, standing at the top of the gangway.

Why did men always wink at girls? Lizzie thought she might have to watch herself with Captain MacHeath. She did not see the way his mate glanced at Albert, then quickly looked away, coiling his thoughts up fast and tight before they could snarl on the startling beauty of the boy.

At last came the squeak and creak of pulleys and halyards, and the ghostly rising of the mizzen sheets. The jibs unfurled, almost at once. The mainsail soared into life. A crack like a bullet, as the hot wind caught at an unwary sheet and, ironed by air, the canvas uncreased and billowed. The ship began to roll, the wooden decks to breathe, and they were off.

8

MR PEACOCK STARES ME UP AND DOWN, YET HIS thinking seems far away. My wet skin chills. I have again the sense of a man unfathomable, whose powers are hidden, one who will always lead and never follow. I have met no other palagi like him. Then he speaks aloud once more, and I know he is back with me, all sharp eyes again, and my fears gather.

'This is it then? No more of you?'

Disappointment in his falling voice. And irritation. Does he want me bigger, stronger?

'I will grow a little more, perhaps,' I say.

He shakes his head and sighs.

'All this waiting and they sent me only one? Man Friday! To clear all this . . . ?'

The dog's eyes follow my master's sweeping arm as it draws out the whole island, the forest that I know rises behind the bluff, all else that lies still unseen beyond the golden stones of this low cliff. I shake my head likewise, and point out to sea, and we move together up the beach, and climb up a little way on the lowest rocks so we can more easily see how fares our vessel.

'You couldn't wait?' he says to me. I could have. Should. I leapt too soon, for little purpose. A lesson there, Solomona will assure me. The small squall passed as I swam through. It's plain to see a small boat can land now where I shored myself, and not be wrecked. The *Esperanza's* sailors have downed the gig and my brothers wait in line to ladder down: blood-brother Solomona, and our four Rock brothers, the most labouring young fellows from our village, whose families bring most cotton to the Church, and still have young men to spare. Broadest of back, most hungry for calico. I lack their years, and have not yet the boldness for further roaming than here, nor desire for plantation work. But still I am no boy. I had my first haircutting some years ago, my mind is big and strong, and my tongue nimble, and that is why I am sent. As for Solomona, he is here for God, to do His ministry, and to put aside his sadness. It is hard to lose a wife to sudden sickness, and harder when it makes you also lose a future long prepared for.

'Look, sir! Now they come. You see we are six, all told. Good workers. Dependable fellows, every one.'

'Good,' Mr Peacock say, thoughts hiding always. 'Six, you say? Good. Six. Quickly! Let's go and meet them.'

Why does he not stir himself? This man uneases me, the way he goes from light to dark like a forest walk. His sharpness blurs. He looks around this place he knows so well as if it is a strange land to him and not to me. His vision wanders, his forearm hairs upstand themselves and he shivers, though this sun is warm for any body clothed and dry. Has he the sickness? I back myself from him a little. Will it be safe to stay? And what of Cook's blighters with their wanting eyes – where do they hide?

A shout of joy comes.

'Pa!'

And here they are, voices before bodies. Three of the five – tall girl, boy, shorter girl – bouncing between the rocks, through a path in the cleft of them I did not see before. The biggest leads, never turning. Across the beach they run and their legs scissor, scissor, scissor, palagi knees flashing, one, two, one, two, legs that swim and climb and jump. These girls do not hide their ankles as Mrs Reverend desires her girls and ours to do.

'Wait for me!' cries the last and smallest one. 'Wait for me!'

Six legs stop and straighten, suddenly. Uncertain, with curious eyes, the children tilt their heads; birds collecting courage enough to peck at a prize. Am I that prize, or Mr Peacock? They cannot decide. I see how the two smaller ones watch him, and guess this is not a soft man, nor a rod-sparer, and also that only the big, bold, bony daughter has no fear of him. Nor of me.

'Pa!' she says eyes bright, mouth wide. A friendly smile she quickly turns on me. I return it, with a head-bow. She is safe and fearless. But I do not shake her hand, and she does not hold hers out to me. This hair-whipped daughter is something between a girl and a woman and I do not know these rules. I have only known married palagi women, with bonnets, and very few. One or two at most have visited our shores. I did not shake their hands.

'Oh Pa!' she says. So happy. 'Here already of course. We didn't see you. We didn't know.'

'I saw the smoke from the forest,' says Mr Peacock, nodding approval. 'You did well, Lizzie. And look – the other kanakas will soon be here.'

The boy, jostling against his sister, is hungry for praise.

'Billy saw the ship first,' she says. 'Where's Albert?'

'With the goat,' say Mr Peacock, shortly. Not a man who must explain himself to any person. The talking quickly ends. Four faces turn to mine. But my tongue grows stiff and heavy and will not obey me before so many listeners. I can only look.

Close-quartered, these children seem stranger still. Not what I thought I saw before, no, not at all. Not as young, perhaps. Needing no urgent rescue. Precious little flesh on bones to spare, yet they are not starving. Nor dressed or cared for like the Mission children: no white pinafores for these girls, no ribbons, no boots, no stockings. Dull clothes which would never please my mother nor our cousins. I hope that is not our bargain. Their hair blows wild under faded palm-straw hats, the tall girl's dark, her sister's light and straight. The brother dresses much like a deck boy. Sun-brown skin as dark as sailors' too, all three, though lighter than my own. And yet I see these children are clean and tidy and stand with pride. Like me, awaiting orders.

'Mrs P coming?' Mr Peacock looks around again, darting eyes, still swiftly moving, disquiet in them now that startles me.

Then barking breaks from the rocks, and two more come down the stony path, one daughter small indeed, still round of cheek, the other grave and careful, her hair darkest and longest of all the girls. With them walks the lady-wife of Mr Peacock, leaning on both. Slow of step and short of breath and red of face, the mother is heavier even than I had thought, closer to her time. Her husband turns before she reaches us: we are ahoyed. Already the *Esperanza's* first boat's close to landing. Mr Peacock runs, first to meet it, and catches the rope the sailors throw him. They heave her up the beach together, children hanging-helping on either side, careless of foam, all fighting the backwards pull. A quick unloading, Likatau and Pineki tumbling with bags and baskets, and then some *Esperanza* men, and Iakopo and Vilipate following more carefully. Finally jumps Solomona, heavy with his dignity, stony eyes searching mine. I have cut across him and though he will say nothing now, he will surely find time to tell me his disappointment later. I take my shirt from him with lowering eyes and put it quickly on, and play my part.

*

When the boat is safely shored, there is a separation, like oil from water. Island palagi and Rock fellows eye the other, all twitched, suspectable. Slippery-gazed, the children mumble behind hands. What kind of hunger haunts them? How will we fare together? Too soon to tell, for all is busyness and shouting, questions, answers, orders, sharp and fast. Nearly straightway the second boat needs pulling up the sand. People and voices mix and muddle, all working hard, crew and Rock fellows and this family haul and hoist. Captain is here now, talking, talking, talking to Mr Peacock, nineteen to a dozen, too quickly for me. Mr Peacock pull his beard and shakes his head and nods it, and push back hat some more to scratch his head. Baggage mounting, hens and cockbird chuckling in their cage, children poking fingers in, and pulling out again, pecked bloody. And Solomona checking and double-sure checking that all our gifts are safely stowed and nothing left behind, counting every mat and parcel.

*

Then all together we become a great snake of folk, children and parents and then sailors and last fellows, from the beach up through the rock cleft, where now I see a rough path winds. Baggage passed hand to hand, from sand to stones to rocks – up, up, up – and then we are high, and marching across thick grass and under trees through planted gardens, neat and fenced, to the Peacocks' settlement, and roast meat salty smells. Not far. The trees are tall behind, and tufted scarlet. Small cottages huddle, talking each to each, built not of wood or coral, but fading leaves, growing from the ground. Ready to blow away. Nothing painted. No verandas. No window frames. No glass. Poor dwellings.

9

'Too much,' murmurs Mrs Peacock, smoothing the stretch and ache of her belly with one hand. 'A miracle.'

She all but collapses into the chair Ada brings, while Lizzie fans her. Ma, so swiftly felled? But she is an ironwood tree, spreading her roots deep and wide beneath a canopy that endures all storms and shelters all. Where no sustenance is visible, nor can even be imagined, she seeks it silently, out of sight, below ground, wherever you are not looking, threading towards moisture and worming out the tiniest pockets of soil. Above ground too, she makes new roots, that reach through air, twisting and multiplying in emptiness; if a branch topples, her knotted outriders are ready to grope and grasp solidity wherever it may be. She can anchor herself on bare rock, plant herself on pumice. She is indomitable. From time to time she blazes.

But now she seems more like a gigantic tree fern, knocked horizontal by a storm, a feeble mass of roots revealed, majesty unsupportable.

'It's not the baby . . . ?' Lizzie whispers.

'No, no, not that . . . ' It's not the settling of a small head in a bone cradle that's sent her flying but the chance of change at last. The shock of hope's arrival, unannounced and out of nowhere. Her mother sets her trembling mouth to a smile of welcome.

'Welcome to my island,' says Mr Peacock, and Lizzie's proud to witness awe in the sailors' eyes, though she notes a strange unsteadiness in her father. What a day! Everyone upside down and topsy-turvy! She pulls herself straighter.

'Delighted to see you here,' continues Pa.

'Pleasure's all mine, Mr Peacock. I confess I've been full of curiosity to meet you, ever since I first heard of your endeavours here.'

The captain, an East Coast man named Hawthorne, drops to his knee theatrically to present Mrs Peacock with a new pipe and a pouch of fresh tobacco. Ma eases open the drawstring to inhale delightedly, and Lizzie breathes in rich spiced leather.

'Thank you kindly.'

Captain Hawthorne is quickly back to business. 'A whaler's been putting the word out for you, the *Magellan Cloud*. I'm told she called on you, some time back? Well, these kanakas will be just the ticket. You'll find no harder workers in all the South Seas. Recommended by the resident missionary, no less.' He leans forward, voice dropping so low Lizzie can barely catch his words. 'Cheap too. Pay 'em in calico and they'll be quite content, God bless 'em. I'll take your orders before we go. In writing.'

Everyone stares at the six Islanders, who stand with shifting feet and hanging arms kept in order by Solomona's stern anxiety, his capacity for wordless reprimand, and their own astonishment.

'Over here, boys,' says Mr Peacock.

They shuffle towards him warily, little by little absorbing more and more of the state of this out-at-elbow palagi family. Their threadbare clothing, too tight, too patched and mended, and their work-worn hands. The children's faces betray an eager, complicated kind of appetite – can it be satisfied? The Islanders' alarm surfaces slowly, in glances hurriedly exchanged and barely visible, unnoticed by the *Esperanza* crew. The sailors sprawl on the rough benches behind their captain, smoking and chewing and growing sentimental, knowing their hours ashore are numbered.

'Plucky little castaways,' one murmurs, too audibly. 'Thank the Lord we came.'

Ada to Augusta, known as Gus, all the children line up beside their parents, framed by the low and leafy hut. Queenie tells Ada and Lizzie to leave a gap for Albert.

'He won't be long,' she says to Pa, half questioning, half hoping. She wants completeness, and to know there'll be no unpleasant-ness to taint this glorious day.

'He'd better not be,' comes the quick reply. 'We need the goat he's butchering all the more now.'

'Yes,' whispers Ma. 'What are we to feed everyone, Joseph? Where will we house them all? This is all so sudden.'

Across the gap, Ada whispers, listing, in Lizzie's ear. She wants to run back along the track behind the outhouse that leads up into the forest and yell for their missing brother. Is it too late? This strange occasion has stiffened, turned so formal. Better Albert returns while there are witnesses to curb Pa's anger? What does Lizzie think? Albert must know the *Esperanza*'s landed. Surely, surely he'll be here soon. Why doesn't he hurry? He must come before the longboat grinds out into the surf for the last time, before sails unfurl and fill. He must. He must.

Lizzie keeps her head turned from her sister's soft mosquito moan and her hand itches to slap Ada's words away. If Albert misses out, it's his own fault. Ada can't make excuses for him for ever. Lizzie has better things to think about today, and she won't let her babbish brother spoil anything. He'll hobble home. She inspects the new workers surreptitiously, wondering how they will measure up. What changes they will help to bring about. Excitement surges, trembling inside her, so delicate and strong she mistakes it at first for fear or pain. She vows she will remember this moment, always, this turning point, this fresh beginning, this glorious new start on Monday Island which will obliterate or make worthwhile all the months of struggle. This, this will be the day they bury every setback, bid farewell to disappointment, this the afternoon their future truly begins. Everything is opening up again before them. They are no longer alone.

She beams loyally at Pa, who is talking in a low voice to the captain about the practical matters they will need to discuss – what the *Esperanza* will bring back here on her homeward voyage: bolts of cloth, all colours, more grass seed, and lead for bullets. Maybe even the first sheep. The hotel money would pay for that.

When he first set sail on the Pacific, Hawthorne tells Mr Peacock, his holds were packed with sandalwood and bêche-de-mer. Now it's men he moves more often, from island to atoll to island: free men, he assures them, seeking new lives, dreaming of bounty. Rarely men returning. He looks about him, admiring all Mr Peacock has managed already, with 'just a handful of girls', if he may say. Billy scowls but Lizzie's radiance grows, accidentally landing on the youngest Islander, who smiles back so directly that she looks away, confused.

Boys, Pa had said, echoing the whaler mate, all those months ago, and boys were what Lizzie had expected. Yet how could such a word – so slight – ever conjure the life and strength that stood before them now, the energy beneath oiled skin, the shoulders so broad and muscled they could lightly bear two or even three times any load she could ever hope to carry? Their faces are not long razored. No boys, thinks Lizzie. To be a man, in these parts, perhaps you need more than whiskers. To the captain and her father, would these fine young Islanders always be children?

'This fellow will introduce you to your kanakas,' says the captain. He does not know their names, thinks Lizzie. 'You might not guess to look at him, but this one here's a man of the cloth.'

Lizzie senses mockery. The one he thrusts forward is, like his companions, dressed neither in parson's black nor the barkcloth of the islands, but in simple sailors' slops. Flannel shirts, red and blue, loose breeches. Legs coppery-brown as burnished nutmeg, and just as God made them, which she knew would please Ma and disappoint Billy. No sign at all of drawing on their skins, no patterns in blue or black criss-crossing their calves. Their hair is short and straight and not quite black – sunshine reveals a ruddy glow. A yellow mass shines in their leader's cupped hands, a pile which unloops into softly clicking swags of polished snail shells. Mrs Peacock bows her head, and the man steps forward and gently places a necklace around her neck. There is one for each of them, Billy included, and some to spare. The new arrival steps back smartly with a waiting air about him, but Ma knows what to do. She whispers to Queenie, who runs into the hut to return with an armful of woven palm-leaf hats, still green, six in all.

The Islanders approach Mrs Peacock, one by one, the 'man of the cloth' the last to receive his gift.

'God bless you. My name is Solomona,' he says with dignity. 'We are all most pleased to meet you. This is my brother, Kalala, here is Iakopo, this Pineki, Vilipate and also Likatau.'

His hat is tiny. It was made for Gussie and it perches on the back of his head. The captain coughs and hides a smirk, and one of the watching sailors laughs out loud. Lizzie's fury flares and she glares at him.

Kalala is the swimmer, she sees – a slightly shorter, scrawnier, younger version of his brother, with the same broad cheekbones. Also the same eyes, dark and shiny as newly scooped pawpaw seeds, but Kalala's are more curious, less cautious. Lizzie notices grey grains of sand still stuck to his collarbone, and he feels her looking, and brushes them away. His understanding is greater than the rest, she guesses. Of English, but also other things. He sees Ada looking behind her, up to the high forest, though Solomona waits with hand outstretched to shake hers, and Pa frowns at her.

'Ada,' hisses Lizzie. 'Come *on*. Never mind Albert now.'

'How do you do?' Solomona says five more times, shaking five more hands, each one smaller. Gussie takes his fingers gingerly, then, marvelling, reaches out the other hand to stroke his arm. She had all but forgotten that other people exist. The watching sailors melt like tar.

More gifts follow. Barkcloth, decorated in a patchwork of squares and lines in black and ochre, patterned like shells and leaves and starfish. Mr Peacock's eyes widen greedily when he shows his wife the next package, and her voice is soft with joy.

'Banana?'

'Yes,' agrees Solomona. 'From our island. For your island.'

Knotty brown corms, briefly revealed and explained, then quickly covered against the sun.

'You'll like bananas,' Queenie whispers to Gussie, self-importance swelling as the second-youngest Peacock basks in her superior knowledge and experience. 'And look,' she continues. 'Look at the pretty chickens.'

Somewhere in the shade of her mind, Lizzie half remembers chickens just like these, birds safely cooped, angled heads pecking for grain. No more clambering on cliffs to steal the terns' eggs, freckled and fishy, thinks Lizzie.

'Oh, thank you. Thank you. We cannot express our gratitude enough for your bounteous gifts,' Ma stammers.

'Thank the Lord for all His bounty, for He is good,' says Solomona.

'So very good.' Mrs Peacock is almost beyond speech. Ada begins to sniff. For Lizzie, it's like a mist lifting. In the depths of toil and moil and heartbreak, she had only ever let herself see a little way ahead or behind, refusing to contemplate how close or how often they had teetered on the edge of nothingness. Now, witnessing Ma's shaking hands – even Pa was unlike himself today, one moment here, the next his spirit wandering – Lizzie's own faith in her parents is shaken too. In their very darkest times, Lizzie had always believed their assurances that all would be well, that because they had survived calamity before they would always do so. She had to. She was less sure now.

'You really are a man of God?' says Mr Peacock.

'Certainly I am in the Fellowship of our Lord Jesus Christ. Two years I have trained to become a native teacher and pastor at the Institute on our island. With Mr Reverend from England, of the London Missionary Society.'

'Ordained?' says Mrs Peacock, blinking joyfully at this fresh news, half rising, as if she would take Solomona's hands in hers.

'Soon to be, I trust.' A glimmer of pride suppressed, a hint of pain.

'But *we* are not heathens to be saved,' objects Mr Peacock, spikily. 'Have you come to plough our land or save our souls?'

'Hush, Joseph.'

'Both, madam. Sir. I am a Gospel Ploughman, here to labour in the service of the Lord, and also to help you as best He sees fit. All our work on earth, we do in His name.'

'And with His blessing on this wondrous day, I am quite certain. Oh, Joseph, is this not marvellous?'

Solomona has not finished. 'When young men travel to other lands in search of work and betterment, they are exposed to many temptations, sir. But there will be no backsliding on this island, I can assure you.' He lowers his eyes, backs away humbly.

'Amen,' says Mrs Peacock, recovering herself a little. Has she been too eager? 'Solomona. We have been so long alone here, so very long. And today is Sunday. Perhaps you could lead us in prayers – a sermon even – this very evening? Joseph, will we have music too?'

Gussie and Queenie clap their hands ecstatically, and Billy cocks a hopeful ear. Dancing as well as hymns! But where's Albert with the goat meat? They're all asking. He should be back by now. Where *is* Albert? Courting trouble. Not one of the other children would like to be in his place when he finally returns.

Promises are made. In six months perhaps, eight at a stretch, the captain will be back with the work gang's pay – bolts of fabric, bright cotton print for gowns, denim for dungarees. If everyone's agreeable, he will return them to their island, leaving this one immeasurably improved. The months will fly. They shake hands, the captain of the ship and the captain of this island. Hawthorne mumbles some words about the baby to Mrs Peacock. An awkward business, to leave a lady in her condition, her time so close, but what choice has he? The men load the longboats with sweet potatoes and oranges and push them into the surf. The sailors sing. The children wave and cheer.

Ada looks after the departing crew with anguish. Lizzie squeezes her hand, guiltily, expecting that drag of parting – so like a shifting anchor – to pull at her own heart. But when she turns to see the semicircle of watchful Islanders, ready for instruction, her breast is deliciously feathered by the wingbeat of possibility. All they need is for Albert to get back with the meat, and their new life can begin.

10

GOODBYE, *ESPERANZA*. HER DISAPPEARING IS OUT OF sight. Is it always so? Well. You cannot watch for ever. When I look for the last time, the sea is only the sea once more, shifting, colouring – now more brass than silver – ready to swallow the sun. In the lower gardens between shore and houses, we fellows idle and toe the earth, filling our faces with air that tastes of grass and leaves and carries sap and blossom with it. Fresh, yet without home's sweetness. I pull a weed from a row of beans – only one to pull – and crumble a pinch of soil between thumb and finger. Vilipate sniffs its richness, nods his head.

We are suddenly forgotten and our master leaves us here untended.

'Solomona?' I say, thinking to ask him why. But my brother, I see, is off balance still, mind-swaying, finding his new land-feet. I must take care not to knock against him with my doubting. Indeed, will guard him from more questions until he has means to answer them, just as he has always guarded me, more father than brother all my life.

On our voyage I grew to be a goer-between. The other fellows look to us both, a little, for we have served palagi many years, our mother too, and we know their ways and words, or so we thought. But Solomona has been raised somewhat more in our friends' eyes. In his own too, I fear. He is now some special somebody, the preaching man, not anymore the Solomona who dived and fished and swam and dug and sowed with all of us from small times. Nor the new-married man, hands joined in church. Nor Pioneer, ready to take the Lord's Word across the sea to heathen lands. Nor yet the new-widowed man, mourning, stranded, his boat-place taken by another, his future clouded, no longer serving the London Society. All that is past. We plough new furrows. We are his Mission and must look for Solomona's guidance.

Thinking already of the Peacock wife's request, he fishes up his Holy Bible from our sack, the Book in English, bran-span-new and sent from London. Mr Reverend gave it him before our departure. (Morocco-bound, he said.) Then Vika made parting garlands for our necks. Vika – my cousin, who is like a small sister to me since her mother was lost to sorrow – whispered as I bent my head that when we come home she will have the prettiest robe in Church, and I whisper yes she will.

The sun's heat fades. My brother frowns. This volume is too creaky-new to fall open at the much-loved parts, the spots of study, and seeks to close itself. Solomona nods, as if a someone is speaking in his head, and his lips keep wording silently. He is testing sentences for strength before he is called to speak them loud, inking sounds into his head. My brother is a fellow who has always chased perfection. This is surely not the time to miss it, the first time he is called to lead prayer in English. He must win this new flock with his words, offer whatever comfort they are seeking.

Asking leave with upping eyebrows, Vilipate spreads his mat out on the grass, under a tree, and Luka joins him to wait and watch. Iakopo and Pineki sit down too, complaining of hunger, and soon after that they out with their strings, and while the time with swapping figures. Pineki makes a crab, and Iakopo a catch. He holds its criss-cross to me and my fingers play the fish for him. Waggle, waggle, I tease, and he knots me, hard. I whip my hand away, and try to pull the string but I am trapped and my finger swells and whitens. They pretend they cannot untie me, so I wrench off the cord and walk away. When their circle of string is straight and whole again, they start once more, facing each other, and step by step, together, use all their toes and teeth and fingers to make a house. Vilipate looks at it.

'A house of string?' he says (in our language, for he speaks no other yet). 'It's a real house we must start building. There is no place for us here yet. They are ill-prepared.'

'Perhaps they did not believe we would come,' I say. 'We sent no word ahead. And something else seems wrong. I can't tell what. We have to be patient.'

I am anxious to see this island, to know how we will live, and where, and when the palagi will set us to work, and what our work will be. How will matters lie with this father, Mr Peacock, a man like a grouper fish, his colour always changing? I thought this landfall would end all sudden tiltings, but our course alters quickly even here. This family is done with welcoming. Of a sudden they look through us like livestock. We see head-shaking and hear upped-voices. Something new fills out their minds. When they talk, they talk only to each other, mouths slit straight as mussel shells. We are told nothing. So we wait, at the edge of the huts, outside their circle.

Scattering, scurrying, the children look about and run pell-mell across the headland. They stare up at the forest, and scan its leaves, and run again to find a better view, all calling and calling at once. 'Al-bert!' one shouts, and then another: 'Al-bert! Al-bert!' Back and forth they go, like ants trapped in a flooded nest.

'What have they lost?' asks Pineki. 'An animal?'

'Albert! Albert! Albert!' Plaintive cries, ever faster, ever higher. The tallest girl is all a-trimble-tremble, and the smallest holds her hand.

'What is Al-bert?' asks Iakopo. 'A dog?'

I shrug.

They run up into the woods, and some return to the shore. The two dogs we have seen chase them back and forth, barking all the while. I do not think Albert is just another dog. Then they are back again, all the children, and the big girl is pleading with her father, weeping now. Still Mr and Mrs Peacock pay us no attention. Their eyes stir with a thing unseen, of which they cannot speak. The father man is angry with the girls. They are fussing, he says. He shouts so loud we cannot mistake his words. A fuss about nothing. Albert will come back. It's not been so long. If Mrs P insists, yes, the father will go to find him himself, right away. Then they will see. No more fuss now, he says.

'They have lost a son,' says Solomona. 'That is their problem. I hope it will not be ours.'

'A small boy or a big boy?' asks Vilipate.

'I cannot be sure. He must be big to carry so much, but the sisters speak of him as if he is small.'

'We can help them look,' I say. If we find this son for them, it will be another gift, and we will be rewarded. But also I want to learn where we have cast ourselves, and consider how these coming months might be. In looking for the boy we can measure our task. The son's finding will keep the mother calm and gentle. Birthing mothers must not be anxious. I know this from my own mother, who has helped half our village into this world.

'Ask the father man,' I say.

'Call him Mr Peacock,' Solomona tells me. 'Respect him with his name.'

Solomona is still angry with me because I did not wait. On the ship. I was not obedient. I like my own way too much, he says. I lack humility. I risk growing proud.

'Yes,' I say. 'Mr Peacock. Ask him how we can help. You are our elder here.' I sit down on the mat, head bowed. Then I stand again, and follow Solomona to the mother and father. I do not want to argue. And I want to hear their words.

'Hungry?' barks Mr Peacock when we reach him, not letting Solomona speak. 'You want to rest, prepare for the night?' No hole for our reply, he turns to Mrs Peacock. 'See? We have other priorities. Tell the girls to get some mutton-birds ready to eat tonight and tell them to stop this nonsense about Albert. I'll go and fetch him and the damned goat meat now, if that's what you want. I'll find out what he's playing at. If that boy listened, he might find it easier to follow orders.'

'Joseph, please,' says Mrs Peacock. 'You know—'

'I know what I told him to do. And he will remember well enough when I find him. Take care of our kanakas, Mrs P. They're hungry and they're tired.'

He walks away and up towards the forest behind the huts. The second girl, the one they call 'Lizzie', this girl hangs back a heartbeat, then runs after her father, and pulls at his sleeve. We watch her make him turn and listen. Quickly moving lips and hands and arms. Mrs Peacock watches too. He shakes his head. Keeps walking.

'What did you say to him, Lizzie?' asks the taller girl, when her sister returns, smaller, shrunken. 'What did he say?'

'I asked him not to be too hard on Albert. I reminded him his leg still hurts him. Perhaps that's why he's stayed with the carcass, I said. It doesn't mean he hasn't butchered it yet.'

'And?'

'Pa told me not to make excuses. He said we can have no shirkers here.'

Ada's fists curl. 'He won't listen to us,' she says. 'He won't even listen to *you*.'

'Maybe he did listen,' says Lizzie. 'And he *is* right about shirkers.'

Their mother is quick to stop this kind of talk.

'Enough, girls. They'll both be back soon.'

Kindness comes again to her lips as she turns to us, holding open her hands, and at this moment I see something of Mrs Reverend.

'I fear we are neglecting you, boys,' says Mrs Peacock. 'You have found us all at sixes and sevens. Now, let me see. Billy and Lizzie will help you with the tent. Tomorrow you can make a start on building your new dwelling.'

'Sorry, sorry,' says Solomona, noting her fretfulness.

'No matter. We are glad you are here. So glad. All of you.' She loudens and slows her voice as Pineki and Vilipate near us, Luka and Iakopo close behind. 'It will make the world of difference to us to have you here, even just for a few months. A world.'

What next? She hunts our faces. She wants to know if she can trust us with her daughters, if she will need eyes everywhere now we are here. Uncertainty hangs all around us.

'Tell me your names again. I could barely take them in before. I am forgetting everything. Slowly now. Who will speak first?'

'Show her,' I whisper. I pick up a stick, and hand it to Solomona. 'Write the names.'

I know our names are hard for some palagi, but I do not want another's. Everything else we have left behind, in hope of greater gain. I will keep my name.

Solomona looks for a place to write and sees the ash patch, powdery grey. He holds a hand above, feeling for heat, then strokes it smooth and makes the first mark, a curving snake and then a circle and so it goes.

'Solomona,' he says, pointing to himself. 'S-O-L-O-M-O-N-A.'

'Like the king,' says Mrs Peacock. 'In Kings.' All the children join the circle round the ashes, craning and shoving to see the marks we make. Their eyebrows bend, and their eyes round in wonder.

Solomona says his name again, three times. An easy name to start, a Bible name. Then he smooths away his letters and begins afresh. He points the stick at me and says:

'Kalala.'

I whip the stick from his hand to write my own name.

'K-A-L-A-L-A.' My letters are straight and perfect.

The children stare at me. I point again at my letters, and repeat my name. 'Kalala,' they say. A breeze reaches in between us and a silvery cloud rises. My writing dusts over. Its lines drift and fill. No matter for these children. The blankness in their eyes tells me a strange thing. They could not read my letters when they were full clear. These children do not read at all.

Solomona passes his hand across his mouth. He has seen this too, and he is astonished. When I pass the ash-stick to Pineki, Mrs Peacock interrupts.

'You know your letters? All of you?'

Pineki nods, not because he understands her question, but because he wants to please. He scratches a slow P in the ash. Very slow.

'On our island we have a school in every village,' says Solomona. 'And many teachers. We love the Word above all things.'

'Remarkable,' says Mrs Peacock. 'How remarkable.'

Solomona is a polite fellow. He addresses himself to Mrs Peacock as if her children's ignorance does not surprise us by any means. 'We will show you the names of all our brothers so you can learn them all. After, you will show us yours?'

'Yes. Yes, of course.'

Meanwhile, Solomona quickly scratches the letters for Iakopo and pulls him forward, repeating his name.

'Like Jacob?' says Mrs Peacock.

Solomona scratches Vilipate and Likatau for speediness, and Likatau writes Luka too, and Solomona tells Mrs Peacock he has turned his name towards Jesus now. Then all we fellows bow in turn and smile and repeat our names and point, and the children say them back to us, and the girl that is not so big, not so small, talks of the missing boy.

'When he comes, you'll see. Albert can write his name—'

Ada shushes her.

'Come inside,' says Mrs Peacock.

One by one, we fellows follow her into the hut, where there are beds and chests and suchlike, and a table and stools, but not enough for all to sit. Sturdy, but roughly made. Nothing to delight the eye. I think of the birds and fishes of our island, gold and silver, that swim and fly and shine on Mrs Reverend's double-seat, inlaid with pearl and tortoiseshell. The pride of our village at its presentation, and the months of making. Then I cast off these thoughts, which cause my heart again to waver.

One girl fetches for her mother a vast book, a Holy Bible, battered and streaked white in patches, which she clasps for some moments to her swollen belly, resting it on the mound of child. A golden band, her marriage ring, bites her finger's flesh. Then she shows us all the names inside.

The first is the tallest girl, Ada Mary Peacock, she explains. Then comes Albert Francis Peacock. He is not here yet, she tells us, as if we had not heard the calling of him, or felt anguish in the air.

One name, with a little change, can become another. Sidney, the Reverend's son, my friend, who was sent away to school to England and is lost to me, who will learn to be a doctor like Dr Livingstone, we once called Sid. Fine playmates, used to say Mrs Reverend, once upon a time, until the days for play came to sudden ending.

Elizabeth Jane Peacock is Lizzie. To say her name, you stretch your lips out twice, like when you feel a pain you cannot speak of, and in between you make your tongue like a wasp in flight. I practise saying Lizzie. Then she says my name back to me, and then begins to tune it, up and down: 'Lalalalalalala'.

'Your name is like singing,' she says.

I smile and she looks harder at me, a little longer than before.

'*You* are the swimming one,' she says. 'Thank you.'

I am surprised. I did no good by diving, except make a fool of my-self, says Solomona. Thank you? My face asks why, and she replies:

'You gave us hope.'

Quickly my brother says the next name, William Edward Peacock, and the boy says:

'William. Billy. That's me.'

'Me next, me next,' says the girl who fetched the Bible, hopping and bobbing. 'Show me, Ma?'

She keeps her finger planted carefully under the H while she takes the Bible round.

'Harr-eet,' reads Solomona.

'Harr-y-et,' Mrs Peacock corrects him. 'But now we call her Queenie, because she is queen of our island. Our little queen.'

I tell her that my small cousin Vika also has a queen's name: our Reverend Minister's queen, who is called Victoria and lives in London. In the parlour in the Mission House there is a picture of her, sent from Sydney with the printing press. Her face is like a swollen taro and she is rich and fat like an old islander. All this thinking wings my mind again to the Mission House, now grown so big that it has doors inside as well as out, and rooms that join one to another, and lamps of glass, bright-burning. I recall my first sight of the looking glass, and my mother's bright laughter when I jumped from myself. This hut here . . . so poorly furnished . . . I did not think palagi could live like us.

Another name, Thomas Charles Peacock, and the air grows sudden still. This baby was Thomas for too short a time to shorten. Likewise Alfred Henry Peacock. The last name in the Bible is the longest: Augusta Emmaline Peacock. The big children all point to the smallest one and say: 'Guess! Guess!'

Solomona and I show empty palms. What test is this? We cannot guess her name. And they laugh, for we do not have to. They are telling us. Her name is Gus.

Mrs Peacock claps her hands and we scatter. Billy takes us

to the storehut, where the good wood lives, and tools and suchlike. Its front is wide and open. I think we are to move the wood so that we fellows can sleep under its roof this night, but no – he is looking for a sail, and rope, and from time to time behind him too, for the coming of his father, and absent brother.

'Ma says to make a tent for you. Over there?'

Head-shaking. The canvas does not smell good. It is damp and dotted black with mould. We will sleep on our mats under the stars tonight, I tell him.

*

Mr Peacock returns with falling shadows and barking dogs, bent by some burden on his back. Ada speeds to greet him with a falling cry. But the flesh and bones he carries is only goat meat. No Albert, he tells her, angry-stiff. No sign of him.

'Then we must look,' says Ada.

'No!' Mr Peacock is loud and sharp for all to hear. 'Too late tonight. It's his own fault for wandering off. I told him to stay with the carcass. He must take the consequences.'

'Oh,' says Ada. A small sad flinching sound.

'We will search in the morning. A night in the forest won't hurt him, but it will make him think twice next time.'

'You mustn't worry, Ada,' says Lizzie, uncertainly. 'Albert will be fine for just one night.'

'I suppose it *is* too dark to look for him now,' says Mrs Peacock. The sky is turning inky, spark-scattered. 'Joseph? Is it? But in the morning, if he's not back – and I'm sure he will be – we will all hunt together?' Her voice ripples like wind-blown water. 'We will hunt over the whole island, until we find him.'

We fellows look at one another, thinking of all the spirits and devils and unseen things that live in the high forest on our island, and nothing to keep safe this boy all alone, no dog even. We clamp our mouths. We fellows would not be in that forest in darkness for all the calico on this earth or ocean. 'Tonight we can pray for Albert,' says Solomon, hesitantly.

Lizzie brings one of the new candles from the house, flame bright and strong and beckoning, and I hold it for my brother, to make amends, tipping it between my fingers so the sliding wax can fall on earth and do no harm. Solomona reads with downed eyes, always down, and the verses come slow and flat and dead. His voice does not ring like a bell. It does not rise and fall. Dark dull mumbling – a task to make out where one line ends and one begins. I think how Mr Reverend holds a chosen word, and how he sees into each body one by one, when he speaks, into each heart, with eyes you desire to rest only on your own person. When Mr Reverend sermonises, you think God is sending the words into your own head, filling each ear with holiness. You may not hear or know the words before, and yet you feel their meaning. But I know also that this is a kind of trick, which Solomona too must learn.

Mr Reverend, he sits at his desk long time, and scratches down words in ink, and scratches them out. He tears up paper, starts again, sometimes angry, sometimes sad, always perseverant. Here on this island, there will be no desk for Solomona, no lectern for his Bible, no time to search for words. To travel far and wide to spread the Word and bring light to our heathen brethren on every island, a native pastor needs only his voice, and the Word.

He has been chosen, and the Lord will take care of him. Not yet. You see, Mr Reverend say pastors need wives, to be two-handed men on their Mission. But last year Solomona became a one-handed man once more. A few weeks later, the new *John Williams* came to take the new teachers away to New Guinea, in new dark suits, as Pioneers of the Cross, all with their wives, and my brother was left behind, alone. God proposes and also He disposes. Here, perhaps, on this other island far away, he will fill his soul again and put aside his sadness with usefulness. This is Mr Reverend's hope.

As we pray, restlessness infects us all. Our ears open for sounds beyond, for noises in the dark, desiring to hear again the voice this family knows so well but we have yet to hear. Solomona's eyes never rise. Mark. Chapter ten.

'*Suffer little children to come unto me, and forbid them not: for of such is the kingdom of God*,' he says.

The little girl Gus has fallen asleep where she sits, head tilted, mouth catching insects. All is disorderly here today, everything out of kilter. Once more I try to fix my mind on Solomona's words, and the fellow who comes running in the story, and kneels to Jesus, and calls him 'Good Master'.

'*What shall I do that I may inherit eternal life?*' he says. '*Honour thy father and thy mother.*' Mr Peacock lets out a growl like a guarding dog. Fire-lit faces turn and tighten.

Jesus tells the man to give all he has to the poor so that he might have treasure in heaven. He goes away, sorrowful. He has great possessions, many things. '*How hard it is for them that trust in riches to enter into the kingdom of God*,' says Solomona. Camels. Needles. I puzzle how Solomona will guide us now, and tell us how we must think. For have we not come here, we six, we

Islanders, in hope of great possessions? Is this *not* the way to enter the kingdom of God?

'Let us pray,' he says, shortcutting his service. No lesson.

Every pair of hands is quickly clasped. Eyelids close over all the dancing flames.

'Let us pray to our Lord for our safe delivery to this island, and his blessing upon the work we come to do here for Mr and Mrs Peacock.'

'Amen.'

'Let us pray for fair winds for the *Esperanza* to return for us when our task is done. And let us pray most fervently of all that the Lord in his mercy is keeping Albert – Albert Francis Peacock – safe in his bosom.'

'Amen,' we all say again. Tears glitter on Ada's face and, trying to hold her silence, she shakes. Her mother comforts her.

'Amen,' says Mr Peacock, a final stop, and bends to attend to the long box which lies at his feet. Two clicks. The darkness softly twangs. From a dark, silky shroud he uncovers a curved, wooden, golden thing, which glows a little, throwing back the firelight. Mr Peacock tips his head and places it beneath his beard, and stands like a tree with two new branches, one fat, one slender. He takes the thin stick and moves it across the shiny boxy thing, and right away we fellows squat down, and cover our ears with our hands.

This noise! To see off evil spirits? But quickly he turns some twig-like part and the thing begins to sing instead of moan, and I find I know its song. So we sing together, Rock fellows and palagi family. Two languages. Luka's eyes are shining, and I remember that although he is strong and brave, he is also very young, like me, and somewhat frightened by this place, I see, and I move closer to him.

'Abide with me . . . '

We fill our lungs with hope, and sing the louder, as if the unseen boy, Albert Francis Peacock, might hear our voices, take comfort in them, and find his way quickly home.

BEFORE

In the early days of the voyage, the *Good Intent* stopped often to trade and take on fresh water. They passed plenty of small islands, and Lizzie always begged to go ashore with Mr Peacock when he went to barter for seeds and roots – potatoes, maize, yams, taro, kumara. Sometimes he agreed. At Nuku'alofa on Tongatapu, the red-whiskered Scottish storekeeper greeted them warmly and asked after Albert, and of course to be remembered to Mrs Peacock. *How could anyone forget this man?* thought Lizzie. When, months back, all but Ada had lost hope, and Albert's spasms were at their worst, his fever spiking, his tongue furred, his stomach sunken, the storekeeper had searched and found an ancient bottle of Dover's powder. It somehow eased the boy into slumber. Most likely saved his life. Pa lit up with fresh gratitude, cagily revealed something of the family's plans and his aspirations for Albert, and accepted the storekeeper's offer of beans, black and wrinkled. He was on the point of buying up four months' supply of flour, salt, tea, tobacco and sugar too when Captain MacHeath stopped him. No need for that, it seemed.

'We've fair stocks still in the hold,' he said. 'If the island's not to your liking, you may not want much. But I'll give you a good price and all you need, should you choose to stay.'

'Nothing to lose,' Pa muttered.

'How kind he is,' Lizzie whispered to her father as they settled themselves back in the ship's gig, shaded by an ivory-handled silk umbrella the captain had produced with a flourish as they'd set off. As if she were a lady who needed a parasol!

Ahead, the sea's fury broke in a dull haze. Beyond, the ocean darkened. Half a day later, the *Good Intent* passed leeward of the last and loneliest island, and on they sailed south.

*

Albert spent more and more time hanging over the taffrail with every passing day. He could keep nothing down. Ada was always at his side, supporting his shoulders, dabbing at his clothes when the wind blew the wrong way. His cheeks gradually hollowed, and his skin took on a tin-glazed pallor, pockets of violet spreading beneath his sinking eyes.

During better spells, Albert followed a pair of vast tortoises as they roamed the main deck. They had been brought on board some islands back, destined one day to become soup, salvers and tureens. Meanwhile, they dragged themselves onwards, seemingly exhausted, never able to see any way round the obstacles in their paths. Whenever he could, Albert removed their blockades, quietly setting each item back in its place once the creatures had passed. Several times he found an animal encircled by laughing sailors, its head slowly hammering against a locker or mast, its claws sliding and scraping.

'It's not funny,' he muttered defiantly, his own head lowered like a bull to hide his eyes' betrayal. But the tortoise was too big for Albert to move by himself, and he had to call Billy to help him shift the animal onto a new and safer course.

'There!' he said, with satisfaction. The small cheer that immediately went up from his audience surprised Albert. Why hadn't they just helped? He took a brief, blushing bow, shivered, and rushed dizzily back to his place at the rail.

Time began to drag as one week turned into two. Again and again, their parents warned the children to stay out of the way of the crew, or there'd be consequences. 'Keel-hauled and hung out to dry,' Billy assured the others, thrilled by the threat. He was learning more than Ma would have liked from the deckboy, who was also called Billy. Tucked out of the way between watches with his new friend and a marlinspike, sheltered by a tarpaulin stretched over the ship's smallest gig, Billy Peacock picked up splicing tricks along with shanties and rich language and stories of crippled mainsheet men. He showed off his Turk's Heads to anyone who'd pay attention, and stacked other knots up in his memory, ready to amaze his father when he needed. When Deckboy Billy found out where they were bound, he taught his apprentice a song called 'The King of the Cannibal Islands'.

> One day the king invited most
> All of his subjects to a roast.
> For half his wives gave up the ghost,
> The King of the Cannibal Islands.

Billy Peacock sang it in turn to his family, Pa picked up the tune on his fiddle, and they all tapped toes.

'I'm going to be Queen of the Cannibal Islands!' shouted Queenie, yelling out the chorus, her favourite bit.

Hokee pokee wongkee fum,
Puttee go pee kaibula cum,
Tongaree, wongaree, ching, ring, wum,
The King of the Cannibal Islands.

'No you won't,' said Ma, 'for there *are* no cannibals where we're going, and if there were, we'd not be stopping.'

The bosun was passing by. He gave Queenie's plait a tug.

'They won't eat you if you're a good girl and say your prayers,' he said. Ma smiled and frowned all at once, and pulled her daughter closer.

'A good girl? You'll be their long pig,' said Billy, pretending to eat Queenie's arm. Then he sang the verse about headless wives. A day later he was calling Albert a lubberly haymaker, which made Ada furious, for by this time Albert had lost the strength to stand. He lay on deck, eyes restlessly closed, a basin beside him. He refused all food and turned his head away when his sister tried to tempt him to drink a little cold tea.

Mrs Peacock's concern grew hourly. Albert winced and groaned as she pinched up the skin on the back of his hand, again and again, and sighed at how slowly it flattened. She and Ada begged him to try just a nibble of biscuit or a scoop of water. Pa watched sternly from a distance, his face darkening. Eventually he pushed Ada aside, and knelt next to Albert himself, deaf to his clammy protests.

'Stop this, Son. I'm ordering you to drink.'

'I'd rather die. Just want to die,' moaned Albert, feebly shuffling away from his father's raised hand.

'I'll clatter thee first.' Jaws clenched. One great hand held the back of Albert's head, the other thrust a flask between his lips, and stinging brandy splashed the boy's bared gums. 'Now drink,' Mr Peacock commanded.

Lizzie heard the harsh clunk of metal on teeth, and a choking gurgle. Ada wept loudly. Ma turned shakily aside. 'Biscuit!' ordered Pa, holding out a hand for the piece of hard tack Albert had rejected earlier. Lizzie passed it to him, and watched, compelled, as he smashed it into crumbs small enough to force down his son's resisting throat and then held his jaw shut until he swallowed.

'That's better.'

Later, Pa took Lizzie aside and told her of the steerage deaths he'd witnessed on his voyage out from England over twenty years earlier. Vomiting without respite, grown men and women had starved themselves before they ever reached land. Emigrants who'd saved for years for their passage. What a waste, thought Lizzie, seeing for the first time that it was love and fear, not anger, that made her father so fierce when he saw the death smear moistening his own son's face. No wonder Ma had thanked him for his roughness.

The ship plunged on through teeming nothingness, as full as it was empty. Albert kept forcing himself to eat, and Lizzie spent hours simply observing the horizon dip and rise, rise and dip, or slowly tip from side to side, as mesmerised as Gussie. The vastness seemed more marvellous and more hard to bear each time the sun rose, yet still there was no sign of land.

Then, almost imperceptibly, the horizons ceased to shift.

Slowly, slowly, everything else stopped moving too. The crew threw pails of water at the sails, to stiffen them into service against the slightest breeze. But none came calling. The *Good Intent* was completely becalmed. No amount of whistling made the slightest difference. The whole ship seemed to droop, and all that was on it. Even the gliding birds, which usually scraped the waves, had vanished. The heat rose, the smells rose, and the water became a sultry mirror. Until you looked straight down, at the clarity and depth and enormity below. Albert, happily leaning over still water at last, was the first to sight a jellyfish, pulsing, trailing, absurdly bright and oddly purposeful. The others joined him at the rail.

From time to time, Billy sucked on a finger and held it up to test the air. Nothing.

'What if we're stuck here for ever?' he said.

'I wouldn't mind,' admitted Albert. The calm had given him a glorious reprieve.

'But what if we run out of food?' Queenie was always hungry. 'Or water?' She sounded panicky.

'Shhh,' said Ada, wondering, worrying.

Lizzie wanted to ask Pa, but he was in the cabin with Captain MacHeath.

There was nothing to do but wait. Bodies sprawled on boards. Talk wilted. Nearing the evening, when it wasn't cool but it was cooler, and the only sounds were the sigh of shrinking timbers and the odd whistle of a moving block, Mrs Peacock sat on deck, the baby in her lap. She took her yellowing meerschaum pipe from its soft leather case, and packed it with tobacco. At first she smoked in silence, nose to nose with the carved dog that clambered on the pipe's flaring stem. Lizzie sat nearby, breathing in sweet woody smoke which rose as straight as a mast from the bowl.

'Tell me about when *you* were little,' she tempted at last.

'Oh, it's too hot for stories.' Ma blew on her daughter's face.

Queenie crept round to Ma's other side, and leaned in to listen, stroking Gussie's hair with an idle hand. Mrs Peacock gently tapped her fingers away, and told her to mind or she'd waken her, and then there'd be no peace.

'Please tell us a story,' whispered Queenie, undeterred, prepared to be patient.

'Tell us about winter,' said Lizzie. They both knew it was just a question of getting their mother started. 'Winter when you were little I mean. In London. When it was cold. Really cold.'

'Cold enough to see a crow's breath? Oh, that's too long ago. I can hardly remember those days.'

'Yes, you can,' said Queenie, lifting her skirts a little to encourage the air in, and letting them fall. 'Tell us about snow. That'll cool us down.'

'Snow?' Mrs Peacock sucked on her pipe and smiled. 'What can I possibly say about snow that I've not told you before?'

Queenie thought for a while.

'Does it really melt the soonest when the winds begin to sing?'

'That's just a song,' Ma told her. 'But I suppose it's true enough. If it's a warm wind.'

'And what does snow feel like? Is it hard or soft?'

Billy hovered nearby, wanting to listen, not wanting to admit it. He cocked his head, and appeared to concentrate on his whittling. Voices carried easily in this stillness. Low laughter came from the captain's quarters, where MacHeath was once more entertaining and advising Mr Peacock, over brandy. Ada and Albert also settled themselves within hearing distance of Mrs Peacock, sitting back to back for support. They'd been playing draughts, their set borrowed from the second mate, but Albert always beat Ada, and anyone else he played, including the second mate.

'Snow can be hard or soft,' said Mrs Peacock. 'It all depends.'

'Please, Ma, can't you just tell us?' begged Queenie.

'What more is there to say? I've told you often enough how it sparkles in the sun.'

'Like the sea?' asked Lizzie.

'A little like. Not much.'

'Like stars?'

'No, not like stars either.'

'But how does it sound?' Queenie asked, deflated.

'Like nothing at all. Quite, quite silent as it falls. It hushes the world, at first, though when you walk on it, it makes a kind of crunching sound. And by the end of the day, it's made everything noisier than ever. When it's melted.' She could hear that peculiar gritty splash made by wheels and hooves and boots, cobbles and kerbs, sweepers and omnibuses, soot-stained slush collapsing from gutters. But she couldn't put it into words. 'Dirty stuff, snow is, in London. And perishing cold.'

'Oh, I want to see snow. I want to see the world all white . . .' Queenie blew out her lips and closed her eyes.

'You don't have to go to England. There's snow enough in New Zealand, up high. There were blizzards on the gold fields not long after I came to Napier Town. Terrible stories in the newspaper – avalanches, and miners swept away, and skeletons found months later. Ask your father. No, don't. What am I saying?'

So Lizzie led the talking somewhere else, to her own old days.

'Tell us about New Zealand now. Tell us about where *I* was born,' she coaxed.

'Ah, Nuhaka,' said Ma, with a dreamy sigh. 'There was a spot you could see out your days. Full of promise, Hawke's Bay: lovely climate, natives so hardworking—'

'Wasn't I born there too?' came Albert's voice from behind Ada.

'That's right.' Mrs Peacock gently stretched her stiff legs. 'Yes, we had high hopes then. We thought flax was going to be our future.'

The first few years had gone well enough, she told them. The satisfaction of seeing the paddocks round the mill draped from top to bottom with drying fibres. The scream of the new stripper sounding all the day in the sheds – like music when you thought of the money it would make them. Why, its speed was a miracle! Soon they bought a scutching machine too.

'And then . . .'

Albert bit his lip. He could just about remember the night the flax mill burned to the ground, along with the newly dressed harvest, and both machines, and who knew even now if the first spark had been malice or ill fortune? He remembered Pa snatching him up from slumber, a bonfire smell indoors, a threatening crackling roar heard through a wooden wall. The mill was a tinderbox. Nothing could be saved. Lizzie was convinced she also had some memories of the fire – black billowing smoke and crashing timbers and screams to pierce your heart – but maybe it was only the telling of the disaster she recalled, and Ada's sobbing afterwards. And so the ever-growing family left Nuhaka, and pressed north, and now Ma admitted for the first time how close she'd come to turning back on the long overland trek to Ohiwa. On and on they plodded, sodden and chilled by endless rain, the horses' heads getting lower and lower. But Pa had strength and will enough for all, she told them. He'd walked for hours with Albert on his shoulders, talking all the while about the new venture, keeping them going, despite the wet and cold and the never knowing where they'd sleep next.

'And what was it, Ma? The new venture?' Queenie always wanted to know what happened next.

'A harbour hotel, in a new settlement, in the Bay of Plenty. On a beautiful spit. But Ohiwa had everyone fooled. You wouldn't know to look at it but that sand was always on the move. You can't build a settlement on sand. We didn't know till it was too late, and so many people were buying up land round there, and they had such grand schemes, so we thought perhaps we could make it work . . . Anyway, your father doesn't give up without a fight—'

'No,' said Lizzie, proudly.

'And he did his best.' Ma sucked on her pipe, and Gussie sighed in her sleep. But even Mr Peacock's best couldn't make that hotel pay. North they went, then along the Bay, to try their hand at farming. This was a life that suited Ma and the little ones much better – raising maize and potatoes under vast skies in Whakatane – and that was where Billy and Queenie were born.

Plenty proved not enough for Mr Peacock. It wasn't his, you see. Land was scarcer there by then, and the acres they farmed belonged to another man, a speculator, Ma said, far away in England. Not many more years had passed before they abandoned Whakatane too, leaving only the smallest of graves behind, setting sail with trading-post ambitions, first for Auckland, then to the South Seas.

Perhaps they shouldn't have pressed on when they found they had missed the moment in the Friendly Islands. Perhaps they should have known better than to take on another hotel in Apia. But who can ever predict what you'll find, anywhere you go, and by the time they reached Samoa, Gussie was well on the way and they had to stop for a while . . .

Ma's voice died away, as if she blamed herself for the timing of things. Pa will be happier now, farming again, thought Lizzie. He was surely made to coax life out of land, not coins from strangers' pockets.

'It *is* good to settle,' said Ma. 'But sometimes it's better to move on. You have to settle in the right place, you see, or there's no point. I'm making you no promises about Monday Island, mind. You can never know it's right until you get there. So now we shall see what we shall see and put our best foot first.'

Then she made their scalps tingle in a different way, ordering all the girls to brush and plait their hair again, as she wondered aloud what on earth had led them to imagine that there could be any reason here, in the middle of nowhere, with nothing happening, to be letting standards slip.

Each night, they bedded down on deck among the stacked copra sacks and stared at the stars until sleep came. So very many to see, more and more the harder you looked, and so much brighter above sea than land. They might have been flung there, seeds cast by a careless sower, shining in clusters like islands on a Pacific map. Lizzie floated among them for hours, staring at the most distant dot of light, until she noticed that great swathes lay even further beyond, each shining pinprick so minute that together they formed luminous drifting smoke, twisting veils of light or ghostly lace. The sky wasn't empty, any more than the sea.

'Upside down,' said Pa one evening when they were getting ready to bed down for the night, and Lizzie was staring into teeming nothingness, trying to tell reality from reflection, where water ended and where sky began. 'The stars, I mean.' Ma nodded and smiled at Pa, and the blanket she was shaking out hung slack for a few seconds while their meeting eyes shared some memory they'd never tell the children. Queenie stuck her head between her knees and peered upwards through her legs to see what difference it might make.

'The moon's upside down here too,' Pa added.

'To you, maybe. But not to us,' said Billy, bravely, as he lay down. He was pleased to feel his father's hand in his hair. Just a rub and a fond pat. He closed his eyes, and dreamed of a fresh wind coming and ports he'd maybe never see.

Three nights later Lizzie woke, startled: the ship was on the move again. She staggered to her feet, head spinning with relief, guided by the gleam of brass fittings, the starlit glow of billowing canvas, until she saw her father beckoning her. Together they paced the quietly creaking ship and stopped to watch the stern wave raging with light, millions of sparkling particles in a stream of water. At the bow, the same mysterious radiance rushed in a silvery stream from the wing-like fins of flying fish, skimming the water in threes and fours, aloft for impossible distances and leading the way, it seemed, like guardian angels.

BEFORE

Landfall.

A word to trip a seafarer's heart.

Lizzie heard it in the early morning, called out from the top of the mizzenmast, then echoing round the ship. What could Little Admiral Billy see with those sharp dark eyes of his? Lizzie could make out only the faintest smear, just a snagged thread on the horizon.

Hours later, the snag took shape. Another full watch had been rung – 'All's well!' – before their island passed from ghostliness into anywhere you could imagine landing. It slowly grew into clarity. A line of hills – here was a mountain, even, green with forest. The peak disappeared into wispy cloud, making its height hard to judge. Darkness pooled purple in front of a curving ridge. Closer the ship came, until the pale rocks of cliffs could be distinguished rising in humps like the coils of a sea monster, divided by shadowy green ravines. At first they appeared to drop straight down into the sea, but as the *Good Intent* made headway, a few strips of beach appeared below, and they could see a line of breaking surf. Lizzie shielded her eyes with her hand and longed for Pa's spyglass. Though she had put the waving palms and milk-white sands of the Friendly Islands far behind her, she had never anticipated a sight as inhospitable as this.

Mrs Peacock emerged from the hold, where she and Ada had been making sure everything was packed up again, and nothing forgotten. Queenie, silent at last, leaned against her mother's stiff skirts for comfort, and Gussie, now on Ma's hip, pointed at something with a soft sigh and twisted herself round to search her mother's face for clues. Was this a time to be happy or sad? To laugh or cry? Mrs Peacock betrayed nothing, but her grip on the baby tightened.

Mr Peacock was on the poop deck, standing beside Captain MacHeath. Both looked grim. The first mate shook his head, face closed; the bosun gave the gathered children a pitying look, followed by a phoney grin. Robson's last advice had been to land on the North Beach: in a westerly the surf wouldn't be half as heavy. Clapperton Bay, on the other side, was a poorer place to land by far. If only he'd known himself, all those years ago. Pa had told MacHeath all this.

Except today the wind was coming from the north-east, and blowing hard. Vast, navy blue rollers crashed onto the shore, as if commanded to smash stones to sand by nightfall. It was difficult to imagine how the surf could be higher anywhere.

Mr Peacock turned to the captain, shouting to be heard: 'Can we wait till the wind changes?'

More head-shaking. More shouting.

'Could be days. I'm in a hurry. We lost enough time when we were becalmed. I can afford to waste no more.' MacHeath clapped a hand on Mr Peacock's shoulder like a sympathetic friend. 'I'm sorry, but that's how it is. We'll have to see how we fare on the other side.'

So the schooner swung west, following the line of pale, stiped cliffs around a jutting bluff. ('Not too close! Keep her away!') With its jagged pinnacles, and sharper drop, this coast looked even less promising. As they rounded the westernmost point of the island, Lizzie's stomach began to knot.

'Do you think—' she whispered to Ada.

'No,' said Mrs Peacock sharply before she could finish. 'Wait and see. Then we will make our judgement.'

That was when Queenie shouted out: 'Sharks!'

A pack of ten or twelve was following the ship, or so it seemed, swimming swiftly just below the surface, the curved fins on their backs breaking through the water one after another in a rippling rhythm.

'Is this the place?' asked Billy, doubtfully, looking at a tiny cove beneath a curve of towering cliffs.

'No – look!' Lizzie shoved him in the right direction to look beyond the next bluff, where the stretched crescent of a wider bay was finally beginning to show. A good strip of sombre grey streaked with brown – sand, or shingle. Hard to tell. To be sure it was at the foot of an ominous wall of cliffs rising higher than any they'd seen yet – at least a thousand feet – with eye-fooling flat lines of grey and yellow, looking like Egyptian pyramids from the illustrated newspapers. Sailing in, you saw the steepness from a different angle, and the illusion vanished. Then it seemed the mountain had been sliced in two, immeasurably long ago. You couldn't help but wonder what had happened to the other half. Perhaps the trees wondered too, for they seemed to peer down to look, slowly falling from the top, straggling down the cliff face in their efforts to join the greenery at the bottom.

All along Clapperton Bay ran a wide and inviting strip of land, almost flat, and green as you liked, and this was backed by a more gentle-looking grove of trees, streaks of crimson against the dark leaves – the fiery flowers of the pohutukawa. The same trees covered the side of the mountain.

'It looks like New Zealand,' said Ma, with some satisfaction. 'After a fashion.'

As if in welcome, the wind dropped to a useful breeze, while the thunder of surf from the north of the island was muffled enough to be put out of mind. Coloured a deep blue of rare intensity, the waters sparkled here under a high midday sun.

Desperate to be first on shore, the younger children set up a clamour, quickly shushed. Pa would go first – and check there was *really* nobody there, thought Lizzie, nervously – and then the others would be landed with all their baggage when he'd grasped the lay of the land. A jolly boat was lowered, and one of the sailors shimmied down to it. Just as Pa was about to swing his leg over the deck rail, his eye fell on Albert.

'Three will be better than two if those sharks get curious,' said Pa. 'Down you go.'

'Not fair,' mouthed Billy. As the boat backed off, Lizzie waved tentatively, hoping to catch Pa's eye. But he was busy rowing on one oar, looking over his shoulder with every other stroke, calculating where they'd be best to come to shore, while Albert held on tight and watched the water, rigid with tension.

The captain had already ordered their baggage to be brought up on deck, along with the stores from the hold.

'Will there be time enough to get it all ashore today?' Ada wondered quietly to Lizzie.

Ma didn't like whisperers. She separated the children with a few quick orders – a last blanket to be fetched, the puppies – so much bigger now – to be muddled back into their crate. Meanwhile, the gig was lowered and loaded. Sal began to whine.

*

The first they knew of Pa's return was a thud and a flash of orange. A juicy citrus had landed on deck, tossed up from the boat below, and Pa's head soon followed. The children ran after the rolling fruit.

'Save the pips.' said Pa. He nodded at Ma, then ducked back down for more.

Lizzie beat Billy to rescue the orange from the coil of rope where it had come to rest, and dug her nails into the thick peel, greedily inhaling the sharp sprays of oil that hit her cheek. The first mouthful of flesh was every bit as sweet and juicy as Robson had promised. She handed out a pig to each sibling and a few leftovers to a handful of crew members whose curiosity had brought them hovering.

'Tip-top!' said Deckboy Billy, as if that decided everything.

For a short time, Albert, left on the island with orders to flag the next landing, was its only inhabitant. At the north end of the bay, where the surf was less ferocious, though the slope of the beach even steeper, he waved his arms and shouted. At last a second boat shot grittily through the foam with a decisive thrust of the oars, Ma and the children hanging on to the sides.

Lizzie didn't need Albert's hand. She jumped out by herself into an advancing wave, and despite her readiness to resist, was pulled sharply backwards by its undertow. Wet to the thighs, she forced her way up onto the beach, took a few tottling steps towards the top, and stopped, feet planted. The ground lurched beneath her. She had been at sea too long. She had to root herself again. Hands on hips, she surveyed the towering cliffs, the ridge of grey sand and pebbles immediately ahead, and the trumpeting pink tangle of morning glory which sprawled and crawled towards them, outermost tendrils eagerly criss-crossing in beckoning haste. This way, this way, the plants implored. She threw back her head and laughed.

'We're here. We're here at last. The island's ours. We're home!'

'Lizzie!' Ma was calling from the boat, reminding her that she couldn't just run off and explore. Someone needed to get the baby away from the water, and the boat dragged up the beach before it could be pulled back by the waves' strong undertow, and everything unloaded.

Mr Peacock, arriving on the first returning gig, walked towards his wife and stood beside her. He took her arm in his and touched his hat and scanned her face.

'Will it do, Mrs P?'

How could she know? She didn't answer at first. Nobody else would speak till she had. Lizzie held out a hand to Ma's flailing arm, balancing her as she staggered up the steep beach, feet sliding lawlessly until they reached the knotted flowery mass at the top. Fleshy leaves, glowing emerald where the light shone through, creaking like cut cabbages under their bare feet. Ma squinted up at the rock face, took in the flat, grassy land nestling below, the swathe of blue beyond – a stretch of water – the trees. The lushness of it all. The beauty. Almost familiar, but yet not quite. She nodded.

'It will, Joseph. I think it will do well, for now.'

That was it. It was the reply he wanted.

They all rushed back to the water's edge to help Pa and a couple of sailors take off the first necessities: carpet bag, fiddle, camp oven, blankets. The emptied boat returned to the ship with the news that the Peacocks were here to stay, and was quickly reloaded.

Crates, boxes and bags soon lay scattered among the pink flowers at the top of the sandbank. Against the vastness of the surrounding cliffs, their possessions looked insignificant. But they were hardly castaways, Lizzie reminded herself, gathering her skirts to climb up further so she could see what lay beyond.

11

ALL THAT FIRST UNQUIET NIGHT, MEMORIES OF HOME tide in my mind, keeping me from slumber. Times all is confusion and I feel I voyage in a strange ship yet see nothing. Times I am back at the Mission, the day of our departing, Mr Reverend sitting before me, clear enough to touch, our many-day-back talk rolling back and forth inside me.

All was busy-busy then outside the window. The *Esperanza*, three days already at our island, was loading at last, after one day waiting for the sea to calm so canoes can come to her, one day with much worry that all is now too calm – perhaps the vessel could wreck itself with drifting, like the old missionary ship, the old *John Williams*, still not broken up, all these many years. Next day, cotton dusts hair and Jew's ear scents, the air, for the day has come for all the gifts for the Church, brought to the Mission by the Fellowship, to go on board before us. At the jetty arrowroot heaped. Our Church must pay its way, Mr Reverend always tells his wife, and in my hearing. We cannot be a burden to our London brethren. He worries in his heart about the price he'll get for all these goods.

And I have also glimpsed the letters he writes to London, when
he is careless and leaves 'em unfolded and unsealed. (I could not
help but look.) Our minister reaps great praise for wondrous
changes wrought upon the Rock – nowhere else on God's whole
earth has every islander been brought from savagery to the
Christian faith in so short a season. But he sorrows still, mourning
a new feeling growing ever stronger on our island, that mood he
calls the mercenary spirit.

For this reason I never asked him about our payment for our
work away. I would not have him think me mercenary, laying
up treasures only here on earth, pining for great possessions. I
do not tell him what the other palagi here said to me when we
walked by the store that morning. How my family goes up in
world. News quickly scampers in and out of all the houses, and
Vika puts on airs even before our sailing. Such fine customers
my family will be when we return, Solomona and me, says Mr
Head, storekeeper, whose wife, an islander like me, wears clothes
as fine as Mrs Reverend's, with white lace collar and shiny stripes
for Sundays. No Mother Hubbard dress for her, make no mistake.
She is bombazine and satin. So longs my mother.

And still Mr Reverend look at me and say:

'You will certainly come back a wealthier man, Kalala.'

Fingers raking beard with slow patience, as if to find something
hiding in its wispy strands, waiting like fish in weeds.

*

I wake again and again and wish we had never come to this place.
It seems to me that we have broken into the middle of a story
and now we are part of it.

12

THE SKY IS PINKING NEXT MORNING WHEN I HEAR double-click of knees – Solomona lowers himself in prayer nearby. He means us to hear his murmuring words – some in our tongue, some in English. Again and again, he repeats the name Al-bert. So the boy is not back, and now he prays for him again. I roll away, and my brother's mumbling ceases.

'No sign yet?' I say, up-sitting.

'Amen,' he finish. 'No, not one sign that I can see.'

We have made our little camp a small distance from the huts. Not too far, nor yet too close. My stomach growls for food but I think there will be no eating this morning. And we must delay our housebuilding.

Soft whistles like birdsong come from Vilipate, who lies on his back sleeping still, mouth open. Luka and Iakopo waken and stretch full slow, throwing their blankets off, rubbing eyes. When they remember where they are, they sit up straight and shivery. This place is cooler than our island. Pineki stumble back from the bushes he has watered, loud-yawning and buttoning himself as he walks. His gaping jaw clamps shut and he pull down his shirt when Solomona tsks at him.

'What?' he ask, scratching his head and then his buttock.

'Be full of respect. We are guests here. Our hosts are suffering a loss.'

Pineki's smile drifts, and he turns to tidying mats with Luka and Iakopo. It is light now and soon perhaps the naughty boy will return, and he will be beaten for his disobedience, and then we will see what our work will be and we can build our house. I hope this is so.

'Maybe he is messing, not missing,' I say. I do not want him gone much longer. We balance on a narrow ledge, between lagoon and open sea, and it uneases me, and Solomona too, I see. 'Or maybe both.'

'We will see,' said Solomona, looking again towards the Peacock huts. 'We will see. I have begged the Good Lord for His help, and I am sure He will see fit to answer our prayers.'

Vilipate wake up, and stand, and straightway begin to fold his blanket, as if to tidy away himself with his belongings.

'I am ready,' he say. 'What now?'

'We must wait for orders,' I tell him.

I know he wants to start work. He does not desire distraction. Vilipate wants to show how strong and quick he is, at every task.

So there we stand together, one body with many legs, looking across the grass towards the family, who huddle too. One girl comforts another, the smallest child holds the baby in her arms, and the father is pointing here, and there, and everywhere, anger in his voice. The mother stands hand on belly, with pain-pulled face.

'Be careful,' I say. 'Remember the palagi do not like us to stare.'

'Yes, yes,' say Solomona. 'Kalala is right. It gives them discomfort. It is not polite. At times like this, they trap their thoughts inside themselves. Yet when they talk to you, remember: do not drop your eyes then!'

'Ask them how many vessels come by here,' I say to Solomona as we stand making circles in the sand with our toes to hide our uneasiness.

He reproves me. Hardly here, and I am wanting to be home. This will not do.

'Ask them yourself, if you must. You speak their tongue as well as I do, or better.' Then Solomona regrets his impatience, and softens himself towards me. An arm on mine, eyes steady on eyes. 'But not now. Later. When the boy is found.'

Vilipate and Pineki give me an eye-corner look, to say they know why I never will. It has been too many months since a ship came here last. It may be many months yet before the next one passes. Just as the *Esperanza* cook often told us, we must play our cards till then. But first learn the game. And meanwhile, today, all thought must be with the missing Albert.

Everyone waits, balancing between the after and the before.

And then a wordless mourning cry cuts the air, and turns all hearts in wonderment. It is the oldest girl, the one called Ada, who is still more pained with fear than all the rest. She pull away, runs up towards the forest, but the father call her, voice loud as a cracking sail.

'Come back at once, Ada!'

Mr Peacock's voice grows somewhat softer, like he is trying hard, hard as he can, to make it kind and gentle, yet also shouting after her for all to hear. 'You won't help Albert or anyone else by rushing off on your own.'

She longs for her brother.

'We will organise a search party,' he tells her. 'The time is right. We have left it long enough.'

Solomona hangs back, like a fish who feeds on fragments, and circle-swims for any morsel that might float up when big killer-fish have had their fill. Ada eyes him as she passes, brow suspicious, wondering what he might know. Swish, swish. Her angry, frightened arms brush against her dress as she marches.

'Boys!' Mr Peacock calls over to us. (Always boys.) It is clear he means to use us in the searching too.

'Come on,' I tell the others. 'Come on, Solomona. Time to start work. This is where it begins.'

Even Pineki grows full serious now, seeing all the family gathered so quiet and grim. We join them with no more ado. A map is drawn on sand. The island is divided. The parents tell us again about their Albert – mother interrupting father, Ada breaking the speech of both. Something more than child and less than man, they say. Taller than the others. This big. The girls show us with their hands flat above their heads. Blue eyes, they say, as if we could mistake him for a different fellow who is also lost. Such blue eyes . . . such beautiful blue eyes, like china, and such a handsome boy, his mother tells us, and her hands shape his absent face in the air before her, as if she would cup his cheeks and draw him towards her for a kiss. Too much beauty for a boy, I think she means.

'Any sign of him, report back to Mrs P,' orders the father. 'She will stay at home with Gussie.'

'And if we find him?' asks Billy, who is to search with Queenie and Ada. Cloud-white faces all.

'Light the bonfire again on the bluff if you bring him home. We will see the smoke. If not, make a noise, of course. A hulla-baloo. As loud as you can.'

Mr Peacock turn one final time towards us, staring deep into every pair of eyes, his own snake-narrow. He means to know our hearts. Can he trust us? He has no choice.

'Understood? You know what you are doing, boys?'

Together we mutter: 'Yes, sir.'

Solomona bows his head.

'We will do all in our power to find your son and bring him home. Rest assured that wherever he may be, he remains in the loving care of our Lord.'

'Yes. Of course. I sincerely hope so.'

He walk away. Our chests empty of held breath. Solomona and I start explaining to our fellows but we see at once they need few words. The sudden heartache of this family penetrates all, slowing blood flow, turning over minds with horrors. Our finding must be fast and certain. We will go in pairs. We must not sep-arate. All times together. Beware dangers unknown.

'How will we know these unknown dangers?' ask Pineki.

'Just beware,' Solomona tells him.

'Can we eat before we go?' Luka is hungry.

'No.'

'And tapu places? Where are they? How will we know them?' This is Vilipate's question.

Heathen superstitions, I have heard Mrs Reverend say from time to time. Mr Reverend hush her, gently. We have our own, he say. We simply give them different names.

In English, Solomona whisper quickly to me:

'Shall we ask Mr Peacock?'

I reply in our tongue. Not to chastise but to be fair and free with our knowledge.

'No. I think he is not a man with patience for tapu.'

'Yes. You are right,' Solomona put his fingertips together and cough a little before he answer. I nod my head, gather attention.

'I think you will know a tapu place when you see it. There will be a sign. Just must beware. Take care with every footstep.'

He coughs, uncertain of his next words. But I know what they will be. Mr Reverend frowns on fornication. Since our island saw the Light, this sin makes an outcast of you. It will have you expelled from the Fellowship of the Church, weeded and thrown away like a tare come up with wheat. We have learned to skip clear of fornication at every cost.

Now Solomona whispers his reminder: 'And never forget the strong request of Mr Reverend: watch yourself with the young ladies at all times. Do not be alone with them.'

BEFORE

There was nothing to show another person had ever walked this way before.

'Come and see the lagoon. We have a lagoon.'

Albert, colour returning to his cheeks, swept an arm behind him. Queenie, suddenly awed, slipped a hand into Lizzie's. The children hung back so that Ma could lead the way, as Pa would expect.

'Never waste a journey,' she reminded. Everyone picked up as much as they could carry, Billy unsteady under the weight and bulk of the camp oven, while Sal made circuits of them all, full teats swinging, and called quietly to her puppies, which Ada carried in their crate. The sailors made ready to follow.

Beyond the sandbanks they found a vivid meadow of shimmering blue. Mounds of billygoat weed stretched before them, flowers like fluffy pincushions. Around the edges of the lagoon – more of a swamp, in truth – the greenery grew lighter and lusher. The waters themselves were already dark and dull, for the shadow of the mountain and the cliffs behind was moving steadily across the bay. In a few hours' time the sun would go completely, and soon after that the light. The *Good Intent*, her captain and her crew would also quickly vanish. Could they delay that moment, Lizzie wondered, wavering?

Pa strode behind his family with the captain, carpet bag in hand, oblivious to his daughter's trepidation. It seemed to Lizzie, turning back to watch the two men, that their roles had shifted: her father had grown in stature in the short time since they had landed on this island. With every step, each sweeping glance, Mr Peacock was taking possession of Monday Island. The idea strengthened her resolve.

'We'll berth in the shelter of those trees tonight,' said Mr Peacock, turning the procession towards the head of the bay.

Leaving Ma and the baby encircled by trunks and cases, the children headed to collect firewood in the cool shadows and fresh scent of the gnarled and twisting trees that grew behind the camp and beneath the cliffs. They found plenty of fallen branches, and kindling, all good and dry. Loud cracks and snaps echoed out across the bay as they stamped and jumped, breaking up the smaller sticks into manageable lengths.

By the time the last crates arrived from the last jolly boat, full of the promised provisions, a welcoming fire was burning.

'That's the lot, Mr Peacock.'

The captain and Pa then turned their backs for a low-voiced negotiation over the carpet bag. Coins were counted out – eighty for the Peacocks' passage, and ten gold sovereigns more for flour and beans, tea and sugar, candles and soap. MacHeath looked up at the sky, still clear but darkening fast, and shook his head as if in sorrow. 'And we must be on our way.'

It should hardly have come as a shock. Yet it did, to everyone.

'You've a powerful fine family, and no mistake, Mrs Peacock,' he continued. 'Top to bottom. I admire you all and I'm sorry to bid you all farewell. Oh, but I nearly forgot. Cook gave me this for the kiddies. While you get yourselves on your feet. But I can see that won't take you long.' From inside his brocaded jacket, he brought out a couple of greaseproof packages, which he sniffed approvingly before handing them over to Ma. 'Salt beef sandwiches and plum cake, I believe. And now all that remains is to wish you every success with your new island home.'

It sounded so final. Until that moment, Lizzie could persuade herself it was all a game, an adventure. Even Pa had danced back and forth from shore to camp with a playful air, ruffling Billy's hair and swinging Queenie on arms of steel. As faces grew suddenly serious, Lizzie's stomach flopped like a fish. Soon they would be completely alone here.

Ma stumbled over her thanks.

'We will see you very soon, won't we? You will come by on your way back from Auckland with the new supplies we ordered? And . . . to take us off, if . . . '

'Oh yes, Mrs Peacock,' he assured her. 'About three months, I should say. Now, coming to see us off, little birds?'

'Of course,' said Pa.

The surf was a good deal higher already. The family stood close together at the top of the sandbank and watched as the jolly boat pulled away. Even once out at sea and well on their way to the ship, not one of the rowers could spare a hand to return the children's waved farewells. Only the captain briefly tipped his hat.

Then Lizzie wanted to call out to him (as if she'd ever be heard): 'Wait! Come back! We've changed our minds. Don't leave us here!'

She clamped her mouth shut with her own hand. Queenie's face was already a picture of confusion and alarm. Billy was pale and drawn. Lizzie was old enough to pretend, and for the sake of Pa, she'd do her best.

'This is it then,' said Albert quietly to Ada. Standing with thin arms folded, face serene as an angel's, he betrayed neither fear nor regret as he watched the departing crew. Perhaps it was the relief of dry land, however lonely and remote, a horizon that kept still, and the prospect of eating heartily again, nausea and fever reduced to bad dreams. Perhaps it was simply the hope of staying put. But if Albert could stay so calm at such a moment, how could Lizzie fret? Pa was there, right behind her, and Ma next to him, the cleverest, strongest, bravest people she had ever known.

In the middle of the bay, where the mightiest currents collided, the little boat paused, as if she had forgotten something, and the watchers on the shore held their collective breath. But she soon regained its course.

A hiccup in Lizzie's heart as the jolly boat was hauled up. Another when they saw the anchor weighed. All alone now.

No more words from anyone, even when, with a bellying of canvas, the *Good Intent* sailed south.

At last Gussie began to cry and arch her back.

'No point in watching for ever,' said Pa, brusquely. Though his reassuring hand dropped from Lizzie's shoulder, she noticed he still did not move his feet. The family stood on shore, all eight of them, in silent vigil, until the ship was completely out of sight.

BEFORE

The camp took shape quickly. Before it got dark, Lizzie helped Pa rig up a makeshift tent at the edge of the grove of ironwood trees using an old sail donated by MacHeath. Sal settled down to feed her squirming puppies. When Ma was satisfied everything else was where it should be, she rescued the apron that had been protecting the big china mixing bowl, tied it round her own waist, and announced her intention to bake scones.

'Flour, Ada. And salt. Over there.' She waved her spoon at the food crate.

Ada rolled across a heavy fifty-pound tin, one of twelve Pa had bought from MacHeath, and set it by her mother. Then she found a knife to prise it open. The top was stiff, and there was a hint of rust round the edge. Hardly surprising after a few months sealed in a damp hold. The blade curved in protest, but eventually the lid shifted.

For a moment Ada could only stare. 'Look, Ma!' she said, crossly, shaking the tin as she tipped it towards her mother. Pa came quickly to inspect. Lizzie followed, peering over her sister's shoulder. A soft fuzz coated the surface – vivid blue, almost green – Ada gave it an angry poke, and her tin spoon bent. The flour was a hard, solid mass. Inedible.

'Unfortunate,' said Ma, in her measured way. 'But can't be helped now, and we've plenty more. Let's try this one.'

It was Ma's turn to recoil from the musty smell. Without a word, Pa grabbed a third tin. No fresher. He only needed to shake it to realise that their entire flour supply was in the same condition. He threw it down in disgust, aiming a kick at the cylinder that sent it spinning. Ma tried to calm him.

'Never mind. It must have been an accident. But we've hard tack too, and that'll keep us going until we work out what the island can provide.'

Lizzie had already started rummaging.

'Here . . . this should be it.'

Pa's lips twitched and tightened as he emptied a mass of moving crumbs onto the ground, specked dark with weevils and their eggs. Ma shoved the ruined cabin bread into the fire with the edge of her foot to burn the pests as fast as possible. Queenie and Billy leapt to help her, aiming sharp, angry kicks at the mess.

No tears. No tears allowed.

Albert and Ada checked the sacks and shook their heads. There was barely a bean that hadn't been hollowed out by pests. The rice too was infested, the lard rancid, and as for the promised tea, that was nowhere to be seen. Lizzie's throat felt blocked, her lungs airless. She swallowed, and turned a face, falsely bright, towards her father's. He would have a plan. Pa was never without a plan. The other children were already cowering.

With a vast roar, Mr Peacock booted one of the tins into the air and out of sight. Grabbing a stick from the woodpile, he whacked another in the other direction, into the woods, where it rustled through the leaves and got stuck in a branch.

'He knew, the scoundrel. He knew. The—'

Gussie launched into screaming. Glaring at her husband, Ma jerked her head towards the beach. Pa made a strange animal noise at the back of his throat, and strode away, shouting, cursing, and kicking another tin before him.

'Wait, Pa,' called Lizzie, but he pushed her away from him, his rage like a scorching barrier, and left her shaking. He let fly with his foot again and again, until he'd been swallowed by the dusk and his grunts and shouts of anger were inaudible.

'Come, children,' said Ma, and they obediently turned back to the fire. 'Let him be.' Her voice took on a lilting tone, as if she were telling a story to the little ones to pass the time. 'We have the sandwiches from Cook. Here, help me lay out the cloth, Lizzie. We'll sit over here to eat them.' As she laid them out, carefully dividing the rough hunks of bread into fair-sized portions, setting some aside for her husband, giving herself the small end of the loaf, she murmured to herself, half under her breath: 'A terrible mistake, of course. No decent Christian would do a thing like that on purpose. But that awful climate. Destroys everything. How happy I am to be out of it. I'm sure it'll be no time before the captain's back with our new supplies – and plenty of them.'

'Will he give our money back?' asked Queenie.

'Certainly. Why would he want to cheat us?'

Lizzie could think of lots of reasons. Those tins must have lain in the depths of the *Good Intent* hold for years, mouldering away in one tropical island station after another, rejected by the ship's cook, never thrown away, and nobody but the Peacock family foolish enough to make an offer for them, sight unseen.

'Why didn't Pa check?' whispered Albert, voicing what they were all wondering, now.

'Shhh,' said Lizzie. 'They came out of the hold so late. Maybe MacHeath showed him a different tin . . . Or maybe he just trusted him.'

She remembered the two men drinking together in the captain's cabin, long into the night, during the calm. She remembered MacHeath's exaggerated wink when they first stepped on board weeks ago. It made her want to poke his eye out.

Mrs Peacock nodded at the children and closed her eyes.

'For what we are about to receive, may the Lord make us truly thankful, Amen.'

Lizzie nibbled at her sandwich, determined to make it last as long as she possibly could. Sal bounded over and sat up on her hind legs as Albert had taught her, and the puppies staggered around in the crate's sudden emptiness, whining and yapping and falling over.

'She can smell the meat,' said Albert, whose own hunger had returned with a vengeance. 'Poor old Sal. She can have mine, I don't mind.'

'We'll all give her a bit,' said Lizzie, quickly, peeling open her sandwich with a pang, and passing a string of beef to Ada, who was already doing the same. 'That's only fair.'

Billy was a little more reluctant, and Queenie was eventually shamed into giving up some of hers too. She gulped down the rest and then turned to her mother, with eyes remarkably like Sal's.

'Is there any more?' she asked.

'No,' said Ma, firmly.

'Nothing at all?' persisted Queenie, ignoring her sisters' warning glances. 'Not even another orange?'

'What will we eat tomorrow?' said Ma. Gathering herself, she regained her familiar authority. 'I've boiling water here, good and hot. That'll fill you up.'

'Just thinking there might be nothing to eat makes you hungry,' Albert remarked.

'Don't think it then,' said Lizzie.

Round the fire, the children's faces glowed and darkened, foreheads and cheeks picked out and then abandoned by the light of flames as heads moved to listen to the shadows beyond. Ma rummaged in the carpet bag for the big Bible, but she kept it shut on her lap, and pressed her lips shut too. Family prayers were family prayers. They couldn't start without Pa. But it wasn't just that, thought Lizzie, humming a few consoling lines of 'Nearer, My God, to Thee'. Billy joined in with the words of the second verse:

> Though like the wanderer,
> The sun gone down,
> Darkness be over me,
> My rest a stone . . .

Ada put a warning finger to her lips.

'What's that?' asked Queenie.

Tantalising silence. A few crackles from the fire. Then a series of guttural squeaks and splutters came from the woods. Leaves murmured, edge to edge. Twigs cracked. Lizzie clutched at her sister's sleeve.

'How do we know there's nobody else living on this island?' she said.

'Do stop that nonsense,' said Ma.

'Where's Pa?' said Queenie, very quietly.

She and Billy stared at Lizzie and Ada and Albert. A low whistle came from the darkness.

BEFORE

A parson-bird had briefly deceived them. It was singing again at dawn, as familiar in daylight as so many other things here – flowers, trees, ferns and fowl – familiar, yet not quite right. Or perhaps a different bird, for the call Lizzie heard as she woke was stranger and closer, awkward wheezing and cackles interrupting outraged hoots, its flight as noisy as its call. Then she saw it: glossy dark feathers, almost black, tufts of white quivering at its throat. It eyed her curiously where she lay, stiff and chilled, a few feet from a pile of ash and embers and a cold cauldron. Not far off, Ada and Albert slept on, huddled together for warmth like the babes in the wood in the song. Blackbird Island, remembered Lizzie.

That first, unforgettable evening, Mr Peacock materialised re-assuringly from the night after a few hours. You'd never guess how he had raged earlier. Ma quickly lit a candle and read a passage about taking no thought for the morrow, and Pa recited a psalm: *'Weeping may endure for a night, but joy cometh in the morning'.* After that, the usual hymns. One by one, the children's voices dropped away as sleep overwhelmed them, until only Lizzie sang on with her parents. Pa carried Queenie to the sail's shelter, draped across his mighty forearms, and came back for Billy. Lizzie watched drowsily while Ma banked up the fire for the night, and then covered Albert and Ada where they lay. She must have done the same at last for Lizzie, for she didn't remember falling asleep and it was light when she woke.

Ma was still asleep, unusually. Once again, Pa was nowhere to be seen. Lizzie moved carefully and quietly around the camp, turning over a half-burned log to uncover its hidden heat, feeding its glow with the dried ferns and twigs Albert had tucked away from the damp night air the previous evening, and building up a sturdy teepee of sticks and logs, so that Ma would wake to a good cooking fire.

Lizzie wasn't sure what she'd be cooking, but they'd need fresh water. She picked up the billycans without a clink, and set off across the damp, dewy tussocks, anxious to get an impression of the island entirely on her own. By the time she reached the marshy edge of the lagoon her hems were drenched. In she waded, moving slowly and scooping water from the surface while winking bubbles spun up from the mud below. She meant to go straight back to camp. But she could hear the breaking surf, and surely it wouldn't take long to climb to the top of the sandbank to see how the beach and the bay – their beach and their bay – looked in the first coral-flushed light of the very first day.

The sand bore the mark of an even earlier visitor. And here came Pa, striding towards her from the rocks, rod balanced over one shoulder, two substantial fish in his other hand. He smiled as soon as he saw her, holding his catch a little higher, waggling the fish so their scales flashed and sparkled. Lizzie waved and ran to meet him.

'What beauties, Pa!' she said. It was no exaggeration. The fish were big, and bright blue, one more silvery than the other, both with tiny yellow spots scattered like stars across their solid bodies.

'Oh look at their faces! Don't they look at you so crossly – those funny lumps are just like eyebrows! I've never seen anything like 'em.'

'Nor I. Reckon they must be some kind of drummer fish. Anyway, he let himself be caught easily enough. Maybe that's why he's so fed up. Got the fire going have you, my spadge? Let's see if they taste as good as they look.'

They did. Their flesh was firm and sweet and there was plenty of it. Once they'd finished off the last of the ship's cook's sandwiches, everybody was satisfied. And breakfast had come easily enough to fill the children with a new confidence about the meals ahead. While they were clearing up plates and mugs, and heating water for washing up, Ada did what she and the others often did. Brushing past Lizzie, she leaned into her ear. 'Go on. Ask Pa now. He'll say yes to you. Quick, while Ma's in a good mood too.'

Pa was unrolling a large tent which had first seen service in the Maori wars. This would be their home until they had built something permanent.

'Can we explore now, Pa?' she asked.

A brief glance at Ma, an even briefer nod back, and Mr Peacock replied:

'Off you go. Not too far though, and not too long either. There's far too much to be done.'

But when Albert stood up to follow them, Pa blocked his way.

'No, not you,' he said. 'I need you here to hold the pole up. You don't need strength for that, just steadiness.'

Ada hesitated, then raced off after Lizzie, with Sal at her heels. They looked back to see Albert swathed in canvas, while Pa shouted instructions, and Billy counted out tent pegs.

'Which way?' said Lizzie.

'Let's look for Pa's orange tree,' suggested Ada, wisely. 'There may be other fruit trees nearby too.'

Mr Peacock had left only ten or twelve fruit on the single surviving orange tree, and some of these yet to ripen fully. Creepers entangled the citrus. Soon it would be shaded completely by the crinkly, shiny leaves of matipo bushes. Yet Ada's instincts were right. You could just about make out where the old orchard had once been planted.

'Do you know what peach trees look like?' asked Lizzie.

'Only when they've got peaches on them,' admitted Ada.

Sal dashed ahead on some invisible trail, followed by Ada, scrabbling through saplings. The girls pushed through, trying not to let the branches spring back in each other's faces in their eagerness, ducking under the climbing tendrils. It was Lizzie who first noticed the grapes, hanging down in graceful bunches, almost thrusting themselves into her hand when she reached up for them, perfect in their misty translucence. She shoved three or four into her mouth at once, bursting tough, sour skins on her tongue, and called Ada back.

'Do you think the Garden of Eden was like this?' Ada asked, wiping a trickle of juice from her chin.

'No, tidier,' said Lizzie.

'At first, maybe. But it must have got out of hand quickly. I mean before Adam began to delve. Let's ask Ma.'

Lizzie was reminded of Pa's dry question to Robson in the bar, just before she was forced to dart away. Where *was* the snake?

'Hold out your skirt,' she said. 'We must take some for the others.'

'In a minute.' Ada ploughed on. 'We need to find Sal first.'

They found themselves back on something that might once have been a path, and followed it into an area that must once have been a clearing.

'Sal! Sal!' Ada called. 'Sal!'

A faint yap-yapping came back to them.

'She's after something. I wonder what?'

'Something she can eat, probably.'

'Hope it's something *we* can.' Lizzie didn't blame Sal for wanting to rush off. 'Let's leave her be, and we'll see what she comes back with. The poor thing's been cooped up at sea with those puppies for so long.'

Heading back to the vines, Lizzie tripped over something hard, hidden beneath the ferns and scrambling weeds. A rock? She held her bleeding shin and hopped around while Ada pulled away at the vegetation.

'Look, Lizzie! Bricks! Who could have left them?'

'Robson, perhaps? Why didn't he say? Or have they been here even longer?'

'There were other settlers too?' said Ada, surprised. 'I didn't know. Can you find any more bricks?'

Scattered though they were, there were probably enough to build a fireplace, but not even the smallest of houses. Anyway, something to please Ma and Pa.

'Shall we take some now?' Lizzie said.

'Later. Better to come back with more hands, and something to carry them. Oh, but look at those . . . '

More berries, black and juicy these ones, hanging in long strings from a tall straggling bush with dark glossy leaves. Lizzie picked one, rolled it in her fingers, sniffed at it. She was about to eat it when Ada stopped her.

'Do you have any idea what they are?'

'No,' she said, undeterred. 'But they look delicious.'

Ada knocked the berry out of her hand, and crushed it underfoot. 'Don't be a fool. You've no idea what they could do to you.'

When they got back to the camp, and Ada told her story and showed the leaves, Pa raised a hand to slap Lizzie and she felt her legs turn liquid. But he let it drop, almost as quickly, and called all the children to come at once. They shuffled their feet and made their faces solemn, and even Gussie stared so intently at her father you'd think she understood too. These were tutu berries, he told them. No need for punishment if they had actually eaten them: they'd not be there to punish.

'Don't even touch them!' he said, fiercely. 'Never, ever. They are deadly.'

'I'm sorry, Pa. I didn't know.' Hot and flushed, Lizzie held her hands behind her back determined to wash them thoroughly.

'So that's what killed the other children?' Ma said, unable to stop herself.

Pa nodded, and admitted that Robson told him that one of the earliest settler families had lost three children to tutu berries. Lizzie couldn't tell if ignorance or desperation had made them eat them and didn't want to ask.

'Where are they buried?' asked Albert later. He shivered. 'Did Pa say?'

'No. He probably doesn't know,' said Ada. 'Fancy not telling us before.'

'He has so much on his mind. And he probably didn't want to frighten us, not when we've just arrived. Or make us sad,' said Lizzie. 'It's very sad.'

'You were lucky,' said Albert, in a tone of wonderment. 'I thought you were in for it then.'

'Oh, Pa would never hurt Lizzie,' said Ada, confidently. 'You know that.'

She took his arm, and they wandered off together, looking round from time to time in a way that made Lizzie certain they were talking about her. Left with Queenie, she told herself she didn't care, and told Queenie that she'd certainly help her look for the poor dead children's graves, just as soon as they'd collected more firewood for Ma.

'And if Billy says anything about ghosts, you're not to listen,' she added, meaning to comfort. 'He's only teasing. Ask Pa.'

13

LIZZIE KEEPS PRAYING THAT ALBERT WILL SUDDENLY reappear and put all their hearts to right again. Hers is beating somewhere near her throat. She's not even sure what scares her most, but she knows she'll forgive her brother anything and everything if he'll just come back now. He doesn't. The search parties set off, all in their different directions, with Ada, Billy and Queenie first to leave, with Spy. Pa and Lizzie are the last pair to go, and the sight of Ma standing by the fire, hand in hand with Gus, watching everybody else vanish, hardly knowing what to do with herself as she waits, makes Lizzie want to run back and offer to keep them both company. Except Pa has chosen her, and she can't let him down.

She's surprised then, and a little disappointed, when he suggests they separate almost as soon as they are both in the forest and out of sight and earshot of the others. Of course. He's right. This way they can cover more ground between them, without causing her mother unnecessary anxiety. More chance of finding Albert faster.

'It's like fishing,' she agrees eagerly. You have to spread your net, as wide as you can.

'And you know the island better than all the others,' says Pa. 'It won't take long to get to Goat Point and then you can work your way back. I'll go straight to the lake, with Sal. We weren't far off when I left him. All those odd cracks and crevasses in the rocks around the crater. It'd be just like Albert not to see the danger in taking shelter there, though heaven knows I've warned you all. I'll make a thorough search.'

His sudden embrace briefly crushes the breath from Lizzie, and a few tears too. Released, she swallows, and almost confesses that she's more familiar with the perils around the lake than he knows, but there's no time to waste: Pa's already wishing her luck, and telling her not to worry. She nods, and wants to tell him the same. He's drawn and haggard this morning, horribly so, as if he can't admit even to himself how much he's worrying about Albert.

Setting off as instructed on the track towards the western bluff, she soon reasons that if Albert were on this or any path, he'd have found his own way home. She will have to hunt harder if she's to be the one to find him. Of course she doesn't need Pa to find her way, she tells herself, flattered. She surely knows each rock and promontory almost as well as her father, the fissures and the paths and the gullies, the dead ends that stop you short and also the winding, goat-trodden loops that take you back upon yourself and spin your senses round. But it seems she doesn't.

After a night of little sleep and half-heard voices, she is easily tired. An hour or two into the hunt, she has lost the track completely. Her familiarity with the island is weaker than she believed. Of course she knows the ways from here to there and back again, but there are more in-between places than anyone could guess, and they get harder and harder to tell apart. And now that she's searching alone, she can see it's not like fishing at all. You can hardly take a net through trees and undergrowth, and the wider they spread themselves, the bigger the holes they leave between. Maybe it's more like hunting, she decides, but she doesn't like to think of Albert as prey, and she pushes the thought aside. She begins to run, as fast as it's possible to over ground that's so uneven, so up and down, over narrow, vanishing paths made only by goats.

Under the thickest canopy, where the light is almost green, Lizzie cannot see the sun. Down in yet another gully she cannot see the sea either. Deprived of clues, she calls yet again, shrieking now as resentment turns to terror:

'Albert? Where are you? Can't you hear us? We're all looking for you! Answer! Can't you just answer?'

Sounds inside and outside her ears become hard to tell apart. A seedpod bursts open and startles her. The rustling whip of a lizard's tail leaves her breathless. Or perhaps a rat's. It could be nothing else. Or have other new arrivals slipped ashore, unseen, while children and parents were distracted by the *Esperanza*? Lizzie chastises herself for this crooked way of thinking, and then the whispering starts and stops again. The faster she thrashes through the undergrowth, the harder it is to track the noises. Time and again, strange sounds send her flailing, beating her way through rattling leaves. Striped tree trunks flicker.

Lizzie stops trusting herself. She begins to doubt the island. Its noises have not changed but now she is alone in the forest Lizzie hears them freshly. Birds whose unremarkable cries have kept her company on hunting expeditions for nearly two years squawk like frightened children among the fleshy leaves of mousehole trees, whose branches meet high above her head. She catches something of Albert's voice; misrecognition pierces her just below the ribs. The air itself feels violent, as though the island is gathering itself for something. She imagines it breathing, heaving, maybe shifting. Unless she's the one who's been tilted off balance by the throbbing pressure inside her own head and lungs, from running too fast, too full of fear.

She cups her hands around her mouth and shouts, twice: once from her strangled throat, the second time forcing the sound out from somewhere deeper, lower.

'Al-bert. Al-bert. Can. You. Hear. Me?'

Not a sound.

As Pa so often complained, Albert was clumsy. Even before the accident that lamed him, he used to trip, or barely make it to a rock he leapt for. Those strange aches and pains in knees and ankles he kept complaining of – ever since the flux – his swollen toes and fingers . . . Lizzie wished she had taken them more seriously. He had probably tangled himself up, and fallen. Perhaps hit his head and staggered off too mazy to find his way. How frightened Albert must have been, lost and alone in the forest all night.

But surely – with so many searching – someone must have come upon him by this time. Lizzie wants this to be true. She is impatient for this fuss to finish so that their new life on this island can finally begin. Albert has probably sauntered home with Ada, she tells herself, and even now Ma and Gussie are fussing over him. While the rest of them behave like fools, Albert is eating the first batch of biscuit warm from the camp oven. She wants to scramble down to North Bay, and hear a fine hullabaloo, and run between the huts and see Albert's face look up.

Lizzie feels the empty groan of hunger. Her anger towards her brother reignites and festers. She should have taken Ada aside, and questioned her, properly, before they separated. They had so many secrets together, Ada and Albert. They were always disappearing somewhere, always together. She must have some idea where he could be. Lizzie has had enough. She wants to go home.

At last she calms enough to notice landmarks. A pile of rocks, the particular contortion of an ironwood tree – an elbow rather than a knee – all these give her a better idea of which way to go. And finally, unexpectedly, she is back on the path itself, and it's widening out, and here are fresh goat droppings, and she's getting higher and briefly lower and then much higher. Soon everything feels familiar again, and she realises how far she's come. Almost to the western tip of the island.

Lizzie decides to keep going, right to the very edge, where the trees thin. To come so far and not look out to sea? It would be a waste – a squandered opportunity. At Goat Point she'll check for ships, the coming weather . . . and something else as well. Yes, here, just as she was expecting, she meets that other path, zigzagging like a line of scalp wriggling through hair parted and plaited in a hurry, which will take her to the flat, rocky promontory which makes her shudder, but also thrills her.

Today the sea is a blue so intense and luminous you could lose your mind gazing at it. It's the blue of Albert's eyes in sunshine. She has to raise a hand against the glare of it, and hold back whipping strands of hair with a crooked elbow. There's nothing but sea to see. No sails, no clouds. Hundreds and hundreds of miles of unbroken ocean. A milk-white foaming rage directly below beats loudly and invisibly against sharp shoreline rocks also hidden from sight.

Cowardly, she tells herself. To come all this way and leave without certainty. If she doesn't look, even if there's no proof of anything, she will never stop imagining what she might have witnessed. So she crouches down and begins to crawl, knee by knee, palm by palm, towards the edge of the rock where she's been standing, finally lowering herself to slither, belly-down. She's done this before, a few times, to frighten herself as much as anything, but only with Ada or Billy holding on to her feet, and urging her on. A few more inches. There's nothing here her grated fingertips can cling to. The slope of the rock remains in her favour and she knows she cannot tip. Her stomach lurches anyway. Stiff-necked, she raises her head a fraction, inches on a little further, and then peers over and down.

A whistling roar engulfs her, and then a crash. Another hard on its heels. In her mind, the noise pulls her down, all the way, tugging at her reason. She almost wants to fall. She pictures herself hurtling through space, flying like a pirate bird, plunge-diving with a purpose. Her body feels leaden and light at once.

But there's nothing there to see. No sign. No sharks. It could not be cleaner, whiter, this moving tracery of foam, rising and falling below, all feathery down and scalloped lace, hiding and revealing the black rocks beneath, and the dark depths that surround them. Lizzie retreats, only partly relieved: if Albert had fallen here, would he be washed away by now, or worse? She edges backwards until she feels safe enough to stand. Then she turns and runs back down the path, twisting and jinking like the goats they once saw leap from here. The day they first discovered the point. When, after a desperate chase along tracks far more overgrown then, a pursuit so frenzied the memory of it made her heart beat now, she and Pa and Albert came so close to capturing the milk goat Ma had begged for. They'd thought they had her cornered, that there was no way out. Lizzie will never forget her horror at the animals' panicky leap, how the whole small herd had kept on going, plunging from the clifftop as if winged. Nor can she obliterate the ruby-flecked foam, the triumph of the sharks below, quick and bloody and messy and clean at once. They came so fast. You'd think they had waited all day.

Lizzie runs again, on and on, away from there, running back home, until an urgent swish and snap of leaves and twigs and branches brings her to a lung-heaving halt.

14

PINEKI IS MY SEEKING-COMPANION, FOR WHICH I AM glad. Though not a serious person, he is quick and sharp. He notices how we come – they send us first on Rough Haw Track – and turns it round in his head, always keeping a measure, so we can find the proper way back. Pineki tells me how he would delight to be the boy's finder, how this would crown our glory in Mr Peacock's eyes, and smooth all paths ahead for all the gang. This hope quickens our step and sharpens our looking.

When we were deck-watchers on the *Esperanza*, it seemed to us a fellow could swiftly circle this island. Landed, we see that Monday is indeed many times smaller than the Rock, our fortress atoll that stands alone. Yet walking is harder, slower here, paths are fewer, fainter, more scrambling. No circuit road. No fringing reef to calm its fury, the sea is more violent, but by some trick often seems more distant. Less of beauty here in my eyes. The ocean does not break through holes in the land in rainbowed plumes of spray, or creep into our multitude of coral caves. No arches, no canyons, no patterned, pointed rocks twisting towards the skies clad with green like forests, nor vast tree roots like sheltering walls, where a fellow can sleep, or hide, or meet a person, unseen.

This kind of thinking will not help my soul to settle. It brings so clear a picture of home to my mind I feel a yearning hunger in my belly. My heart is overcast. I hear in my head my mother's voice, and Vika calling back to her, and I see them as they move through the Mission House, talking to Mr and Mrs Reverend, collecting laundry, sweeping, tidying. All the little everyday jobs. For all the years I can remember, my mother has kept house at the Mission. Since first our father was taken. And since our father's father sorrow-sickened. They look after us and we look after them, and they say we are their island family. Perhaps we brothers have the greater luck. Knowing home so well, at least I can hold this picture in my heart. Our family cannot see where Solomona and I now stand. They can only wonder. But there is a pattern to their days worth cherishing. We cannot tell how even this day will end.

Pineki asks if I think this boy is hiding, and why, and what sort of boy he is. How can I tell? I say. What do you think? He shrugs and tells me there may be many secret spots we cannot see. If a body wants to hide on this island. We walk, considering. Always looking. White skin. Blue eyes. Open or shut? Pineki still harks on about hiding. Easy for some short time only, he says. Or maybe as a game. Yet hiding can never be easy without help, I tell him. All bodies need food, and water. And I think Albert cannot be playing. No boy, not even a larrikin boy – if he is one, and that I doubt – no loving child could want to hide-and-seek so long, making his parents white with worry, and his brother and his sisters weep. Yet the way his sisters and mother speak of him . . . like a child, not a man. A child in need of help; a strange and beautiful boy.

Well, this is a mysterious way in which for God to move, I think, to conceal this Albert boy, and stop his homecoming. (I must learn to think more like Solomona, I tell myself, as I have often done before. He is my elder.) We must keep faith and hope in our hearts, until revelation is granted us, I say to Pineki. And then I tell him that with so many people looking, we are like a third hand. When we return to the houses, we will find the Peacock family whole again, unbroken, and all will be well.

We climb higher, into cloud-mist. Sweat cools quickly here, where moss drip-drops and sparkling webs stretch branch to branch. We swing our arms and twitch when wetness lands from nowhere. The path is not so clear. It stretches longer between us. And then, all at once, it seems – maybe I was too slow to follow or my friend too fast to lead – I cannot tell – we have lost each other. How long has it been since I could not see or hear Pineki? A little too long. I hold myself quite still. Listen. Only to dripping. My mind is set not to move until Pineki finds me, as I guess he will, in time. Unless this is his game. To show me how easy it is to hide here, and how hard to find.

Waiting, I sit on a tree fallen long, long ago, now soft and green with growing things, smothered by living ferns and moss cushions, star-pricked. I look around me without moving, marvelling at branches and trees damply draped, clothed in soft wisps of emerald and silver. Pale, papery bark hangs like rags. I push my curious hands into black, black soil which lets me in so easily and smells so strong, of life and death together, I think there must be witchery in it. I wonder how Solomona fares.

A crash – a flying fox? – and then Pineki calls, and I reply, with breaking voice, and he appears before me. For a moment we clasp each other, while our heartbeats slow. We speak only of our happiness in finding, and say nothing of our fears.

15

PEOPLE ARE COMING TOWARDS LIZZIE. TWO OF THE kanakas, these Islander boys who look so much like men. Two of them, and one of her. When they arrived on the island, surrounded by burly sailors, they did not seem so tall and broad.

She watches as they emerge from the bushes which means she sees the precise moment when they see her, and come to a sudden halt. On the path, knees open and bent, as surprised perhaps by her appearance as she is by theirs, they make her think of animals prepared to spring. They've tied their shirts around their waists and the sweat of effort gives a sheen to their chests. One says something under his breath, and the other answers, but of course she doesn't understand. They are also on their guard, unsmiling. Lizzie has no experience of being alone with men. She remembers, of course, from the hotel, that Ma forbids it, but this is different. These men are not drunken strangers. They have left their own families to come and work with hers. She should surely welcome them. Yet when she moves towards the Islanders, they edge away.

Lizzie closes a dry-as-biscuit mouth. Not the pastor, who speaks English. She knows him by his careful air of wisdom. Nor the other English speaker, the preacher's brother, whose name made her think of the sound of singing, singing without words. She tries to remember other names, and fails. Disconnected syllables muddle in her head. Was there a kind of Luke? A Jacob? The shorter Islander – she's right, it's Likatau, and the other is Iakopo – Likatau speaks again, and Lizzie understands he is telling her something, something important. She panics. Something has scraped his upper arm, and it's bleeding, but he doesn't seem to notice. He speaks again. She doesn't understand. She shakes her head, and he takes a step forward, and it's her turn to back away, although there is nowhere to go, only Goat Point behind her.

The men talk to each other again, swapping sounds, and she hates the fact that she has no idea at all what they are saying.

'What is it? Where is he?' she shouts at them. 'What have you done with him? Tell me! Please.'

She misreads their contorted faces. They cannot make out hers.

'What do you want?'

They have come to a decision. Their eyebrows are in accordance. One on each side, they come towards her, as if they mean to trap her. She turns to flee, but then they take her arms. She struggles and squirms, trying to pull away, but they're far too strong. Just as she is about to bite Likatau's hand, he lets her go, and so does Iakopo, and she staggers. They both step back, shaking their heads, clasping their hands as if in prayer or supplication. They look more frightened than she feels. It's all a misunderstanding, she realises. They're pointing. Their faces do not threaten but question.

They don't know where Albert is.

They don't even know where they are themselves. They need her to show them where to go.

'Follow me,' she says, heading home.

Lizzie talks to keep herself brave. It doesn't matter to her that the Islanders can't understand, or that when she turns around next, there is bewilderment in their eyes. She notices they have put their shirts on. No doubt the missionaries have told them they must cover themselves. She knows that, like her mother, missionaries hate nakedness.

'It's not so far now,' she tells them, in the soft way of speaking to fear she learned from Albert – the way he'd talk to the milk goats. They both nod, as if they understand. They understand at least that she's offering friendship. 'We follow this path all the way along the ridge until we reach the edge of the crater. That's how you know. When the land rises and drops in two directions. You'll learn your way all over the island soon enough.'

Their heads jut forward as they try to catch and disentangle her intentions.

'Is there a lake on your island? Or a volcano? Is it really a rock? How big is it, I wonder? I wish you could tell me. How many people? Is it as big as Tongatapu, where we used to live? That seems so long ago now. Did this island seem tiny, like it did to us, when we first saw it from the ship? We've been here ages now, since Gussie was a baby. Well, she's still a bit of a baby, but she was much smaller then. We were all much smaller then, of course. And Albert hadn't been well, and he needed lots of building up. It wasn't easy, that first year – you know we used to live on the other side? Maybe that's where Albert was last night? Well, Ada and Billy are sure to have found him and they'll be bringing him back by now. With all of us searching, all this time, *someone* must have found him, don't you think? But we must keep looking, just in case.'

Desperation mounting, she calls again:

'Al-bert! Are you there?' Iakopo and Likatau copy her obediently, Lizzie urging them on, conducting with her hands so that they can all time their calling, and make it as loud as possible. A last great shout, and then they all strain their ears with exaggeratedly tilted heads. No answer but the noises of the island. When the men look at Lizzie for reassurance, she answers more emphatically than she feels.

'You'll see. He *must* be home by now. Come on. Let's hurry. I hope Pa isn't too angry with Albert about all this trouble he's caused. Poor Albert. Pa *can* get cross, I ought to tell you, but that's only because he sees how things *should* be. You'll see what I mean. He wants everything done just so. You do, of course, when a thing's your very own, don't you? You want it perfect. And Pa says Monday Island is ours now, make no mistake.'

'Monday Island,' repeats Likatau, and Iakopo nods, eagerly, because these are two words he knows. The path broadens and they join her, one on each side, watching her lips move, taking it in turn to catch her approving eye.

'Yes, Monday Island. And when we've cleared enough land, thanks to you, and you'll be so quick at that, I can see you will, then Pa will send to Auckland, and we will finally have plantations as we've always planned, proper plantations – lots of fruit, all kinds of fruit – and also sheep, and then there'll be wool to sell as well as timber. We really will make it a paradise. That's what Pa has always said.'

She looks for further signs of understanding.

'Never mind,' she says. 'Solomona will explain. Or Kalala.'

She quickens her pace and lowers her voice.

'Maybe it's God's will?' Lizzie turns briefly to beam at Iakopo and Likatau. She likes this idea. It makes her feel that the whole family has simply been blown off course, a little way, and they are just on the point of finding their bearings again. 'I mean that you've come now, after all this time, because now we truly have been tested and we've never given up, not once – not even Albert – we've always persevered, as Pa says we must. So God has sent *you* to us, like a reward. We've earned it. It's meant to be.'

16

RETURNING TO THE FLATS TO SEE NO BROTHER HERE, and her mother's asking-face fast falling, the girl Lizzie stops, rock-still, silent. Iakopo and Likatau nearly knock against her in their tumbling hurry to be back with us.

Solomona shouts out a warning, in our language: 'No touching, no touching!'

'Nothing?' calls her mother, and now her voice is breaking. Lizzie can hear it too. We all can.

Lizzie goes to her mother and takes her oily hand – she has been barrelling up mutton-birds all the morning. Mrs Peacock firms her mouth and brushes her girl away.

'I thought you were with your father. Where is he?'

'He's not here?' says Lizzie. Her face is red, uneasy. 'He must be coming soon. We went different ways to cover more ground.'

Mrs Peacock's eyes close. It seems to me she is talking to herself, in her head, and then she nods, and brings an end to that matter, and she is another person.

'Food now. Everyone needs to eat,' she says. She reties the

apron which stretches across her belly, and drives a fist into the hollow of her own back, as if to firm her spine. 'Get the paring knife, Lizzie. We must get on.'

'Where's Billy?' asks her daughter, not moving.

'Digging taro.'

'Queenie?'

'With Billy.'

'*Everyone* else is back? Even Ada?'

Mrs Peacock nods over her shoulder, into the darkness of the hut. Lizzie looks around, as if she is counting. She sees Solomona and me, and also Vilipate and Pineki, safely returned, but no Albert.

'Nobody's seen anything.' Her voice like a cave.

Hunting without finding is a hollow thing. While you are away looking, it is easy to hope another has had the finding, and so no wonder your own hands are empty. With the return of every failed looker, the hollow space grows bigger.

Unearthly silence hangs. All movements slow. Still there is no weeping to be heard, not since Ada's mourning cry at dawn. As for us fellows, we watch, on hand, no certainty of our tasks, or even if we are to sit or stand.

'You rest, Ma. I will cook.' Lizzie talks soothingly, and steers her mother to a stool, but Mrs Peacock has had her fill of waiting.

'I cannot do nothing.'

Bustle. Bustle. Fingers flying. Lizzie's shoulders sink. All hope now rests with the father.

We fellows eat in silence, sitting apart from the family. Fatty smoked fowl and taro mash. Smack of lips and gulp of throat. We keep our eyes to the ground, and do not question. Our only task now can be waiting. From time to time Solomona's lips move in prayer. I must speak to the Lord too. I will speak plainly. I ask him to help another father find his beloved son.

Luka, by my side, head low, whispers his thinking aloud.

'When Mr Peacock next returns, all this will end. You'll see. Is he not a man of strength and vigour?'

'Yes, surely,' agrees Iakopo. 'If any person can bring home the boy Albert, must it not be his own father?'

'Certainly,' says Solomona.

I recall my first meeting with our master on the shore below – but a day ago, so very long a day – and I think of the force I saw at once in him, light and dark together.

More hours pass. The barrel of birds is full-packed and weighted. Oil upward-seeps, enough that Mrs Peacock can draw it off. Always busy, yet always watching, listening, and all the children too. Hushed voices so any calling will be clear.

Queenie is first to catch her father's steps and runs at once to meet him on the path. Mr Peacock does not speak to her before she reaches him. He drags his feet. He comes alone. And it is not hard to see, even from afar, that he brings no good news with him.

BEFORE

On their second day on the island, Pa woke the children with an enticing shout:

'Who's coming to help me build our house?'

Ma had let them sleep in their clothes again, so Lizzie was quickly on her feet, and first to chase after her father. Breakfast forgotten, the others followed, and soon they were all running along the edge of the sparkling lagoon towards the stream that fed it, where it was most swampish. When they were sloshing ankle-deep beside the tallest thicket of velvet-headed bulrushes, Mr Peacock stopped.

'Rappoo,' he said, handing out three stout knives to the eldest children.

Then Lizzie understood that they were to make a whare, a thatched hut made of reeds, New Zealand-style. They would live like Maoris here.

'Cut them right at the base,' Pa instructed. 'We'll need the roots too. Then bring it all to camp. You and Billy too, Queenie. You're big enough to carry plenty. I'm going up the cliffs.'

Bringing the back hem of her skirt through her legs, Lizzie tucked it into the front of her bodice so that she could bend over without getting it soaked, and waded out. She grasped hold of the nearest, fattest reed, and set to, hacking away just below the water. She wanted Pa to return to great piles of reeds. The house took shape in her mind.

'Lizzie's wearing a nappy!' chanted Queenie, but she copied her sister, and so did Ada. Lizzie was only shin-deep, but Queenie's short legs meant the swamp water was over her knees, so Ada shooed her back towards the shallows.

'I want a knife too,' said Billy, trying to grab Albert's. He jerked the blade out of reach.

'Pa gave it to *me*.'

'Stop it! There's no time to mess around!' Lizzie shouted through her legs. She stood up, scowling, having finally got the knife through the first tough white base. So much effort, and all she had to show for it was a single stem. She held it out to Billy. 'Take this and lay it down over there. Just wait, Queenie, and I'll give you the next.'

Billy looked at it, disappointed.

'It's a start,' Lizzie snapped.

Back under the water to ease out the root. Her fingers groped in the mud, detaching the fine tendrils first so she could get hold of the solid lumpen thing she could feel sticking sideways out of the plant. A wriggle and a great heave, and it was out. She staggered backwards, splashing.

'Come on, Billy, don't sulk,' said Ada. 'You can have a turn with my knife soon. We'll all get plenty of turns, don't you worry.'

They did. The children spent the whole morning hacking at the reeds. Queenie did her best to help, earnestly toing and froing from swamp to pile, but eventually she headed back to the camp, saying she was going to help Ma instead. Later, Lizzie saw her wandering off to the shore with a bucket. When they had cut and pulled enough reeds and roots, Ada, Albert, Lizzie and Billy took it in turns to carry them back. Doubled over with their loads, necks crooked backwards to see the way ahead, they wove up the gentle slope as if they had sunstroke. Someone always stayed at the swamp to keep on cutting. By mid-afternoon their hands were cut and blistered, their bellies rumbling.

'When can we stop and eat?' asked Billy. He wriggled toes so white and shrivelled they looked like maggots in the mud.

'When Pa comes back,' Lizzie said, without encouragement.

'When Ma tells us,' said Ada, at exactly the same time.

Albert was too tired to speak. He dropped another reed on the pile, and splashed back into the swamp, shoulders slumped. One high cheekbone was smeared with mud. His golden hair was matted.

A few hours later, there came a shout from Queenie, and Lizzie looked up to see Pa emerging from the woods.

'Food!' cried Billy gleefully, dropping the knife he had finally got his hands on, and running off to meet him. Lizzie picked it up with a sigh. It was obvious that Pa could have nothing substantial with him, dead or alive. She loaded herself up with the next bundle and followed the others back to camp.

Pa still hadn't sat down when she got there, and his hair was stuck with leaves and twigs.

'What did he say?' she whispered to Billy when she reached them.

Pa lowered his tin cup of water and addressed Lizzie directly.

'I said I'm going to need your help if I'm ever going to get a goat . . . and yours . . . and yours too.'

He nodded at Ada and Albert.

'How many did you see?' Lizzie asked.

'Plenty. But I can't get near them. They're fast and they're wild. We'll need to take the dog up.'

Albert stared at the rock face.

'Are we going up there now?' His voice quavered.

'Don't be nesh,' snapped Pa. 'Of course not now. We need to start on the house frame first. I've just found plenty of nikau – the trunks are sturdy and we'll get thatch and mattresses too from their leaves. Where did I put the axe?'

Ma broke in.

'Nobody's going anywhere till they've eaten. So go and wash your hands. The towel's over there. Girls – tidy your hair. Albert – your face.'

No matter where they found themselves, cleanliness remained next to Godliness in Mrs Peacock's book. Observing the fundamental rules of life kept chaos at bay. Still she offered no clue as to *what* they were going to eat. When they were all sitting down, Queenie lifted the lid of the bucket with a triumphant flourish.

'Look what we found!'

Billy leaned over to look, and recoiled, nostrils quivering. 'But they're alive,' he said. 'Don't we have to cook them?'

'No need,' said Pa, firmly, and reached in. Limpets, in their shells. Gigantic ones, some almost as big as a hand. He held one out for inspection, and turned it onto its back to reveal a shell apparently lined with shiny white porcelain, wavily bordered in purple, cupping a mass of glistening flesh that made Lizzie think of slugs. The flesh seemed startled when Pa's knife plunged in. He smacked his lips when he tasted it and was a long time chewing. The children watched Mr Peacock's slowly grinding jaws and marked his eyes, until at last he swallowed. More lipsmacking followed.

Ma handed the bucket round, and the children surged forward.

The limpets smelled of sea, and they tasted of it too. Leathery and tough, slimy and gritty, but definitely edible.

'You have to creep up on them,' boasted Queenie. 'Take them by surprise. I'll show you later.'

Lizzie and Ada pretended that they had never tasted such a delicacy, and begged her to collect more the next day.

'Pass me the shells,' ordered Pa. 'They'll be useful for something.' As he stacked them, he noticed that plenty had a second, smaller limpet cemented on top of their ridged domes. They roasted the passengers on the embers to release them, and Albert collected up the small shells in the hope that one day there would be time to play draughts again.

The only other food was roast bulrush root, another dish that couldn't be eaten in a hurry. Ma scooped the lumpy blackened sticks away from the heat with her long tongs, and Pa showed the children how to peel off the charred outer layer and pick out the fluffy white flesh, separating out the stringy fibre in the middle. His teeth moved methodically, delicately. Cobwebby strands stuck to his beard like spun sugar.

Lizzie was too hungry to concentrate. The limpets had released her appetite, but failed to satisfy it. How many lumps of root were there? How much could she claim as her share? Too impatient to work through each mouthful with the attention it demanded, and too afraid of missing out, she was left with a dry, chewy mass in her mouth. When nobody was looking, she spat it into her hand and threw it into the fire where it landed with a treacherous sizzle.

BEFORE

Within a week the westerly winds had returned with a vengeance. They tugged at the tent all night and blew up the surf so high that fishing was impossible. At low tide the rocks below the shoreline were dotted with bare circles, cut out of the green and red algae all around the bay. The limpets were finished. At least there was nikau, Pa reminded the children. It turned out you could strip off the palm tree's long, tough outer leaves, and find a pale, tightly folded heart nestling inside. Ma said it tasted of celery. Lizzie had never eaten celery. It *was* good to eat, though not for every meal. Like the limpets, it never quite filled you up. And there was never enough. The fruit was soon gone. Pa found fern roots for Ma to roast. Afraid of the look in their parents' eyes, the children stopped speaking of their hunger.

*

One morning, the family woke after a restless night, filled with growling stomachs and the intermittent whining of the dogs, and Queenie found one of the puppies cold and stiff. Sal had disappeared. She must have followed a promising scent too far and lost herself, thought Ma. 'She'll find her way back,' she added, reassuringly. Later, Pa sent the children to hunt for her in the woods, but all their shouts and calls were in vain.

Queenie and Billy wanted to baptise the remaining puppies, which kept nosing around the empty space they were left with, their legs more unsteady every hour.

'Think of their lost souls.'

'Animals don't have souls,' said Ada. 'They can't be heathens.'

'Then they can't go to heaven,' Lizzie pointed out.

'Where do they go?' wondered Albert. Nobody knew.

'We can still have a funeral,' said Queenie. But when they looked for the tiny body, Ma told them Pa had already taken it off to bury, and nobody dared ask him where. It seemed too late for prayers.

Queenie knelt with Albert at the crate, gnawing at her bottom lip.

'They're starving, aren't they?' she said, sucking in her own stomach, trying to think how they could keep the tiny hearts still thumping. Albert nodded. He stroked their wrinkled, plush-felted skin and sent Queenie for a shawl to cover the remaining puppies. At first they kept staggering out from underneath it. Then they lay and shivered. Then they lay still. By that evening another was dead, and Pa was chastising Albert for being mawkish.

In the night, the whimpering grew more feeble. Lizzie planned to wake extra early, before Pa even, so she could go and search for Sal again before they had to get back to the housebuilding, if she could find the energy. She listened to the fading whines, and Queenie's breathing – too light, too rapid – and knew that she was not asleep either. She reached a hand out across the groundsheet, tiptoeing her fingers from Queenie's shoulder, along her arm, until she reached her hand. Her sister lay flat on her back with her palms pressed into prayer, her lips forming silent amens. Lizzie stroked her cheek lightly, and leaking tears dripped into Queenie's ears and overflowed into her hair.

'Shhh. Shhhh,' Lizzie whispered. Queenie hadn't made a sound. 'They're going to sleep now. Listen!'

Not sleep. Only one puppy was still breathing in the morning. With eyes of steel, Pa strode off into the woods, slung with rope and tools, ordering Albert to follow. His son hesitated while Ma removed the cold companion, and then he sighed, and told Queenie to look after the last puppy.

'I have to go, or Pa will . . . Pick the puppy up and don't put him down at all, if you can help it,' Albert told her. 'You'll keep him warmest with your own body. See if he'll take a little water and sugar, on your finger. Some rappoo porridge maybe, if there's enough to spare?'

'Can't you help me?'

Albert sought permission from Ma. 'I can't stay long,' he said.

A short time later the distant rhythmic thud of Pa's axe broke off abruptly and didn't resume. When he came back to camp, he was carrying Sal.

'She's a bag of bones,' he said, putting her in the crate. The terrier's fur clung to corrugated sides, and her stumpy tail curled tightly between her legs. 'Those pups should be weaned by now.'

'But we've nothing to feed them,' cried Albert, panicking. 'We've hardly enough for Sal.'

Pa's eyes quickly quelled his protests.

'I told you to come with me. Don't make me tell you twice. We've a house to build.'

Back to the woods.

'Go on, Albert,' said Lizzie. 'Or shall I go?'

Albert shook his head and ran after Pa, followed by Ada's helpless gaze.

Queenie laid the last pup back in the crate with Sal, hoping it would do them both some good.

'Can she count?'

Ma shook her head.

'She knows something's wrong,' said Lizzie, who found herself at that moment in the grip of a chilly, skin-crawling shiver. 'Sally, oh, Sally, what are we to do?'

The terrier could barely find enough energy to raise and turn her head, but she managed a few licks before flopping back, exhausted. Her teats were swollen and sore. Without thinking, Mrs Peacock pressed her hands to her own breasts, which hung like empty skins. She looked at Gussie, sleeping in a crate of her own, her chin moving in her sleep as if she were feeding, as it used to when she was tiny. She had spat out limpets and bulrush roots alike. Feeding the dogs was the least of Ma's concerns.

BEFORE

Soon the children could barely remember how to stand upright.
Lizzie walked like an old woman. If she wasn't stooped under a
load of bricks, or a vast bundle of rushes, she was dragging a tree
trunk through the woods, fighting with the greenery that caught
at her knees and ankles and sometimes at her throat. Like all the
family's, her hands were raw and blistered, her legs slashed with
reed cuts. One day her bubbling, squeaking stomach went quiet,
as if it had given up on hunger.

But at least the frame of the first hut was up, and the back
wall in place, green at the top and pale at the bottom. When Pa
came back with a fistful of clay – to cement the fireplace bricks
in the outdoor kitchen and firm the floor, he said – and explained
every bucketload had to be dug up from the far side of the swamp
and carried back too, Ma folded her arms and shook her head.

'Enough. It will have to wait. Just look at the children, Joseph.
Pale as death. And Albert was half starved before we even got
here. You'll wear them all out if they eat no meat. As for Sal . . .
there'll be no hope for her, let alone the pup. We must have a
goat, right away. Two or three, if possible. For meat and for milk.'

'Now, Mrs P?'

'Yes, now. We can't wait another day. I'm only sorry I held you
back before. And the pup—'

'Spy,' reminded Queenie, and Ma smiled and kept talking.

'Spy's strong enough to manage without Sal for half a day now, I believe. Take this.'

Slowly and laboriously, without a word, Ma had been gathering pollen from the bulrushes. That morning she had made the dusty flour into scones.

'A picnic!' said Lizzie. To her and Ada, it felt like a holiday. They could stand up straight! The sun was shining! In high spirits, they skipped ahead on what was already becoming a track through the woods, Albert more or less keeping up with them. Pa's pace was more measured. He knew to preserve his energy for the climb.

The path ran out. Albert called to Sal, and the children leaned against the base of the cliff, waiting in the cool of the overhang for Pa to catch up and tell them what to do.

'Keep going,' he said.

'What?' said Lizzie.

'How?' said Ada.

'Where?' asked Albert.

'Up.' Pa nodded at the vertical rocks. 'Up there.'

Lizzie looked up, and down again, then up, and along. She was so very tired.

'Will you go first?' she asked.

Mr Peacock thought about it, then spat on his palms and heaved himself up to the first ledge. He edged along a little way, and reached down a hand for her. She shook her head. They'd never get up if they couldn't do it on their own. Lizzie spat into her own palms, supposing it would give her a better grip, or courage, or had some other purpose that would become clear. She tucked up her skirt and swung herself up, and then along, and up again, and once more along till she was standing beside her father.

'Take your time, pet,' advised Pa. 'There's a long way to go yet . . . '

The cliff was too sheer for Sal's stubby legs, so Albert passed her up to Ada, and then Ada passed her up to Lizzie, and finally Lizzie held her scrabbling claws away from her face and heaved her up to Pa. She weighed so little. After that, Pa took charge, lifting the terrier up in front of him at every stage, until she conquered her trembling fear.

Lizzie shifted again, to make room for Ada on the ledge. Pa was right. No point in rushing it. Albert seemed to agree, for there he was, still on the ground, tightening his belt and gathering strength. Lizzie caught a glimpse of his white translucent face, and turned her attention to the next ledge, refusing to think about how frail he'd so quickly become again. Perhaps it would be better if he stayed below. But Pa would never hear of that.

The lime-streaked rock face was pitted with hand-holes. You never had to reach far to find a place you could edge your fingers into or tuck your feet inside. She felt like a spider, stretched and taut, after too many days of feeling like a beetle. As they persevered, the vegetation thickened, until you could hang on to bushes, and at last small trees. The sea's backwash diminished to a faint sucking shush.

'Wait, Lizzie! You're going much too fast.'

She looked down between her feet, and laughed at Ada, calling from the ledge below.

'Too fast? Your legs are longer than mine! Why don't you hurry up?'

'But what about Albert? You're being unkind.'

Lizzie knew she was. It wasn't the length of Albert's legs that caused him problems. It was the way they trembled. The strength of them. His swollen ankles.

'But you know we've got to keep up with Pa,' she called down. And kept going.

The next ledge was wide enough for Lizzie to turn round completely. She grabbed hold of a root above her head and flattened her back against the wall of rock. You could see so far from up here. You could see how alone they were. Frameless, the ocean looked bigger and more infinite than it ever had from the beach. Just one great rock right out in the middle of the bay, and the distant rise of another, much smaller island, far off to the left, too small and treeless for human habitation. Maybe another beyond that. Nothing else at all. Directly below the cliffs, the pale tent and the fire looked tiny, and the small figures of Ma and Billy and Queenie moving about the camp seemed barely human. Insignificant in such an expanse of ocean. Nowhere lonelier.

'Lizzie, wait!' Ada shouted up again.

'Can't you see I *am* waiting?' said Lizzie, cross because she didn't like the thoughts that came when she stopped and because she knew Ada was right. But where did she find the patience? At last a job that had some pleasure in it – a chance to see the rest of their island, to stretch their legs, a chance of excitement – and their brother didn't care if he ruined it.

'Hurry up, Albert!' she shouted down. 'What's keeping you?' And why did Ada always have to speak for him?

Soothing noises from Ada. Nothing at all from their brother.

'You can,' said Ada. 'I'll show you. I won't let you go. There . . . that's right . . . feel with your left foot now, yes, just a bit higher and you'll be there. Don't look down. And that's the difficult bit over, I promise.'

She kept talking cheerfully to Albert, pointing out bird burrows splashed with guano, enticing him on. Eventually Lizzie helped her to heave Albert up to their ledge, and he leaned against the cliff with eyes closed, spectre-faced and limbs unsteady.

Of course Lizzie arrived at the top first, where Pa was waiting at the edge of the forest, looking out to sea, and Sal was already exploring.

'What can you see?' asked Lizzie. 'A ship?'

'Nothing. But it never hurts to look. Sit down and get your breath back, my spadge. You've done well. You always do. But be ready to move like lightning on my say-so. There'll be no time to lose if the animals appear.'

Lizzie flopped down, gratefully, jumping up again as soon as Ada and Albert reached them.

'Seen any yet?' asked Ada.

'No,' said Pa, shortly. He looked Albert up and down. 'What took you so long? Lizzie was far quicker, and she's younger than you. You're going to have to get used to this climb. Now, let's find these goats.'

Of the many faint tracks leading in different directions, one seemed better used than the rest, so they set off down it in single file. Several hours passed looking, a few scattered droppings the only sign of their prey. The longer they marched, the less often Pa looked round.

When Sal suddenly made a backtracking dash off the path into a clearing to the right, provoking a crashing in the undergrowth, Pa was quick to raise his gun. A fierce little goat, brown and white, stood with lowered horns, cornered in a sharp crevasse. Pa fired. The animal staggered and fell. Lizzie gave a cry of pride and relief, and Pa strode forward, a satisfied grimace on his face.

'About time,' he said, pulling out his knife. There was no point in carrying any more than they needed back down that cliff. Mr Peacock grabbed the goat's back leg and set to work, skinning the animal there and then. At the first cut, Sal set up a frenzy of barking. As soon as Pa had separated the thigh hide, he hacked off a foot at the joint and threw it to her. She dragged off hoof and bone to chew contentedly alone, growling quietly.

Then Mr Peacock remembered the children, and reached inside his jacket for Ma's parcel of scones. Ada unwrapped them, offering him the first, but he shook his head and bent back over the goat. Lizzie squatted next to Pa to watch while she ate, as slowly as she could. Next time, she wanted to be able to do this job herself, just like Pa. He steadily slid his knife into just the right space between skin and fat, systematically pulling, unpeeling, cutting again, revealing marbled muscle, membrane, lard, and the white, white underside of skin. He cut off the tail, slowly eased away the back hide. Limbs and head slapped against earth.

'Is it really a wild goat?' she asked. It didn't look different from any other she'd ever seen.

'Wild enough,' Pa grunted. He reminded her how the early explorers had left goats to breed on islands so there'd always be something for passing sailors. 'Or castaways.'

'Or shipwrecks?'

'Umm.' The goat was quite naked now. 'Goats are survivors. That's the point.'

'Like us?' said Lizzie.

'Like us,' agreed Pa.

Albert hovered queasily.

'I'm thirsty,' he said.

Lizzie was afraid Pa would be harsh, and roll his eyes. But the kill had improved his mood.

'Well, you're in luck.' Mr Peacock jerked his head towards a bush with lacy, heart-shaped leaves, whose branches were stuck all over with orange berries like squat little candles. 'Eat those. Kawakawa,' said Pa. 'Tuck in.'

They gathered sweet, peppery handfuls of berries far bigger and juicier than they'd ever found in New Zealand. After a while, Lizzie's tongue was tingling. She stuck it out and pinched it. Her fingers could feel her tongue, but her tongue couldn't feel her fingers. They all began to slur their words, on purpose, laughing, and Ada pushed her tongue down to her chin, and opened wide her eyes, and then all three children spread their knees and tried to dance like New Zealanders.

Meanwhile, Pa gutted the goat. Great grey sacks, and snakes, still pulsing, spilled out like eels hitting the air. When their father reached in to wrench out heart and lungs, and laid them carefully on the hide, Albert turned away, retching. Lizzie gave the organs a curious poke.

'Do I look like that inside?' she asked.

'Not so different. You've only got one stomach.' Pa flicked a fly from the subsiding entrails. 'But it's a strong one.'

Lizzie felt triumphant. Until Pa added, in Albert's earshot: 'Unlike your brother's.'

Albert walked quickly away from Lizzie and Pa, pushing into the forest on the pretence of answering the call of nature. Ada kept her face blank and would not meet her sister's eye. How had the day soured so suddenly?

17

THREE DAYS NOW . . . FOUR . . . WITH NO SIGN, NO breath, no fingernail.

The skies hang low and grey and heavy for hours on end. We rarely see our shadows. We live in limbo, all together, Rock fellows and palagi, and spend each day looking under leaves and roots, searching cliffs and rocks, calling and praying and weeping, yes, there is more weeping now, and more and more each night, and we are becoming closer and yet more distant to this wounded family. We hush our steps and still our voices, hardly knowing how best to show kindness. No track, no trace of the boy on this island can be found. No hair. No whisper. Nothing. I can no longer believe that Albert can return, but nor can he be buried. We fellows will never see this boy we have never seen. And still we cannot step forward. We cannot go back.

The worst to watch is Mrs Peacock. Her grief floats in her wake. Every day there is more labour in her walking. Lumbered with the growing child inside her, lumbered with living, limbs barely at her bidding, she wades through each hour like one trying to remember how bones and muscles work. On the fifth morning, as we break our fast, Mrs Peacock breaks her silence on her son. She speaks of the lake. Like a fruit bat's wings brushing the treetops, thoughts pass sluggishly across her children's faces before they hang. What if her beautiful boy is underwater? Mr Peacock protests, says he has looked there, several times, and surely would have seen him. How hard has he looked? Hard enough, he says. But the mother is firm; she knows the drowned take time to make themselves known. She finds me out – the swimming fellow – with beseeching eyes which do not leave me until, with Solomona's blessing, I agree to search.

We make our way there together, two by two. It's a strange bare lakeshore of strange light stones, and the water is warm and green, soothing at first to my open eyes, used to saltier swims. The bottom falls away sharply and is quickly lost to me. I see nothing but weeds. I feel nothing. Each time I swim a little further and dive a little deeper, and each time I rise, failing, gasping more, until Solomona pulls me from the water.

'Enough,' he whispers urgently, holding me fast. 'We do not want a second body gone. I need you.'

I have been under so long this time that I have barely breath to answer, but I tighten my hand on his wrist, and nod, and agree to swim no more. My brother needs me. It is enough. I need him too, never more than when his heart is here with me, in this world, seeing me as I am, not as he would have me. Stay too, Solomona, rush my thoughts. Let us both live fully our lives on earth together. We cannot always think of heaven, no matter who waits for us there.

As we return, Mrs Peacock leans on her husband, every step

a breathless effort, a kind of sob. For the rest of that day, we say only what we need, only to each other, and there is no more talking palagi to islander. The work of eating and living does not stop. We fellows, still here and hungry, must be fed, and sheltered before the weather turns. Day six, we search again, from dawn, and harvest nothing. What more can we do?

At long last, Mr Peacock summons us to speak of our other work, the work we came here to do. I cannot look at Mrs Peacock then, or at the children. When they see this other work commence, they will know that our master has surrendered expectation of finding Albert living. We have crossed a threshold to another place. Life must continue on this island without the boy. Mr Peacock quiets our murmurings with flattened hands. Accepts this truth, unspoken. Bows his head in reverence. And then resumes his talk.

'Time and tide wait for no man.' Pronouncing each word with care, he tells us that he works as hard as he can, always, from sunrise to sunset, and so does Mrs Peacock and so do all the children, great and small, and we have seen all this, and thus we too must work. There can be no easy come, easy go South Sea nonsense here, he says.

Vilipate catches, somehow, his drift, and indignation lights his face. But Mr Peacock is quick to say he has no worries on that score. That is why he sent specially for us, not some other kanakas from some other place. He knows our island, our truly Christian island, and how different it is. Why, all the world now knows this! Sponging dry his flattery, we nod, and tell him it is so.

A stern man, it is clear, but also fair and often kind, and he may prove a decent master. We have little to compare. *Judge not,*

that ye be not judged, I tell myself. We will look for the best place
to plant the bananas before they shrivel, we tell him. He listens,
heeds our thinking and advising. We say we will make for him
a fence to keep the chickens from scitter-scattering, and also a
small hut because they like to hide their eggs.

Yet tomorrow cannot be the day to start these labours.

'One moment, sir,' begs Solomona, and the time is granted.

After long talking with us, and much more head-nodding, and
when he is full certain all our gang have understood every important thing, Solomona face again Mr Peacock. We wait to hear
what has taken six full days to say. What he promised Mr Reverend
he will say upon our landing.

'Sir . . . ' says Solomona.

We wait. I push my brother forward with my thoughts. Go
on. Say the words. Be bold.

'Yes, Solomona?' For Mr Peacock, Solomona is an easy name
to remember and repeat. He uses it often, just to show he know
it.

'Sir, you must know we can do no work on Sundays. We always
remember the Sabbath day and keep it holy.'

'Of course, my friend.'

Bluster, I believe, but soon I soften.

'Tell me,' our master says. 'What day is it now? I am losing
my way in the week a little, with all that's passed. Anyway, it's
Mrs P who usually keeps us in line on such matters.' He need
not say more. His wife's voice has barely sounded since our return
from the lake. And she hides her heart too, her ever-sorrowing
heart. The children – all but the smallest – tiptoe about both
their parents.

'It is the sixth day, today, sir,' says Solomona, standing tall, his church face frowning. '*But the seventh day is the Sabbath of the Lord thy God: in it thou shalt not do any work, thou, nor thy son, nor thy daughter, thy manservant, nor thy maidservant, nor thy cattle, nor thy stranger that is within thy gates.*'

Mr Peacock's flickering eyes fix on Solomona till he quails.

'Sir?' What can I say to strengthen my brother? Then our master quietens us both with a dark-lined palm. No explanation needed, he tells us.

'Of course, of course, I understand. There will be no work on Sundays.'

'And there will be prayers and thanksgiving,' insists Solomona, more bravely.

I see Mr Peacock does not like to be told what to do. The fumbling noise in his throat could be yes, could be no. Be careful, Solomona, I say in my head, more cautious now myself. Do not push this man, at this delicate time. He is quickly vexed. I hope not one of us fellows has ever cause to kindle his anger.

But all is well.

'As always,' Mr Peacock agrees. 'Prayers and thanksgiving.'

We walk further on Georgina's Flat, the lower terrace named for his wife, already planted with grass, which here grows lush as I have never seen before. I smile at Solomona, seeing that he and I share one thought: of pastures green and quiet waters. The surf below this terrace rages, but the pasture here is pleasing. Vilipate kneels down to crumble the earth between his fingers. He smiles, for he thinks this will be easy work, easier by far than at home. The work is closer to the houses too. No walking through bush for hours to reach it. Fine metal tools to work with. All could yet be well. If it were not for the missing boy.

'You will grow cotton here?' he ask Mr Peacock, and I turn

his words to English, and the new master's reply back to our tongue.

'No, no, not cotton . . . cotton boom's been and gone. Didn't you know? Too much from America back on the market now. Since the fighting ended. Is it cotton still you grow back home?'

We all nod.

'We grow it for the Church,' explains Solomona. 'Copra and cotton. And also we send arrowroot. And we pick fungus for the Chinamen – Jew's ear. We give it to Mr Reverend, and he take care of everything and send all moneys to London to pay for our missionaries and pastors and teachers.'

Mr Peacock looks at Solomona, and turns down his mouth. He hardly believes what he's hearing, I think.

'I'm sure he does. He's blessed indeed. Well, coconuts don't grow here and arrowroot I haven't tried and Jew's ear I've never seen – though I know the celestials can't get enough of it. It's fruit trees I'm after. All kinds. Oranges I've ordered – more oranges that is. And a little flock of sheep is what I'm set on.'

Oranges we see on ships, but they grow not on our island. Sheep we know of, because Mr Reverend has drawn us pictures, because the Lord is our shepherd, and we shall not want. The absence of coconut we feel in our tightening, unoiled skins.

'First things first.' Mr Peacock slaps palm against palm, cleaning something away. 'Can't have you living here like gypsies. Need to build another house for your gang, don't we? And after that we can start to clear the upper flat and make the new terrace.' Something else said over his shoulder, words to the wind: 'And I suppose you'll be wanting to build a church here too, and you won't do that labour on Sundays neither.'

I wonder if he will also build a mourning hut. Then I remember that Mr Reverend has told me this is not the custom for palagi.

*

Eight days missing. Sucking his cheeks, Vilipate looks sideways at Mrs Peacock (slower, slower, and yet slower, all the passing hours). He whispers to me that even as she grows larger, she also seems to shrink.

*

Not too close to the Peacock dwellings, and not too far, we frown and rub our chins and move some rocks, and pace out our spot, and we look at the other huts to see how they build here. After breakfast Mr Peacock will return us to the lake, where we will cut reeds, and these will be the walls to contain us. The children must show us where to find nikau palms, he says, to weave the roof. We set off smartly, and I whisper to Solomona my fear that this may be the time Albert has chosen to rise up through the water, floating, bloated.

'Indeed,' he murmurs. 'We must pray also that the Lord in His mercy will give this family a body they can bid farewell and bury as a Christian.'

'Nobody speaks of Albert now.'

'No, but he is there in their thinking, always. He always will be there.'

It has been weeks, maybe months, since I spoke to Solomona of his wife. I thought it was a kindness. Now I do not know.

I quell my worrying there and instead try harder to believe in this boy we have never met. This beautiful beloved boy, precious like china, whose voice has never sounded in my ears, has turned into a broken quockerwodger in my head, a puppet of a person, and I cannot pull the strings to make him dance. I work to conjure him. I open my heart to his spirit. I cannot tell what I am searching for. I feel nothing.

18

OUR HUT IS BUILT — MUCH LIKE THE OTHER FOUR, but rougher because more hasty — and we reach the end of the first day's clearing.

'Well, they weren't wrong about you fellows,' Mr Peacock tell us. The whole gang shines with sweat, chests and backs full scratched and filthy. Behind us the scrub is lying, dying, drying. Such a fire there will be here when this felled underforest is ready for the flaming. The spark is in our master's eye. 'Fine team of bushwhackers I've got myself.'

We wipe faces, and roll back the aching from our shoulders, and swing our arms free. Billy does the same, and Luka say proudly:

'Thank you, sir.' (Each day I teach the others some few more palagi words to make life smooth and easy.)

'We'll break in this island yet, make no mistake,' says Mr Peacock. 'We'll slaughter this forest. Give me another year, and nobody'll know the place. Our Garden of Eden. Tamed.'

He push back his hat and look up at the mountain rising above the flat and I see in time he means to conquer that, steep sides and all.

'Sir,' say Solomona. 'Our work here is finished for this day?'

'It is indeed. We'll head down now and wash up and cool down and see what Mrs P has got ready for our tea tonight. You've certainly earned it. Shirts on, boys. Don't let her see you like this.'

Walking back, Solomona promises Billy that he will play with us when we've eaten. The tide is low, and we will teach him cricket on the beach, as Mr Reverend taught us, and Sidney too. Vilipate is surprised he does not know the game – is it not an English game? he asks. Seeing some likely branches a few days ago, he fashioned an ironwood bat, wound with threads, like a short, smooth-ended katoua. Iakopo has sought out softer wood to make our kilikiki balls. A little out of hearing, Luka and Pineki talk of Billy's father: praise long his courage, his powers of seeing and determining so far ahead, his rock-like will. Such a man, they marvel. Such a man. What could not such a man accomplish? And then we near the huts, full of hunger and thirst, and nothing is ready for the evening meal, and no one to be seen. The goats are noisy. Queenie runs, flapping her arms.

'Go away, go away!' She tries to shout and whisper all at once. She has become an important somebody. 'You can't come back here now. We're busy.'

Mr Peacock is in laughing mood, like we've never seen before. He tries to swing his daughter to his shoulder to carry her back, but she fights and squirms from him.

'No, no, Pa, please. Lizzie says it's not right. You must all leave us be for now.'

Brave, like Lizzie, this one. Her fierce gaze strikes her father, making his sinews stiff. Anger is always quick and close with Mr Peacock. Understanding may follow later.

'It's time, is it? I see.' He puts her down, speaks gently now. 'How is she doing, your ma?'

Queenie bends her head and softens her voice. And at last I understand that the baby is coming.

'I don't know, Pa. Ada is with her. And Lizzie. They're inside.'

'Has it been long?'

'I don't know. Since this morning. Is that long?'

No answer. His burning is all quenched. Queenie takes his hand.

'Come with me, Pa. Ada says we must go for a walk together. You and me and Billy. A long walk.'

Solomona tell all the fellows it is time to take ourselves away also. Vilipate smalls his mouth, head-shaking. We take the long way back, on the forest path, disappear into trees, and when we come to the other side, we take our time, washing in the hot spring on the beach, out of sight and far away from the huts. Hunger makes holes in us, but this is not a time for men, and we must have patience. Then Solomona leads us in prayers for the baby coming. They have lost one child, he says. We must beg the dear Lord that they do not lose another.

19

I T SLITHERS OUT WITH UNEXPECTED SPEED, WHITE AND
veiled, eyelids pressed shut; a bloodied package of tucked-up,
trussed-up limbs and slicked black hair, trailing a glistening,
blue-tinted rope. The sight of this marble child in her sister's
hands freezes Lizzie's veins. She cannot speak, cannot tell her
mother what she sees. The silence terrifies. All this time, for this?
Ada is too stiff, her eyes too wide, her breathing too quiet.

'Thank God,' sighs Ma, who cannot see, who has laboured
sheep-like, on the ground, bleating only at the crowning.

'Ada?' says Ma, more sharply, lifting a hot and shining face
from the pile of blankets in front of her. She reaches quickly
between her open thighs for the uncanny parcel of flesh and bones
her daughters fear to touch. In the same movement she sits back,
without a word, and her fingers peck urgently at the baby's
shoulder, breaking the thin skin which encloses it. She peels the
covering away from a blank, unfamiliar face which she holds a
few inches from her own, and blows, sharply, on the pale skin.

Her breath seems to give life itself, and Lizzie breathes again.

It opens eyes which fail to focus, quickly covered by crumpled lids. Purple thighs flop open, and the knotty, pulsing tube stuck to the baby's belly only half hides the ungainly fruit between them. When the tiny gummy mouth opens and a thin mewling begins, Lizzie and Ada paw at each other, giggling and gasping, almost weeping. Alive! All is well! Ma smiles too, a crooked, teary smile.

'That's better. Now, quickly, girls, get a shawl for your baby brother.'

Ada is soon back, with covering for mother and child. She wraps them up together, and rubs the double bundle. Lizzie stands transfixed, the piece of skin which moments earlier contained her brother hanging from her hand. She knows it's special. She knows her brother Albert was also born veiled like this. His shrivelled caul is somewhere safe. Ma knows where. The last bit of him she still has. The story always repeated was that it was his luck, that he would never drown, but Albert had not been lucky, and it hadn't saved him.

20

TO PASS THE TIME WE TELL STORIES OF HOME AND it seems easy to forget roaring bellies in our hunger to be elsewhere. When the first stars shine, a lurching figure comes through the dusk. Rolling and ringing and singing, it stops and starts. A belch. Then a call to us.

'Kanakas! Hey, you! Kanaka boys. Come over here, my kanakas!'

We have lost our names. He thinks to own us.

Like a foreman, not a pastor, Solomona raises us to our feet with a quick head-jerk. Mr Peacock stand before us, swaying. He stares most hard but his eyes wander.

'Here. This's for you.' He hold out a bottle, and wipe its lip. 'I wan' you to toas' my boy. My new boy. My little boy. My baby boy. My boy Joseph.'

Pineki starts forward, eager-face and pleasing, so I hold him back with a fistful of shirtcloth. Solomona speaks for us.

'Thank you, sir. No, sir. No liquor for us, Mr Peacock.' Quietly, in our language, he remind us: 'Liquor is an abomination in the sight of our Lord. We have not come here to be educated in vice.

Remember what Mr Reverend has preached to us. Remember
the Mission ship wrecked on our reef by the drunkenness of its
captain? Remember Noah.'

I remember reports of the wealth in the hold of the old *John
Williams*, the surprise of it. The questions it provoked. The needle's
eye. I remember too the day when Mr Reverend spoke of the
state of some of our boys in Apia, talking of vice and habits and
disease, and started to say – then quickly stop himself – that it
might be better if some of our Rock's wanderers never returned.
Forgive me, he said. Do not concern yourself unduly. The risk
of degeneracy must be lower of course when a Fellowship fellow
travels from a small and remote island to another which is smaller
and yet more remote, he told me.

'No liquor? No liquor?' say Mr Peacock, his eyes blurring then
fixing, his brow lining like a piglet's nose. He sweats out a smell
both foul and sweet. Some movement in the trees behind and
there stands Billy, the last boy left, who has followed his father,
but is now afraid to approach. He duck back and away from us
not to be seen. I sense his shame.

Our heads refuse for us.

'What, none of you?' Mr Peacock say, rocking between anger,
doubt, surprise. He think we judge him. He is not mistaken.
'Not a little drop, when we have such celebrating to do? Such
celebrating. Come on now . . . don' vex me now.'

Mr Peacock speaks like a man calling to a chicken he wants
to catch for the boiling. Wheedle, wheedle. Pineki has still some
desire to peck – I see his unsteady feet, and he never hides his
admiration for our master – but he holds himself back.

'Not a drop, sir,' say Solomona, shaking his head most firm,
hand raised against Mr Peacock and his odours, as though he

would push his body from us. I wish he would. 'It is not our way, sir. But truly we thank God for the safe delivery of your son and we will pray for him.'

We nod and mumble, all a gang. Mr Peacock throw back his head to drink some more and his next words spit at us.

'Well, aren't you a Sunday school collection! Suit yourselves. I'll thank you kindly for your congratulations, and toas' my son myself.'

One last swig, and this bottle is emptied. He falls backwards, like timber.

21

THE WHARE SMELLS FAINTLY OF BLOOD AND EXCRE-
ment. The stool Pa knocked over when Ma sent him
away points its legs at Lizzie accusingly, so she sets it
on its feet. Her head sings. She does not want this to happen to
her ever, but can't think how to stop it. Does Ada know? And
yet . . . the astonishment of it . . . the glow of Ma, whole again,
lit from inside, so serene and purposeful despite her splitting.
Lizzie starts to roll up the goatskin rug, to hide its dark, matted
stain, but Ada, returning at just that moment with a clean bucket,
takes it from her.

'Not yet. There's more.'

'More?' Lizzie's eyes follow Ada's to the twisting rope still visibly
looping between mother and baby. The cord now looks dead rather
than alive, its blue pulse stilled to white. But her brother's breathing.
She notices a few smears of blood – a small archipelago – on Ma's
inner thigh.

'Yes . . . it'll be here soon,' Ma agrees, mysteriously, offering
her vast, brown nipple to a mouth that glistens like a small, wet

petal but shows no interest. 'Come on now, come on. Just a drop.'

She milks herself efficiently with thumb and finger, and smears the baby's lips with the oozing yellow trickle. The creature turns his head away.

'He wants to sleep, Ma,' says Ada. 'Look at him. The darling. Can't you let him sleep? He must be so tired.'

'No, not till he's fed, and we're all done here, and then I'll sleep too.' She doesn't say more than that, but there's a determination in her voice that scares Lizzie.

'Shall I make you tea, Ma?' Lizzie asks.

'Soon.'

Ma holds the baby up, inspects him, hungrily. His eyelids flutter, and then she turns him round to face the other breast, and strokes his cheek, very gently.

'Try this instead. Come on now, just a little. Be a good boy for your mammie.'

'Why doesn't he want to eat, Ma?' Lizzie lowers her voice. It seems to her, obscurely, that Albert is to blame. His absence hangs in the hut. Perhaps his new brother feels it too. Perhaps Albert needs to be found and buried before this child can live. Lizzie tugs at Ada's sleeve, wanting to ask her, but then a face appears at the parted shutters: Queenie, questioning, mouthing. She wants to come and see the baby. Lizzie sends her away and tells her to leave Ma alone. Queenie needs to take care of Gussie. She retreats, whimpering, leaving Lizzie wishing the thing in her mother's arms looked more like a baby, and less like a sea creature. His eyes are a milky version of Albert's.

'Is the baby . . . quite right?' she asks. 'Is something wrong?'

'No, but none of you were like this. Not even Albert . . .'

Her voice stumbles at his name, and her breath whistles into her, as she winces at something Lizzie can't see or feel and doesn't want to.

'Ready, Ma?' says Ada.

'Look!' says Lizzie, before their mother can reply. 'Clever thing!'

That tiny mouth has at last discovered what it was made for. The tiny chin begins to move forward and back in a slow, steady rhythm, and the baby's wandering eyes find his mother's. Before long, his lids droop, and everything gradually slows, until even a little poke can't start it all up again. Its tiny chest fills visibly with air and empties itself, over and over and over again. It's unmistakably alive.

Ma says 'Ow', half stands and hands the baby to Ada, and then up she starts again with that animal breathing and unearthly face, silently stretching.

'Bucket, Lizzie,' she pants. Her hand grabs at her baggy belly, as if to stop it from sliding away. Her body – soft and loose and messy – is falling apart. 'It's coming.'

Confused, Lizzie dashes for the pail, and helps her mother to crouch over it, standing before her so Mrs Peacock can lean on her shoulders, steadying herself in a long, drawn-out, near silent moan.

'Twins?' whispers Lizzie. Slowly dancing, her sister shakes her head, and rocks and soothes the baby.

Lizzie touches her mother's forehead with her own, afraid she's dying, hoping love and longing will keep her on this earth, desperate to bring an end to this agony, whatever its cause. Ma grimaces again, her face darkening, sweat squeezing briefly from her forehead. Something squelches out below. 'Afterburden,' she mutters, sucking in her breath and reaching for a cloth to dab delicately at herself. Even as Ada removes the heap of meat and membrane her mother has deposited in the bucket, Lizzie is none the wiser.

BEFORE

Lizzie and Albert followed Pa shakily, hardly knowing where they were going. Ada, waiting at the top of the cliffs with the captured nanny and her two bleating kids, jumped to her feet as soon as she registered the numbness on their faces. Nobody wanted to talk about what they had just witnessed, not right away. Who could have imagined such a stampede, or how it would end? Talking wouldn't change it.

Still, at least they wouldn't be coming back from another goat-hunt empty-handed. Ma couldn't be disappointed this time, not with one for meat and one to milk.

Mr Peacock unloaded the only goat they had killed before it leapt, and creaked his head from side to side to loosen his stiff neck.

'No time to butcher this fellow properly tonight. We'll need the last of the light to get the milker down the cliff safely.' He hoisted the carcass into the tree, working quickly and efficiently, checking each knot with care. Its yellow eyes stared and swung.

'Will we all go back now?' said Lizzie, quickly. 'Surely we can't leave the meat here all night?'

'You think it's going to run away . . . ?' said Pa, laughing. It was his way of lightening the air, Lizzie understood, so she tried to smile.

'No, Pa. But you never know what might take it. Ada and I can stay and guard it.'

'What do you think, Albert? Can the two of us get these three back on our own?'

To Lizzie's surprise, Albert nodded.

'Yes. I think so. If we've got their mother, the kids will follow.'

'Good lad.'

Albert approached the nanny. 'Shh . . . Shhh . . . steady on. You'll have the tree over if you keep pulling like that.' She stuck in her heels and lowered her head. He lowered his own, kept his hands behind his back, breathed gently into her nostrils, undismayed by her rolling eyes. Slowly, slowly, she began to calm – just a little – until she had ceased to fight her captors and merely stood and trembled.

'That's the way,' said Pa. 'We'll rope the kids if need be.'

'So Ada and I can stay?' said Lizzie.

Pa gave them both a narrow look, then jerked his head towards the skittering kids.

'These two are less likely to panic with fewer people around to put the wind up them. We can't have another stampede. Though what your mother will say when we come back without you . . . '

She could say what she liked, thought Lizzie. It would be too late by then. A whole night of freedom ahead. Nobody telling them what to do until morning. And Ada to herself for once.

'You girls going to be warm enough? Here – have my flint and coat.'

Pa shrugged his jacket off into Lizzie's waiting hands. He stood in waistcoat and shirtsleeves, considering his daughters, while

Albert held on to the nanny goat with all his strength. She dragged back, resistant, locking her knees against him, while the two kids pranced and danced around her, springing up with straight, stiff legs.

'This way,' said Pa, when Albert's patience had calmed her again.

'We'll get the fire going right away,' said Lizzie, handing the flint tin to Ada. 'Thank you, Pa. Thank you so much. We'll be very good.'

'Sleep well. I'll be back at first light. And don't you dare move from here.'

'Of course we won't.' Ada managed to sound almost bored. Lizzie looked indignant at the very thought.

BEFORE

Ada collected dried bracken for kindling and broke up twigs, and Lizzie made a circle of rocks.

'I don't think we should light the fire yet,' she said.

'No,' agreed Ada.

'Though maybe he'll be back if he doesn't see the smoke.'

'Once they're over the edge of the cliff, he'll not see a thing. Anyway, he'll need both eyes for Albert and the goats.'

'So I reckon we can go and explore now,' said Lizzie, with tilted head. 'Just a little, before it's too dark.'

Ada nodded. 'Which way?'

'Where Pa showed us. To the crater lake,' Lizzie said. It was obvious.

'That far?'

'Let's sleep there,' said Lizzie, snatching up the coat. 'What's going to happen to a dead goat? And then we can swim in the morning too. When did we last go in the water? All the way?'

'He did promise to take us when there was time.'

'There's time now. At least for us.'

'I hope Albert will manage,' sighed Ada. Lizzie swallowed a sharp retort. She was certain Albert managed better when Ada wasn't around to fuss over him, and she was pretty sure Pa thought so too.

It turned out that once you were up and over the first ridge, pretty much all the goat tracks led down to the water. The girls let momentum carry them down the last stretch, as though they had no choice in the matter but to let one leg follow another, just to keep up with their hurtling bodies, lungs at full stretch with no one to hear their squawks and yells.

Ferns and loam gave way to mud and pumice and a skeleton regiment of trees, stark white and splintered. Barren devastation after the lush excess of the forest. Awed into stillness, the girls stared bewildered at jagged limbs hanging at uncomfortable angles where they had been half ripped off, branches like bones, not an inch of bark remaining, not a leaf left dangling. The eruption could have happened last year, or twenty years ago. The girls had no way of knowing.

'Did Pa say anything to *you* about the volcano?' asked Ada, uncertainly.

'Not exactly,' admitted Lizzie. 'I suppose he talked of the crater lake. I never thought to ask what had made the crater.'

'And Mr Robson?'

Lizzie had long ago confessed her early notice of their moving plans to Ada, and sworn her to secrecy.

'I couldn't hear everything they said. But Pa would never have brought us here if it wasn't safe. And now we've got the lake!'

The ghostly forest was reflected in water the colour of bright moss. Lizzie bent to pick up a stone. Light and airy, it could hardly summon the energy to cut through the air as she hurled it into the lake. The water swallowed it with a whisper of a splash. Two red-beaked birds with purple plumage flicked their tails and staggered into flight. Lizzie pulled Ada closer to the water, hanging on to her for balance while she stuck out a heel, and then a toe, and finally plunging in a whole foot.

'It's warm!' she said, delighted. 'Warm enough. Not cold anyway. Like a giant bathtub.'

'Any fish?'

'I doubt it . . .'

'Will it make us go green all over?'

'Don't be silly.' Lizzie swung her foot into the air, and pointed and flexed it. 'Come on!'

Ada stepped in too, and wriggled her green toes, and wobbled a few steps from her sister. They eyed each other, grinning. Then Ada pulled back one leg and swooshed forward her foot in a strong, satisfying arc which sent a bridge of droplets slashing across the water surface. Lizzie sent another out, and then Ada a third. For several minutes they stood holding up their hems and gleefully kicking the water not at but across each other, forming slow, sparkling intersecting patterns, making scoops of their green feet.

'We're free!' yelled Ada, grabbing Lizzie's wrists and beginning to spin. The sisters twirled on the strange, bruising beach, lurching and colliding and finally collapsing together in an exhilarated heap, with the sky whirling above them.

'Nobody to tell us what to do till morning,' gasped Lizzie. 'Heaven.'

They lay watching the clouds slow down, enjoying their unusual liberation. Ada sighed.

'Oh, this is lovely. Don't you feel sometimes we're hardly more than servants for Pa?' She looked sideways at her sister. Lizzie contemplated the idea briefly, and dismissed it.

'He's our father. We have to do what he says,' she replied.

'Don't we? And what Ma says too, of course. That's always how it is. And anyway, it's not just for him. Everything we do, all our work, it's for all of us.'

'Ye-e-s,' said Ada, slowly. 'It's just that sometimes it seems . . . '

Lizzie sat up very suddenly.

'What's that?'

She pointed across the lake to a twisting thread of steam which rose from a crack in the pink-flushed rock face opposite. Made visible – though barely – by the cooling evening air, it vanished almost before you could see it.

No need to consult. The rough, sliding stones muttered gently as they moved hastily across them. Picking their way round the shoreline, the girls' arms kept flying up at the sharp pain of bruised soles, but they would not stop.

Standing right below it, they could see that the steam was trickling from a crack much higher up the rock face than they'd first imagined. It opened out into a wider crevice some way below. Ada put on Pa's jacket to keep her hands free – Lizzie told her she looked like a scarecrow – and they began to climb, up and along, up and along, edging and stretching and pointing out handholds to each other. Lizzie knotted up her tunic skirt to stop it catching and reached the ledge outside the opening first. Undeterred by the whiff of brimstone at its opening, she felt her way, cautiously, one hand raised above her head, into a narrow cave. She hallooed down it, ready to duck if necessary, but the way her voice sounded suggested that this cave opened out again inside.

'Careful,' called Ada. 'How big is it?'

'Big enough for both of us, easily, I think. Definitely bigger once you're a little way in. And the walls are dry. Feel the rock.'

'I'm feeling the ground,' said Ada, bending behind her, letting a little more light in as she crouched. 'It's warm, isn't it? Toasty. What do you think?'

'About sleeping here tonight?' Lizzie understood instantly. 'Oh yes! I've never slept in a cave. And this one's an oven. Perfect! No need to bother with a fire.'

'We'll be up early? We'll get back to the goat meat before Pa, won't we?'

'Of course. We'll have to. Lay the coat down here.'

Lizzie helped Ada spread it out. Old sweat and fustian and working bodies billowed up. The comforting smell of Pa.

'Do you think they're back home yet?' said Lizzie, envying Albert's triumph, exulting in her own.

'Home,' said Ada, trying the word. 'Yes, I should think so, by now.'

'I wish I could see Ma's face. She'll be so pleased with that nanny.'

'And Queenie. I wish I could see *hers*. Two more babies for her. Though one's for eating.'

'Unless they've all got stuck on the way down? Or fallen. You know Albert's joints are playing up again?'

She hadn't noticed. And like Pa, Lizzie found it hard to believe in pain whose cause she couldn't see.

'Don't worry so much. Pa always knows what he's doing,' said Lizzie, shoving her hip at Ada. 'Move up.'

'I wish we'd brought a candle.'

'What do we need to see once we're asleep?'

The sisters huddled against each other, looking out towards the tall blue pyramid of sky at the mouth of the cave which turned velvet, then darkened to navy.

'I hope he's not made Albert take the rope. I hope that stupid nanny hasn't pulled him off the cliff. I hope the kids haven't run away,' said Ada. 'I hope Sal hasn't lost herself again.'

'I hope you're not going to spend the whole night worrying. It won't make any difference.'

'Really?' said Ada. 'Thinking makes a difference, doesn't it? Isn't it a bit like praying?'

'I don't think worrying is like praying.' Lizzie ignored the quiet twang of guilt. She didn't want Ada to be thinking about Albert when he wasn't even there. 'Anyway, right now Albert will be a hero for bringing back the nanny goat. Nobody to steal his thunder. They'll all be singing hymns and saying their prayers down below, and the nanny will be feeding her babies, and soon everyone will be asleep, and we will be too.'

'Maybe.'

Ada's voice shrank. Lizzie blundered on, trying to cheer her up.

'You worry too much about Albert.'

'Somebody's got to.'

'If only he wasn't so obviously afraid of Pa. Albert needs to stand up for himself. Seeing how scared he is – that's what annoys Pa more than anything, I think.'

'Hmmmph.'

'What do you mean, *hmmmph*?' Lizzie gave Ada's shoulder a little shake.

'I mean it's all very well for you. You don't know what it's like. You're his favourite.'

Lizzie didn't have an answer to that.

'I have to work just as hard as anyone else,' she pointed out.

Ada replied slowly and carefully.

'That wasn't what I was saying.'

'I didn't ask—'

'But you're not frightened of him,' said Ada. 'What have *you* got to be frightened of?'

They lay and listened for a while, absorbing the deadening silence of the rocks that contained them.

'Is Billy frightened of Pa too?' asked Lizzie.

'Of course he is. Everyone is. Maybe not Ma, so much, but that's because she knows how to handle him. And Queenie doesn't notice everything.'

Lizzie turned prim and distant.

'I don't think we should be talking like this.'

'See,' was Ada's only reply.

Lizzie looked for diversion. A gurgling sound somewhere far below them was so like a stomach rumbling that it made Lizzie giggle.

'That's God. Asking when *we're* going to say our prayers,' she told Ada.

Ada pushed her, but she laughed too. Nervously.

'Are you sure?'

'No, of course not. I don't know what it is. Has it stopped?'

They listened. Faint hissing and bubbling from deep within the cave reminded her of their old room above the kitchen at the hotel in the Navigator Islands. There was always a big pot of water coming to the boil on the range below, and the room was warm and made you sleepy in just the same way. When the thumping became louder, more like a distant steam engine's pistons, Ada slid an arm around Lizzie. By then both girls were floating with the uncontrollable exhaustion of physical labour, their breath slowing and deepening. Ada jerked once, like a dog smelling rats in its sleep. And then Lizzie was asleep herself, dreaming Sal was on her chest, curled up with Spy, her half-grown puppy, and she couldn't push them off.

*

She woke feeling still weighed down, impossibly leaden, as if caught in a kind of dream: you see the danger, but can do nothing about it. Her muscles would not respond. She could hardly move at all. She groaned and poked at Ada, whose eyelids fluttered. Nothing else stirred. Something more than sleep was trying to drag them both towards oblivion. Sulphurous steam had gathered around them in the night in a warmly tempting, invisible cocoon. She couldn't give in to it, but she desperately wanted to, and her eyes were closing again. No. She had to resist. Lizzie forced herself to sit, and that made her choke, and at last, just in time, she grasped the situation.

'Quickly, Ada! Wake up.' She shook her sister as hard as she could, shouting in her ear, slapping her face, smacking down the hands which pushed her away. They were both coughing and gasping. Lizzie heaved Ada to her knees and pushed her, still struggling, towards the entrance. 'Move! Get out!'

At last Ada understood, and they staggered out together. Gulping down the fresh morning air, they clutched at each other, choking and laughing and crying all at once. Until their skin iced over as they understood the spider-web strength of their luck.

'I thought I'd never wake you,' said Lizzie. 'I thought you were dead already. Your lips . . . they were nearly blue just now.'

'I didn't want to wake up, ever,' Ada replied. 'I thought I

couldn't move. Don't tell Pa, will you? Please, Lizzie, please don't tell him. He mustn't even know we came in here. We were meant to stay by the fire. If he finds out we slept here . . . '

Lizzie nodded.

'Of course I won't tell him. We mustn't tell anyone about the Oven.'

They shook hands solemnly.

'And let's get back as fast as we possibly can,' said Ada.

'But it's still so early. And just look at the lake now the sun's on it.'

They scrambled back down from the rock ledge with only one thought. Helping each other off with their clothes, the girls waded into the water in shifts and drawers, white cotton and pale limbs turning ever darker.

Long before they heard Sal barking, they were back in the clearing beside the hanging goat carcass, with a fire nicely burned down to embers, underthings just a little damp. Ada grabbed Lizzie's arm. Her eyes were still watering from the cave's fumes and her voice was hoarse.

'Remember you promised?'

'I'll never tell anyone,' Lizzie agreed fervently, wiping her running nose. 'Never.'

22

IT IS FORTUNATE FOR THE PEACOCK FAMILY THAT THEY have my brother here. As Mrs Peacock often say: 'a blessing indeed'. One child in limbo already, body unfound, soul unblessed, untalked of now except in dreams it seems . . . (often I hear murmurs in darkness, restless turning) . . . it would be bitter indeed to lose another to that place between worlds.

The baby, Joseph, is a big-eyed, small-boned yellow thing, which does not fatten. His skin stretches over his skull, and light glows through his tiny hands. When he cries, opening, opening and opening toothless gums, white-coated tongue curled back, it is a worry to all. But when he is silent, and cannot be woken, the worry is worse. For some days, hope is frail. Palagi babies are much weaker than ours, I think. Passing strange how rarely God and medicine help them. Mrs Reverend has buried two since they came to our island. The last, four years distant, a small infant, a girl-baby again, who did not live to see the world one week before she went to the arms of Jesus. The palagi find our customs strange, so they bury the daughter by the church, and call that place the graveyard. But there is no church here on Monday Island.

They sent my friend Sidney away from the Mission House when he grew too old. So often do I think of him these days and nights. Something in that lanky-limbed girl Lizzie brings him to my mind. She is like him in her movements, so quick and certain, and also in her zest and thirstiness, how she looks about the world thinkingly. Like Sidney, she lacks fear to speak her mind. For some past days Lizzie has been kitchen-mistress, chopping, stirring, counting, with Queenie at her elbow. Ada guards the baby like a treasure, and Mrs Peacock, soon busy again, moving faster and faster day by day, watches her daughter watching over him. She sees how Ada cannot bear to put him down, and how she whisper in his pink shell ear night and day, telling him to stay with us, not to leave us. Mr Peacock walks away from the crying. Iakopo ask me why the mother ate no ti before the birthing, but I cannot say and he shake his head with sadness and regret.

Some more days pass. Sunday again. In the days previous we have caught fish and dug an uma in preparation for the ceremony. This is but a small feast and we have found no crabs here of a size to make them worth the cooking, yet the smell of the buried food, slowly cooking in its parcel of leaves, takes me home in my head, and Solomona too, as he tells me softly. How is our mother faring, we wonder.

It is time for my brother to bless the waters of the warm springs, and wash sins away, and say the words of the Lord, and it is time to name this boy. In rain, may he be able to run, in gales, to run away, by night or day. Let him not be swept away by the waves, let him be swift to escape when his enemies pursue him. Let him live long on the surface of this earth.

Solomona performs well. My chest swells, and I let him know my pride. How hard Mrs Peacock listens, head forward to miss nothing of a prayer she has not heard before. How joyful her smile. We sing together, and Mr Peacock play his fiddle, and later other songs, not hymns but toe-tingling dances and jigs. A sideways, lilting air he calls a schottische. When a new tune starts, the children rush up and down and round and round like little cyclones. This is a polka, Lizzie tells me, laughing at my surprise. They try to teach us how to turn and step like them, and cross arms, even Solomona. Mr Peacock flash his eyes and make the music go faster and faster and the dogs bark and jump until everyone fall over, laughing and tumbling on the meadow. I love to hear the girls' laughter. We fellows cannot sprawl long. Up we jump to our feet when the fiddle tunes, and I offer a hand to Ada, who shakes her head, and then to Lizzie, who takes it, and I swing her to upstanding, and her palm is hot and she looks straight at me and it seems to me too long. Albert's absence is set aside for a few hours, perhaps.

Will Mr Peacock drink tonight? I glimpse another man within his skin, one I am loathe to trust. But when sleep gives me no solace, and I face each coming day a little wearier, what faith can I have in my judgement?

*

The christening brings a change in the baby.

'Look,' say Ada one afternoon, a few days later, when we fellows return from our daily labour on the flats. 'Look, Pa.'

She hold the bundle close to her face, and she look into his blue-as-sky eyes, and tender-thumbs his cheek. Crowding all, we see that life has come at last, and those eyes are steady and seeing and no longer roam regardless. His gaze latches to hers, and I see he understands that this is the world he is meant for, not the other, and he is curious what it might contain. After that, he begin to thrive. No more do you see in his thin skin every blue vein-river, like a feeding breast swollen with milk. And now they use his name. They call him Joey. A few days more, I see his mouth twitch like a smile. A curse is lifted, we fellows tell ourselves. He is blessed. Mrs Peacock call this smile wind, a sore tummy made better, but then she naysays: no, we are right, it is a miracle.

'A true miracle, and we will give thanks to Our Lord that He has heard our prayers.' Solomona duck his head in happiness like I have not seen since his great disappointment.

And after that the days go easier. One child is given life, another death. As the youngest shows himself determined to stay with us, to embrace this world's blessings, so comes the time for the family to mark the departing of the lost one. Mr Peacock spends some hours alone, near the storehut, sawing, hammering, and he returns with a wooden cross to remember Albert. It is an English kind of gravestone which marks no grave. The father carves and burns his son's name and years of life, and that evening we watch, and the other children watch, as he walks slowly around their settlement with Mrs Peacock alone. They are choosing the place where their son will be remembered. The next morning, before work, he summons Solomona.

When Solomona returns to us, all the fellows are curious.

'Tomorrow,' he tells us. 'We will have a funeral service.'

'Without a body?' I ask him privately that evening, when the others have gone to wash. My brother does not like to show any weakness before them. 'How can it be?'

'It must be,' says my brother, with twisted brow. 'All hope is passed. A funeral will be a comfort to the family.' And, as ever, he sees how I am thinking. Ministering to heathens is one thing: they cannot know your slips. But a palagi family has expectations, harder to meet. 'Mr Reverend is not here to consult. I can only ask for guidance from the Lord. And I am satisfied. And perhaps you will sleep better too, Kalala.'

Yet when the moment comes, and Solomona faces the empty space before the cross, he shakes a little, and speaks too quickly. He wants this business finished and set aside. '*We brought nothing into the world, and we can take nothing out. The Lord gave, and the Lord has taken away; blessed be the name of the Lord.*' Much weeping and sadness follow, lasting all the day, and even after the sun has descended. Not all the family has lost hope yet, I understand. Not Ada, I believe. But the cross is also an anchor, and it marks an end to these days of drifting.

23

'PLAIN SAILING NOW,' SAY MR PEACOCK IN THE week after the funeral that was not a funeral. He has praised our work, how well we have cut and laid the underforest where his orchards will grow, and Luka and Pineki are buoyed with joy. 'When this lot is fine and dry, and the weather just right, we will be ready to burn.' He look at the sky with a measuring eye, and see how fast the clouds pass. 'Not long now.'

So here we are, all moving forward together, this island a boat in open water running before the wind. We have left behind the hidden reefs that might wreck us. Only at night do other currents pull at me, when I hear cries from other huts telling me I am not alone in my ghost-sick state. By day I try to put all that aside. I am mindful of my promise to Mr Reverend that I will forget neither my letters nor my learning. I must be prepared for any 'opening' on our return, whenever that may be, a teacher's post at a village school. I think about things I have already forgotten, or hardly known. The face of my father, and his voice. I wonder how forgetting happens. Could I wake one morning and look at a printed page and find that no longer do I know how to make letters fit together into words? Is this talent not like swimming, or fishing, or walking or talking? (Not sleeping, for it seems I've lost the trick of that.) Such a chance makes me fearful. I must take care to guard my talents.

One afternoon, late, on a day when we have made great progress with the clearing, and Mr Peacock has rewarded us with early freedom, I tire of games with Iakopo and Luka and the others, boys' games of throwing tika and spinning tops and such. Solomona, who shares my fears, I see, has borrowed a pencil stub from Mrs Peacock, and scratches thoughts for a sermon on a raw slice of wood. He frowns. He pulls his ear.

'Haia!' our fellows cry. I pluck another curling leaf from the fern frond to keep the score. Disquiet will skew their play if I walk away from them alone. They find it strange. 'What is your trouble?' Luka ask me. Only palagi prefer to keep their own company. Pineki often taunts me with turning palagi. So I tell them of my promise, like a rainbow, and how I must keep my word to keep my words. And then I beg from Solomona his English Bible, whose pages reach so great a number I think of stars and sand grains.

'Solomona?' I say, before I leave him.

He looks up, his mind still churning with his sermon. So many things I need to say. What does he make of our new master? How fares now my brother's heart, with so much more distance from his sorrow?

'What will be your lesson?'

He is pleased.

'I will take my text from Luke's Gospel. Either chapter nine, or chapter fifteen. What do you think?'

I consider. 'Not the Lost Sheep,' I say. 'Nor the Prodigal Son. Better the Greatest in Heaven. Matthew. 18.'

By his smile, and soft-closing eyes, I know I have made him happy. And though he has not found me wanting, I resent that he tests me in this manner.

As I walk I recall the heavy sighs of Mr Reverend, sighs which flitter the pages binding him to his desk into the night. He makes his translations into our tongue, line by careful line, slowly, taking notes, asking questions all the time of me and Solomona and others who are teachers or becoming so, whenever he catches us, questions we all try to answer as best we can, so he can render better the Bible's meaning to our people. We talk of promises and covenants, salvation and slavery. We count the ways to count. The English Bible is a book with many books within, each book with chapters, each chapter verses, and much work needs to be done to have it all translated and printed on our island.

As I left, Mr Reverend was finishing the story of a man called Moses. With the Lord God's help, Moses led his people out of cruellest bondage in a place called Egypt. He told them of a land promised to them which flowed with milk and honey. I recall the day I offered words for this story while together we sat and studied, and considered cows and coconuts, and nectar made by flowers and insects, and when it may be right to leave one land to seek another. Mr Reverend's mind circled round slavery. To think . . . he said, eyes on paper, as if a picture appears there which he alone can see. How easily it is done. One man taken captive by another. It takes a moment. And then they are gone. Then Mr Reverend locked my eyes fiercely, and sorrow brimmed in his. I cannot forgive myself, he told me.

'You must take care, always.'

'I understand,' I told him smartly. Only because his hard looking-search discomforted me and I wanted it to finish. I did not understand. Still I do not. But now I have time to think and ponder. Is it chance, or God's purpose, that Mr Reverend offers such a special kindness to my family? And now I see freshly how all that loving kindness has fished me from my waters and left me dangling, gasping in an air I barely breathe.

I think of him working on without me. By now, the book called Exodus may be complete. Soon printed, crank by crank, and bought with joyful hearts by brethren in every village. Our printing press is a most beautiful and noisy machine, made up of many parts and sent to us from England by the LMS. It came by way of Sydney, Australia, when I was a small boy. It lay idle many years, for want of parts. Writing on the press, in metal letters, raised, formed words which now I know: 'Albion' and 'Fetter Lane'. But for too long my mother flicked her feathers at the dust which gathered in the corners of these letters, as Mrs Reverend taught her, and clicked her tongue when I asked about this strange and silent machine. She answered with a command to go away and play, and let her do her work in peace. Finally another boat from Sydney sailed with the last, lost case. It came through the reef to our jetty on a double vaka which sat low in the water with the weight of the box, and was brought to the Mission House with pomp and singing and ceremony. I was there when Mr Reverend unpacked tympan, ink and rollers, and all the sundry little things wanting for the press. Faces crowded at the window. I was there when he found the type, and there was much rejoicing, and we drank tea. And that is how my reading life began, at seven years old, with backward metal letters, on blocks, in rattling cardboard boxes, marked 'Lower Case' and 'Upper Case'. And also labelled 'Blomfield Street'.

First Mr Reverend asked me to sort loose letters, see which goes with which, matching-matching and keeping all in good order. A game, invented perhaps to allow my mother to finish her work of cleaning and cooking and washing with no more interruptions. Naturally, when Mr Reverend's son Sidney saw me playing, he wanted to play too. That birthed our friendship. We learned together.

His father taught us the letters' names. An alphabet, he said they were, and held them to a looking glass, to show us how each sign would look when printed. Later, when I went to school, I learned to see them better the other way. In time, I would help Mr Reverend to put the letters in the right order to make our words, and it was my task to bolt the tray to keep the lines all safe. He called me his compositor. You have to think backwards to do that work, he said, but I had started by thinking backwards, so it was quick and easy for me. The 'k's and 'l's always finished too soon. The letters for my name. We never had enough. He asked me if I ate them. It took me a moment to see this joke. He made many jokes with serious face. Sidney too. It is a thing for which I hunger now. Mr Peacock is a serious man all through, inside and also outside.

Mr Reverend wrote to his people in England, which sometimes he calls Albion, asking for extra 'k's and 'l's . We are still waiting. Mr Reverend is a man of great patience. It is long and slow work to make our island's Bible. So there are many stories I yet know nothing of, and much to ponder and discover in the book I carry.

Up on the bluff, the breeze teases the printed paper, so thin and light, each page holding the reversed shadow of the next.

Maybe these new stories will push away the ones that come for me each night and make me fearful. Flickering Bible leaves turn into noisy wings which cause my heart to flutter. I catch and pin them down, fearful they may rip and fly away and vanish into the heavens. Directly above my nails, square and lined with the day's dirt, I see my brother's name is printed. The Song of Solomon. A sign, I think. The place I must surely study first, the place perhaps to ease my doubting. What is the Lord's purpose in snatching children to his bosom before they are grown? Fathers from their children? Wives from husbands. How must we under-stand the shape of His justice?

I start to read.

Sounds rise faintly from the beach but do not pursue me: the fellows hurling clubs and shouting. Soon I am in another place entirely, a place of curtains and chariots and myrrh. A great heat burns my neck, but it is not the sun. It comes from within, from the Song of Solomon. Many words here I hardly know how to say – like camphire and Kedar and spikenard and En-gedi. There are words which make me hot and shifty – lusty words I wonder at. Does Solomona know they hide here, Holy, beneath his name? Has he read this talk of kisses and mouths and beds of green? And what of Mr Reverend, who preaches chastity with such passion? *Behold, thou art fair, my beloved.*

I have no Beloved. But when I read this, my body aches for such a person, better than wine. My body aches to be Beloved. These verses intoxicate me until I close the Book, stare out to sea and think of cold waves to drench my loose desire. Doves' eyes. Behold, thou art fair. My finger still rests between these pages, marking this magical place I have found. I cannot let these words vanish.

I cannot resist. I read on, and on.

Apples and flagons, and yes, I *am* sick of love. I long to sing this song. Lips like a thread of scarlet make me weak and shorten my breath. *O my dove, that art in the clefts of the rock, in the secret places of the stairs, let me see thy countenance, let me hear thy voice; for sweet is thy voice, and thy countenance is comely.*

But then I hear the swish of cloth that tells me a female comes, and a shadow falls across me. I crush my arms around my legs and hide my pages. Half-remembered words hold their sweet echo: *I am black, but comely . . . Look not upon me, because I am black, because the sun hath looked upon me.*

'What are you doing?' says Queenie. She stands with her hand in Lizzie's.

'He is reading the Bible, like Ma used to like to do,' says Lizzie. 'Can't you see?'

'Yes,' I say. 'I am reading.' The sun hath looked upon me. My feet buzz where I have squashed them and I stagger upright to stamp the feeling into them again, losing the Song and falling instead into Chronicles, where name after name after name is numbered on the pages and all these names mean nothing to me. I show the Book to them.

'Don't stop on our account,' say Lizzie, not fully pleasant. 'Sit down again.'

'*What* are you reading? Is it Psalms?' Queenie ask, jiggling like a boiling pot.

'No, not Psalms,' say I.

'So? What? And will you read it to us?'

'Hush now, Queenie. Kalala doesn't want to be bothered with reading to us.' Lizzie give her sister's hand a little shake, the telling-off kind, not too strong, and she explains as she lets it go:

'Ma used to read us psalms from the Bible, and sometimes stories, but now she never has time.'

'No. She's very busy. She has much to do,' say I.

'Yes.'

She waits with folded arms, stands planted, and Queenie the same.

'You can go on if you like.' A kindly nod from Queenie. Both still standing.

I remember the stick in the ashes the day of our landfall. That strangeness I quickly forgot: these palagi children who do not know their letters. Even Vika know her letters. Mr Reverend took care of that. You cannot enter the Fellowship of the Church if you cannot read. Everyone wants to be in the Fellowship. Always better inside than outside. So all the children on our island learn. Some fellows learn chapters and verses by heart better than they can piece them out, word by word, but that is their secret.

'Ma's got newspapers in her trunk. With pictures.' The little girl sways with her boasting.

'Quite a number,' says Lizzie. 'English ones, left in our hotel in Apia. Called the . . . the . . . the . . . ' She looks in the sky to remember, eyes scrunched up. '*The Illustrated London News*. The stories aren't new now, of course, but we don't care.'

Then Queenie sadly adds: 'But we never look at it. Ma doesn't have time.'

Like a song.

'Let's ask her if we can show them to Kalala? Can we, Lizzie?' Queenie spins from me to her sister. 'There's an elephant on the front of one . . . a dead elephant. Do you remember? The soldiers shot it to eat it. In Paris. All that meat! Have you ever seen an elephant? I haven't.'

'No,' I say. E is for elephant. That's what the schoolroom chart says. So I too have seen a picture.

'Such a big animal. From a country far away called India, where the Queen is Empress now, Ma says. A nose like this that can hold a bun,' Lizzie put her arm in front of her face and wave it, and I step back, and Queenie jump and do the same with her arm. 'And great big ears like this, Ma says.'

Both girls put their hands to their ears and flap them, and then use their arm to make their noses long again. They look very funny and I am soon laughing. And then I am sad for I know what Mr Reverend would be thinking. These children will be in darkness until they can read for themselves.

'Are there any stories about elephants in your book?' Queenie ask.

'I have not found one yet. But there is a story about a devil, and another about some fishermen. Do you know them?'

Queenie shakes her head, and Lizzie looks uncertain. I open the Bible again, and I find the verses, the ones which are safe and which I know how to find. 'I will read them to you, if you want me to. This is Matthew. Chapter four.'

24

THE IDEA OF READING PURSUES LIZZIE. SHE IS
disturbed by a sense of outrage, which settles in odd
ways and lets in draughts, like a blanket in the night
tugged between sleepers. Outrage, or shame? She pushes aside a
memory of Albert in the kitchen at the hotel, tracing flowered
letters with his fingers and begging their mother for help, and
all she says is: 'That's St Paul's', mysteriously, before seizing the
paper to stare greedily at the pictures herself. Why had Lizzie
never cared to read before? She suspects Kalala pities them.
Certainly he looks at them oddly. We do not meet his expectations, she thinks, any more than he meets ours.

There's been no time. It's not been needed. It's hardly needed
now, she tells herself. It didn't help Albert. Her thoughts turn
ugly. Could every savage read nowadays? They'd been left behind.
What else had they failed to learn?

A few days later she kneels in her parents' hut, pressing
fingertips into gilt, then opening the cover of the family Bible,
and letting pages slither by with a sense of hopelessness and the

smell of age. How difficult could reading be? Ma made it seem natural and easy – almost unimportant. Lizzie had assumed one day, when she was older, she would simply open a book and know what the marks meant. Pa only read in his head, when he needed to, never aloud, never for anyone else's pleasure. Kalala read beautifully, slowly and deliberately, curving his voice to the meaning of each phrase, pausing not just to take a breath, but to give breath to the words he uttered. He made them live. A few tripped his tongue, from time to time, and he had to run at these twice or maybe three times. The obstacle leapt, he then sped up, as though reading downhill, carried by his own force. So different from his brother Solomona. Solomona the solemn, the even-handed, who landed on each word with so little distinction you might think he was fearful of giving one more weight than its share, as if such a thing might bring chaos and retribution.

Lizzie puzzles over Kalala's verses when she is fishing from the rock with Pa, one rare afternoon; preoccupied with the plantation, her father rarely calls on his daughters for help now he has a gang of fine fellows working for him, muscled and tireless and obedient. Men, not boys. She doesn't miss the sudden eruptions that shattered the air whenever Albert had messed something up, but she misses Albert. To judge from Pa's brooding silence, he must too. Lizzie baits his line for him, and hopes he will talk to her, like he used to. But he stands hunched and concentrating, all focus on the water and their catch.

Lizzie thinks about the stories Kalala tells them. The net thrown from the boat in Galilee one last time, that net which came up full and flashing with fish. When she watches the black silhouettes of pirate birds as they plunge into the water and soar up again with wriggling silver trapped in long, hooked beaks, she thinks of the fowls of the air who sow not, and neither do they reap, and yet are fed. She thinks about the lilies of the field, neither toiling nor spinning. She wriggles her sticky shoulder blades and longs for fewer clothes.

Back among the women that afternoon, stabbing her needle into workcloth, taking up a pinafore for Gussie which fitted Queenie when they first arrived on the island, she wonders exactly *how* long those who mourn must wait to find their promised comfort? Ada's new tranquillity amazes and angers Lizzie. The small rip she noticed in her own chest when Albert first went missing is behaving like an untended tear in an undergarment; out of sight, it lengthens a little day by day, thread by frayed thread, catching on things as she passes, and getting only bigger.

She's doing a lot more sewing now than she ever used to. And washing, and ironing too. The girls don't dig and hunt much now. There's time for other things, and Ma calls this a blessing. They can prepare for hungrier months, cure goatskins, make rugs and covers for when it gets a little colder. Ada and Lizzie will learn the womanly arts, and Queenie too, and not before time, for one day they'll be wives themselves, though how that might chance is never touched upon. Mrs Peacock feeds the baby and issues orders, and watches over the girls as she never has before. No more slapdashery around here. Something else is making her keep her daughters close, but Lizzie can't tell what. Lizzie doesn't call it a blessing. She is beginning to feel like one of the island's rats, running round and round and round the old metal buoy on scrittling claws, unable to leap back into her old life.

*

A few days later, Lizzie tips out a basin of bruised taro peelings, fish heads and mashed-up tonga beans. The chickens dart forward, heads jerking, as if someone has told them to walk not run. She squats by the birds, chin in two hands. The two speckled hens always step aside for the brown one. The preening rooster stands a little to one side, keeping an eye on the others. You'd think he owned them.

'Ladies first,' says Queenie, joining her, squatting down to watch too. 'He always does that. Any eggs?'

'Not yet.'

'Do you think there's something wrong with them?'

'I don't know. Ask Ma.'

Albert would have known, thinks Lizzie. If he were here, he'd devote himself to watching them, crouching motionless for hours until he had worked out the problem, then found a way to solve it. Queenie sighs, stands and stretches.

'Look,' she says, pointing towards the shade of the tree by the Islanders' hut. Kalala sits, legs outstretched, head bowed over Solomona's English Bible. Solomona is asleep, and so is Vilipate. Iakopo, Pineki and Luka are swimming, out of sight. They are a good match for the surf. 'Shall we ask him for more stories?'

She runs off. Lizzie follows with less enthusiasm, and lets her sister do the talking, content to hide behind her keen demands. Kalala is obliging, and the girls sit down. This time he reads them a new story: about a brother who cheats his brother and deceives his blind father. When Queenie asks Kalala about his own father, he tells them that he was taken away on a ship long ago.

'Didn't he want to go? Why did he let them take him? Why didn't anyone stop them? Where is he now? Will he come back?'

Kalala looks to his lap.

'Too many questions,' whispers Lizzie. 'You'll make him sad.'

'I don't know,' says Kalala, honest and matter-of-fact. 'Nobody knows. Solomona was just a small boy, no bigger than Gussie now. He knows only that it was the will of God. That they were deceived and stolen.' His fingers scrabble idly while he talks and when they find a stone, he tosses it in the air, as if to mark his thinking.

'And your mother?' Queenie tips her head, frowning at Kalala.

'She also does not know.' A thoughtful pause. 'But she keeps hope alive,' he adds. 'She watches every ship. Perhaps he will find a way to return to us one day. What is life without hope?' Lizzie feels that word as an admonition. Have they given up all hope, since Albert's empty funeral service, so settling and unsettling both at once? His speech finishes with a hollow flatness that does not marry with its claim. She senses he's repeating another's words.

Then Kalala tells them another story. Not from the Bible. More trickery.

'Once upon a time,' he begins, because this is how Mrs Reverend used to begin all the stories for children. 'This one is about a rat and a land crab and a shorebird. Together they build a canoe, a vaka, but before they go down to the sea with it, they wonder what they will do if it turns over in the water. "I will swim," said the rat. "I will fly," said the bird. "I will sink," said the land crab. They set off on their voyage, and sure enough . . . ' says Kalala, because this is what Mrs Reverend always says. His words float in the air, like a lure in water.

'What?' Queenie leans forward.

'Sure enough,' says Kalala, 'the canoe capsizes. And the rat swim, and the bird fly, and the land crab sink. The rat swim and swim and swim, almost as far as the reef, but . . . but . . . but

. . . he begin to sink.' Kalala makes small plopping noises with his lips. The noises of a drowning rat.

'Good,' says Queenie, with satisfaction, sitting back against Lizzie. 'I hate rats.'

Kalala holds up a warning finger. His story isn't finished.

'Just in time the octopus swim by. "I will help you," he tell the rat. With one long arm, the octopus place the creature on his head. He hold it there safe, and with the other seven arms he swim careful, careful to shore. He set the rat on a rock, and the rat shake himself, and thank the octopus, and then he say: "I left a present for you! It is on the top of your head."'

A short dramatic pause.

'What? What has he left?'

Kalala cannot say. But he is smiling, wickedly. A short breath from Queenie that turns into laughter, as she understands Kalala's struggle to find the right word for the last part of the story.

'He's left a . . . a turd? Dung? Droppings?'

'Yes! Can you imagine the anger of the octopus? He can never forget such an insult. He is still chasing the rat to this day. So if you want to catch an octopus, you have to make a rat for him to catch, with a cowrie shell for body, and legs that sweep the water like little rat feet, and a long tail. And when he comes out from the rocks and the reef to catch the rat, quick as quick, ready to throttle his old enemy, then you have him! You can catch the octopus.'

'We must tell Pa,' says Lizzie.

Kalala shrugs. That's up to them, he seems to say. It's not his place to tell Mr Peacock anything.

'This story isn't in the Bible, is it?' Queenie asks, doubtfully, and Kalala shakes his head.

'From my island,' he says. 'But I tell you another story from the Bible soon. I will find one you like.'

'Come on, Queenie. Time to leave Kalala in peace. Thank you for the story.'

Queenie turns to Lizzie and says again, quite crossly now, inviting Kalala to hear:

'Why can *he* read and we can't?'

Heat flushes Lizzie's cheeks.

'I told you.'

'Tell me again.' Creeping alarm makes her sister petulant. The natural superiority this small island queen has always taken for granted is looking shaky.

'We've just never learned.'

'*Why* not?' asks Queenie, lower lip jutting.

Lizzie is making excuses. She won't say a word against her father in front of Kalala.

'There's never been time. Too many other things to do. Anyway, what would we read?'

'Is it too late?' Queenie asks Lizzie, but she is really asking Kalala.

'No,' says Kalala. 'Everybody learns to read on our island. Of course. All ages too. So that we can all receive the Word of the Lord. It is never too late for light. Ask Solomona.'

They settle begging eyes on Kalala.

'Can you teach us?' asks Queenie.

He glances at Solomona's sleeping back.

'If Mrs Peacock say yes. And Mr Peacock.'

Lizzie is shaken by a rush of bitterness, which shocks her. 'Mr Peacock won't notice.'

*

Ma makes rules. Lessons are not to interfere with Kalala's plan-tation work, nor with the children's chores. 'No Sunday work,' says Solomona when he wakes up. But he's proud of his brother.

'You'll be a real teacher soon,' he tells him, walking back from the flats, one arm across Kalala's shoulders. The next afternoon Queenie, Lizzie and Billy gather on the beach, where the sand is hard and damp. They take it in turns to copy Kalala, making shapes with sticks and chanting the names and sounds of letters.

Kalala shows them the word in the Bible and how to spell out G-O-D. Then Sally and Spy bounce up, and chew the sticks, and their paw prints scuff the children's work, and Kalala uses the same letters to spell out D-O-G. Ada hovers at a distance, with Joey slumped over her shoulder, rubbing his back and peering over his bundled form, and Lizzie knows she is thinking of Albert. She feels unaccountably guilty, as if she is responsible for his vanishing, as if unkind thoughts could snuff out life.

Mrs Peacock observes the lessons from above, one eye on the horizon.

BEFORE

Albert's triumphant return with the milk goat was tempered by an accident on the way back down the cliffs. They almost lost her. The rope had jerked from his hand, he told the girls later, looking at Pa. I wouldn't have let go, thought Lizzie. Ada pressed him further. Well, then he'd fallen against a rock, hadn't he, and landed so awkwardly he'd gashed and bruised his leg. It had swollen quickly, despite Ma's bathing of it, and for days Albert kept stumbling, and crying out in pain when he walked on it. Ada found him a stout stick to lean on and did as many of his chores as she could.

No time to rest, for Albert was now goatherd, finding new shady spots each day to tether the nanny where the foraging would be sweetest. The male kid they ate, the female they kept. He gentled the goats by degrees, with infinite patience. Quietly scratching the kid under her chin, when he thought nobody was looking, his jaw softened and his eyes cleared and Albert was calm and beautiful again, his pains forgotten.

'Shhhhh . . . shhhhhhh,' he soothed and tried to teach Queenie how to work the same magic.

'Have you milked her yet?' asked Pa after less than a week.

'Not yet. In time,' said Albert. 'I don't think she's ready.'

'We've not got time,' replied Pa. 'Queenie can be our milkmaid.

I need you delving.' He mumbled something else under his breath. Something like 'not shirking'.

Albert knew it would take even longer, left to the little ones. They would try to rush things – it had been hard enough to keep them calm when he was patiently training young Spy – and the work he had already done would be undone. A few days later, while he was dragging cat's claw to make a thorny, goat-proof fence for the new vegetable garden, still wincing as he walked, he heard a scream and then a wail. A lightning kick from Nan's back leg had caught Queenie in the side of her head. Milk soaked into the ground. But that wasn't the worst of the waste in those early months.

*

Robson was right about the growing of things. The first shoots of sweetcorn appeared within days. Beans really did behave like fairy-tale vines. Every day they pushed back the wilderness of Clapperton Bay a little further, and the island felt more inhabited. Every morning Mr Peacock surveyed the garden with satisfaction. Billy had found some sweet potatoes in the undergrowth, and Ada joyfully uncovered a patch of purple-stemmed taro plants, which had been quietly growing and reproducing themselves for years; tubers vast and hairy, the size of a baby's head, flesh speckled violet. Soon it was taro cakes and taro stew and taro porridge. That filled you up, for a while. And then the hunger returned.

At mealtimes Ma noticed a dullness in their eyes.

'Surely Robson must have planted sugar cane – didn't he say we'd find everything we needed?' Mrs Peacock said, with a moan in her voice.

'Do you think I'd not have told you if I'd found it?'

Mr Peacock stomped off with pickaxe and shovel, and didn't come back for lunch. Ma sent Lizzie and Billy with taro cakes and dried goat meat to find him, and they reported he was digging up a tree – or its roots, anyway.

'They're huge. He'll be ages.'

'What kind of tree?' Ma asked.

'I don't know,' said Lizzie. 'It had a trunk. Leaves.'

Ma narrowed her eyes, checking for cheek, and bent over her mending. This place was so hard on clothes. Even denim ripped too often and too easily. And washday was coming, but what would they do for soap if the *Good Intent* wasn't back soon? If she never came back?

'He said to start digging a pit,' said Billy.

'Well, you know where the other spade is. You'd better start right away.'

Whatever his plan, it would become clear in the end. She had to trust to that.

*

When Pa returned with a full sack, and told them to look for rocks, for the pit was deep enough, Lizzie realised what they were making: a hangi, an earth oven.

'Why is Pa being so mysterious?' whispered Ada. When the flames were roaring, Mr Peacock finally emptied out a sack of uneven logs – thick and heavy and very hairy – and a load of leaves. Albert cut short a disappointed sigh and reached for one to throw on the fire. Pa caught his arm.

'Stop! That's not firewood. That's ti. Cabbage tree. That's what we're cooking.'

'That!' said Billy in disgust, sick of roots. Pa smiled and set to with the axe, splitting the lumps, then hammering at the glinting slabs to crush them into tenderness.

'Get on with it then,' he said, with impatient scorn. 'All this needs to be wrapped in leaves. Don't want it burning after all the trouble I've had digging it out.'

The fire subsided into a rippling mass of glowing coals, a heat so fierce it sweated up your face if you bent too close, and when the stones were good and hot, Ma laid over them a frame of green sticks, piling that with a layer of nikau fronds. Pa arranged the heavy, leaf-wrapped parcels on the platform of leaves, put more leaves on top, and finally shovelled the loose earth back to form a damp, steaming mound.

'There!' called Billy. From a tiny hole, a wispy ribbon was worming out.

'And there!' said Queenie, enjoying this game.

They patched and watched, patched and watched.

'That's it now. No touching, mind . . . No roast children here.'

Then he walked off to find his fishing rod. For two and a half days, no mention of the oven.

*

'So shall we look?'

'I'll get the shovel!' Queenie cried.

'And the tongs,' called Pa.

A line of children followed him to the hangi. Pa drove the

blade into the earth with concentrated tenderness and the pile crumbled inwards like a suet piecrust, releasing a cloud of steam from the new-made crater, a fragrance which made the children sigh. Honey-sweet. They licked the air, inhaled, and when Pa opened the first blackened bundle and they breathed in syrup, they groaned with ecstasy.

'Joseph Peacock, you're a magician,' declared Ma.

Lizzie reached out a bold hand, but Pa shook his head.

'Not ready yet. Have to wait. Need to boil it down. This is Maori cooking. Can't be hurried.'

'Can't they just taste it first?' said Ma.

Ada nudged Lizzie.

'Please, Pa,' she said. 'Just a little.'

And suddenly it was like Christmas on Monday Island. Moans of delight fell from the children's mouths. They chewed the strips of root until left with nothing but a tasteless, stringy mass, a memory of sweetness to pass from cheek to cheek.

'Will there be more, Pa?' asked Queenie.

He answered in a strange language: '*Ehara i te ti e wana ake.*'

They looked at him blankly. 'Unlike man, this tree grows up again even when you cut it down. Yes, there'll be more.'

25

F IVE MORE SUNDAYS PASS, AND OUR WORK PROGRESSES
well, until we are pitted against a difficult stump. It refuses
to be uprooted, and yet its sap is scorched so it cannot
grow. Mr Peacock sends me back for ropes. I have his trust now,
I believe, and I mean to keep it. I understand him, he tells me.
I am not like my brother, referring every question to Him above.
There are times when a man has to decide a thing for himself,
he says. I bow my head and decide some other things for myself,
like not to cross him, and also to watch my back, and to watch
Solomona's for him. I will not let him divide us.

And while I am bent-backed in the outhouse, two coils of ship
rope already on my shoulder, and measuring out a third from
hand to elbow, I hear the sisters passing. Little pitcher, Mrs
Reverend used to call me. How else can a fellow learn?

Lizzie's pleading voice trots behind Ada's steps. She bleats her
sister's name over and over again. The younger girls come to me
for stories, to listen and to wonder, to fill up that hole in their
family which I know may otherwise swallow them all. They love

to talk to me because I cannot talk of Albert. Ada never comes to hear my tales, and remembers her brother all the time, but never speaks of him. There has been some falling-out between her and Lizzie over Albert. Like wheeling birds, their wing tips never touch however near they swoop. There is a strangeness to this oldest girl, a taut and twitching sorrow. When I see how the other children watch her, I know she has changed. I think of raindrops pearling and sliding from a banana leaf, never wetting its flesh.

'Please, Ada. Please talk to me. Please stop.' Then, almost to herself, Lizzie mutters: 'Oh, please stop all of this. You can't go on like this for ever. What have I done?'

They will both pass by and never see me, I am certain, never think to look. I will hurry back to work when they are gone, before trust snaps and sours the air. I do not expect Ada to stop a few feet from my ear.

'What?' she says.

'I – I just wanted to talk to you.' Breathless. Lizzie catches up. 'Didn't you hear me calling before?'

'Calling?'

'Yes. Are you listening to me, Ada? You never seem to hear me.'

'Yes, I'm listening. What is it?'

Her voice is sharp and dry and wounding.

'Where are you going?' Lizzie asks.

'*Where are you going? Where are you going?*' A mean mimic. 'You never stop asking. Nowhere. I'm not going anywhere. Look. I'm not moving. I'm talking to you.'

In my head Ada stands arms folded, head tilted back, eyebrows upped in challenge. And Lizzie is a riser.

'But you *were* going somewhere? Nightbell Gully?'

'Maybe. No. I don't go there anymore. I don't like going on my own.'

'Then I'll come with you.'

'I don't want you to.'

I shift my weight.

'Ada. Please stop,' says Lizzie.

'Stop what?'

'*This* . . . ' Lizzie stamps her foot. A dull thud. 'We're all sad. Not just you. We all miss him.'

Then Ada says something so hard and sharp it stops Lizzie's mouth.

'But I'm not sad, you see. I'm glad.'

Clack go Lizzie's teeth.

'Glad?' she asks. Perhaps Ada nods. 'Glad Albert's dead? How wicked. You don't mean it.' The woven walls of the storehouse shake and whisper as Ada is pushed against them. 'How can you say that? How can you be glad?'

Now I cannot move.

'I'm glad Albert's gone,' says Ada, each word careful clear. 'I didn't say I'm glad he's dead.'

'What?'

'I don't believe he is dead.'

My astonishment nearly uncovers me. Thought soaks into Lizzie's head, like water into sand, unfirming her. A rush of questions, no time for answers, and her voice grows testing. 'Where is he then? Is he hiding? Have you seen him? Is that where you're going now? That's why you never want me with you! Why you're always trying to get away from me now.'

'No, no. Shhh. Listen now. No. I haven't seen him. And I

didn't say he was here. Of course I'd have told you if he was. Don't you see what must have happened? He's not on the island. He's escaped! He's gone.'

I pray that Mr Peacock does not send Billy to find what's keeping me. Not now, I beg.

'Escaped from who? From where?'

'From us.'

26

'FROM *US*?' LIZZIE IS UNCONVINCED.

'From all of us. From here.' Ada hesitates. 'From Pa.'

Lizzie can only laugh, but it's not really laughter at all, and with every gasp her world feels less real. 'Why would he want to leave *us*? We're his family. You can't escape family.'

Even as she says these words she doubts them.

'It's mostly Pa,' said Ada. 'Albert hates Pa.'

Lizzie flinches.

'That's wicked. To say a thing like that.'

'Not as wicked as what Pa has done to him.'

Ada looks at her with a kind of contempt, which Lizzie doesn't even notice because she has just realised something else.

'You hate him too,' she says, drawing away. 'You do, don't you? Your own father.'

Ada is unrepentant.

'Of course I do. If only you knew, you'd hate him too.'

'Stop it! Shut up! I never will. I love Pa, more than anyone or anything else in the world.' Lizzie's proud of her devotion. It's how it should be. 'I feel sorry for him. How dare you talk about him like that? He doesn't deserve either of you.'

Ada shakes her head, sadly triumphant. 'I knew you'd be like this.'

A fearful sensation sweeps through Lizzie, waves of heat and ice rushing from the roots of her hair all the way down her shaking legs, interrupting her outrage. Albert is alive. Somewhere, her brother is breathing, thinking, seeing, hoping.

'Tell me, Ada.'

'Oh, I should never have said anything.' Ada retreats. 'And I promised, I promised I wouldn't.' Her eyes dart here and there, as if she has brought a curse upon herself. What are its rules? When will it strike? 'Albert begged me not to.'

Lizzie reaches out an appeasing hand but Ada shrugs her off. Lizzie persists, holding on tightly this time, because she needs to stop herself shaking. She has to tread carefully. Lizzie isn't certain whether to tear or to tease the truth from Ada. Rip it out, fast, like a sea urchin spine, or untangle it knot by knot, picking each one apart, so the thread stays whole and good and usable again?

'Oh, please don't be like this. I won't say anything. To anyone. I just don't understand. Please tell me. Quickly! What do you mean?'

No revelation Ada can offer could be as terrible as this antici-pation, this dread, this not knowing.

'Ada . . . please?'

Ada hasn't always hidden things from Lizzie. Only since they came to this island. In fact only since they moved to the North Bay. That was when she and Albert started taking themselves off without the others. Sneaking away, Lizzie used to think resentfully.

'I can't tell you,' says Ada suddenly. 'I can't. I promised. You'll tell Pa. I know you will.'

'No, no, I won't,' Lizzie protests, pulling her closer, into a kind of embrace.

Ada shakes her head and cries: 'I shouldn't have said anything. I knew I shouldn't.' Snot strings in her hair and onto Lizzie's pinafore, while Lizzie awkwardly rocks her, back and forth, back and forth, and blotches form beneath her sister's skin. Sun and salt have blurred the outline of her lips. She needs to put on balm, thinks Lizzie, absently. They need to gather more kawakawa leaves for Ma to crush and mix with mutton-bird fat. The baby needs it too. She keeps rocking and soothing, mind and body strangely separate.

'Shhh . . . shhhh . . . stop,' she murmurs. 'Someone will hear. Ma will come. We mustn't upset her. Look, here's your hanky. Wipe your face. Shhh.'

When Ada's gulps have slowed to hiccups, Lizzie tries again.

'Albert . . . ' she prods. 'What did Albert not want to tell me?'

A long pause.

'He couldn't stay here. So we decided. Next ship that called, he'd beg for passage. Whether Pa liked it or not, and wherever it was going. Whatever happened, whoever came, he would find a way to escape.'

'Oh, but Ada, how could you? How *could* you?' she says. 'You knew and you let us think he was dead.'

The gap between them widens.

'I told you,' she said. 'I promised him I'd never tell.'

'It was wrong of you to promise. You've betrayed us all.'

'And I told you that you'd never understand. You're just like Pa. That's the trouble. And now I've betrayed Albert too.'

'But you let us search, all those hours and days, and said

nothing. You let Pa make his gravestone. The funeral service . . . Solomona . . . You've lied to everyone. How *could* you, Ada Peacock?'

'Because I promised,' Ada protests, weeping. 'It broke my heart when he first told me he wanted to leave. It's breaking my heart still. You've no idea how much I miss Albert.'

'Ada, that's not the same.' Lizzie's voice sharpens.

'It feels the same.'

'It's not. And to think you let Ma believe . . . And all the rest of us. How terrible you are.' On the verge of dragging her sister to confess to their mother, Lizzie is scared by the wild panic distorting Ada's face.

'Shhh, Ada. I'm sorry. I didn't mean it. I won't say anything to Pa and Ma. Cross my heart . . . ' She finishes her oath with a finger sliced across her throat. 'But only if you tell me everything . . . '

Ada seems to have decided to believe her. Maybe her cautious confession will bring relief.

'What do you want to know?'

'Why? Why was he so desperate to go? And why now? Everything on the island is better than it's ever been. We're making so much progress.' She's bewildered, all the more when Ada's shiftiness returns. Her fingers pluck at leaves.

'You won't want to know.'

'Yes, I will. I do.'

A huge sigh, another long silence, and Ada begins to speak, thinking long and hard as she frames each sentence.

'It's Pa. You don't see it. You've always been his golden girl. No, don't deny it. You know it's true. He thinks you're perfect. Oh, Billy and Queenie and Gussie . . . they're all right, I suppose.

And me. Sometimes. He knows we won't let him down. But he can't forgive Albert.'

Lizzie's lips open, but she thinks better of speaking.

'However hard he tries, it's never enough,' Ada continues. 'Pa always thinks him nesh. A disappointment.'

And how can you blame him, Lizzie wants to ask. After all Pa's done for us, and for Albert most of all. To have a son like Albert when you're a man like Pa, of course it drives him wild. Everyone has to get on with things. Make the best of the hand they're dealt. They all knew that, and they all did get on with it, as best they could. Why should it be any different for Albert? It wasn't fair. Except it was impossible to deny that he was different. Marked out not just by his fragile beauty, but his health; such a sickly boy, Albert, on land and sea. He never quite recovered from each new blow before the next one came along – the flu, the flux, the swollen joints, the vomiting. Always marked by his careless injuries. Always hobbling. Always wimbly-wambly. It was harder for him, she had to admit. So however much she wants to protest, Lizzie doesn't dare.

'He's tough on all of us,' tries Lizzie. To think that Albert had actually given up, had run away from their promised land, from all of them . . . nothing could anguish Pa more. Ada was right. Better Pa thought him dead. 'It's for our own good.'

'Not Albert's. And he's ten times harder on Albert than he is on us. Twenty times harder than he is on you.'

Lizzie thinks of denying this.

'That's because he's a boy.'

'Does that make it right?'

Lizzie doesn't answer. She's not sure. It makes it worth it, maybe. A bit of her still thinks Albert might deserve Pa's anger. Some of it.

'Albert was on the wrong side,' says Ada, surprisingly. 'I think I am too.'

'Families don't have sides.' Lizzie is incredulous.

'You think that because you're on the right one,' says Ada. 'I was before. But now I've slipped through. Not for Ma. At least not yet. Only Pa. But you know Ma. She'll never be on the other side from him for long. She can't. Then what? But it's always been different for you. That's what makes you so blind.'

'Blind to what?' Lizzie asks slowly. That queasy, shifting, slippery sensation's back with her. Whatever Ada is about to tell her, she doesn't want to hear.

'Blind to Pa of course. To what he's really like. When you are on the wrong side. When Ma can't see.' Ada's hands are sweaty with anxiety and she tries to dry them on her tunic. Then Ada looks straight at her. 'Lizzie, do you remember when Albert first hurt his leg, ages and ages ago?'

Lizzie thought back. There had been so many accidents and aches and pains. One merged into another.

'Do you mean when he nearly lost the nanny goat? Before we moved to this side of the island? He fell. He's always falling and making everything worse.'

She thinks back to the pinched blank look Albert often came limping home with after a day spent digging, or hunting, or fishing with Pa. Not glowering, or angry or resentful. As if he'd been emptied out. His silences. Pa's too. She always used to feel sorry for their father.

'He fell, yes. But he fell because Pa knocked him down. After he let the goat go. And then he hit a rock.'

Pa was often free with his belt. What father wasn't? Discipline. That's just the way it worked, and always had. Albert had the worst of it of course – because he made the most mistakes. But he'd thrashed Billy a good few times too – for cheek, or forgetfulness, and sometimes for taking the Lord's name in vain. The girls usually only got a slap. Lizzie rarely. More likely a pinch on the ear from Ma. Seeing the dismay on Ada's face, Lizzie hastily concedes: 'But of course he was unlucky to fall.'

'No. Listen to me, Lizzie. Listen. You don't understand. Because Albert didn't tell you. He didn't say how hard he'd hit him, and why he'd hit the rock so hard. Hard enough to break a bone, perhaps. Or that Pa went on belting him even then, even when he was on the ground, and screaming. And that wasn't the first time he'd hit him like that.'

'No,' Lizzie says quickly. 'No. Albert must have . . . Pa couldn't . . . '

Lizzie's head begins to shake. Side to side. Over and over again, in waves of denial. Her whole body saying no.

'I don't believe you. Pa would never . . . Make Albert lame? It makes no sense. Why on earth . . . ? And that's still an accident. I mean . . . Maybe he hit him, but . . . Albert said he'd fallen.'

'Pa told him that if anyone found out, he'd beat him again, even harder. He knew it was cruel. He knew it was wicked. But he didn't want Ma to know. And he thought he could hide it from the rest of us.'

Lizzie is still shaking her head. All those cuts and bruises. But Albert was awkward and clumsy. Everyone knew that. Anyone could see.

'Albert was frightened, all the time, Lizzie. Couldn't you see? He was desperate. He hated being alone with Pa. And Pa never stopped testing him.'

Lizzie's fingers cover her eyes. Every part of her has begun to tremble. She doesn't want to hear or see or know any more. Ada gently moves her hands so she can see again, then turns her back on Lizzie, and lifts her tunic. She's hitching up the hem of her drawers, and Lizzie can see the backs of her thighs, quite clearly now, just below her buttocks. There are dark pink stripes zigzagging, criss-crossed, five or six, overlapping like fallen sticks.

'They don't hurt now. But Lizzie, you don't know what it's like, when he comes for you. With that look in his eyes. And you know you haven't got a chance. I didn't know till he came for me.'

'Ada . . . ' Asking permission with her eyes, Lizzie stretches wandering fingers to feel those thin raised lines, fine cord against smooth hairless skin. 'When . . . ?'

'A few months before the ship came. They were cutting wood, just Pa and Albert, and Ma sent me to tell them it was nearly time to eat, and she was cooking fish. But when I finally found them, Pa was thrashing him, over and over, with the buckle end of the belt too. He'd made him take his shirt off and his back was bleeding. I don't even know what Albert had done. And I rushed to stop Pa, and then he looked at me, that way, that horrible way, and right away he ordered Albert to cut a switch for me, and then he beat me too, and Albert could do nothing.'

Lizzie is trying to remember. What had she noticed? A night Ada went to bed early, and slept all crouched and huddled. And Lizzie had imagined another kind of blood had brought her low, the kind you couldn't talk about, and she and Queenie had left Ada alone as Ma instructed.

There's a certain kind of shiver in Oceania that tilts you off balance before you know it. Your soles and stomach feel it both at once, and the air shimmers, and also your ears and eyes and nostrils. It's inside you and outside you; sometimes to give notice that a pot will fall or a plate will break, sometimes that trees will move and the earth will gape. Even if it only lasts a second, even if its beginning is also its end, right at the heart of that very second balances the nauseating prospect that nothing might ever be the same again. Ada's last words give Lizzie that sensation now. Something inside her slides away. The hairs on her arms stand upright, one by one.

Ada tidies herself up, and looks at Lizzie. She's all closed up again. 'So now you know. But just you remember your promise, and don't go sneaking off to Pa or Ma.'

'No, Ada. Stop. Don't go now. We've not finished. I can't . . . I'm sorry . . . I didn't mean it.'

She is alone. Hundreds of questions hum and thrum. Lizzie wants to retreat, go right back in time and start again so that everything can come out differently. Back to the day before Albert vanished, even before the day they landed here. Maybe to a time before the night she crouched in the hotel bar and listened to Mr Robson talking, laying out temptation for the tasting. When did Albert decide he had to go, come what may? How on earth did he manage it, and how did Ada help him and nobody realise? Most of all, how could Lizzie herself have failed to see what was happening to Albert? Not just Lizzie, but Ma, and Queenie and Billy too. How had they all let this happen?

BEFORE

'It's getting closer!' Ma said, blinking. 'It's coming our way! Oh yes! They've seen us!'

'What'll you tell Captain MacHeath, Pa?' asked Billy. 'What'll you say to him?

Pa paused with a palm frond in his hand, then threw it on the bonfire.

'Nothing,' he answered gruffly. 'It's not the *Good Intent*. She looks to me like a Yankee whaler.'

'But is she coming in?' asked Albert.

'She's standing to shore all right.'

The sky, so blue and bright when they first sighted the ship, had turned a sallow yellow. Haze veiled the sun, creating a sickly glare. The sea looked as greasy and stale as the sky above, and its grey was flecked with white where the tops of the waves broke into spray.

'They'll not be put off by a bit of dirty weather, will they, Pa?' said Lizzie, trying to read his face, trying to read the sky. Already the clouds, the colour of rotting plums, were banking up, and gusting wind blowing the coppery smoke this way and that. 'Not a whaler. Aren't they tough as old boots, Pa?'

'We'll see.'

'Will they come ashore this afternoon? Will they have food for us?' asked Queenie.

'Might they take us away?' risked Albert.

Pa stared at the white lines forming ever further from the beach; the surf had begun to break a long way from shore.

'They've not turned back.' Ma shouted to be heard. 'They'll not turn back if they see the children. They won't . . . will they?'

Her tears ran unchecked but Pa offered no reassurance.

'Pray, children! Right away!'

She knotted her hands and clenched her jaw with effort, and all five dropped to their knees to copy her.

'She's dropping anchor!' Billy shouted, running down the beach. Pa snatched him back with a furious yell. Surf like this could whip a child away faster than a frog's tongue scooping up a fly.

'Stay here, I tell you. Just wait.'

The family huddled together, watching and hoping. Another cry of joy went up. The barque was lowering a whaleboat, pointed at each end, narrow as a Viking vessel. Oars out, the boat plunged from the shelter of the ship and into the heavy sea.

'They're coming,' breathed Albert. 'They're coming to get us.'

Minutes later, the sea was almost too dark and mountainous to make out the boat at all.

'It's no good,' groaned Ma.

Queenie pulled her hand from Lizzie's grip and rubbed her crushed fingers.

'No!' shouted Lizzie, cowering, when she saw the stern tipped up so high the boat stood almost vertical. Against the odds, the sailors brought her crashing back down, but then she slipped sideways, briefly lost to sight again in the trough of the waves. Capsized? Swamped? A gasp from the children when they saw it again, oars like scrambling insect legs. But the retreating sailors had given up the struggle. The barque seemed to leave them without a backward glance, sailing away towards the spindrift. Lizzie sat down and sank her face in her skirt.

Hope was something physical, Lizzie understood just then, and could drain from your heart faster than rice spilling from a torn sack. It fell through your fingers, and scattered itself, and couldn't be caught, and when it was gone it left you flapping and empty and wounded.

'At least they're safe,' said Ma.

'Can't blame 'em. Nor must you,' warned Pa. 'She had no choice. *Our* lives are in no danger.'

'They soon will be if we don't take cover,' said Ma, grabbing Queenie's hand and marching her up the beach.

The family hurried together through bending trees back to their hut, dashing here and there to get everything under cover before the rain came, while the goats bleated like banshees. They piled up anything that might blow away inside the hut or the new outhouse.

Fear blew into Spy. He flattened himself and whined at the door, until Queenie dragged him inside, Sal shrinking silent at his heels. Ma only nodded, and told the children not to get undressed. Wrapped up in blankets, they shuddered with the walls' shuddering. They hardly heard Pa hammering tight the shutters, but at last the door opened, letting a lurid light and wilder roar fall briefly into the dark hut, and slammed shut.

As if far out at sea all night, their hut shook and whispered. How little it cared for those who had built it. Defiant, disloyal beyond belief, it would have been happy to tear itself loose and fly free. Into the roar of wind and sea, indifferent and indistinguishable. In darkness, Lizzie silently begged their shelter not to

abandon them now. Exposed, they'd be thrown into the heavens
to weep and whirl among the stars for ever.

Small, invisible comforts kept their minds from bolting: Pa's
arm round Lizzie, and the warm, breathing bulk of him; Ada
and Albert's interlocked fingers, reining in their galloping hearts;
Ma squeezing Queenie, who in turn held Gus; Billy's fingers in
his ears. Pressed so hard together, their bones felt sharper, more
in need of flesh than ever.

And all the while the whaler ran before the storm, alone on
that vast ocean with all the rocks and small islands of the
Kermadecs on which to wreck itself.

*

The sky barely lightened until noon next day. Before long nobody
could remember when their heads didn't roar. The few hours of
brightness and racing clouds they were granted on the second
day Pa snatched to rethatch the roof. The following night the
rains came even harder, bringing scree and stones slithering and
bouncing down the cliffs, to be swept away by the torrents of
the flooding swamp. Chasing the wind, the rain at last departed,
and only then were the children allowed out.

The island smelled of fresh-hewn timber. Uprooted tree trunks
and fallen bushes careened across the path through the woods.
Nikau palms stood shocked and headless, amid piles of litter, or
with broken fronds that hung like injured bird wings from trunks
which tilted away in shame. So full of promise the day before,
the vegetable garden lay in a tangled, flattened mess. The parson-
bird had nothing to preach. As for Mrs Peacock, she was
committed to despair and the dark holes of her eyes looked right

through you in a way that made the children wary of asking anything. Lizzie wondered if she might be ill. Except Ma was never ill.

*

'We have to forget we ever saw the ship,' Ada counselled, as they squatted in the bracken of the lower woods, elbow-deep in earth. Pa had said it might be weeks before it was safe to climb the cliffs again. He had spent the morning inspecting the damaged vegetables, trimming back broken stems and lacerated leaves, searching for undamaged buds, re-staking, earthing up, rescuing plant by plant all that he could. Foraging was once more the order of the day. 'What if it had come ten hours later and passed us in the dark? We'd be no worse off than we are now.'

One by one, Lizzie's fingers were snapping the threads that bound each fat aruhe root to the soil. She twisted to look at her sister as though she had lost her senses.

'Can *you* forget?' asked Albert.

Ada shook her head, and dropped her attempt at piety.

'I never will,' Lizzie said, and chucked her precious lump towards Albert, who clubbed it to a pulp with gritted teeth.

'At least they saw us,' he said, when he'd finished. '*Someone* knows we're here.'

'True,' said Ada.

'And if they're on their way somewhere, they must be on their way back sometime,' Lizzie persisted, fingers working away at the next root.

'Unless they were already going home,' said Ada.

'But Albert's right,' said Lizzie. 'They *saw* us. Maybe they'll tell another ship?'

'And that ship might tell another? And then?' said Albert, ever more eager. But Ada was firm.

'We mustn't get our hopes up again. It could be another seven months before the next one passes.'

So Albert tried to change the subject.

'Maybe Pa will get his fiddle out tonight.'

Even that didn't lift Ada.

'He always says he's too tired.'

'I'll ask him,' offered Lizzie.

'Oh, I'm sure he'll do it for *you*,' said her sister, and looked at Albert with her eyebrows raised.

BEFORE

And then the ship came back. A week later, strangers shipped oars in unison and hopped out as light-footed as dancers, swiftly heaving the boat through the coarse sand in a single practised movement. They knew exactly what they were doing, said the awe in Billy's eyes, and Lizzie knew then that one day she'd surely lose her brother to the sea. These were big men with chests twice the width of her father's, voices three times louder, and even on that broad empty bay, they took up so much space between them that Lizzie found herself shy. Ma stood stock still, breathing fast, her gaze fixed queerly on the giant of a man who led the crew, whose ears were like sails. He tipped his cap, and made her a brief bow.

'Herb Higgins, mate of the *Magellan Cloud*, out of Nantucket.'

His voice, so new and different, cast a spell on the family. They stared back blankly. Higgins glanced at his crew. Perhaps these unlikely islanders had no English. Germans? His jaw briefly twisted and a dark stream of chewing tobacco shot out onto the beach.

Mr Peacock was first to find his senses:

'Joseph Peacock at your service.'

'You folk shipwrecked? Or castaways?'

'Certainly not,' said Mr Peacock, taut with indignation. He

might as well have called them beachcombers. 'We're settlers. Came from Maoriland. New Zealand.'

'By way of the Friendly Islands,' added Mrs Peacock, coming at last to herself, and moving forward, in front of the girls, as if they needed protection.

'A roundabout route to here,' one of the other sailors said.

'By way of the Navigators too,' said Billy.

Pa thrust Lizzie and Queenie forward.

'Say how d'ye do. Where do you think you are?'

The first mate's courtesy was serious and universal. He crunched Billy's fist, bowed to the curtseying girls, then turned to Albert, and hesitated. It had been long enough for Lizzie to forget how it always was with Albert and strangers, to be surprised afresh by that passing uncertainty. To her eyes, he looked more gaunt than angelic these days, and his curls were tarnished. But his beauty still brought the visitors up short.

'Dang my buttons,' said Higgins. 'Settlers on Monday Island again! Never thought I'd see the day.'

The other men moved closer, eyeing Albert, winking at Gussie, nodding at the older girls. Then came so many questions, all at once, nobody knew who or how to answer.

'We always heard this place had a curse on it.'

'If we'd not seen the smoke, we'd have given you a wide berth.'

'The sight of your little ones, dancing round the bonfire! Heartbreaking!'

'How're you faring?' asked Higgins. 'Short commons?'

Pa shook his head, but it was no denial.

'It's not been easy. Every day banyan day for a while. Then we got ourselves up the cliffs –' at this they both glanced up, and Higgins whistled '– and tracked down some wild goats . . . we've fish and mutton-birds, and eggs of course, in season, and goat's milk, and taro . . . corn and pumpkins coming.'

'My, oh my. Regular Swiss Family . . . what did you say the name was? Peacock? Well, we've brought you some provisions.'

Then he turned and yelled to the crew in a topsail voice. 'Set to, my livelies! We've got ourselves a Swiss Family Peacock here . . . What are you waiting for?'

Quickly forming a chain and breaking into song, the sailors started tossing crates and boxes between them.

'Are you coming to live here?' asked Billy.

'We'll help you build a house,' Queenie said.

'No, miss, this lot's for you,' said a dark-skinned sailor with a plait down his back. Seeing her mouth fall open, he added, 'And the rest of your fine family.'

Higgins quickly turned to Mr and Mrs Peacock. 'Hope we wasn't presumin'? We figured you could do with supplies. Brought you . . . now let's see . . . ' He checked the items off on his fingers. 'Flour, sugar, a few potatoes . . . ' A collective gasp. 'Somewhat wormy now. What else is there? Salt beef and pickles. Couple o' sides o' bacon. Biscuit. Molasses. A tin or two of coffee too – not much, I'm afraid ma'am . . . and the smallest packet of tea, but better than nothing.' Here he turned to Ma. She let out a whisper of a sigh. 'Some baccy. Oh, and a barrel of brandy. And we'll have no talk of payment.' Higgins glanced at the children. 'We've had a good haul in the Solander Grounds, and our own supplies are grand.'

Pa began to bristle.

'We're no charity cases,' he said. 'We—'

Higgins stepped back, hands raised soothingly.

'I see what you're saying,' Mr Peacock went on. 'But the strength of the matter is—'

'The strength of the matter is that we're very grateful to you,' interrupted Mrs Peacock. 'I don't know what we'd have done if you'd not come back, I really don't. Hush now, Joseph. You know quite well the truth of it.'

At last Pa nodded, and looked at the sand, and then the sky, and nodded again.

'Very grateful,' he said, his voice choked.

Mrs Peacock sniffed and rummaged in her apron pocket for a handkerchief.

Higgins's hand closed about the monkey bag round his neck, as if he didn't trust the Peacocks not to fill it up with coins regardless, and he and his crew followed the children up to their battered home.

'Not surprised we didn't spy this place from the *Cloud*. Sure looks like a cosy spot up there by the woods.'

To Lizzie, the hut looked small and shabby.

'Show them the gardens, Joseph, while I make the tea,' said Ma, pointedly.

So many deep voices, so many men at the table on their best behaviour, awkwardly silenced by white linen and blue china. Two golden hoops gleamed from a single ear on the shaven dome of the biggest man of all, the boat-steerer. He shook his head when Lizzie offered the milk jug, as if he didn't trust himself not to crush it between his timber-dark hands. Billy couldn't take his eyes off him.

'Stores are in the outhouse, Mrs Peacock. Everything you could need, we hope,' said Higgins, joining them at last.

'We don't know how to thank you.'

'Anyone would have done the same. Anyone but that hufty-tufty toe-rigger of a captain who brought you here.'

So Pa had told him everything.

'Why, if I ever run into . . . Still, you must be mighty proud of what you've managed here. You've raised yourself a plucky bunch. If you can survive what you've had to so far – and you'll get through this winter, now – I reckon you'll make a go of it here.'

'I believe we will.'

'But have you never thought about moving to the other side? Landing's much easier on North Bay.'

'Perhaps. But we've planted so many vegetables here now, and they're growing so well.'

He looked at Ma, expecting her to agree, but the mask of tranquillity she usually wore was sliding away. Her lips twitched. Her eyes were unreliable. Then out she burst:

'Mr Higgins, I must ask you. I wasn't going to, and I know I shouldn't, but really I have to. Could you not find a little room for us on the *Magellan Cloud*? I beg you, sir, could you not just take us off this wretched island?'

The children held their breath. The slurping stopped. Saucers hovered mid-air.

Ma turned to Pa. He looked at the mud floor very slowly. His fists, hanging by his side, uncurled and stretched out all their fingers. Queenie slipped her hand into Lizzie's. Albert's eyes were huge. Pa will never leave here, thought Lizzie, chilled and fearful. Does Ma intend to flee without him?

'Mrs P,' Pa said, slowly and sadly shaking his head. 'Oh, Mrs P. Can you really mean that?'

Ma put a hand on his arm, looking for forgiveness.

'It's too much,' she said, turning from Pa to Mr Higgins. Her fingers trembled. 'We've given it our best, but who's to say what's around the corner, when these folk have gone, and not another ship till Lord alone knows when. We've never been quitters by choosing.' A last anxious glance at Mr Peacock, and then she said it again, and nobody could doubt she meant it. 'It's too hard, this place. It's too much. Won't you take us off with you? All of us, I mean.'

The silence deepened. Mr Peacock turned his back and gripped the window frame, as if he did not trust himself to speak. Lizzie burned with sorrow. Slow seconds passed. It seemed to take forever for Higgins to stammer out his answer. He couldn't look at Ma.

'No. We can't.'

Mrs Peacock wilted. Just for a moment. And then recovered herself so quickly you'd think she'd never even asked.

'Well. That's that then. Not to worry. Now, if I can just get to that flour you've brought us, I'll have a plate of scones on the table before you know it, and at least we'll send you on your way well fed.'

Mr Higgins stood in the doorway and didn't move to let her past, even when she tried to dodge his bulk. He addressed her sincerely and directly.

'Mrs Peacock, I'm dreadful sorry. If I could change matters, I would. But like I said to your husband, we're on our way north now. We've come from the cruising grounds the other side of En Zee, and we're working our way north, but we'll be dead off the shipping routes all the way. There's not an island I can think of to put you down on . . . leastways not one a jot better than this, and plenty worse . . . the whaling season's nearly over, and . . . I lied to you before, God help me . . . we've only taken five hundred barrels, so we're hard-pressed as it is. If the odds were with us, I'm sure the master would take you up to Feejee, or some other semi-civilised kind of port . . . but we'll be going nowhere near. You wouldn't want a shoddier spot than you find yourselves in now?'

'No, indeed,' agreed Mrs Peacock, awkwardly.

Lizzie wished Ma had never asked. The shame and regret on Mr Higgins's face was something awful. And the humiliation of begging like that. Poor Pa. Not even to be consulted. She spoke up without thinking.

'It's all right, Mr Higgins,' Lizzie boldly soothed him. 'Really it is. It's not your fault. And like Pa says, we're not quitters. It's a fine island when it's not so stormy. We love it really. It's ours, you see.'

Her father turned round when he heard her words. His eyes, their clarity always startling, had acquired a peculiar charge. They fell on Lizzie with a look of such loving intensity that she felt her powers limitless. Almost weightless. She knew then she was right, and Pa agreed. This was no time to be giving up. With all the new supplies, and more hard work, they'd make a paradise of their island yet. Defeat was unthinkable. She didn't even notice she'd given Ma's words to Pa.

'It's *not* your fault,' Mrs Peacock agreed, blushing. 'And we can't thank you enough anyway. You came back, didn't you? And you didn't have to. We truly appreciate your kindness.'

'And yours to us.' Mr Higgins nodded at the party of sailors, who had set down their empty cups, and were eager to leave such high emotions on the shore. 'We must be making our way now, but I'll tell you this: from here to Nantucket, wherever we go, any ship we meet will hear all about you. We'll tell 'em all to come and call if ever they're near.'

'Very good of you,' said Mr Peacock. 'And they'll soon get

something for their pains. I came here with plans, you know. Growing plans. Trading plans. Another few years . . . Albert's helping me . . . might look a bit puny now, but he's growing, aren't you, boy?'

'You've a strong team indeed, Mr Peacock.' Doubt scudding, Mr Higgins took in the labour force lining up outside the hut, all knobbly wrists growing out of too-short sleeves. Too many bones showing altogether, he must have thought. 'But a few kanakas would make it stronger still. Had you thought of that?'

Pa shook his head.

'Well, I'll put the word out for you. The boys from Savage Island are all good workers, from all I've heard.'

Ma shook her head in a different way. 'Very good of you, Mr Higgins. But every kanaka I've seen on a plantation has been a lazy kind of fellow.'

'Oh no, indeed, not these ones. Trust me. You won't find better the length and breadth of the Pacific. Don't fret, ma'am, Savage Island means nothing now. Those boys work hard, and live clean. No drinking. No cursing. As God-fearing as you or me and maybe more so.'

'It's an idea, Joseph. What do you make of it?'

Mr Peacock pondered, weighing up two different versions of independence.

'Yes. We'd like that,' he said. 'Very much.'

BEFORE

They came in the night, with no warning. Where had they been hiding before? What had they been doing? Breeding, certainly. Watching perhaps, peering out from the shelter of fallen palm fronds, straw-dry yellow, waiting until the pale silky strands were sprouting from the cobs in the stand of Indian corn, and the first sweet squash forming from bright orange flowers below, waiting until the baby beanstems were winding skywards. They had bided their time with infinite patience, somehow knowing that it would be worth it. The beasts could not have planned it better. Now they could have the new crop and the old. Nobody heard the scuttle of tiny claws, the crunch of rodent teeth on fresh, sharp stalks, the slide of a bare tail.

*

'Why's Pa cursing?' asked Queenie, looking over to the garden. 'Is he angry with Albert?'

'I hope not,' said Ada. 'Anyway, Albert's fetching wood.' Unless it was something he'd done earlier. Or failed to do. You could never tell.

'Is Pa hurt?' Lizzie joined them, Gus on her hip.

There was something animal in the tone, something between

pain and anger and despair. Mrs Peacock dried her hands and said they should all go and see if Pa needed help. Her voice was low and clipped, her mouth hard and shrunken. She could never bear bad language.

Mr Peacock seemed to be praying. He was on his knees, bowed over the fresh earth which Lizzie had helped dig and rake the day before.

'Joseph?'

Ma began to run. Pa looked up, raw-faced as the children had never witnessed, and flicked a despairing hand at the tidy rows of tiny craters which now marked the soil.

'Gone. Every one. Every single one.'

Every newly planted bean, every kernel of maize, every creamy pumpkin seed. Taken with the precision of a long-planned military operation. The same could not be said of the attack on the growing vegetables. Here the rats had left a careless mess. Morsels of scattered squash flesh, double-grooved by incisors working pair by pair. Empty corn husks, and half-chewed cobs. Discarded bean pods, bright green and torn, tangled strands of golden thread. The whole garden laid waste.

Queenie began to cry, Sal and her scrawny puppy to scratch and sniff and growl. Lizzie felt herself shaking. 'Why? Why?' she moaned uselessly, at nobody in particular, in no hope of an answer. Albert found his legs could not support him, and collapsed against Ada.

'Can nothing be saved?'

Pa didn't answer Ma's strangled question. He was turning over a cob he'd picked up, checking to see if any kernels had survived. A few. The children stood in a half circle around him, waiting for his reply.

'I don't know, Mrs P. I don't know.'

'Oh, Joseph, Joseph, we did not deserve *this*,' whispered Ma. 'How can we go on?'

Pa shook his head, looking again at the ravagement around him, and his devastated children. He bent to scoop away Queenie's tears with a rough finger in the dark dip below each eye: one, two. And he knelt again, fixing his eyes on his small daughter's face, devouring her, determined to rouse her from despair. 'So what do we need now?'

She stared back, frowning.

'Breakfast,' she replied.

'Traps,' Pa corrected her, already reaching for a shovel.

*

More digging. Great, deep holes all around the devastated vegetable garden.

'The bottom must be wider than the top,' ordered Pa. But the sides kept crumbling. Eventually only Billy was both strong and light enough to dig. He scraped away at the bottom, out of sight for hours. Pa said that he would end up in England. Nobody laughed. The others held out hooked sticks to hoick out rich billycans of rich earth he filled up for them. Eventually Pa stuck a long bare branch into the hole, and Billy clambered up it like a terrified tightrope walker, hanging on with all his might to Pa and Albert's outstretched hands. The branch would become a ladder for the rats, Pa explained, and they started to dig the next hole.

'Where have they all gone?' Queenie asked later that morning.

'They're sleeping off their feast,' said Ma, bitterly, and disappeared inside so the children would not see her face.

Pa took the children into the bush to show them the beginnings of rat runs – tiny paths and tunnels in the vegetation, not four inches wide or tall. All led straight to their vegetable garden.

'They must think we planted everything specially for them,' he said.

Rotten fish heads and goat offal, all the detritus they usually left on the mountain or on the beach to be swept away by surf, became precious bait. At dusk Pa tied up Sal and Spy and left them whining in the shade of the outhouse. He smeared the rat-ladders with entrails, and slopped more guts and lungs into the wide bottom of the pits below. Then it was a question of waiting for darkness to fall.

'They'll be back,' he assured the exhausted children.

That first night Ma made them all stay in the house. Lizzie didn't see why, and crept out as soon as the others were asleep to stand under the shadow of the trees, out of the moonlight. She soon heard skitter-skattering and squeaks – the rats were arriving. Her fingers curled. The terriers began whining to be released. But Pa shushed them. Waiting. Waiting. Till the time was right.

And then he untied the dogs.

They were in the nearest pit in a single bound. A moment later, the scrapping and scratching and screeching and killing began. Lizzie hugged herself, her eyes bulging and her heart galloping. What had she expected? Not enemies in these numbers. The invisible frenzy seemed endless: sharp, sudden movements, the occasional yelp and high-pitched screech, but for the most part intense, efficient and chillingly quiet. From time to time Pa's growl overlaid the circling, scratching, rooting, scrambling sounds.

'Drop it, Spy! Good dog, Sal!'

Until there were no rats left to kill, and all that could be heard was the snap and crunch of tiny bones as the dogs ate and enjoyed their reward.

The morning revealed abandoned tails and corpses. The rats were smaller and darker than English ones, Ma told the children. In New Zealand, where Pa had seen pit traps like these, the Maori called the creatures kiore. Polynesian adventurers, they were said to swim from island to island, their teeth in each other's tails. But Pa said that was just a story; they came ashore with passing ships, and bred so fast, so what could you do but kill them?

'Eat them?' suggested Billy.

Ma shuddered and Pa said quietly, 'Let's hope it doesn't come to that.'

Lizzie saw that he actually thought it might, and wondered too. The taro and kumara were all finished. All fruits and berries stripped from the trees. The goats were getting ever more canny. If they didn't defeat the rats, they'd be back to milk and fern roots. Or the rats themselves.

So many corpses, yet still more live ones came. One hundred and twenty-three one night. A hundred and seventy-six the next. A few nights later the dogs killed two hundred and twelve of them, Pa said. Ma worried that the terriers would get fat and lazy. The rats started foraging by day as well as night. Pa made swinging larders for Ma to keep the food in, and Lizzie and Billy joined Sal and Spy on the warpath, collecting the rodents in baited tins, hidden in bushes and tilted towards the rat runs. On a command from Lizzie, just as the rats came swarming and leaping inside, squirming and crawling over each other in their eagerness, Billy would jerk the tin upright. In the blink of an eye the creatures tipped into a seething mass of tails and claws and sleek black fur which the children presented to the dogs and then turned away. Though it was hard not to look. There was a fascination in seeing one animal so effectively dispatching another, even if nobody would admit it.

'It's hideous,' complained Queenie.

'It's their nature,' said Lizzie. 'Would you rather starve?'

'I don't want to be Queen of the Kermadecs now.' Her sister pouted.

'We can't let the rats rule us. And look how many Sal and Spy have killed today.'

The catching became more efficient still when Billy found and baited an old mooring buoy, rusty, holed in, washed up years ago. Even the most cunning kiore could not leap up to safety once it had thrown itself inside.

By day Pa continued to clear the land, Albert and Billy at his side, replanting what they could. Albert listened to his father's talk of fleece and foot rot, Leicesters, Lincolns, Longwools, Romneys and Merinos. What was he supposed to say about the new half-breed on the South Island?

The grass seed sprouted, a fine, luminous emerald green, patchy at first, like a young man's beard, colouring the earth more confidently with every day that passed. Then, one morning, long before there was any hope of it setting seed, Pa found the delicate sward half nibbled away. That was when he took to night-watching, staying up with the dogs and a raging bonfire, guarding and patrolling and occasionally dozing, though never for long. Sometimes Ma would take him a mug of fireweed tea sweetened with ti syrup. His temper grew ever shorter. He tried to make Albert take his turn, but too often the others were woken in the night by Albert's cry, and hissing leather, and all Pa's noisy fury at finding his son fast asleep on duty while the rats returned to feast.

'I'm doing this for you,' he raged. Another thwack. 'Do you care so little for your future?'

Albert could only whimper. Lizzie's heart ached for her father. For all of them. If a second ship had shown up in those dark days, there wasn't a soul on Monday Island who wouldn't have begged for passage.

*

A few weeks later, Lizzie noticed a stillness in the air when she went for water. What had happened? What was missing? It was the birds. All that clatter and clamour they'd got used to on the sandbanks and up the cliffs and on the rocks, the fussing and flapping of black burrowers and wideawakes, the clacking chatter that went on all day and sometimes into the night too, all that cacophony had died away, almost from one day to the next. The birds were departing, flying away. The island was emptying. Soon the Peacock family would be alone with the goats and the rats. Winter was coming.

27

LIZZIE STILL OFTEN WAKES SHAKING, THE COLD DAMP-
ness of sweated cotton sticking to her back and breasts.
In daylight, rare moments of dreamed clarity mockingly
return: a falling axe; a cry, hardly human; Albert, shrunken,
staggering like the starving puppies, whining with them for Sal,
who is nowhere to be seen. Something is always on the verge of
happening to Albert, something monumental. She can't tell what,
so she can't stop it. And dreaming hardly seems adequate a word
for these night-frights.

Ada shifts beside her and only pretends to sleep. The barricades
are up again. All day her sister, busy with the baby, keeps herself
so close to the others that Lizzie cannot prise her away for a
moment. Question after question bubbles up and bursts un-
answered. Lizzie seethes and weeps inside by turn, so angry and
so sad she almost blurts out Ada's secret to their mother. Mrs
Peacock has settled into sternness. Confession would be hard.

Unsettled weather. Queenie looks at both her sisters oddly, and
decided to ask Lizzie outright.

'Have you and Ada argued?'

Lizzie shook her head, wide-eyed with false surprise. Lucky for her, Queenie's so taken by the wonders of letter-learning, her mind is always elsewhere; looking for print on rusting flour tins, stencilled on packing cases, plastered on trunks, and moulded in iron on the frame of the sewing machine, which is out every day now. Mrs Peacock is making up new shirts for the Islanders with the last of the calico. She won't have them lounging around 'half-naked' on washdays. Wertheim, the machine is called.

'Worth-heem,' suggests Queenie.

'WHIRR-TIME.' Ma corrects her, and her daughter nods. That makes sense.

She reads the letters on the buttons she finds wrapped in a scrap of cloth on the bobbin shelf of Mrs Peacock's sewing basket. One button matches the six on the jacket Albert used to wear. IMPROVED – FOUR HOLES. That makes sense too. Four holes would make a better fastening than two. GUARANTEED NOT TO CUT. Ma has to explain. Who would have thought a button could be mistaken for a knife? That it might slice through a thread? Another button reads A. LINNEY. 23 REGENT ST. This confuses Solomona and Kalala too, until Ma explains ST can mean both Saint and Street. She talks briefly of London, of pavements, people, shopfronts, gaslights, glass. Kalala asks if she knows another street in that great city, a Blomfield Street, where there is a museum of idols, where Englishmen and Englishwomen come to wonder at heathen curiosities, but Mrs Peacock shakes her head and pounds the Wertheim's pedal so she can hear no more questions, and fills her mouth with pins.

Very soon, to Lizzie's annoyance, Queenie's reading has overtaken everyone's. Billy laughs at the strange contortions of her lips. 'Gwah! Gwah!' he growls at her before huffing off to the new plantation grounds, asking what good is reading anyway. You can't eat books.

'It's *guaranteed*, stupid,' Queenie shouts at his back. 'It's like a promise, isn't it, Ma? Isn't it, Lizzie?'

Mrs Peacock nods as she lays the baby on her shoulder to rub his back in slow, upward circles.

'What else can I read, Ma?' Queenie asks. Her mother assesses her. Joey lets out a belch, opens shocked eyes, and promptly slumps into a drunken slumber. Mrs Peacock disappears into the hut, and swaps the baby for a fat book. Lizzie vaguely remembers the swirling patterns of inky waves on its closed pages.

'*The Family Shakespeare.* Lots of stories in here,' says Ma. 'Plays.'

'What's a play?' asks Queenie.

'A story told by actors. In a theatre. They pretend to be the story people.'

Lizzie looks over Queenie's shoulder at the first page, as she reads aloud.

'*In which nothing is added to the original text, but those words and expressions are omitted which cannot with propriety be read aloud in a family.*'

'Here,' says Ma, flicking pages to a picture. 'This is where the first play begins.'

'What's it called?' asks Lizzie.

'*The Tempest*,' reads Queenie.

'It's about an island,' Ma tells them. 'Starts with a storm and a shipwreck. Read it to us, Queenie.'

*

That evening, Lizzie notices more grey hairs in her father's beard. He is stacking firewood but she hasn't offered to help. She watches, wonderingly, the stretching sinews of his arms and his movements' swinging rhythms. He never stops, never rests, never has done. It used to make her proud to think that she, of all the children, had inherited that restless determination. What has it cost him? She detects a kind of wilfulness in his resolve. Something worse than wilfulness, perhaps.

When Pa looks back at her, disturbed by the force of her inspecting gaze, eyebrows raised in a question she can't answer, Lizzie turns away as if caught stealing. For days she has battled with her instinct to deny what Ada has told her, and her fury at her sister's new evasions. Fathers were always fast with their fists when it came to sons. Weren't they? Lizzie is no longer certain. The family has lived so much apart from others. Hard to know what was too much or not enough of anything. In her indifference, in her failure to imagine another way of being, perhaps she had been as cruel as Pa. She ought to feel comforted by Albert's escape. But she could not yet believe in it. How had he managed it, and how did Ada help, and why on earth wouldn't she just explain, instead of trying to avoid her all the time? It was infuriating.

At last she corners Ada walking to the spring, while Queenie's lost in Shakespeare. Their pails clash together, dippers rattling. Lizzie switches sides. Ada and Albert are the only left-handers among the Peacock family, and it roused Pa's anger whenever he tried to show Albert how to do anything. Hold it like this, he would say, and Albert would obediently swap hands to copy Pa. But then the swing of his axe faltered, or the blade of his knife slid uselessly away, or his shovel would lose its force. Yet Pa never used to mind how Ada tackled anything. Once Lizzie thought it

was because Pa liked her more than Albert. Now she wonders if
he doesn't care because Ada's just a girl.

'I keep thinking about Albert,' Lizzie says. 'Poor Albert. I see
things I didn't see before. I wish I'd known. I wish I could have
stopped him going.'

Ada makes a movement of her lips too harsh to call a smile.

'But now he's free . . . '

'Yes,' says Ada.

'Did *you* say goodbye to him at least?'

Her sister is slow to answer.

'Well?' Lizzie insists, nudging her with an elbow.

'No,' she sighs. 'No. In the end I didn't see him.'

'What! Then how do you know he's gone?'

Ada falls silent. Lizzie burns with frustration. An unpleasant,
threatening note edges into her voice, which she can hear but
can't conceal. 'Ada, you have to tell me what you saw.'

'Nothing. I don't know for certain how he managed to escape.'

'You don't know?'

'Of course not. I was with *you* all that time, remember? That's
why I wanted to look for him right away. To be sure. But he was
so determined. And no sign of him anywhere. So he must have
gone. Either the ship came back for him,' says Ada. 'What was
she called? The *Esperanza*. After she left here—'

'When? In the night?' Lizzie is instantly dubious, too impatient
to wait for Ada's 'or'. 'So where did she pick him up? Not from
here, that's for sure. From Clapperton Bay?'

'Maybe. If he hid there when Pa first went up to look for him
. . . started another fire?'

'But we all saw the *Esperanza* go . . . we saw what course
she took.'

'You know how clever Albert is. He'll have worked something out,' Ada insists. 'He told me he'd do anything. He said he'd stow away if he had to. Maybe he hid in the gig before it left.'

'But you didn't see him?' Lizzie wants a witness. Proof. You can't know something you've not seen.

'Of course not. Oh, how I wanted to look, but I kept thinking about Albert staring at me from wherever he was hiding – at the rocks at the head of the beach? – willing me not to turn, not to give him away. So I didn't. It would have ruined everything.' Ada's voice rises defensively.

Everything *is* ruined, thinks Lizzie bitterly. She thinks back. How preoccupied they had been that day, how busy with things that now seem petty, excitements like the yellow snail-shell necklaces, and the banana roots, and the noisy chickens. She imagines Albert up in the forest, abandoning the goat, disobeying Pa almost for the first time ever, and setting off into the world alone, more alone even than Pa himself when he left England so many years ago.

In her head he darts through the trees, and clambers down the rocks as fast as his lameness will allow, always finding somewhere to hide. And as soon as all the family and sailors and Islanders have left the beach, he climbs into the prow of the beached jolly boat, to tremble under an airless tarp, curled up in darkness, waiting for the boat to slide back into the water. How long did he imagine he could hide before he was sick? Did they haul the boat up with him? Possibilities ribbon away like little eels.

'And nobody saw him? Nobody at all?'

'Of course not,' says Ada. She always had more faith in Albert than anyone else in the family. 'Because we weren't expecting to. But he knew the chance might never come again. So he took it.'

Stowaway stories were a favourite in the Pacific. Boys stashed in barrels and trunks and sail-bales and whale carcasses, picked up at one port, by accident or intent, let go at another, halfway around the world, months later. So she had underestimated her brother. Lizzie nods. 'Good for him. I suppose. If that's what he wanted. So that's what you were always talking about?'

All those times they had abandoned Lizzie.

'The trouble was we could never quite agree. Albert always said Pa would never let us go.'

'Us?' says Lizzie, stock still, dropping her pail in shock. 'Let *us* go?'

'I knew it wouldn't be easy, but I always said we should come clean, not sneak away. All out in the open. We could say goodbye, and then everyone would know where we were and there wouldn't be all this upset and confusion. Poor Ma.'

It hadn't struck Lizzie for a moment that her sister had ever planned to leave with Albert.

'You'd *both* have gone?' She looks at Ada, gentle Ada, who never used to qualify her kindness, who once upon a time only hurt feelings by accident. Always patient with Queenie, and Billy and Gus – and now Joey – but most of all with Albert, while Lizzie champed and sighed, her stomach knotted with meanness, soured by Ada's sweetness and her own impatience. Yet Ada would have left them.

'I had to. I thought Albert needed me. Oh, but I was furious when he left without me . . . at first I thought I could not hold it in. That I'd *have* to tell you. But now I understand. He had to take his chance. And some day he will tell us where he is.'

Lizzie doesn't want to hear this.

'You didn't tell me. You didn't ask how I would feel.'

Her sister's face is oddly innocent.

'We had to go. And I thought you wouldn't care.'

'Care?' Lizzie can hardly speak. This discovery has pushed everything else aside.

'I knew you'd never leave here. Like Pa. I've always thought this is really your island, right from the very beginning. You knew about it first. You cared about it most. Albert never wanted this. He never wanted . . . things. Land. Just to know more, see more. Not to have to pretend to be something he never could be.'

They reach the spring. It's shady here, and fresh. Almost like being underwater the way light streaks softly through the thick air and makes it dance. Lizzie kneels first among the ferns, pressing her dipper into the wet grass under the rock, letting it slowly fill, and bowing her head while she rearranges everything inside it. All this work has always been for Albert. It's all Pa cared about. Not him, exactly. But his name. Securing the future for the Peacock family, a tiny empire nobody could ever take away because it belonged to no one, where nobody else could give orders. Peacock land for generations.

But that meant the boys. Albert and Billy, and the sons they would one day have, and the sons those sons would produce in time. Perhaps Pa planned to bring them wives one day, to ship them in with the sheep and make them breed. Lizzie doesn't know. She realises of course that she has been useful, tough and bold enough to have secured her father's admiration, but now she recognises that she is also dispensable. This land never would or could be hers. It has taken Albert's vanishing to make her understand.

'Albert never belonged here,' Ada continues.

'We all wanted to come.'

'We wanted to leave the hotel. We didn't all want to stay. Remember the whalers?'

Of course. *She* would have stayed then, she knew. Even if Ma had gone. She'd have stayed with Pa. Lizzie refills her dipper. This slow trickle of water on metal could be a heavenly sound, but today it sounds forlorn and makes her shiver. Angry and also ashamed, betrayed and guilty both, Lizzie cannot help but shift away when she feels the heat and weight of Ada against her, leaning like an animal seeking silent reassurance. She thinks again and then returns the pressure.

When both buckets are full, Lizzie stares down at the rippling version of her sister's eyes. They always used to trust each other. They somehow need to start again.

28

WHITE BELLY, WHITER STILL IN MOONLIGHT. SHE flaunts it as she falls back, crashing against dark water in a wild sheet of spray, every ridge and furrow on show. Foam and froth runnel down and down and down. The joy of her. The song of her. I watch, half dreaming, drawn to the bluff by this gigantic slap of flesh on sea, and I feel myself unravel as this whale pulls longing from me. To me she calls, only me, it seems. She knows I am here this night – high, alone, in darkness. She surely must – for I know her, this mother of all mothers with tooth-marked tail. I saw her first, far away, from my own coral cliff, when I was half the height I am now, half this heaviness, and I have seen her since from my vaka, night fishing. She must return on the ocean path we took here. The thought tightens and twists my unhomed heart.

Up flicks her boat-vast tail. There are the old wounds healed again, familiar scars scratched like writing, ragged, uneven marks grooved into skin as tough as bone. The blackness churns and another beast breaches, a smaller echo of my old friend. Her calf, new this year, now arching backwards, in a slow fall, flippers stretched like wings. Whale and child defy air and water . . . and look, here comes another – a father? – hooting, honking, snorting, making merry. I laugh with love of seeing my mother-whale again. And weep that I cannot follow her home at will.

Catamarans, Mr Reverend calls our claw-sail boats, our double canoes. Soon before our sailing, I asked him if there are catamarans in the Good Book but he said no, he did not believe so, and then he talks again of fishers of men. I tell him I am a fisher of fish.

A smile.

'This Mr Peacock . . . ' I said, thoughts flitting, circling, unwilling to land. 'There are . . . catamarans . . . at his island too?'

Eyebrows twitched up, in, down. The Reverend shook his head, pushed back paper and put down pen.

'I can't say for certain. Most unlikely, I'm afraid.'

My mother-whale breaks through the sea once more, and my thoughts journey fast between here and there, now and then, reminding me of a German word Mr Reverend once taught me: *Wanderlust.* Something like an affliction among my people, he believes, and yet he confessed it was this spirit, this appetency, that brought him to our seas from far away so long ago. Then he offered me Solomona's place at the Institute.

'You are so quick to learn,' he told me then. 'A natural teacher too. Your English the best by far, I do believe, of all the fellows on the Rock. Stay.'

I have his son Sidney to thank for that, but we did not speak of Sidney. Nor did we speak of my ever-doubting heart. I will never be ready to follow Solomona's Pioneer path. Instead I seek to please the Reverend with a psalm. '*They that go down to the sea in ships, that do business in great waters . . .*'

And he pick up the words:

'*These see the works of the Lord, and his wonders in the deep.* Yes, you will indeed see wonders of all kinds on your travels, Kalala. And in time you will enjoy the fruits of your toil. Fair enough. God bless you all.'

God bless us all. Bitterness now rises as I think of Sidney with his new friends, all missionary sons, all dressed in black in the English school, learning all I will never learn. I think of them talking together of the savages they used to know.

Our island is emptying. Full ships leave new diseases and body-prints on sleeping mats. Infants without fathers and mothers without sons. The elders shake their heads, and Mr Reverend sermonises, but who can stop this spirit of change, when young men choose to go? When so many places call us, that call comes so loud and clear, and strangers make such promises.

With the world's wealth comes new friends. I see one walks this way: Lizzie, summoned to the lookout by whalesong too, no doubt. Blanket-wrapped and billowing, she sails towards me, but inside is a thing of skin and bones, body a mast, wrists like sticks. I am certain she comes here, like me, to flee her dreams. I know how restlessly she sleeps. I hear her night-time voice, and how it cries. Towed by hoot and splash, she looks out to sea as she walks, never seeing me. I wait till she is closer, and then I call.

'Lizzie.'

'Who's there?' she answers, piping. 'Kalala?'

'Yes.'

'Have you seen? Have you seen the whales?'

'Yes. They called me here too.'

I feel her easing as she walks towards me, still watching the water. Our book-sharing has made us comfortable together, in silence and in speech, and we sit again, she beside me, knees tenting, flesh parcelled in wool, our four eyes glistening with wonder. Again and again the double spray appears. Again and again the path of moonlight stretching out towards the sky's dome is torn to pieces. Silvered shards like a broken looking glass. The fourth new moon to rise since first we came.

'We are so small,' she says.

'The world is very vast.'

'How can we know if we matter?' she asks.

'To the world? We can't.'

'Can't know or can't matter?'

'I don't know. Maybe both.'

All her questions are too large for me. I want to ask Solomona, or Mr Reverend. I want vast, gigantic answers, greater even than the Mission school's coloured map. But more and more I fear that Mr Reverend and Solomona have only one answer, and it is always the same, and it will never content me. We see what we can see, and what we see we know. And what of what we cannot see? The world is full of infinite, invisible, unknowable mysteries. Where do these great whales go when they are not here or there? God knows, Solomona says. But I would know this too. To what depths do these leviathans vanish? How far does this ocean of islands stretch and how can I keep in my head all that I know or believe to be here?

I think of all the words I know that stand for greatness. Astonishing, magnificent, omnipotent, omnipresent. I think of the different things greatness stands for. One, above all. Lizzie speaks again.

'And if it is true – if we are of no significance – how can the world be just and fair as we suppose?'

Until she looks at me, I cannot tell if her question is for me, or for herself, or maybe for the ocean. Her mouth and teeth are formed in such a way that she cannot easily close them. Her lips rest always a little open, shining. I used to think she was on the point of speaking, and I would wait for her words. Tonight she waits for mine. Though her sister Queenie is quicker, Lizzie is an eager learner, and she expects me to know bigger things. I fear to disappoint her.

'This world?' I say, surprised. 'It is not *this* world, only the next, that is just and fair.'

'*The Lord executeth righteousness and judgement for all that are oppressed,*' she says, and looks at me, upper lip curling, questioning.

Solomona read this psalm last Sunday.

'*Like as a father pitieth his children, so the Lord pitieth them that fear him.*' I reply. She shivers. '*For he knoweth our frame; he remembereth that we are dust. As for man, his days are as grass, as a flower of the field, so he flourisheth. For the wind passeth over it, and it is gone; and the place thereof shall know it no more.*'

'Now I feel smaller still,' Lizzie says. She raises her eyes to the heavens, and sighs, and rests her chin on her blanket-wrapped knees once more. I swallow. This waiting between us is a space I do not know how to fill. The hollow hooting from the ocean becomes loud again. Edge-eyed, I look at Lizzie, and her face is split by an open smile. Another great slap from the ocean, a crash of bubbles, and she laughs, throat throbbing.

'How do they do it? How do they dare? They think they can fly!'

'They nearly can.'

'We saw them last year. I didn't know if they'd be back.'

A chain of whales has linked us through months and oceans when we knew nothing of each other.

'Albert heard them first, and Billy saw them. And now here they are again. The same mother, I'm certain. But a new baby. Oh, Kalala, look at that!' She claps her hands, like Gussie.

Her delight delights me.

'Look! More . . . over there,' I say, and with my hand I softly turn her head so that she sees the plume of glory for herself. The dark shape moving just below the waves.

'Four! No, look, there are five tonight!'

'There'll be more tomorrow, I think.'

'Do they know we're here? Do they watch us like we watch them?' she asks.

'I don't know. Maybe. I feel it is so.'

'I do too,' she says. A long sigh shudders her body, and I catch its slipstream in my own.

'They're going home,' I tell her. 'Of course they are happy.'

'Home? What home does a whale have? And how do you know?'

She's right. I don't know.

'They're going to *my* home.'

'Will they take a message?' she asks, but she is smiling as if she doesn't believe they can.

'I hope.'

She glows as she watches. She hugs herself.

'Oh how I love them! More than anything, I think. Oh look! Look! She is rising again. How great and grand she is. I'm so happy they are back. Why do we have to be people when we could be whales?'

'Or goats? Or limpets? Or any creatures without souls?'

'Limpets? Oh, it would be easy to be a limpet. Can limpets dream? Or do they only dream of sea?'

Then I confess, as much as I am able.

'I dream of sea,' I say. 'But in truth, I dream of ships. Not our kind . . . these are palagi ships.'

She frowns at me. She sees at once these are not good dreams.

'I don't like to dream,' she says, shoulders hunching once more. 'I never sleep.'

'Never?'

Lips pressed hard, she shakes her head.

'Almost never. I'm afraid to sleep. When I close my eyes . . .'

Her slow words stumble, and her fear returns. I know this fear.

'Tell me,' I say. I would not dare ask such a thing by day. But in the dark, even this bright darkness, words can fall more freely. 'If you wish.'

'Pictures come,' she says. 'So many pictures, one after another, pressing and pushing into my head. They make no sense. When I close my eyes I see things I don't want to see.'

Yes, I know.

'I hear things too. Oh, you'll say it's just bad dreams . . . but I know what a dream is. I used to dream of falling. When I was small. Falling and falling and falling. Not every night. Just sometimes. I only remember how it felt now. I never knew where I was, or what had happened just before, or why I was falling. Sometimes Ada would hear me cry, and pick me up from the floor, and put blankets round us both to keep me safe. Or just the rush of it woke me. And slowly I learned to know this feeling, and to know that I could stop the plunging and wing out my dreams, scoop myself up before I reached the bottom – though I never did – and fly away.'

'Falling and flying?' These are dreams I also know. And sinking and drowning.

'Yes. But now everything's changed . . . I can't tell if I'm awake or asleep. I can't change what I'm doing because I'm not in the dreams myself, not part of them. Only watching. Always watching, from the outside. Something is happening that I can't stop, and nobody can hear me, or see me, or help me. That's why I hate to sleep.'

We sit in silence until the singing starts up again; hooting and whistling, the whales roll and splash. They dance for life and freedom and the open seas and homecoming. I plunge deep into myself for words but I come up for air with empty fingers. I am silenced by a kind of shame in what I see at night, and what I feel. And yet I'd have her know it.

'You hear weeping in your dreams?' I ask.

She nods.

'Oh yes. Weeping and pain. Teeth held tight like a steel trap. Violence. Someone being beaten. I can't tell who. I can't stop it.'

She turns from the sea, and dares me with her eyes to tell her more.

'Wounds,' I whisper, and my breath sucks quickly in.

'You know,' she says. 'How do you know? About the weeping. And the beating.'

'And sickness. And pain.'

'What is it, Kalala? What does it mean? Is it the same for you? Do you know what this means?'

I know what Solomona would say, for once I asked him, most quietly. It means we have to pray. He prays for me to be relieved, and made me promise silence, not to trouble our fellows here with these notions. Imagine, after what has happened here, after a boy disappearing, imagine how Luka and Pineki, even Iakopo and Vilipate, who are steadier sorts of bodies, imagine how their hearts would race at this. Remember, he tells me, quietly, firmly, remember the old ways, remember how evil may be expelled. How they may seek to crush wickedness from my chest. Say nothing. Not to anyone. He begs me. But I have tried to pray, tried so often, and it brings no relief. Breath like breeze, as if Solomona listens from the shadows, I tell her my secret thinking.

'I believe it is the aitu.'

She kneels and leans forward with urgent eyes.

'What do you mean?' she asks.

Mr Reverend does not like talk like this. Heathen ideas, he says. He would tell me now to forget the aitu, and think only of the one, true spirit. How hard I have tried. So I only whisper the word again to Lizzie, and look about me.

'Spirits.'

She shifts closer.

'Like the Holy Spirit?'

Have mercy on me, O Lord, according to thy lovingkindness . . . blot out my transgressions.

'No, no. These are not good spirits. Spirits of ancestors, family. Spirits that come when something bad has happened.'

She seizes my arm. Hot breath. Cool, damp fingers. I hardly breathe.

'You mean ghosts? A kind of haunting?'

'Perhaps. I believe so. Because every night it is the same for me. A confusion of voices, half known, and the shout of strangers too. The fall of despair in my gut. Throbbing pain and a feeling that I must choke, that I can find no air. I feel the weight of chains on my legs, and I think I will never move again.'

Darkness and foul smells. Always I feel the ache of parting. Sometimes when I wake, I drag myself outside, and vomit until my stomach is void of everything and my head is throbbing and light as air. Aitu. The aitu are taking possession of me. I am ghost-sick.

I feel her fingers tighten, and she shakes her head, and stares. 'Who are they?' she asks me.

I have told myself a thousand times that aitu cannot exist. Only in my mind. Aitu are heathen things, and should not bother me. Who are they then? What is it that comes for me here? And although I pray, and make the sign of the cross before I sleep, and I never whistle at night – I do nothing, nothing at all that may court these spirits – yet they prevent my sleeping. And Lizzie's too. I slide my wrist from her hand, remembering the Reverend's warning, more harshly repeated by the captain to all our gang, on the deck of the *Esperanza*. These girls are not for you. Make no trouble if you want to come home again. Not this kind of trouble, I think, but still I must take care.

'You think that is what makes me dream of Albert?' she says, paired hands pinned between thighs, her prayers upside down. 'Is it him? His spirit?'

Thou shalt not bear false witness against thy neighbour.

I answer cautiously. 'Perhaps.'

This single, uncertain word stops her, and unstoppers her.

'No,' she says. 'It can't be. I will tell you why. It's not my secret. But you must keep it for me.'

I see she needs to tell me. 'I will.'

'Albert isn't dead. So it cannot be his ghost that haunts me. He's gone from here, Ada says. Escaped. Stowed away on the *Esperanza* on the day you landed. That's why there's no trace of him.'

Yesterday, when I watched them after supper, it seemed to me that the two big sisters had healed the wounds which divided them. This resurrection has been their bandage.

'In a few months,' she continues, 'when the ship returns with our orders, and your payment, and to take you home, why, then we will have word of him at last, we hope. The captain will tell us where he is.'

'Did Ada see him go?' I ask, with care.

'No. Did you?'

'No.'

'Did anyone?'

'We have never seen Albert in all our lives.'

Lizzie will not be daunted.

'But he was clever, you see. And patient. He had waited so long already, and that day he waited longer . . . until all of us were looking somewhere else. Then he concealed himself, Ada says, in the boat on the beach. She says this has been his plan, for months. It's possible, isn't it? Where else *can* he be?'

Outrigging hope has kept her sister from capsizing. I want this to be true. I want Lizzie to stay afloat too. I like this girl, bold like Sidney, who lives so full of wonder at the world. But my eyes betray me.

'You think it's not possible.'

I cannot lie. 'Certainly, it would not be easy.'

'But it is possible.' She wants to right herself.

'Perhaps. If that is what Ada believes.'

There. My doubt is in the open. I cannot unsay it, so I push at her thinking another way.

'Why has she kept this secret? Your sister is not cruel. Why has she let your mother believe her son is dead? Your father too?'

And then Lizzie's spine slackens.

'I know. I know . . . sometimes I fear his vanishing has turned her mind. But when I am with her, it makes sense. There's no certainty, no proof of anything . . . And if my father ever knew she had hoped to go with him . . . even that *she* knew Albert had planned this day for so many months . . . You promise you will say nothing, Kalala? Not to Solomona. Not even Queenie. Will you swear to me? Until we know for certain.'

She need not ask me. I am sorry to have pressed her this far. It is not for me to judge her father. I have no father of my own to stand beside him. Had I a father living, had our family not lost its backbone, what would he have said to our venturing? Would he have sought to stop us? His face was never in my head to bind me to my island, and I have been raised by other men. But mostly women, for we lack men more and more. I know that fear rules many families, sending judgement into hiding, twisting bonds. I try to calm her clutching hands. I promise, 'hope to die', and pass my finger across my throat as she requests, and then softly I remind her that we have forgotten the whales.

The sea looks dark and empty. Then, far, far away, we see the waters part; the breaching of a great body grown small with distance. It disappears. A silence falls over us, and our thoughts gather separately, and grow louder in our skulls, until we must release and join them together.

I think of everything I know of this boy. The boy Lizzie tells me is clever and brave and beautiful. The boy who trembles at his father. Who turns his back on great possessions. This island.

'And if he doesn't . . . ? If she never hears?' I ask.

'Or if she is wrong and now he sends word another way, from another kind of place entirely? Not to Ada, but to me, because I am guilty. Ada blames me, you see. I never spoke up for Albert. I always took my father's side. She's right. I never meant harm or harshness but perhaps I caused it. I have become harsh.'

'What other place do you mean?' I ask.

'These spirits you call . . . ' Her face warps, remembering. Should I not have spoken of them? Mrs Reverend hates to hear of them even more than her husband. She forbade me to talk of aitu ever with Sidney or Becky. I say the word again to Lizzie, louder and clearer than before. A challenge.

'Aitu.'

'Yes. Those. Could it be Albert who comes at night? His spirit? I think I *feel* him here still, I think he has never left, but how can that be and how can I know?'

I shrug. I open my palms. It is not for me to say. She needs proof.

Lizzie looks differently at me now.

But I can say no more of my affliction. I can't make words of it. I want her to understand without speech. I shake my head, yet my eyes implore her.

'I'll tell no one,' she promises, kneeling now beside me. 'You can tell me what you want and when you want. But I have a question for you. Do you think it's possible that the same spirit visits us both?'

Once more I shake my head. I am certain it is not Albert who comes to me each night and wrenches at my guts.

BEFORE

Pa grew blacker with each week that passed. Ma's temper short-
ened almost to nothingness. Then one morning Mr Peacock set
off with only Albert, and more food than he'd ever agreed to take
before. He told nobody where they were going, and they were
two days absent. Two nights. Three days. Still Ma never spoke
of them, and the children didn't ask. Even Ada held her tongue.
Then Pa was back, with triumph on his face.

'We're moving,' he announced.

Ma set down her knife.

'To the North Bay? Higgins spoke true?'

'He did. Do you want to see it first?'

She shook her head. 'Where's Albert?'

'Coming. Not far behind.' Mr Peacock sat down, and Lizzie
joined him at the table. Ada dried her hands and stepped out to
meet their brother, who came in vacant with fatigue.

'Well?' said Mrs Peacock.

'Well . . . I've had a good look round. There are things we have
here we'll miss, to begin with. But there's more we stand to gain.'

'Like what?' asked Lizzie eagerly.

'No rats, I hope, if we're careful. Better land, and a better
landing. Closer to the lake. Other things I'll show you when we
get there. Ready for some hard work?' her father asked.

She nodded.

'When do we go?' she said. She should have guessed the answer.

'Tomorrow.'

'Can we move our house?'

He planted his palms flat on the table top.

'No. We have to start again.'

*

As the day wore on, Albert's lameness, still not healed, showed more and more. Ada swapped packs with him, lightening his load, but this made little difference. Pa shook his head despairingly.

'Always the same with you and your cranky legs. Still can't carry more than a girl?'

Albert rolled anxious eyes at Ma, but she was busy helping Gussie, who kept begging to be carried. They tramped the inland tracks, damp-backed, weighed down like pedlars. More trees and branches had fallen in the winter storms and blocked the paths. Up the cliffs, over ridges and ravines, past Crater Lake. Lizzie lost count of how many times they crossed the island, over how many days. Yet each time Lizzie reached that point on Prospect Ridge where you could hear the surf again – and then, a little further, when she had a clear eye of those white-capped rollers – her heart lightened a little. At last they reached a turning point: more trunks and crates and bundles gathered on the north side than the west. No going back then. There would be an end to this.

On the new beach, there were hot springs. A little burrowing on a warm spot and you could splash in a warm bath whenever you pleased, and soothe aching limbs and backs. For the brave, a chance to swim, and swoop in on the surf, without a furious undertow pulling you from land. A new sense of openness. A shelf of rock which jutted like a jetty from the base of low cliffs. Lizzie quietly cursed the wind that a year ago had made landing here seem so impossible, and she cursed MacHeath – as Pa now did, openly, inventing fresh punishments to be exacted if he ever set eyes on him again – and wondered afresh at the captain's cruelty.

To be sure, they had further to go for fresh water and building material, but not so far as all that. And on the fourth day they discovered a secret gully, a deep-sided valley filled with arum lilies and scented nightbells. A charmed, enchanted spot which made Queenie talk of fairies. Where, too, Ada and Lizzie came upon a pile of old pig bones, which Pa quickly buried, and never spoke of.

When they came to build their first new whare, on the strip of land looking over the beach, the cutting and carrying were endless as before, but now the journey back was even harder. The children were already blank-eyed with weariness when Mr Peacock announced a new task.

The grass had to be moved.

They had no seeds that could be gathered and resown, he told them. The rats had seen to that. And the grass was too young and fine to lift as turf, but if left unguarded it would be destroyed. So Pa insisted on saving their new-grown pasture root by root, stem by stem, blade by blade. With delicate probing fingers, Ada, Albert, Lizzie, Billy – even Queenie – eased every single stalk of meadow-grass out of the soil of Clapperton Bay, one by one. Each pale stem wrapped tenderly in damp linen, in bundles of forty or fifty or sixty. Each bundle strapped to a child's back and carried on a journey that could take nearly half a day.

'He's crazy,' muttered Ada, weeping one day as she worked. She tried to wring out the pain in her back, and Albert leaned over to rub it for her.

'Shhh,' he said. 'Don't let him hear you.' It had become a habit to think that way. But Pa was on the north side of the island, digging and harrowing, breaking and raking the rich earth into the finest tilth, ready to receive the tiny plants marching his way.

Ten acres transplanted, shoot by shoot. Three weeks later Lizzie called the others over to see.

'Look. He's not crazy at all.'

Emerald-bright once more, the grass was growing, spreading its vibrancy over the earth like a velvet cloak.

29

AFTER THE WHALE NIGHT, ANOTHER SUNDAY DAWNS. Thanks to Solomona, the pattern of the Sabbath has changed completely. The children are only too happy to play by the Islanders' rules, and Ma also agrees there should be no work on Sundays. Pa resists without words, without much fuss, and simply disappears, a pack on his back, and sometimes his gun too. He's often gone for hours and comes back red-faced and swaying. Though his mood is light and he is quick to joke and laugh – teasing Queenie, swinging Gus on his shoulders so she screams, offering to get out his fiddle – Ma does not join in the laughter.

Once morning prayers are over, goats milked, chickens fed, and all those small chores no day can do without are done, Sunday unexpectedly becomes a day for swimming and expeditions, rounded off to Ma's satisfaction with an early evening service and plenty of hymns. They all look forward to it, Queenie more than most. Because as long as it is the Bible lying open on her lap, on the seventh day, nobody will stop her reading.

This Sunday Lizzie feels unsettled, full of expectation.

Something has changed. Something is going to happen.

Releasing secrets, even just a little, even when perhaps she should not have done, has brought her a sense of ease. She hopes that Ada feels the same. A trouble shared is a trouble halved. Except Ada has one half, Kalala another, and Lizzie is left with pieces that don't quite match. To seal their reconciliation, Lizzie asks Ada if she will come with her to Nightbell Gully. After all, it was always Albert's favourite place on the island.

'Ma says she'll make us a picnic.'

But Ada looks startled.

'No, no . . . I . . . ' Her voice trails off. Evasion is one thing, but Ada has never been good at an outright lie. She bites her lip before whispering the truth. 'I don't want to. It makes me think too much of him. Go on your own, if you like. Take Queenie and Billy.'

Before Lizzie can say anything else, Billy is at her elbow with the food.

'Gus has a sore throat, and Ma wants to keep her home. Pa's asleep. Could he be ill?'

Pa was never ill. He never slept during the day.

'Maybe,' says Lizzie.

'I'll stay and help Ma with Joey,' says Ada. 'We don't want him getting ill. What about the kanakas?'

'I'll ask Kalala,' says Queenie, running off.

'You'll have to ask the others too,' Billy shouts after her. He gives Lizzie a sidelong look. 'Won't she?'

'Of course,' she agrees defiantly.

Solomona needs time to prepare that evening's sermon, but

the rest set off with the dogs in a noisy gang, laughing and pushing at each other and chucking things, sending huge flocks of kakariki squawking up to the treetops, in flashes of green and red. Ki-ki-ki-ki-ki-ki-ki.

'Where shall we go?' Lizzie calls to Billy, who is swaggering ahead and a long way up the track already, thrashing joyfully and heedlessly at the undergrowth, turning occasionally to see if the others are admiring his progress. Pineki and Luka play along. Before long Iakopo and Vilipate break into song, and soon all four are clapping and swaying and whooping behind Billy. Only Kalala hangs back with the girls.

A sudden shout from up ahead: the others have surprised a solitary goat. Blood up, they crash after it through the bush, soon out of sight, eventually out of hearing.

'They'll be back when they remember we've got the food,' says Queenie, patting her pack.

'Hope they catch the goat,' says Lizzie. 'And hope it's a milker. We need more milk.' Though how will Queenie tame a new nanny without Albert's gentle guidance?

'Lake or gully?' Queenie asks Kalala. 'You choose.'

Lizzie interrupts.

'He knows the lake, remember? And we've not been to Nightbell Gully for months. Come on.'

Like most places on the island, getting there requires some exertion – a sharp climb up, over Rough Haw, followed by an equally steep and rocky clamber down past a series of quietly trickling waterfalls. Kalala is sure-footed and strong. Lizzie never imagined he'd struggle here. Yet he stops repeatedly, twitching and shivering where he stands.

'What's the matter?' she asks. His smooth brown arm is stuck with tiny bumps like a plucked chicken. 'Do you want to go back?'

He closes his eyes briefly, and shakes his head.

'Keep going,' he says.

Queenie, slowed by her pack, scrambles down towards them. 'What's the matter?'

'Nothing,' says Lizzie quickly. 'You go on. We won't be long. Here . . .'

She guides Queenie's bare toes towards a foothold in the rock, and helps her jump down so she can overtake them. When Lizzie turns back to offer a hand to Kalala, she finds his palm is clammy, his eyes unsteady.

'What is this place?' he asks, his voice thick with uncertainty.

Lizzie answers lightly. 'A valley we found when we came to this side of the island. A special place.'

She begins to descend, but he does not follow.

'Why do you come here? Why special?'

Lizzie looks down into the lush vegetation.

'It's pretty. Wait till you see the flowers and waterfalls. It's different from everywhere else. Beautiful.'

Magical is the word she wants to use, but stumbles over. Brought here by instinct, perhaps, by their talk the night before, of ghosts and dreams and spirits, she's now uncertain.

'You are permitted to come?' he asks.

'Yes, of course. Ma knows this is one of our favourite places. And Pa likes it too.'

But that is not what he meant. His body is disturbed by a shudder, which he shakes away, before making another determined effort to continue. His face a mask, he pushes past her towards a flapping wall of hairless ferns, layer upon layer of hanging leathery tongues, taunters all, and flinches as he scrapes past them, as if he can hear them whisper.

The floor of the gully opens into a dell, fragrant with fleshy white lilies. Queenie is already on the far side, heading for their favourite rock, flat and mossy and big enough to spread a picnic on. Even the birdsong seems more delicate here. But Kalala is frozen on the penultimate ledge, struggling to breathe. He can no longer force himself onwards.

'Are you coming?' Lizzie turns, bewildered, and he questions her so fiercely she almost cries out her answer.

'Tell me, Lizzie. What has happened here?'

'Nothing. Nothing that I know of. Why? What is it?'

'You're sure?'

'I don't know. Tell me what . . . '

He bends, hands braced on thighs. From time to time he flinches. Lizzie is afraid to come too close. And then his misery passes and he raises his head, and stares at her.

'This place,' he says urgently. 'We should not be here.'

She looks around for some kind of sign or mark, and sees nothing.

'How do you know?'

He puts a finger to his lips to hush her. His breathing is still laboured.

'Your sister—'

'She's reading. Look. Tell me quietly, tell me quickly, what's wrong? What is it, Kalala?'

'You feel nothing here? Nothing at all?'

'No. No. Of course not. I never have. Nothing.' She feels dizzy and sick, but that's with worry, fear and guilt. This place has always been a retreat for her, for all the children. Seductive

and mysterious in its seclusion, but hardly threatening. Except
for the pig bones. She has not told Kalala about those bones,
stained green, half buried when she and Ada found them. Why
would she?

'Shall we go back?' she asks. 'Do you want to find the others?
I'll call Queenie. We can invent some excuse. We don't have to
stay here. Let's go.'

'No. Stop. Wait. I feel I know this.'

'Know what?'

His behaviour frightens her. Of all the newcomers, Kalala has
always seemed the steadiest. Self-possessed, calm and wise. Like
the Rock they call his island. But now he seems to shift uncertainly from mood to mood. Lizzie wants to go home, right away,
before his terrors return.

'Too much like my dreams,' he says, but he is slipping away
from her again already. 'Nightmares – the one I could not speak
of last night. I feel it returning.'

Before she can help him, his knees give way, and he falls back
against a tangled mass of tree roots. His eyes flicker open and
shut, and he flinches, once, twice, three times.

'*Nakai . . . nakai . . . fakamolemole . . .* ' Kalala pleads,
shielding his face as if from attack, and then cringing again as if
he is being beaten. He doesn't seem to see her anymore.

'What is it?' she asks, desperate to understand. 'What can you
see? What can I do?'

'Stop,' he begs. 'Let me go.'

He suddenly grabs her wrist, encircling bone and skin so tightly
that it stings. She can't shake herself free.

'Let go of me, Kalala. Stop!' She pulls herself free. 'Wake up,
for God's sake. There's nobody here but me.'

'Let us out!' he cries. 'Stop!'

Lizzie shakes him hard, a hand on each shoulder; his head jolts on his neck.

'Listen to me, Kalala. Please. There's nothing here. Nobody. You're safe.'

His eyes snap open. First he looks dazed, and then alarmed.

'You're hurt?' he asks. 'Show me your arm.'

She nurses her wrist, rubbing away the redness.

'It's nothing.'

'What happened?' he says hoarsely. 'I can't remember. Lizzie! Tell me! What have I done?'

He knows something, but not enough. Lizzie is reluctant to say anything which might return him to the incomprehensible, fugitive place from which he's just escaped.

'Nothing. Everything's fine now. Nobody's here.'

Kalala shudders. Something is coming back to him.

'But I know I felt . . . I heard. All in my head? All those voices?'

'What did they say? What did they tell you?'

But everything is sliding away from him. He's left wordless, lost, marked only by protean sensations he can't retrieve, and now would hardly wish to. His guts feel twisted, he tries to explain, his tongue swollen. He thinks of unseen bodies emptying of breath.

'I can't tell you. I don't know.'

'I can't see anything, Kalala. Let's stop,' she says, terror rising. 'It's getting worse, isn't it, this . . . this thing? Do you feel it getting stronger? I mean the further we go? Oh, let's go back. Let's not stay here.'

'Yes. Yes it is,' he says, squatting on his haunches. 'I'm sorry.

I cannot . . . ' And then it overwhelms him. A few more words of protest die away into a low, guttural moan, a face-buried keening.

'Shhhh . . . shhhhh.' Lizzie is struggling with tears herself, and the intolerable but unanswerable urge to reach out and touch Kalala, to offer him physical comfort. 'We can go. I'll get Queenie.' Except she can't leave him like this. She waits, her own skin icily shrinking, until whatever ungraspable vision grips him begins to recede. At last Kalala shudders and knuckles his eyes, and looks at her with relief and recognition. He seems to have shut out his enemies.

'Last night . . . we spoke of the aitu on this island,' he whispers.

'Yes.' Lizzie drops her voice too, holds him with her gaze.

'They are here, I'm sure. My head, oh, my head. Can you see how this feeling grows again? It's because the aitu are unhappy. They hope to possess me.'

'Can they? Can you stop them?' Lizzie knows her panic is showing.

'I don't know. I don't know what they want of me. I don't know even if I believe in them. Warning or punishment? The Devil's work or God Almighty's? I can't tell. I don't know who – if anybody – hears my prayers. But all the time I find myself thinking of the Stolen Ones.'

His head flops, as if too huge to bear upright.

'Kalala. I should have told you before.' She talks quickly, without looking at him. 'There *is* something here. There was. Long ago. We found bones. Scattered by the last earthquake, we thought. Pig's bones, Pa said. There were settlers here before us, years ago. They must have kept pigs, he said.'

'Pigs, you say?'

'Yes. We buried them. We didn't want to frighten Queenie and Billy. I think I can remember where. Shall we look for them? Perhaps—'

'No!' He shouts, shaking again, uncontrollably, his hunched form wracked by wave after trembling wave, which he can no more stop than he can prevent the beads of sweat from breaking through his skin.

'I'll talk to Pa,' says Lizzie quickly, consolingly. 'Ask him again about the bones. Perhaps he knows more than he'd tell me then.'

He nods. She waits, shakily. And once more the affliction seems to pass, like a fever breaking.

'They are leaving me,' he says, standing and shaking out his limbs, wiping his face on his shirt. 'Come. I have had my warning, I believe, and now perhaps will have some peace. But I think they will return.'

'To me too?' Lizzie asks, drawing back.

'No. I believe . . . ' He shakes his head. 'No, I wonder . . . I think . . . I feel your aitu must be your own.'

'Albert?'

He nods, with a disarming muddle of conviction and pity.

'But I told you. Albert's gone. He's not on this island anymore. You know what Ada said—'

He fills the space she leaves.

'I think she's wrong.'

'No!' Too loud. Lizzie stares at Kalala. Unbearable that Ada could be mistaken. But, if Lizzie is honest with herself, the story became less plausible the moment she began to tell it to Kalala in the moonlight, and registered the doubt in his face. She tries again, slowly and quietly.

'Ada insists he has escaped.'

'Of course. She wants her brother living. She has to believe it. But you know it's impossible. One of us would have seen him.'

'Even in all that excitement and confusion?'

Kalala is blunt.

'Yes.'

'He could not have stowed away after we left the beach? When the rest of us came up to the flats?' Her pleading voice betrays her desperation.

'I went back myself. I helped to push the longboat off. There was nobody hiding there. I'm certain.'

There is something miraculous in the sheer certainty of Kalala's calm, firm disavowal. Lightheaded, Lizzie tries to mimic his steadiness while she absorbs this new shock. She thrusts her hands deep into the pockets of her pinafore, letting her fingers fidget for a few moments with their contents, turning over a length of vine-twine, a scrunched-up handkerchief, a candlenut, hardly able to let herself follow the direction of his thoughts. Then she tightens her fists. She is still allowing herself hope.

'So Albert is still here, you think? Still somewhere on this island.'

He nods. Kindly, gently, as if he is cradling her with his eyes. So gently that it means she can't avoid taking the next step.

'But . . . he's dead, isn't he?'

'I believe he is.'

A tingling wave crawls over Lizzie's scalp. She squats, quickly, shakily, before her legs can let her down, and stares furiously at the ferns and moss and rocks around her feet – each fine hair and particle of soil seems curiously distinct. She roots herself as deeply as she can. Her mind feels sticky, slow as treacle. Yet only moments pass before her understanding of what must be done slides into certainty.

'Dead,' she says. Assuring herself. 'Then we gave up too easily before.' Her body its own lever, she thrusts herself back up to standing. 'When we searched for him. We will have to start again.' Then she looks directly at Kalala. 'Will you help me? He must be somewhere. Or there must be some sign of what has happened.'

'We searched the whole island before.'

'We were all so upset. Bewildered. Too hasty. I want to look again.'

'Because you feel his presence?' asks Kalala, inspecting her face earnestly, as though it might tell him something her lips won't admit, or perhaps to test the seriousness of her intent. She senses he admires her determination and that thought strengthens her. 'But not here . . . not in this place?' he continues.

'No, no. Not here. Not anywhere in particular. I wish I did. I wish I could.'

At that moment Queenie calls impatiently. She's waited long enough.

'Come back here!' Lizzie calls down to her, hoping her voice will stay firm and clear. 'We need to go back!' Her arms drop back to her sides and she assesses Kalala in turn. 'I'll wait for her. You go and find the others and tell them we will meet them at Crater Lake.'

'Yes. Yes, I will. But first tell me . . . is there anywhere on the island that you feel your brother's presence? Anywhere it is strong? Like this place for me.'

Frustrated, Lizzie tries to think, but all she can do is shake her head.

'No. Nowhere I've been since he vanished. During the day, I feel nothing. The opposite. When I think of him I feel dead and dry and cold inside.'

'But at night?'

A thousand pinpricks fall on Lizzie's neck.

'You know . . . I dream.'

Kalala won't say it directly, but she understands what he is asking of her. Rather than escape her dreams, she must confront them. Instead of avoiding sleep, she must perhaps embrace it.

'But nothing is clear . . . I can't remember. In the morning.'

Don't make me remember, she wants to say. Don't make me sleep.

'If you could know what has happened to him – if we can somehow discover – perhaps he will leave you in peace.'

'Perhaps. Do you believe that? Can it be right to believe such a thing?'

Kalala seems equally confused.

'I don't know. My mother believes it, though she keeps it quiet. Mr Reverend has faith only in the Holy Spirit. He will hear no talk of ghosts and spirits.'

'You really think he is telling me to look for him?'

He shrugs, but hardly carelessly.

'You think I'm telling myself.'

'Whoever . . . whatever . . . I'll help you.'

So Lizzie puts out her hand, as she has seen her father do, making an agreement. And she remembers taking hold of Kalala's arm, in the dark, on the cliff, the night before, and the way he slid away from her, as if perhaps his Reverend has warned him away from girls as well as ghosts.

'We'll shake on it,' she says firmly. 'Yes? I'll ask my father about the bones. I'll *make* him tell me what he knows about this place. And we will both keep looking for Albert. No giving up.'

From out of nowhere, noise envelops them. Spy and Sal barking, all the boys yelping as they career into the gully. They have lost their goat. And Queenie is climbing back up to them, grumpily complaining.

'What have you two been *doing* all this time?' she calls.

Lizzie feels caught out, guilty of anything they care to suspect.

'Say nothing,' pleads Kalala.

30

LIZZIE PASSES THE VEGETABLE GARDEN, AND THE goats. The trees in the new banana grove already rise above her head and at their base sprout new pups which will soon be ready to split and plant again. It reminds her how much time has passed since Albert vanished. Four months now, nearly five. The *Esperanza* could return any day now. And then what? As she walks across the stretch of land burned earlier, old ash billows round her ankles. At the top, new fires are dying down.

Kalala looks round first. At his turning a ripple goes round the others, and a temptation to tease that's quickly squashed. Billy frowns at his sister's invasion, and Pa calls to her.

'Is something wrong? Someone hurt?' He gestures to the others – keep gathering up the tools, no need to stop and gawp – and hurries over. 'Is it the baby? Is it Mrs P?'

'No, no,' calls Lizzie. 'Nothing like that. I just wanted to see the work.'

'You had me worried,' he said.

'Sorry,' she says. Sorry that her appearance has become a bad tiding. 'Can I help?'

'It's heavy work here.'

Lizzie thinks of all the heavy work she's done since they first landed on the island. Building the houses, moving the grass, carrying the camp oven up the cliffs with Ada's help. Won't there be more heavy work for her when the Islanders depart and the Peacock family is all alone again?

'We're packing up now,' adds Pa. He doesn't want her here.

'I see,' she says. She removes a thorny twig caught in his beard, and hands it to him. He tosses it away. His eyes seem to smile. It's never easy to tell what his mouth is doing.

'So, Lizzie. What do you reckon to this? What do you see when you look now?' he asks, nodding towards the cleared land. 'Tell me what you see.'

She stares at torn and blackened stumps and dusty ash, the pits and hollows in the grey powdered soil where tree roots have already been routed. There's a right answer and a wrong answer, she's sure.

'Earth . . . ?' she says, checking his face.

His eyes glitter like the sea behind him as he looks with pride at the devastation all around.

'Our land. Peacock land. Ours for ever now. We're getting closer to taming it all the time. I'll tell you what I see: orchards, orange groves, growing from here to there. Acres of grass. Hundreds of sheep. And what would you say to a little wooden house one day, painted white perhaps, with a veranda and glass windows? What would you say to that, my little Lizzie?'

Lizzie rarely looks towards the future now, the habit her father taught her. It can't sustain her. Her imagination always trips on Albert.

'Do you know what I've decided?' Mr Peacock announces, not noticing her silence. 'We need a new name. I like the sound of Peacock Island. I want there to be no mistake who owns this land. Not ever. What do you say?'

'Can you do that?' Lizzie asks. 'Call a whole island whatever you like? Won't it spoil the maps?'

'It'll *change* the maps,' says Mr Peacock, exhaling satisfaction at the prospect. 'We've earned that right. Anyway, Monday Island's only what everyone calls this place. It's got some Frenchy name on the maps. Don't ask me to remember it. And other names too at other times.'

Kalala, Solomona and the rest are loading their broad shoulders with the crooks of trunk and branch they will take down to season in the storehut: ship's knees. Monday Island's inexhaustible currency. Keels and deckbeams strengthened by wood they've cut will travel the world in years to come, so Mr Peacock often boasts. He shouts a last command.

'On you go. That's the way, Billy. We'll follow down soon.'

Then Lizzie and Pa are alone together, as they've not been for months. She feels affectionate hands on her shoulder, as if they'd direct her gaze, and his breath on her neck, and the force of his attention, and she basks in it all, just as she once used to. Her father's beard is wild again, long enough to tickle Lizzie. She twists and smiles up at him and never wants to move again. He's like a living mountain, a harbour at her back. Lizzie leans against him, pushing away all the uncertainties Ada has planted in her heart, and her loving comes back to life. Ada and Albert never understood him. Content with so little, they saw his strengths as weaknesses. Lizzie knows better. It's hard work to build something that can endure, to make a success of life. You can't give up.

Where would they all be now if their father had let those early setbacks triumph?

'You've done so much these last few months,' she says. 'I hardly know the place.'

'We'll tame this island yet,' he says again. 'We'll have to control the goats, of course, can't have the beasts wrecking my orchard . . . we need to get some of that cat's claw up here . . . maybe some cats too, for the rats, in case they follow us here . . . and in another few years, I'm thinking we'll have to clear a driving road, so we can water the sheep at the lake. Three hundred acres we could have on this side, I reckon. Oh, to think of all the time we wasted at Clapperton Bay.'

'We didn't know,' says Lizzie. 'How long will it be, Pa, before we get the sheep?'

'I'll fetch them from Auckland when we're good and ready. When we've cleared enough ground, and the grass is growing, and we've enough to trade, and can smoke another ship to the bay. We'll need more grass seed too. Finer. Water tanks. What else?'

'Can I come with you to Auckland?'

She turns to face him, and finally he looks at her. He stares at her for a moment, long enough to see her properly, and shakes his head. And there. Gone again, it seems. Whatever it was that held him. Was she too young, too old, too female or simply useless to him now? Would he have taken Albert? Will he take Billy?

'I'd like to, spadge. You know I would.' He holds her hard against him, and surely there's a catch as he inhales. 'But your ma will need you all the more when I'm gone.'

He closes the conversation with one last sweeping look at the day's work, picks up his tools, and starts walking home. He's slipped her mooring, and soon she's running after him, feeling a fool, feeling she has wasted an opportunity.

'Pa, Pa . . . wait for me.' She needs to speak up quickly. She needs more time. 'Will you show me how far you'll clear this season? Can we walk that way?'

'What? Through the burning? You'll scorch your soles.'

But he slows his stride, enough to let her catch him up. She thinks of Kalala and her promise, and takes his arm.

'We could walk through the upper terrace?' she offers.

'We'll be late for dinner.'

He starts to walk faster again, and, panicking, her thoughts spill out so fast she can't even make a question of them.

'Pa, the bones.'

He stops.

'What bones?' He speaks so slowly, with so much hidden threat that Lizzie is silenced. Her arm slides from his.

'I said, what bones?' he repeats, fiercely.

'You know, Pa. The ones in the Nightbell Gully. The pig bones we found and buried. Ages ago. You said . . . you said . . . '

'I said you were not to think of them again. Have you touched them? What have you done, Lizzie?'

'No. Nothing. Why shouldn't I think of them?'

'Too frightening for little girls.'

'Pig bones! *Little* girls, maybe.'

He looks at her sharply, and walks on, speaking over his shoulder.

'Yes, I can see you're not a little girl. Nor Ada. That's all too clear. And that's why I'll caution you now. Keep away from those kanakas, my girl. I'll not say it again. I hope I won't have to. Keep Queenie away too. She's growing up faster than you know.'

It's going wrong. The conversation is swerving from her grasp. She runs after him, calls out her question.

'But they're not pig bones, are they?'

'No. No. They're not. You're right.' He stops, and sighs, and rubs his face wearily. 'Kanaka bones, I believe. From long ago. Men who died before you were born.'

'Here? There were Islanders here before?'

'There were.'

'From the Rock?'

'Perhaps. And other islands too. Robson told me – cautioned me, I suppose. When I pushed him that is. Every Eden has its snake. They had some visitors they didn't welcome. It's why they left. But those kanakas weren't here by choice – theirs or his. Blackbirded, they were.'

He can see she has no idea what he means.

'Forget I told you. Not pretty. Better not to know—'

'No, I want to.'

He can't keep her innocent. He's just said she's not a little girl.

'It was a long time ago, Lizzie. Nothing to do with us. No need to think about it now.'

He starts walking again, and she's forced to follow, but she won't give up.

'Not so very long ago,' she protests. 'Tell me what happened. Who were these kanakas? Why did they come here? To work for Robson? And what do you mean . . . blackbirded?'

'You don't know of blackbirding? No. Why should you? You're such a sharp one, I thought perhaps . . . well, it's a nasty business.'

Such reluctance to come clean. As if he can still protect her from the truth.

'Please tell me Pa. Why "birding"?'

Mr Peacock thought for a moment.

'Because you round 'em up and catch 'em, I suppose.'

Mutton-birds, thinks Lizzie. Fat, glossy mutton-birds. You don't even need to trap them. You can take 'em as you please, just pluck 'em from their messy nests and eat them up.

'Or it's the colour. Blackbirds . . . natives . . . But it's trickery, plain and simple. The blackbirders lure the men with the promise of trade, or Bibles, or contracts they don't or can't ever understand.'

'The Stolen Ones,' she says, echoing Kalala, understanding at last. She takes her father's arm again, for comfort, and his rough skin rasps comfortably against hers.

'Yes, stolen's about right. I've heard of slaver captains dressed as priests. I've heard of crew with guns and harpoons. Outright violence. Either way it's an evil business. It's true laws have changed since then. Boats patrol now. Even kanakas get wiser, perhaps, but how can you blame them for falling for the recruiters' tricks? How do they know what greets them on the other side? Too little's changed, I'd say, and the Lord knows slavery happens still, all over, or near enough. Men will lie and men will drink and men will always scheme and cheat. And be cheated. It's too easy, you see, when all the young men on all the islands want to get on ships and get away. The world needs workers. If it's not sandalwood, it's guano, if it's not cotton, it's sugar. Or silver to be mined. They call it the Labour Trade now, not slavery, but what's the difference? Queensland's the new Louisiana, they say.'

A new thought sickens Lizzie.

'But, Pa, our workers weren't blackbirded? Pa, Pa . . . Solomona and Kalala and the others . . . Nobody stole them?'

'Lord, no.' He squeezes her hand again, and pulls her close, as if he'd like to hide the horror. 'Our boys came here with willing hearts, and they'll go home wealthy. Compared with their brothers at least. Fair exchange. No robbery.'

Of course. Of course. She only needs to ask Kalala.

'And are there other bones, Pa? Have you found more?'

'Full of questions today, aren't you?'

He doesn't want to answer them. Not so long ago he used to praise her for her doggedness. His little terrier, he called her, proudly.

'Bones you've not told us about,' she persists. 'On other parts of the island?'

His face has hardened, shutting her out again. He looks at her suspiciously, mutters about bad dreams. Too late for that. He's hiding something.

'Pa? Where exactly? Tell me where you found them.'

'You'll say nothing to Queenie or Ada? Our secret?'

That was better.

'Yes. Yes, of course.'

He settles his tools more comfortably on his shoulder, and strides on, looking straight ahead.

'Not so long after we landed . . . '

Lizzie nods. A rare, confiding kind of mood has come upon her father, from out of nowhere. It seems he wants to tell her. He wants to tell someone.

'I was digging, soon after we first arrived. Clearing the taro beds. I'd somehow put aside the tale – Robson's story, that is. Well, I wanted to forget it. It was over. Finished. Nothing to be done. And there's been the volcano since, a few cyclones too, I'm sure. I thought everything would be covered up by now. But as I was digging I did hit bones. Pigs' ribs, I thought at first, no, really I did. I took the first skull for a turtle shell. But when I found others, other kinds of bones, well, that's when I remembered. Couldn't forget. And after that I looked out for them, and I cleared and buried decently all I could. Couldn't have you little ones digging up kanaka bones.'

A kind of kindness, then, this secret. Nausea begins to take possession of Lizzie. She hangs on harder to her father.

'And I thought you'd never need to know,' continued Pa, half defensive, half regretful. 'And then we found the ones in Nightbell Gully. Just a few, mind. One man's, perhaps. Or two. But how could I tell you the truth? How could I tell you children what they really were?'

How will she tell Kalala?

'But you knew before we left,' she said, 'and still we came?'

'It happened so long ago. I did not see how it could harm us now.'

'Ma knew too?'

'Of course not. Why bother her with old tales? You know what I've always said. No looking back. But oh, I tell you, I was a happy man when we moved this side of Monday Island. Sometimes I think that bay was cursed.'

'Monday Island,' she repeats, sickened. 'You mean Blackbird Island.' This place is no more named after a bird than she herself is. Perhaps it will never feel like home again. She thinks of her father, telling no one, secretly removing the bones . . . those poor stolen men's bones . . . and pities him for bearing, all alone and for so long, the burden of that dreadful knowledge. 'Tell me more, Pa. Tell me everything you know.'

LONG BEFORE

No single soul could ever tell this story – not then, not now – but that day, at last, Mr Peacock told his daughter all he could. A piecemeal tale, grown from seeds sown in bar-rooms, on board ships, above deck and below, passed from tongue to tongue. Reports and rumours spread by winds and currents. What he'd heard, and what he'd found, and what he'd come to realise. And here's the rest.

*

Twenty years earlier, from the deck of a fine, fast barque, three-masted, a single eye sized up the atoll that stood alone. Over his vacant socket, this slaver's Spanish captain rarely wore a patch. An oculist in Barcelona once tried to trade him a glass eye, but he refused. What did he want with a sightless bauble, when the hole left in his face made others see so quick and clear? Low-lidded emptiness, glimpsed off guard – it could make a strong man blench, and spook a kanaka in seconds. It bought time. It bolstered power. No doubt it would help him here, where he intended to fill the spaces left by a particularly troublesome pack of 'colonists': Islanders who'd died before they could be sold.

From the veranda of the Mission House, high on the coral

cliff, a spyglass watched the ship. As one-eyed in his way as that Spanish captain, as guileless as the other man was cunning, this missionary's vision had always been too partial and too innocent. Mr Reverend, they called him there. He was wary that morning. Not six weeks earlier another ship had kidnapped forty men. Snared by empty promises of fish hooks, paddling out with expectation and high hopes, they found no trade, no choice. They were quickly trapped. A few struggled to escape, were hacked and slashed, and ribbons of watery blood marked briefly their downward drift to the ocean floor.

Lamentation followed, long and loud. Rachel weeping for her children, refusing to be comforted. Meetings were held. The island could not lose more souls to slavers. There could be no more trading in this way. A new law: only one vaka from any settlement could go beyond the reef to greet an unknown ship, and it would carry always letters of warning.

So when this second Spanish ship appeared, the Reverend wrote to ask where she was bound and what she wanted here, and sent his letter with two teachers by canoe, watching them carefully through his telescope as they paddled out. The men went willingly on board the *Rosa y Carmen*; their vaka was hoisted after them. When he looked again, his dark and shaking circle framed a new boat being lowered.

Down to the jetty to meet the seaman in it, a loathsome, bloated sort of man, unshaven and unwashed, besotted and debauched. His English was poor, his mime most feeble, and he could not or would not understand their questions about the missing men. The missionary sent him back as charged with medicine for his captain; a Christian act, no man could refuse. The bloody flux killed quickly. He was glad to see him go.

But the missing failed to return.

Blood up, neck hung with shark's teeth white as pearls, their chief pursued them with a fleet of thirty men. Nine of their canoes flanked the returning jolly boat, yet as they drew near the barque, it pulled away and the air exploded into bullets, spray and splintered, shattered wood. These vaka sank. And down came the Spanish crew, to seize the swimmers from the sea.

*

The watching missionary set down his glass and wept, inconsolable. Nothing left but to live with guilt, and pray to be forgiven for trusting too much. What a poor shepherd he had proved to his flock. He cursed the mania for emigration, and he blamed himself. How high the price of light. His own presence had made a beacon of this island. And all he could promise was safety in heaven, not on earth.

*

Over the water, unseen, the men were bound and kicked under bolted hatches into a placeless place, a floating prison. Pushed into air unbreathable, foul enough to taste, the Islanders gasped and fought for breath. Flesh against bare flesh, shoving muscles tight with terror, jostling and recoiling from unseen strangers, limbs and backs, heads and hair, grass and barkcloth, and above all, the rank stench of the hold. Worse than bilge water. This was where the flux had truly taken hold, and it was spreading fast.

Voices from other islands. Voices of sorrow, pain, despair. Much later, a musket firing. The Rock fellows gripped each other harder still at the sight of sudden lines of light. Armed with lanterns, and also snarling, choking, pitiless disgust, sailors descended to inspect the sick. Prodding for life with whip ends and musket butts, they hunted down useless ballast and contagion. Sought flickering lids and glassy eyes. Fullest pails withdrawn, washed out – slime and pus and mucus dispersed to particles in salty underwaves – too quickly refilled. Corpses hauled up. Overboard they splashed, slowly tumbling, sinking, sinking, sinking, hair floating behind, descending ever darker, deeper. The vessel held her course regardless.

Some on board had only just begun to curl round the first dull gripe. Others were doubled up with cramps already, minds and bodies panic-surged, flushing from time to time with the hot-cold sweat which foretold each outpouring. Others, too weak to move, lay matted in foulness, slime-thighed and bloody-buttocked. The Rock fellows cried for mercy and release, and the barque roiled and pitched and heaved through an unseen ocean.

At last they felt their course shifting. The captain would never return his useless cargo to Easter Island, Rakahanga, Pukapuka, Fakaofo. But he did know a lonely spot where he could strengthen the survivors for some weeks or months, and discard the sick. A thriving little shore station, in the middle of nowhere, where it would be easy to take control and never pay for provisions. Then on to Peru, as planned.

The surf was high when the *Rosa y Carmen* approached Clapperton Bay. The settlers came running: three families, stirred first in hope and then in blood. One father's name was Robson. Bare toes mined the sand in terror. The youngsters quaked.

Of fifty emaciated bodies tipped into the first launch, only three could stand alone. Three others died before they reached the shore. The settlers watched the captain jump from the landing vessel with a pistol in each hand and a bowie knife in his belt, and shrank from his officers' bayonets. The sailors dragged men and women from the boat like sacks of rotten produce, revolted by their ruined cargo. Onto the beach and into the foaming tide, they hurled bodies that were barely breathing. Many did not even know they were dying before they were washed away and drowned. Those with power still to crawl were defeated by their fight with the breakers' pull. Corpses soon scattered the sand.

For weeks *Rosa y Carmen* lay at anchor in the bay, no colours at her mast, a strip of tarred canvas concealing her name. Some sailors were left on board to scrub out the foul hold, and float a raft of water barrels to shore for filling. Others set out to seize the settlers' stocks, while women and children cowered in their huts, and men stood helpless, at bladepoint. The youngest, darkest, and least-valued sailors were ordered to bury the bodies on the beach. Before nightfall, eighty or more lay under grey grit, in the shallowest of graves, a mass of strangers from many far-off islands, who had died deformed with pain, stick-thin, tortured with grief. In came the tide, and out again. Bodies were soon unburied, left to tumble in sea and sun.

31

HER TALE ALMOST DONE, LIZZIE TURNS TO LOOK at me directly. We have been walking together on the beach below the bluff, keeping to the cliff, keeping out of sight. Up and down, we pace and talk, scuffing over our own prints, trying to see backwards as best we can, while the cloud hangs so low it cloaks the flats.

'Maybe that's why . . . in the Gully . . . the bones.' Her voice unsteadies. 'Could your father be here? Could he have died here, here on this island?'

Is this enough, I wonder? Dreams and words, instead of bones and bodies. Can these alone convince me? I lack my own eye's witness. I am faint-hearted. Throttled by fresh doubt, my reply chokes in my throat. No. No, no, no. If we know he is dead, we can no longer hope for his return.

'He has found you again,' Lizzie says. 'Can't you see? He means you to know his story.'

Perhaps. And perhaps all stories are like this. Some parts can be told. And something else you must make out on your own.

We know a beginning now. The end, if there is an end, I have to picture for myself. My tears flow freely as we talk, and Lizzie's too, yet even this partial understanding brings some easing to my buried sorrow. There seems enough of substance in this veiled tale to lay hold of and follow with our thinking. A truth worth netting, however hard to spear.

'Perhaps the fellows from my island were stronger than the rest of the Stolen Ones,' I say.

'And so they would have been set to work the sooner here,' says Lizzie. 'The captain stole everything from the settlers, Pa told me. They needed labour to shift stores, you see, load boats, cut cane, dig taro, fetch water, wood. All that. And then the settlers' families began to sicken, and their children began to die.'

Small bodies die most quickly, when sickness comes with ships.

'Perhaps the crew grew careless with their captives,' I say. 'How could they watch them all?'

'The cliffs at Clapperton Bay rise so high. The men so weakened. Escape must have been unimaginable to their captors,' Lizzie says. 'And so many dead and dying . . . how could they have kept count of numbers? The slavers sickening too perhaps?'

'We are quick and agile climbers. We are used to cliffs and chasms,' I tell her. 'Rocks hold no fears for us.'

Lizzie smiles. 'And I think your father was like you. Clever. Watchful. A resourceful man to have sons like you and Solomona. He must have been. He would surely have found a time to creep away, perhaps with a friend.'

She is quick with her imaginings. She wants this story to stand for mine. How can I do anything but chase the same desires?

'Yes, not alone,' I say. 'I must hope, if my father indeed died here, he did not die alone. And at night,' I ask Lizzie, 'when the moon is brightest . . . before sunrise, could they have reached the top? Even so weak?'

'Oh yes,' Lizzie assures me. 'Well before sunrise. And then waited in the forest till it was light enough to see and make their way unwatched across the island, as far away as they could get to. Remember, they knew nothing of what lay beyond, on the other side. And in the gully, they'd know they would be safe. Nobody would ever find them there, so hidden away and secret, so peaceful.'

I remember our earliest days here, searching with Pineki, searching for Albert, and I see the land again through my father's imagined eyes, searching for a hiding place, somewhere to stow away until the man-stealers quit the island.

'So he escaped,' I say, ever more convinced by this clear vision, and its familiar echoes. 'And lived on fern root, and berries, for some days and nights.'

Blessed are they that have not seen, and yet have believed.

'Weeks?' Lizzie wants to give me hope, but I shake my head. I know how the end comes, and how fast. Sickness not hunger. Needles and then knives turning and twisting your stomach. Your guts stretch and spasm and cold sweat seeps as you burn within. Who to pray to for suffering's relief? Death took these Stolen Ones in the gully, and there they lay, till Lizzie found their pieces.

Never closer, never more distant feels my father. I have no proof. I have seen no bones. And what could they tell me if I had? I must wonder, because it is my way. And because this feels something like an ending. One I want to trust, though I cannot see where it might take me yet. We turn again, our shadows lengthening, and walk beneath the cliffs the other way.

'What then?' I say.

'At last, it seems, a whaler passed the island and saw the state of things,' Lizzie tells me. 'Her master grew suspicious when he spied the nameless Spanish vessel at anchor off Monday Island and saw how fast and armed she was. This new ship scared the slaver captain off, Pa thinks. We know the whaler returned to rescue the settlers who'd survived. And by then the captured Islanders, those who lived, now strengthened by their stay, these men had been shipped again. For Peru. Weeks later they were auctioned on the dockside at Callao.'

*

My prayers that night are the whirling waters left by a rising paddle. They circle and spin, back to my father. If he is here, if his bones are here, it is here that we must honour his life. I pray for my father's soul, and for the souls of all the Stolen Ones, wherever they are, and hear in my heart again my island's weeping. The left-behinds' long cry of mourning rises to heaven; this agony swells in the wake of every departure of our men and boys for other islands. Forced or willing, partings like deaths. Some say only ghosts can return. Certainly all are changed by leaving. Am I not changed myself? And mothers and grandmothers tear their hair, inconsolable, and stand on the coral cliffs, longing to leap. Some, like poor Vika's mother, obey that longing.

Mutterings in my memory lie beneath this keening; the voice of Mr Reverend, mouthing numbers, counting up columns, top to bottom, checking and rechecking, taking ten and carrying over, totting up tithes and contributions and congregations, and sighing at his falling figures, composing sermons on the habits of industry.

*

At lesson times, I have begun to notice, Mrs Peacock casts glances at us. Lizzie and I take care not to bend too closely together over our pages, especially when Queenie is elsewhere. I wonder if Mr Peacock has ordered his wife to keep watch.

We talk again of Albert. We must look everywhere, even the places searched before, she tells me.

'I understand,' I say, and shift myself apart from her, and the heat that rises beneath her skin. 'One by one, this is the way. We will look one person by one person, one section by one section.'

'And Solomona?' she asks me. 'What will you tell him? About the bones.'

Words so gentle. She is careful with me, understanding too well how the same blood may flow in different patterns through different bodies.

'Nothing,' I reply. 'Not yet. Nor the others. All this is too newly swallowed. I need time to think more deeply, and to listen, and decide what's best for us.'

Our search is to be a secret which I must keep, as she keeps mine. For I find I trust her as I once trusted Sidney.

32

KNOWING ABOUT ALL THE BONES ON THE ISLAND makes a difference. It shouldn't, Lizzie tries to persuade herself, for – really – nothing has changed. But somehow it has. It's not that she feels unsafe. More that something has shifted, and come to rest elsewhere, like a rearrangement of rocks and soil, sticks and stones. If Kalala agrees, she will talk to Pa again, she decides, and find out where he has buried them all. It isn't right to let human bones lie like that, with nothing to mark them.

She has a long way to go today – to fetch the grape harvest, and bring back oranges from Clapperton Bay. Her plan is to get there as fast as she can, fill up her bag with as much as she can carry, and return by a different route, covering even more ground, looking for clues and signs all the way there and all the way back. She and Kalala have been searching for many days, using one excuse or another to get away, and it is proving a lonely task. She won't think about the bones now, she tells herself. The bones. The bones. The bones.

She won't even say the words.

The bones the bones the bones.

Words or bones, neither can hurt her.

It's faster going than it ever used to be: the paths are so much clearer, with so many more people using them. She knows her father has already searched the bay and the cliffs, and the rocks at the bottom too, long and hard. He used to vanish for hours in those early days – to escape from Ma's silent grief, Ada hinted. But Pa was grieving too, thought Lizzie. Grief has a way of changing everything, she's found. It can sometimes make it hard to do the easiest things, like find the right place on the fire to balance the kettle. Even months later.

They could all have missed important clues during those early, heartbroken weeks, before they settled into their various convictions. Lizzie's nursing a wild new hope: that Albert is still alive but deep in hiding – like Kalala's father, long ago, before the sickness struck. Something had happened that fateful day, something so terrible Albert could not or would not return. He'd risk starvation rather than live subjected to his father's will. He could still be living up on the cliffs at Clapperton Bay, waiting out the days, far from Pa's scrutiny and rage, until the next ship came to carry him away. Couldn't they all survive on next to nothing?

As Lizzie passes the top of the track that leads down to the gully, her own bones seem to wobble like a compass needle, and she stumbles slightly. All that business about aitu. She still doesn't know what to think. So Lizzie decides to make herself brave with song. A hymn? All she can find is disconnected snatches of words and tunes. A sea shanty sneaks into her head to cheer her.

Hokey, pokey, winkey fum
How d'you like your 'taters done?
I like 'em done with their jackets on,
Says the King of the Cannibal Islands.

It's been a long time since they last had a potato, with or without a jacket. 'Taters' hadn't done as well here as Pa had hoped. Their leafy tops drooped yellow, and the potatoes rotted away before they were big enough to harvest.

Last night it rained again. Moisture is in the air like the memory of a kettle boiling. The armpits of Lizzie's blouse are dark and wet and her back is soaked in sweat. She wipes her face on her sleeve, and keeps going, along the ridge, past the turn-off towards the lake. And then she can't resist it. Lizzie doubles back. A swim will calm her down and wash her stickiness away.

The bones the bones the bones. Back in her head, full of vengeance.

When she reaches the shore, she looks around, uneasy still. She sits on a rock, warm with the sun, and feels the navy blue of her tunic heating up against her thigh, heat penetrating flesh and fabric. It is like being slowly cooked.

Inside out, or outside in? She can't decide which garment to remove first. Her tunic buttons run up her back. She'd never thought before how inconvenient this was, or why a piece of practical clothing might be made this way. There was always somebody around at bedtime to unbutton her, and then she would spin round and unbutton her sisters in turn. If they were in a hurry, and Ma chasing them, the girls sometimes made themselves a small circle of unbuttoners, fumbling and bending and racing and unlacing in the shadows before tumbling under the covers.

Lizzie can reach the top button, and there she starts. Then she works her way up from the bottom, and finally she slips her arms out, folds the tunic neatly and lays it down. She finds herself glancing back up the path, although she's heard nothing. Nobody can have followed her. They are all busy with their own work. She can hear the distant fall of axes. She is safe, and free. So just for once, she can see no reason not to take off all her other clothes.

Blouse. Petticoat. Vest. Be thankful I don't make you wear a corset, Ma often tells the big girls. Only because she can't get her hands on them, thinks Lizzie. She wonders if Pa will be shopping for stays as well as sheep when he goes to Auckland. The thought makes her feel peculiar, and she shoves it away. She's his golden girl again. He trusts her. He tells her things that even Ma doesn't know, that nobody on this island knows, except Kalala now.

She will be a crutch for Pa, thinks Lizzie, while Ma is wrapped up in the baby and her silent grief for Albert. She will ask him more about his plans, for the sheep, the orchards, the trading post. Keep him thinking about the future instead of the past. How the loss of Albert must gnaw at him. How he must blame himself.

Looking around for the last time, she removes her drawers, ready to run, quickly, splashingly, into the water. She feels a duty to get herself out of sight, even of herself. But this time, for once, she stops, closes her eyes and stretches. Now she is no longer marching, the air feels cooler. It brushes across her small breasts, hardening her nipples, which seem to freeze in shock at their own exposure. They are no more used to being in the open than the hair which now grows in her armpits and the other place where she has never looked, which is dark and absorbs the sun in a different way, warming the skin beneath. Everything is opening. She stretches again, and looks at herself. So pale, except for hands and feet and wrists and ankles. She makes a very thin mattress of her clothes, laying it right on top of the pumice pebbles and she lies down on top of it. She's not wearing a stitch.

She thinks of the native women she used to see on the Navigator Islands, barkcloth mats wrapped like long skirts around their waists, but above that quite bare, except for a necklace, because nobody has yet told them nakedness is not allowed. Breasts flop or swing or point or float. Bare like Eve. Now Lizzie too is bare like Eve, the sun warming her most private skin for the first time in her life. She likes it. She is at liberty.

Eyes shut, every sensation intensifies. She shifts her legs a fraction, and the movement makes a noise like lips separating from a kiss. Coolness marks the damp spots where her inner thighs were stuck with sweat, and the fine hairs on her arms lift with the faint prickle, as if her body were tickling itself. The island is breathing on her.

So this is sin. She shifts again, letting the sun fall on her stomach and the dark patch of hair beneath it and her pale thighs, which fall open just a little more. Tiny, unfamiliar darts of sensation zigzag across the surface of her skin, and somewhere deeper, less familiar too. There is a sturdy, sensible, practical part of her which completely understands why you can't spend all your days like this. Far too distracting and enjoyable. You would never do any work.

She becomes a drifting cloud, a speck of dust. Floating drowsily, mind light as her limbs, Lizzie has almost forgotten where she is and what she is supposed to be doing. She basks, refusing to think, allowing sensation alone to triumph. Her fingers explore.

Lizzie gives herself up to a flow of disconnected thoughts and images – snatches of voice and light and shade and colour, memories muddled with dreams. From time to time, something undefinable traps this stream; she's held back, momentarily, by an underlying sense of urgency, like a leaf or a stick in water catching briefly on a rock, before being gently tugged away by a stronger, more pleasurable undercurrent. Before she knows what's happening, she's gasping.

The lake looks dark and uninviting when Lizzie staggers to her feet, and she has no idea how late it is. A vaporous wisp, just visible across the water, rises from the cave hidden in the cleft in the rocks above the water, the cave where Lizzie and Ada spent what was nearly their last night on earth. A few weeks later, when they all went swimming together, Pa had gathered all the children round to explain why the lake was always warm, and told them to be sure to stay well away from any caves and craters they might find on the island. 'Just in case . . . he'd said, mysteriously.

Lizzie had kept her eyes on her toes, only glancing once at Ada, trustingly, glad of their secret.

Perhaps she had trusted Ada too much. She had certainly misjudged her loyalties. Perhaps Ada hadn't kept the Oven a secret from Albert. Perhaps Pa hadn't searched hard enough before. Lizzie looks across the lake again, to mark exactly where she had to climb. The steam was gone. Invisible. It always came and went, a moody measure of something far below. What a temperamental, shifty kind of creature this island was, a place where heat lurked unseen under the surface, and contours shifted from one decade to the next, where hot springs rose and vanished, rocks trembled unpredictably and the foul breath of the inner earth found unexpected ways to escape. A land which took in bones and spewed them out again.

Knee bent like a lonely heron's, Lizzie shakes out her drawers, and pulls them on one leg at a time, before wriggling into her vest, which she then tucks in. She hesitates before leaving her blouse and tunic and petticoat flattened and crumpled on the stones. Just for once she wants to be able to climb as fast and freely as she dares, no hems or pockets to catch on twigs, nothing to trap her knees as she ascends.

A stupid place to hide, of course, but, as Pa had said months ago, wasn't that just like Albert? He never did think things through. Lizzie could just see him panicking, terrified Pa would return and discover his disobedience. He'd made a mess of butchering the goat. He'd let another kid wander off. He'd abandoned his duties, and that meant no possibility of escaping punishment. But if he knew about the cave, it might have seemed a good place to hide for a few hours, at least, and maybe Lizzie would find some small clue to prove he'd been there.

Longer-legged, older, and more experienced, Lizzie no longer has to stretch across awkward gaps, although in places the ledges seem narrower than she remembers. The plants have grown up quickly too, and there are more roots to hang on to, but the mouth of the cleft is also better hidden, and more easily missed. A few heaps of goat droppings, fairly fresh, remind her there's nowhere these animals don't venture in search of greenery. Always alert to the panic of trapped beasts hurtling to escape, Lizzie steadies herself in anticipation of a sudden rush of slippery hooves. And then she notices vegetation has been pulled away in places, and now hangs limp and dry.

33

As it gets later and later, Ada, like me, becomes restless and twitchy.

'Do you know where Lizzie is?' Sideways like a crab, she asks me this when she comes to collect our fellows' supper dishes. At once I am on my feet. Five faces stare at me.

'No,' say I. 'I know only that she went to fetch oranges. And grapes. I will look for her, if you want me to.'

'I do,' says she, most firmly. 'Now.' Looking only at me. 'Take the dog, Spy.'

The dog is not accustomed to my command, and tries to follow her back to the kitchen fire.

'Go on, off you go, good boy, find Lizzie,' she orders. 'Go with Kalala.'

She shoos him off, quietly, not letting her eyes settle on me, uneasy at the attention the animal might draw to us. For some few moments he trots from one to the other of us, checking, wondering, head moving like somebody watching a throwing competition. I quickly smack my thigh and whistle through my teeth as Mr Peacock does – as Sidney taught me – and soon I am Spy's master.

Yet I have no chance of a quiet leave-taking. Questions pursue us. Vilipate first. Of all the four who came here with only our language, Vilipate is the fisherman, a most nimble catcher of English words, which he puts together ever faster.

'Another child gone?' he asks me.

Luka catches Ada's backward glance.

'Does this island eat children?'

Iakopo questions only with eyebrows, while Pineki – never serious – asks me where my girl is waiting. I kick him, hush the rest and turn my back on all but my brother. This is not the time to bring so many Peacock eyes upon us. I must find Lizzie. Besides, my head is growing large again. I can waste no more time here. I must be fast and fleet of foot, and I must gird up the loins of my mind too. I do not want to be among the trees of the forest when darkness comes, and I know how fast it will fall.

Solomona walks with me some way, promising me his prayers. But he also presses on me a stick, which I weigh in my hands as I walk.

'Button your shirt,' he tells me, and slaps my back to push me on my way. 'God be with you.'

The dog, Spy, runs ahead – flies ahead – and then worms back to me, begging me to follow faster. At every join and fork, and there are many, he stops. His tongue lolls, and he looks at me sideways. Where now? He does not always like my choices. The main path, I tell him. We should stay on the path that will take us most quickly to the other bay.

When we pass the turning which now I know will take us to the gully I cannot enter, my head pulses like a jellyfish. I must make it small again, small and solid, so that I can think and see clearly, exactly as I must. The aitu have kept silent ever since I met them at Nightbell Gully. With Lizzie's help, I have skirted that place since. But still I beg them to leave me be tonight.

The trees grow thicker, taller. Once I thought this island rich and generous and full of life. I could not help but crumble the soil between my fingers. Dig too far at home, and the rocks resist, breaking your tools, shock-shuddering your arms. The richness here now smells like rottenness.

I ask the dog. Do you smell decay? What do you dream? I ask him. Can you hear the curses of a one-eyed captain? The dog looks up at me with pity, and trots forward faster.

I have never used her name out loud before, only in my head, but I trumpet my hands and I call her. Over and over again, I shout 'Lizzzz-zzzeeeee, Lizzzzz-zzeeee,' louder and louder each time. A saw's teeth buzzing back and forth, back and forth, between my ears, against my tongue. But when I let silence in to hear her answer, only the dog's barks echo.

At the top of the track that turns towards the lake, Spy lies down with head on paws and will not shift for all my shouting. I whistle and slap my thigh until it stings, again and again, and finally I come back to him, and raise my stick. Though he presses himself into the ground, and whines, he does not move.

'I do not need you,' I shout at him, walking away. 'I can find her on my own. I will leave you behind.'

Ai, ai, ai. I know this is not the truth, and so does he. Only Ada's fierce eyes keep me walking through this island, and my fears for Lizzie. My head grows and floats and thumps and before my eyes light dances, but I will not let the other voices in.

I think my path is true. I believe it to be so. It is where she told me she would go. Yet something turns my feet without my granting, and I am walking now on the other side of the mountain, downhill again, towards the lowering sun and towards the lake path and the waiting dog.

He comes running, low, towards my ankle, and I hop and skip, lest his teeth are bared. He nudges me on, and then runs ahead again, and then spins back and repeats all this until I am at the shore of the dark lake where I dived, and dived again, and dived once more, and Lizzie is lying on the stones, and I drop my stick and run to her.

No. Not to her.

I am mistaken.

Only her empty tunic, dark and creased, and her blouse, both topped with a white garment which should be underneath, which I have seen only hanging on a branch or line before, on washday. Lizzie herself has been sucked away. No. I'm wrong. Foolishness. She has taken herself somewhere. But where? Buttons fly from me as I tear at my shirt, and zigzag towards the lake, over the rasp of light and rolling stones. Before I reach the water, the dog begins to bark again, quick and half triumphant, a multitude of blows which slice the air, bounce from rock to rock, and drive into my heart.

He vanishes into greenery and shows again at the other side. I follow.

He scrabbles, loping, leaping ledge to ledge. I pursue him up the rock face, past plants pulled from their roots, knocking off rattling stones that bounce below, a slow measure of passing time that tells me I must hurry.

*

I duck my head through the arch of the cleft and enter a foul-smelling split in the earth I never knew was there. Blocking my own light, I have to let my eyes remember how to see in darkness, while I crouch down and feel my way forward, shirt flapping. Then I reach her hair, and shoulders white as a shark's belly. She lies face down.

The dog barks again, summoning me with a quick dull echo, and Lizzie does not stir. I push the sniffing, nuzzling, poking animal from her head, shove him from us, twice. When I turn her body over, her mouth falls open though her eyes are closed. Then I breathe again, for she is breathing, but this noxious air catches in my nostrils and makes me choke and gasp. So much foulness.

I turn her over to drag her backwards towards the light. The cave is too low and narrow to lift her, and its rough floor reaches for her skin and clothes as if it would trap her. Small, quick backward steps, one two, one two, scraping to the light, bent-backed, head half turned on twisted neck so I cannot see the hanging shelf of rock that hits it. Eyes scarlet and gold. Shake away pain. Keep heaving. Though my load is heavy, my muscles have been strengthened over time by all the trunks and roots and trees that do not want to quit their growing grounds, and pit themselves against me. It is easy to be strong for Lizzie.

Out in air and light, I spit out the stench, and wipe my mouth, and crouch on the ledge beside her. I am thinking too fast for fear, though I know it is close. I push away the dog, and then let him return, and finally I sit with her head and shoulders across my thighs, not knowing whether to shake or shout or stroke her back to life, and trying all at once. Blue branching lines beneath her skin. Scrapes and grazes on its whiteness where she has fought the enclosing rocks. Her linen marked with mud and maybe blood. But her bony chest is too thin and bare to hide its rise and fall. I know at once she lives.

I talk to her, nonsense, in English and my own language, and then I start to pray – the Lord's Prayer first, and then the Shepherd's Psalm, and when I reach the *valley of the shadow of death*, I begin to beg the Lord. Make her eyes open. You have it in your power. Prove yourself if you would not have me doubt you. And I remember Solomona, who tells me always I must pray for grace not favour, the grace to submit to His will at all times. The grace to bear life, and death, together.

Yet finally He hears me. She doubles herself, away from me. I dare not touch her. When she turns back to me she cannot speak; her jaws clatter and click, her throat contorts, and she gags on every syllable. 'I-I-I-I-I,' she says, like an animal. Stuck. She looks to the cave and gulps for air and starts again with another sound: 'He-he-he-he'.

'Tell me,' I say. Her neck is tight. Her fists two stones. She unlocks her teeth.

'Go-go-go-go-go.'

Back into the cave? That is where she points, and then pushes me, hard, so I stumble.

'No, I can't . . . ' I say. 'The air. I cannot breathe the air in there. You must not either.'

'Must-must-must.'

'It nearly killed you.'

'Go-go-go-go-go.' Stabbing with her finger. And rising, swaying, almost falling, she blunders past me, trying to return herself.

'No!' I say, holding her back. 'Stay here. I will go.'

I fill myself with clean air, as if about to dive. I am a good
diver. I know how long I have before I need to breathe again.
And my eyes are good.

I plunge back inside, hands out like paddles, feet shuffling,
and feel my way along the cavern as it opens and narrows and
becomes warmer and warmer.

Lizzie has found her voice. It follows me, but I cannot answer
without losing my clean air.

'Keep going . . . at the back . . . '

Darker and darker. Sweat-salt-stung eyes, back warm and dripping, rock-scoured, my head spinning and floating, all about to
burst. What am I looking for? What has Lizzie left that she wants
so much?

Force myself on. Push feelingly with foot, as underwater, and
open my hands like starfish. I make my fingers wander. Here this
cave is barely a tunnel. Damp, rasping stone. Runnels made long
ago, narrowing into a low arch. It cannot be much further. Nearly
there, nearly there. Keep moving on and on and on, too slowly.
I need to breathe. I cannot breathe. My head throbs with the
work of not letting this place in. Crushed chest. Bursting veins.
I need to surface. I want my face to break through into light and
feel the air stroke my skin. I must be quicker. I cannot be quicker.
Something is in my way. My foot pushes against something that
shifts, but not easily. It's not hard, and nor is it soft. Something
like wood, I think.

Something like bones.

Long bones like hollow sticks. I stumble and recover myself.
I cannot fall here. I turn my back and run for air.

Blundering empty-handed into light fast fading, I try to empty
my head of what my hands have seen. I can't. I can't. I know

without sight that these are not pig bones. Lizzie blocks my way. Her eyes accuse me.

'What have you done? Why did you leave him?'

She wants to push me back into the cave.

'I couldn't breathe,' I say.

Bent at the waist, I hang my head and take in air which smells of nectar, loam and lake, but also a foul animal stink. Drops of sweat slide from my hair to make dark stars on the rock ledge.

'We have to bring him out,' she insists. 'I tried . . . ' A wail of lamentation lets loose.

'The air is poisonous. It must have killed him. It nearly poisoned you.'

He's dead, I think. I can't save him. Decayed dead. The deadest thing I ever felt.

'I know. I know this place. I thought he knew. I've killed him.' Dead voice.

I think of other bodies, in other caves, our burial caves across the sea, stopped up with stones. What if this is not her brother, but one of mine, a blackbird from my land? But the stench tells me otherwise. All the aitu have fallen silent, and I am unpossessed.

'*I* will go back,' she says. 'Wait here.'

'No.' I say, sharply enough to stop her. My hand is on her arm before I know what I am doing, on her bare arm, and she does not shake it off. 'Let me.'

Lizzie seems to shrink.

'I don't want to,' she admits. 'I can't.'

'No,' I agree. 'Better I go.'

'It's nearly dark.' She looks across the lake. The sky is violet. 'We could tell Pa. Come back in the morning?'

'No. I'll try again.'

I can be quick, this time, I tell myself. I know where I am going, and what I need to do. I gulp down air, and raise my arm above my head, and with bleeding forehead and bloodied elbow, I am soon at the back of the cave, where the narrowing tunnel is blocked, and my fingers feel something tough and wrinkled, like the skin of a shark dried out in the sun. My hands circle shin bones, fingers meet thumbs too fast. The roof is too low for me to pick up this body like a baby, but when I try to pull at it, I fear collapse, division, disintegration.

I cannot hold my breath much longer. So I pull off my town shirt and fold his limbs as best I can and wrap him in a shroud his mother made for me. I feel for his head. I need his head. I have his skull. I must keep my head too.

*

On the rock ledge Lizzie weeps and shivers and clutches at the dog. Outside at last, I meet her brother Albert.

34

LIZZIE CROUCHES, EYES PLANTED ON KALALA'S SWEATING face as he tends his burden, but she cannot bring herself to look down at it herself. Her open mouth hangs, drying, and flesh obstructs her throat. His face tells her something of what he sees as he straightens what is left of Albert's twisted, wasted legs, placing knee to knee, ankle to ankle and foot to foot. Then he tidies the boy's loose, unmannered arms. No sleeves to unroll or cuffs to unbutton. Only stained, stretched skin and cloth fragmenting at his touch. Reaching Albert's head, Kalala's eyes startle.

He swallows, with difficulty, and looks at Lizzie. Gently, gently puts his palms on either side of her face. With the hands that have tended Albert, Kalala moves Lizzie's head so that she faces away from her brother entirely. There is something he does not want her to see. Something too terrible. Unspeakable. But she needs to know everything. She has to look. Quickly, just once, before she whips her head away. This cannot be him. This thing that's nothing like her brother, and yet so clearly is.

'Albert. Oh no.'

Albert's skull is crushed.

'He was trying to escape,' she says. 'He hit his head.'

Kalala doesn't understand.

'The poison. You see when Ada and I first found this cave, it used to steam, like the hot spring on the beach. We spent a night here, long ago. It nearly killed us. Something in there – when you breathe it. I don't know what it is. That stink, that terrible smell . . . it can stop you breathing. Why *didn't* we tell Albert? Why didn't I warn everyone?'

'No.'

'What do you mean?'

'I mean the poison did not kill him. This is not your fault.'

'Oh yes, yes, it is. I know it's my fault. Everything's my fault.' Lizzie's hands wrench and turn as though she wants to wash her skin away. He stops her and puts something in her palm. A button. Her fingers close over it and refuse to open.

'No,' he tells her, very quietly. 'It's not your fault. He did not come here by himself.'

'Yes, yes,' she insists. 'He came to get warm, like we did that night, and then, when he couldn't breathe, he tried to leave and hit his head.'

'No. Nobody could hit his own head hard enough to break it like that. Impossible. Somebody has done this to him.'

She forces herself to look again, and her hand moves towards her brother. Her own head is thick and clogged. It must be the poisonous air. She feels as if she is breaking into the smallest pieces. Her body won't hold together. All its parts are edging away, separating from each other, beginning to dissolve. Her mind spreads and thins like a pool of spilled oil. She has become uncontainable.

'Well, we must look after him now,' she says, forcing herself together. 'We must bring him home.'

The pity in his eyes provokes her.

'Come on, Kalala,' she shouts, suddenly harsh, getting to her feet, distancing herself from everything. 'Why are you waiting? I order you to bring him down from here.'

Lizzie points haughtily. It comes as a further shock, even to herself, this cruel imperiousness, coming from nowhere, born of something unrecognisable. When she sees how he recoils, it makes her despise herself all the more. Somebody has done this to Albert. She can't think . . . can't make sense of who or how. But she is to blame. She knows she is to blame. She's certain only of that. A surge of nausea takes Lizzie by surprise. All her joints loosen at once, and she slumps, felled, on the ledge.

Kalala carries her home.

*

Flames approach, flickering in a mess of gathering voices.

'What have you done to her?' her father bellows. As she struggles from Kalala's arms, and pulls away from both men, Lizzie is taken aback by her own near nakedness. She drops to a protective crouch. Ada rushes forward with a moan and an open shawl, holding it before her like a banner, a sail, a bed sheet, a fence. She swaddles Lizzie, and both girls duck heads and flinch when Mr Peacock shoots out a sudden fist, which leaves Kalala sprawling. He coils himself into a curving wall, bare back, hands over ears, ready for the kicking which swiftly follows.

A buckle rings and leather whistles through the air.

Never before such fury. Never before such hatred in Pa's yell of rage.

'What have you done to Lizzie? What have you done to my daughter?'

'Nothing!' screams Lizzie, while Kalala gasps and scrabbles in the dirt. 'Stop. Leave him alone. It's my fault.'

Her father turns on her, but Ada is quick enough to swing between them and push him away, and then Billy appears from the shadows and throws himself on his father's back. Pa hisses and spits and hurls strange words at Lizzie – hussy, slut – shocking, wounding words that make the girls judder and cower and click their shivering teeth. Staring, almost hissing herself, Mrs Peacock puts down the sputtering lantern. Still measured, just, still contained, but barely, she orders Queenie to take Gus to bed, and the baby too, pushing the little ones away from harm as she speaks. Joey's thin wail rises and falls over the girls' departing sobs. Then Ma steps firmly between her other daughters and their father.

'Joseph!' Never before such menace in her voice. If once she blazed, now she scorches. Mr Peacock has become a pacing predator, but she will not let him pass. 'Joseph. Stop! Wait. We must find out first what has happened.'

'Her clothes! Where are her clothes?' roars Mr Peacock. He tries to rush at her. Ma raises her arms but stands firm.

'Leave her, Joseph. Get away from Lizzie. Don't you touch her till she's spoken.'

Another voice from the shadows:

'Mrs Peacock?'

Here comes Solomona, the peacemaker, Solomona the wise, who carries about him an invisible circle of Godliness which keeps Mr Peacock briefly at bay. 'Let me help. Let me talk to Kalala. Let him explain himself.'

The Island fellows are already gathering round Kalala, still fetal on the ground. They help him carefully to his feet, and Solomona interrogates his brother, quickly and efficiently, in their own language, all the while checking his injuries, dabbing at blood, brushing away dirt and leaves, soothing him as he winces, covering him with a shirt. He keeps a close eye on Lizzie's father, who stamps and growls, prowls and paces round the unmarked space that surrounds them. Solomona listens and nods. The other fellows shake their heads and draw in their lips, and try not to look at Mr or Mrs Peacock. At last Solomona clasps his hands and steeples his forefingers. He gathers the fractured family with a sweeping, pitying eye.

'They have found your son,' he says.

Five words hang in the air. Then Ada unfreezes. She's been cradling Lizzie all this time, but now she almost pushes her away, gibbering: 'No, no, no. Someone else. Not Albert.'

Lizzie gropes for her sister's hand. She presses something into it, round and hot and unmistakable. Four holes, guaranteed not to cut.

'Where is he?' asks Ada, turning the button in her fingers. Whispering and arguing with herself, she crawls towards the lantern, to examine it, to be sure the button's his. Solomona puts his own jacket around his brother's still-shivering shoulders and continues as his interpreter.

'He is at a cave, above the lake.'

Mr Peacock stops prowling, and finally listens.

'Albert?' says Mrs Peacock, all fire gone. 'My boy? My sweet, beautiful boy? But what have they done?' She holds out her arms like a sleepwalker.

Lizzie buries her face in her hands.

'They left him there,' says Solomona. 'They had no choice. Kalala had to look after Lizzie. *She* is alive, at least, thanks to my brother. We will have to fetch Albert in the morning. It is too dark and far too difficult to bring his body home tonight.'

'The Oven? Oh no! But you left him?' Ada worries at Lizzie's arm. 'How could you leave him? Lizzie, you left him?'

She's angry with me because she doesn't know, thinks Lizzie. She thinks the strange foul air stopped his breath, while he was hiding, while he was sleeping in the warmth, as it nearly stopped ours. How can she tell Ada that Albert died in pain and violence? She must not ever know about his poor crushed head, his splintered bones. Lizzie can't allow the sight she has seen to worm into Ada's skull, and embed itself in her mind too, taking root inside the cave of her memory. She wants to protect Ada as she failed to protect Albert. Surely that meant she could never name his killer.

'Ada, I couldn't . . . '

Solomona repeats himself.

'Kalala had to take care of the living. Your daughter.'

'Take care?' says Pa, disgusted, still disbelieving, or so it seems.

Mrs Peacock stares without seeing.

'Come with me, Ma?' Ada begs like a just-walking child, a witless creature. 'Come with me to get Albert? Let's go together, now, right away?'

Abruptly, Mrs Peacock returns her mind from the darkness beyond the fire lit, lamp lit space, and at last remembers who she is and what she has to do. She strokes and calms her daughters, first Ada, then Lizzie, and then Queenie, who comes from the girls' hut to be enfolded in a knot of reaching, clutching arms. Finally Billy joins them, snuffling.

'The men will go, in the morning,' says Ma, firmly. 'Isn't that right, Joseph? We must be patient. And it's quite right, what Solomona says. Nothing to be done tonight. Nothing to be done. Nothing to be done. Another night will neither hurt or help him now. So let's get Lizzie to bed.' She slowly remembers the way you have to manage things, how to keep one child occupied with another. 'Look, Ada, see how she shivers. You'll keep Lizzie warm, won't you? She's had a shock, you know, a terrible, terrible shock. We all have. And now we must all look after one another.'

35

Inside and out, I am stiff and bruised. I have let myself slide and sidle far too far into a family I can never be part of. I could have kept myself to myself, thrown spears with the other fellows, let Solomona lead us, had more faith he would, and returned to my island, unentangled and enriched. I could have put my learning to one side. I should have played with string and stones, not storytelling. I pressed my hopes into printed words, ink, and type, and paper. One thing standing always for another, its bond uncertain.

Sleep darts away all night, a fish from a spear, and Albert's broken skull dances before me. Dimly, darkly, I watch again and again the blow which cracked it, as if I now share Lizzie's dreams. A blow from behind. And on the head. Think of that. How you would club an animal to death, not how you discipline a boy. Never your own child. What have I witnessed? Something almost beyond understanding or utterance.

'Solomona?' I whisper in the dark, knowing he lies awake as I do. 'Will you pray that our ship comes soon?'

'I will, and I will pray for you too.' My brother comes to kneel beside me, as if I lay dying.

*

'Not you,' says Mr Peacock, in the morning, early, his arm a fallen branch, blocking our doorway so I cannot follow the gang. 'You stay here. Do not leave your hut until we are back.'

He cuts my protest. What is this new humiliation? His daughter cleared my name last night. And our master no longer hurls lust. No talk now of fornication, nor any sign of why he pins me here alone, apart from all. I would believe this confinement the madness of grief. Some misapprehension time could clear. But I have seen his son, and my suspicions fast ferment.

'Lizzie has told me exactly where this cave is,' he tells Solomona. 'Turns out Ada knew the place already too. They have both confessed as much.' No sign he knows the cave himself. No sign he does not. 'Come on, boys. Pick up the litter.'

A man in mourning cannot be refused. My fellows obey in full bewilderment, looking from me to Solomona to our master. It seems Mr Peacock has been working through the night with axe and chisel – we heard the blows – fashioning a flat kind of bed with handles to bear back his son's remains. Low-lidded, Mr Peacock looks only at me, nostrils widening as if he confronts a stench. Mine flare likewise, and my throat tightens. He is the stench, sweet sickness leaking from his pores. He has been drinking as well as working through the night. Red threads darken his eye-whites and his teeth continually clash and grind, in ceaseless conversation with themselves.

'I will deal with you on our return,' he tells me with disdain.

My fury surges back, and I think to push myself against him. Instead I turn to Solomona, who stands as astonished as the rest. I am certain he will speak at least a word for me before they leave. Yet he shakes his head and makes a movement with his hands like smoothing sand. Fearful, my fellows look down. I think of Mrs Peacock, and all the children, and the depth and freshness of their shock and sorrow, and I see this is no time for protest. I retreat into the shadows of our hut and try, for now, to quell my anger. There's comfort in taking shelter behind walls we have built ourselves, and call our own. All minds must be with Albert today, I resolve. Whatever it may be, when our master issues his complaint against me, Lizzie will take my part. I cannot doubt this.

After some time, footsteps scrape my way. Billy brings me a bowl of taro porridge. Tiptoe, tiptoe, towards the doorframe, eyes down, and then he pushes the dish across without a word. Steam hazes, or perhaps my eyes mist. I feel like a vicious animal, a dog that is sick. If he had a stick, he would use it – not to hit me, but better to keep his distance. I call him back, by name – what has his father told him? – but he pretends not to hear.

Billy goes to sit a little distance from the hut, knees up, head lowered, red-faced. My keeper. The sun shifts slowly. Grief casts strange shadows, truly. It makes you see things which were never there, and also fail at first to see what is before your face. Deception – of self and others – calls with a beguiling voice. I try to trust in Solomona, and gather my resolve, think of Job and his infinite patience. I command myself to wait, feigning obedience, until the time is right, and I can see more clearly where blows this storm. Surely God will show me what path to take? I am no prisoner yet, I tell myself. If I choose to walk out of here, I can. Even if there is nowhere to go.

*

I hear a noise like the cry of a stranger, a trapped animal, an unknown seabird. It is none of those things. Mrs Peacock's heart has cracked, with a sound to shatter other hearts, and I know by this that her beautiful boy is come home.

A moment later her ironwood strength returns and I watch her step out to meet the solemn procession as it descends, her husband at its helm. Pride stretches my jaw when I see the blank, serious faces of my fellow Islanders, and note how they bear themselves. Solomona has trained them to walk just so, heavy with dignity, heads high and eyes unwandering, just as Mr Reverend trained Solomona at his time of grief.

The two parties meet. Mr and Mrs Peacock walk back together, a handspan apart. The girls fall in beside the litter. Ada bears the baby Joe, and Billy joins his sisters, taking the hand Lizzie stretches out to him. All but Gus look straight ahead, away from the shrouded, shrivelled load my fellows carry. When Gus reaches up a hand to pluck at the sheet, Queenie slaps her away, jerking her other arm with rare ferocity, springing tears.

The procession – everyone but me – moves on. Albert is taken to rest in his parents' hut.

Nobody comes near. I have not been told why I am confined.

Later, a little way off, beyond the taro patch, I hear the song of shovels, the stony slide of moving earth.

36

TOO LITTLE SPACE TO HOLD THIS SWELLING SADNESS. Albert's bones lie in the hut which saw his brother's birth a few months earlier, and the family kneels wordless around the bed. Staggered breathing surrounds Lizzie, corrugated inhalations and long, impossible sighs, everyone out of time. She remembers the first nights when they all slept in this hut, newly built on the hopeful side of the island, when the roof and walls were green and fresh, when all their bodies rose and fell as one.

Now the walls have lost their colour. They rustle when the wind blows. Lizzie sees her father has faded too. His eyes have greyed to the dull grittiness of the beach at Clapperton Bay. He is grey all over, beard and clothes and bleached-out skin all merging, like a drawing of himself. When those eyes catch hers, Lizzie retreats. Her insides clamp. Her breathing stops. Her head is spreading again, just as Kalala has described, like a slowly expanding cloud. Feathers. Foam. Air. Nothingness. Her palms press against each other, her fingers lock – she might be praying, but she is holding on, her knuckles and nails whitening with the effort of staying anchored to herself.

Different noises break up fragmented rushing thoughts. Hammering. Sawing. Distant thudding shovels – the kind which usually foretell a feast. Soon the lying wooden cross etched with Albert's name will tell the truth, the marker which all this time has stood like fingers crossed behind a child's back, a sign of something false, signalling only a vanishing.

Her mind muddles. She crashes into blankness. Even moments just passed wash away from her. Her forehead furrows as she tries to piece together shards. Billy was sent to guard Kalala. Billy who every day steps more briskly into Albert's empty place. But why? And where? And isn't Billy here now, kneeling opposite Lizzie, with ash in the parting of his hair.

Her head jerks back. Her thoughts are a mess of maggots, consuming her bit by bit. Each grub has a tiny voice, and it holds forth very quietly, almost undetectable; a ferocious, incessant, wayward confrontation. Still nobody has said anything about how her brother died. Of course not. She's said nothing about his injuries herself. But someone's seen them. They must have. And someone inflicted those injuries. Who is Lizzie protecting with her silence? Ada? Queenie? Her mother? Herself. Someone else.

The maggots are hatching into blowflies, bumping against her skull. They murmur and buzz and whine inside, settling, slowly crawling, rubbing their front legs – washing or wringing their hands – then taking off into the air again just before she can squash them. She can't hear what they're saying. She can think of nothing but the truth Kalala told her the night before. Somebody killed Albert. Had he understood, as she had, that it could only have been one person? Another fly. Splat. Wasn't it obvious to everyone? Surely, surely he would have to confess. Another crack. Everything would break. And then? Oh, go away, go away, she tells the addle-pating insects and their eyes and moaning wings. Bang. Bang. Again and again they hit against her thinking and send it skimming elsewhere. Could Albert go back underground and nobody ever see what killed him? Nobody but Pa and perhaps the Islanders, if he let them? Where is Kalala now? What is he thinking? What might he yet say?

The humming in her head rises. Her fingers wrench apart. She has to show them. Everyone needs to know. And she must be certain too. Because her head feels so sick today she cannot trust it. Lizzie begins to rise, stiffly, joints creaking and clicking. Ada's hand reaches out blindly to pull her back. Her mother mutters an uninterruptable prayer, begging for peace for her unhappy son, calling the dear Lord to take him to His bosom and to forgive his trespasses. The baby snuffles quietly. A stuttering sequence of amens follows. The digging stops. All at once the stillness is broken and all eyes are open, as Pa gestures his family to their feet. It's time.

Solomona waits at the door. He and Luka have patched together a coffin from a tea chest, the last of the treacherous boxes unloaded from the *Good Intent*. Stained and pecked and somewhat dented, it has outlasted Albert, and seen more of the world too. It is too wide and too short to contain her brother. His legs will have to bend. He will lie twisted. What will he rest on? The lid is down, and Solomona has scratched Albert's name on it. Like Queenie, now that she can read, Lizzie looks for letters everywhere. Their brother's name is harder to make out than the faded, stencilled letters on the box's side, which spell out fragments: NCOLOURED, and beneath that JAPAN, and beneath that TEA.

Lizzie puts her hands over her ears and squeezes shut her eyes as the thing is bundled into the coffin. He, she reminds herself. He is Albert. No thing. The flies inside her skull have set up their whining again. She thinks they may soon begin to bite.

Nails are hammered in.

Lizzie asks the flies what she should say, how she can stop this sealing up, but they only whine and buzz. She slaps at her head, and again Ada stills her.

Outside is wincingly bright. The children take up the steady pace of earlier procession, led by Solomona, whose nervous hands juggle Bible and prayer book. Pa takes the front of the litter which now bears the coffin, and Luka – ill at ease – the rear. Then come Mrs Peacock and Baby Joe, Ada and Gussie, Queenie and Billy, and finally Lizzie, last because she hesitated. She has left it too late. She should have stopped them. Past the chickens, past the beans, past the taro beds, past the infant banana trees. The other Islanders lean exhausted on their shovels beside a mound of rich, fresh earth, straightening nervously when they see the coffin coming – one, two, three, but no Kalala. They back away to leave space at the graveside.

Shocked and stiff, the wooden cross leans backwards against a tree. Something is wrong. Solomona's horror is written on his face. No straps. No ropes. That is the way the next part should be done, like lowering a boat. Worse, he has mismeasured: his pacing was too short. He glances fearfully at Mr Peacock, who has also seen the problem and glowers.

Vilipate is the first to jump back into the pit and start to shovel, messily, sweatily, and Iakopo soon joins him, and everything will be fine because in their nervousness, they dig too far, and make room enough for them both to stand and receive the coffin, and clamber out again, pushing and pulling at one another in their haste. Again they back away, and bow their heads.

So everything is ready. It is time. Mrs Peacock pitches, and rights herself. Lizzie takes the baby and stands in the shade with him, swaying deliberately from foot to foot, rocking and hushing and soothing herself as much as little Joe. Her body is not hers. Nothing she can inhabit and nowhere to go. Kalala must have some answer, she thinks again. Looking for him, she sees only something like his shadow in the doorway of the hut, and her confusion increases. Why is he hiding there? She wants cause to doubt herself. She needs to ask him what's true. What's memory. Has she dreamed Albert's wound? Gus, staring and staring at the hole, where a worm twists and turns in sudden daylight, leans over so far that Ada has to tug her from the edge before she slides in after Albert.

Solomona coughs and blinks.

'Forasmuch . . . ' He repeats, 'Forasmuch . . . '

Mr Peacock, who has removed his hat and holds it by the brim, turning it thumb-to-thumb in his hands like a slowly moving wheel, answers with a nod, and the funeral service starts.

Noise and pain grind into Lizzie's head. She doesn't notice when Ada takes the baby from her, as if she needs her own turn with the promise of life the child embodies. Even without that tiny burden, Lizzie still rocks from side to side, soothing only herself. The first handful of earth scatters on the thin, lead-lined lid, with the rattle of heavy rain on palm leaves. All night, all morning, she had anticipated confession and hoped for explanation, all the while torturing herself with thoughts of where this could lead. But it was clear at this moment that her father had chosen another, more unexpected path. And that, as always, it was one that he expected her to follow.

37

I HEAR THE ROPE SLAP AGAINST HIS PALM BEFORE I KNOW what its noise signifies, once, twice, and there is Mr Peacock at the door. On my feet already, I am ready for him. Eager, even, to forgive his trespasses against me. Until I see the rope spring taut between his hands. Then I know I have meddled with strife that does not belong to me. I have taken a dog by the ears when I should have passed him by.

Fear curls my half-sprung limbs faster than flame shrivels a dry fern. I duck away – just like a guilty man – but Mr Peacock moves faster, and catches my arms behind me. Face down on the mat, the taste of flax in my mouth, I struggle as a sharp weight presses my back. Mr Peacock knees me hard while he binds my wrists and I writhe uselessly, unable to force my own knee under myself so I may rise and throw him off. I twist my head and shout for Solomona's aid, just once, before I am shaken into silence. I am a pig trussed for slaughter, but I may not squeal, no matter how harsh my injuries or how deep my humiliation.

'Your brother is praying for you,' Mr Peacock tells me. 'Wouldn't hurt to do the same for yourself, but I don't know how God will help you. Now, get up. Come with me.'

He pulls me from behind up onto my feet.

'Sir, listen to me, please. Sir?' Despite fresh pain, I try to turn. 'Sir, I have not touched your daughter. Not how you think. Only to carry her home. Has she not told you so? Will you not believe her, sir?'

He shoves me in the back. I stagger forward, right myself before I fall, and try again.

'I went to find Lizzie, not to hurt her. She must have told you so. Sir, please ask her.'

'Get out of here.'

'I saved your daughter. I saved her. I cannot hurt her. I would not harm her.'

I don't know how to make him listen. One voice cannot argue. So I stumble on, keeping up my protest.

'Sir? What have I done? Why are you doing this to me?'

'Your confinement has nothing to do with Lizzie. As well you know.'

So Solomona is much mistaken. We need more than patience now, more than prayers.

'You know.'

'No, sir. No, Mr Peacock. I don't.'

'You know.'

I look for answers in the blank, uncertain faces lined up to greet me – the Peacock family on one side, my fellows on the other. They also wait for revelation. But surely Solomona will not wait much longer? Surely my own brother will soon speak out to defend me? If not for my sake, then for the sake of truth and righteousness. With my eyes I try to remind him: he has two masters, one visible, one unseen, and their wishes may neither be the same, nor equal.

And Lizzie? I cannot see her yet.

On either side, swinging glances tell me where I am being taken, and why nobody dare hinder my progress. Passing his wife, Mr Peacock briefly stops to take the gun from her reluctant hands and, watched by every pair of eyes, he lays it across his shoulder. The other hand I feel hard at my back, pushing me away from the kitchen fire and the family's sleeping huts, towards the single ironwood tree beside the storehut.

This they have emptied out already. All tools, all wood, all chests now huddle beneath sailcloth beside the building. A split stake is driven into the middle of the floor, and I see he means to tie me to it while he secures his gaol house.

Then Mr Peacock spins me round to face him. His hunting eyes are on me, glinting between beard and hat-brim, shining like the sweat that gleams and drips around them, unsteady with excitement. When all are close enough to hear his words, he scrubs his face with a darkening handkerchief, ready to speak. I see again how Mr Peacock always measures me. He eyes me up and down, like a vaka-maker before a tree he thinks to fell, considering me from top to toe. He plans to hollow me out, I believe, and soon I will know his chosen tools.

'Kalala,' he says. Stern, solid, sure of purpose. I sense the looming of others, feel the shuffle of feet approaching, hear the nervous throat noises. 'I welcomed you here to work. I gave you a rare chance. You could be far away from here – with your cousins on more distant isles, learning how to curse, no better than a slave. I took you in.'

Understanding is slow to dawn. I wait. We all wait.

'We had a bargain. You have broken it, and your hands are soiled with the blood of my oldest son. If you confess it so, I am prepared to believe you worked alone, without your brothers' knowledge. Can you deny that you surprised him by chance on the first day that we searched for him, and decided then that my fine boy stood in your path to possession of this island. Can you deny that it was then you seized your opportunity?'

My head thunders, loud as surf. I do not understand the question. I want to write it down, to study its meaning, to take it apart again so I can make it clear. It knocks me sideways.

'No!'

'No?' His look of triumph tells me I have misspoken. 'You see. He confesses.'

'Yes, I mean yes,' I cry. 'I *can* deny this. I am no murderer.'

But when I speak again, my words are rattling stones pulled back by sea, foam that flies on wind.

'You cannot change your tune,' he says. 'Too late. You have already admitted your guilt. At last we have the truth about Albert.'

'No!' I shout out my denial, and hear its echo in the voices of my fellows, Solomona, Luka, all the others.

'Too late to gainsay now.' His right hand rests lightly on the broad part of his gun. I cannot stop staring at his fingers, their ridged nails, the polished wood, the metal. Iron and steel and fear control us all. 'What did you imagine?' he continues. 'That I would be fool enough to let you kill me too? That because I am alone, the only man on this island, I cannot protect myself and my family? You're the fool.'

A terrible coldness comes upon me, as when you swim under-water into a cave. He is right. He has fooled me, turned my

words, turned the truth, so that now it is plain only to me. I
look over to my fellows, hoping for help. Understanding only
my fear and confusion, Luka, Vilipate, Pineki and Iakopo beg
Solomona for explanations, and I see he does not know how to
quiet them. He strains to hear his master's words, to understand
himself.

Mr Peacock has no need to silence his wife or any one of his
white-faced children. None dare move a muscle. Their stupefac-
tion is complete. And Lizzie too, half hiding at the back? Surely
she will speak? Surely she knows that a word from her could
change everything? I call her name. Nothing. Lizzie says nothing
and will not look at me. Then a chill deeper than I have ever
known before shudders my limbs. I sense an overturning and
eating away at all my innards. No spirits. Worse by far, more
all-possessing, this is comprehension, dawning only with her
silence. To save me, Lizzie must condemn her father.

I stand as stunned and lifeless as the rest.

'Have no fear.' Our master speaks as from a pulpit. Each word
a wound. 'We are no longer in danger. I will protect us from this
murderer until the *Esperanza* returns (please God may it be soon).
You know me well. I am a decent Englishman, no tyrant, and I
will have justice served on my island. We will try and sentence
this felon before an honest jury.'

Then I have time. My limbs and tongue return to life and I
shout out, again and again.

'I am no murderer! I am no murderer! I am no murderer! And
in God's name, I am honest. He is lying.' Yet even Bible-sworn,
I know my word alone is worthless. This certainty, this understanding that the truth is unspeakable, binds me harder than the
ropes around my wrist which Mr Peacock — this 'decent'

Englishman – now seizes. He pushes me violently towards the stake. I raise my voice again to speak in our language. 'Help me! Stop him.'

Pineki, the first to answer my call, straightway throws himself to the ground in fear, for the gun now points his way.

'You,' says Mr Peacock, staring at all five of them. 'It is time to prove your loyalty. All of you. Your next job is to help me complete this prison. You will make it sound, with ironwood bars that can't be broken. Secure the walls likewise. Or you will find yourselves prisoners too.'

38

'COME AWAY, GIRLS,' SAYS MRS PEACOCK QUICKLY. The unmilked goats have set up an insistent bleat. Caught between possibilities, Queenie doesn't move. 'Harriet!' her mother says, more sharply, using her given name for the first time since they landed here. Queenie? Her daughters are all dethroned. This island has only one monarch.

'I'm coming,' says the girl, but she hangs back even as she follows, edging to Lizzie's side with flickering eyes. 'Kalala?' she whispers, in disbelief. 'You believe Kalala killed Albert? Albert was killed?'

Moving her hand instinctively to the back of her own head, unconsciously fingering her scalp, Lizzie nods. Her eyes are leaking, brimming like a hot spring. She can't stop the salt from pouring out. Ada crowds her from the other side. She seizes her arm with bruising strength, a brutal show of love.

'How, Lizzie? Tell us how?' says Ada. 'How did Albert die? What did you see and how can this be? Why would Kalala want to kill him?'

'Go away . . . ' says Lizzie. 'Leave me alone. I don't know. I can't tell you.'

She wants to push both sisters from her. Without their questions, she has a chance of taking the rope Mr Peacock has suddenly offered. A hope of saving her father – and thereby saving them all, saving everything and everyone, perhaps – except Kalala. If she lets herself believe this lie.

It's possible, perhaps. It must be. And doesn't Pa have an answer for everything? Never defeated. She should have remembered: she could have been readier to steady her weight against his. Yes, she once had faith in Kalala, and now she must teach herself that he has always been her secret foe. It is the only answer. She fell for his tricks because he seemed kind, and was good with words, and full of stories, and he was a friend to her. A mistake. This is Pa's story. When the ship comes back, Kalala will be taken away, and whatever has to happen will happen to him. Life can continue. Her father can be her father again. Who wouldn't choose that? All they have to remember is that Lizzie found Albert, and they will mourn him and forget Kalala. The interlopers will go, the scarred earth will grass over, and the new sheep will graze in the place of the old roots. That's what Lizzie keeps trying to tell herself. She has to make herself believe it. If she can't, everything will collapse. Everything.

But Ada won't let her.

'I thought it must have been an accident,' she insists. 'I thought Albert suffocated. Because I never told about the Oven. He didn't know.'

'What's the Oven? Why didn't you tell *me* about it, Lizzie?' Queenie picks at her. 'Is that where you found him?'

Lizzie's head will come apart if they don't both let her be. Everything is in her hands. She has to choose. She can't. She is tripping and falling over the strange story she wants to tell herself, the one that matches her father's. Her body, surging hot and cold in turn, refuses her efforts. The skin around her forehead tightens.

'I didn't say it was an accident.' She didn't say anything. Nobody did, not to anyone, except Kalala, perhaps, to the Islanders, from whom he has now been barred. As he has from her. Of course. And then she whispers half the truth, just the part she's sure of. 'Albert's head was broken. Smashed in. Before he was hidden in the cave. Now, please, please, leave me alone.'

Disturbed, their mother turns back to look at them again, and the girls spring apart.

Mrs Peacock sets Gussie back on her feet and looks at her youngest daughter with bemusement, as if for a moment she's hardly certain who stands there. She blinks. 'Take your thumb out of your mouth,' she orders. 'Come along, girls. Quickly. Chores won't go away. The kanakas have to eat. They have work to do.'

Domestic rituals need no discussion. The goats are tetchy and restless, obtusely noisy. A kid has pulled free of its tether and pushed its way through the thorn bushes. It has nibbled half the sprouting maize almost to the ground when Lizzie finds and falls on it, blind with anger and fear. Whose fault was this? Who will be blamed? Can these plants recover?

Her rage disturbs the milk goats, whose hot and straining udders are already veined and aching, and can hardly bear the release for which they long. Lizzie pushes the old white nanny's head through the usual forked stake, ties her fast, then blows on her hands to cool them down. She kneads the hard bags like dough, and the goat startles and kicks till Lizzie catches one back leg as she raises it to strike again, and squeezes its tendon hard. The animal's doubly trapped. Lizzie keeps holding on with one hand, and pulls down with the other, releasing a pulsing stream of whiteness. It takes all her concentration. Exactly what she needs. All she wants filling her mind is the zing of milk hitting milk, the ever-forming froth of it. It would be a comfort to lay her cheek against the goat's coarse, musky hide.

39

NOW I HAVE NO CHOICE. I AM A CAPTIVE AS SURELY as my father ever was, the walls around me secured, in silence, by my own brothers, watched over by our master. Billy brings me food, silently pushing a pannikin under the lowest of the bars they built too willingly, but he is too scared to help me eat it, and my wrists are still bound.

'Billy?' I twist from my stake, turning as much as my rope will allow. 'Do *you* believe your father?'

He walks away. I am losing hope that Lizzie will come.

Some hours later, I hear movement, a lumbering thud and rustle just beyond my walls. I strain body and ears. 'Who's there?' I call, low-voiced. 'Pineki?'

'No. It's Luka.'

'Luka!' Tallest and strongest of us all, but he is not the bravest.

'Yes. But I cannot talk to you.'

'You are talking now.'

'It is forbidden. I have come to fetch tools – that is all – I must hurry back. We have to build a new storehut, now, on the other side.'

'Who can stop you talking?'

'I am afraid.'

I think of all that steel and wood, all the tools on this island – too many for Luka to carry alone – spade and hoe, hammer, fork, shovel, pick and axe, plane and chisel. Knives and saws. The whetstone sharpening with a hungry rasp. Mr Peacock is only one man. But with one tool he can control us all.

'Who can hear you?'

A sigh.

'Nobody. I am alone.'

'Then listen to me . . . step to the other side, where he cannot see you talk.'

'No, no. I cannot. I dare not. He watches me now.'

I am impatient.

'Luka! Step where he cannot see you!'

'No. He will come if he cannot see, if I do not hurry.'

'Because of the gun?'

'He carries it always now. Or the boy does. I must go.'

In my mind I take myself to the sea and dive through tumbling waves, striking out with every limb at liberty, cutting with ease and pleasure through the water's resistance. I thump my bound fists on the stake behind my back, and the rope scorches my wrists.

*

The shadows of the bars slide slowly across the dusty floor, narrowing, narrowing, then widening again. Once I hear a snatch of song: Queenie's breathy up-and-down hum, as she clunks up the path behind my hut to fill her water pail. I remember her sisters passing, the argument I overheard that first drew me in. Her tune stops in its middle, as if for a moment she had forgotten all that has just passed, and now remembers.

*

At last Solomona is permitted to come to me. Still he counsels patience.

'All will be well yet. It is like a fever, this conviction. A kind of madness, brought on by fear and the death of his son. It will surely pass in time. He must see his error.' He tells me he has bargained a parley with my accuser, protests again that he believes our master will be amenable to reason in time, when grief and shock abate. As my brother speaks, Mr Peacock stands a little way off, listening and looking on with a sideways slant, his face blank and hard. I wait for Solomona to tell me to pray for this stricken man, and know I never will. We are backsliders both.

'Yet can you reason with mind-sickness?' I ask Solomona. He does not answer. 'Can you?'

Then my words spew out in a chaos of complaint. How can anyone believe his accusations? Can't they see what he is hiding with them?

He looks over his shoulder, and tries to hush me. And then he whispers:

'But, that first day we all looked for the boy, *did* you search alone?'

'No. With Pineki.'

He swallows, with effort, like a man taking foul medicine,

unwilling to remind me of what I had forgotten, and only half remember still: how long I sat in the green light of the clearing, waiting for Pineki to return, listening and hoping but seeing no one. Perhaps I have spent too much time alone all through these months, or only with Lizzie and Queenie. But what does it matter when there is no fono to hear us out, and all our voices all together add up to nothing. Not even Solomona's.

'And Lizzie? She has still said nothing yet?' I ask, recalling how urgently she spoke in my defence on our return, when first her father beat me. Until I can talk to her, convince her, I can risk no accusations. And yet she hides from me. Behind my back my fingernails pierce my skin and my palms weep blood.

'Nothing. It is the madness of grief. He has no one else to blame and he wants to make a sacrifice. Who else here can suffer for the boy's death?' murmurs my brother, pressing his forehead against the bars, his eyes trying to steady mine. 'When the crew have departed.'

'The crew?' I say, incredulous. 'You believe a sailor crept away to kill a stranger? Unseen by all? For what purpose?'

'Who else could it have been?'

My neck, already twisted to look at Solomona, cannot turn far enough to jerk my head towards Mr Peacock.

I see the sudden falling in my brother, the dipping knees and screw of torso that comes with knowledge. I feel the fall myself. Now he has seen what I have freshly seen, and just as suddenly. And the nature of my trap. How carefully I must tread. But Solomona? Who is free and wise and commands respect. Surely he can find a way to set things right?

'Say nothing out loud,' my brother warns. 'He understands more of our language than we know.'

Solomona forces a hand through a gap between the wooden bars, the closest he can come to touching me. He is still a full arm's distant, the space between us vast, and I can move no closer. He says nothing of providence or prayer now. He does not remind me that the pure in heart are blessed.

'Save your anger,' he says softly. 'Learn from this. Be patient and trusting. In this storm, let hope be the anchor of your soul, my brother. Will your anchor hold?'

My ropes are straining hard. I say nothing. An angry dog rips at my chest.

'Remember, my brother . . . ' Solomona puts on his softest, most soothing voice, and I hear the echo of Mr Reverend as he speaks. 'Until the next ship comes, you are safer in prison than outside. Let us wait for a fair and Christian trial, as Mr Peacock has promised us, and then, then, we surely will have justice.'

I curse his calmness. He is not caged like an animal. His outstretched hand crumples and withdraws. Finger and thumb press his nose, jam his eye-corners, stuff the leaking. I will not care. I look away.

The quieter I can make myself, he says, the more freedom I can gain. Little by little. My hands will be bound before me, and not to take to the stake. He will secure me sanitation. He tells me as a comfort, but to me these victories seem paltry. He wants me to love my enemy, but I would rather take the sword and perish by it. Be grateful for this palagi punishment, he tells me. Better caged here than burning in this hut, or sent out to sea in a vaka, slowly sinking. 'Turn the other cheek,' he says.

I turn my back instead. Solomona stands waiting for some time, and calls my name, then leaves me.

40

M R PEACOCK SITS UP AND SMOKES AND KEEPS
guard all through the long dark hours. It is like
rat-watching all over again. Instead of tending a fire,
he cradles a drink. Like Higgins before him the captain of the
Esperanza was generous with his brandy. Mrs Peacock lies wishing
her husband would leave off and come to bed, then falls into a
sleep so heavy she does not hear the baby in the night and wakes
with sweetly leaking breasts, and a milk-soaked shift. So it is
Lizzie who tiptoes with tea at dawn, and finds her father slumped
and snoring under the tree, arms wound round his gun. His
mouth hangs open wetly, a dribbled crust collecting in one corner.

The Islanders' hut is silent still. She glances towards the caged
front of the storehut. Too late to look away: Kalala's seen her.
Lizzie raises a flat hand – a dulled greeting, but one which Kalala
returns doubled, showing his bound wrists. She feels the pull of
him, always. She heats and shivers under his scrutiny. He is
waiting to see what she will do, and she knows that she must
talk to him. But what can she say? For all her doubts, she finds

she cannot tear her loyalty from her father. Her oblivion, once so careless, is wilful. She can think of no other way to protect the family. If Ada and Queenie could only understand.

Mr Peacock does not stir.

The tin cup burns her knuckles; she has to put it down. She presses flat a circle in the grass so it will not tip and spill, and the steam rises. She startles when her father shifts and stretches, and turns quickly on her heel before he catches her in the act . . . of what, exactly? Then she sees that Ada has been watching all this time, leaning against the doorjamb of the girls' whare, arms folded, neck jutted like an egret's.

Doubly watched, Lizzie becomes clumsy, trips on a root and stumbles. Rights herself with reddening cheeks. That hissing's back in her ears, a noisy kind of nothingness she can't unhear.

'You're as blind as ever,' says Ada quietly when she's back. 'Blind and deaf.'

And mute. Lizzie ignores her, brushing past her sister to check the milk she's set out to clabber. Inside, she holds the jar up to the light. The curd has massed together beautifully, and floats above the thin blue whey, like soft high clouds. She drapes a square of muslin across a basin, and scoops out the quivering mass. Squeezing the soft curds into shape, she feels the accusation in Ada's stare more fiercely with every drip of whey.

'Why can't you see?' Her sister moves closer.

Arms winged on narrow hips, Lizzie tries to bend out the aching in her body.

'Why won't you?' They are enemies again. 'Look me in the eye, Lizzie, and tell me you believe that . . . that . . . *boy* . . . could have killed our brother.'

She can't. Of course she can't. Queenie comes to the doorway, the big family Bible held to her chest, reproach on her freckled face. She stands with Ada. They face her together, blocking her escape.

'Lizzie, you know who did it,' says Ada. 'Stop pretending.'

'We *know* you know who killed him,' says Queenie. 'And we know too.'

They all know? Yes. All three of them.

Each girl has worked out the truth, some part of it, quickly or slowly, reluctantly or with relief. And they have each worked out the others know. There's nobody else it could have been. Maybe, in her heart, even Ma knows too. Lizzie is cornered. It's almost a relief. She can't save Pa. But perhaps, she thinks at last, he's not worth saving.

'So what are we going to do, Lizzie?' Queenie asks. 'What are *you* going to do?'

41

I AM LOSING HOPE. I AM LOSING MYSELF. I LOSE HOLD of day and night and every moment is a between time, never one thing nor another. *I am poured out like water, and all my bones are out of joint: my heart is like wax; it is melted in the midst of my bowels.* Forsaken, I press towards light, and see only darkness. In my dreams I am possessed again, or so it seems, and now my visions take forms too close to truth to bear. I roll, sickening, in the foul hold of the slaving ship, the cries of the dead in my ears. I wake to the smell of my own urine. I no longer know who I am, nor where this journey can take me. Even now, when I should be best prepared, I hear nothing. No footsteps. No knock. Break me down, Lord, I cry again. Enter my soul. Show me the path I must tread to reach everlasting salvation. I hear the wind, and the waves, and I hear the beating of my heart, but still nobody calls. Storm without light rages in my breast. I empty myself, and yet I find no space, nor door, nor keyhole for the Lord to enter.

Ever since the day Mr Reverend first spoke to me of such

things, since I was a small child, I have listened for the Holy
Spirit. I have never heard Him speak. I have told nobody. The
fault lay with me, I was once persuaded. I have never listened
hard enough. Surely I would know Him? He has never called.
And now I believe He never will.

I have made a shipwreck of my faith.

Since we came here, other creatures burn my soul, maybe devils
come to tempt me, maybe outcast spirits, perhaps even my own
father. I cannot tell. Why did I not speak earlier with Solomona
of the Stolen Ones? What held my tongue? My doubts multiply.
If I could only hear the voices clearly, I could be guided, I believe
. . . surely then I would know whether and how they may be
honoured – or banished? If they come now to punish me for my
forgetting, or to tell me where they lie. My skull rocks with the
beating of half-seen fists, and I am deafened, and made sore, or
perhaps I cannot truly hear them because they are nothing at all.
Agonies my own soul has dreamed up in punishment. I am
become my own best persecutor.

Hour after hour I keep no thought at bay. Perhaps the worst
is always this: I cannot hear or be heard because there is nobody
beyond to hear me, nobody calling. Nothing but myself. No
other world but this. No justice but man's justice. And Solomona
cannot wait for God to save me. But how can I make him see
this?

Solomona creeps by. He kneels at my bars.

'I have sought permission to pray with you,' he says, seeking
to reassure me.

'Pray?' My bitter laughter frightens him. What binds him still
to our palagi master? What blinds him? It is too late. We have
been betrayed. 'But I am a fish in a net.'

'No, no, not yet. Do not despair.' He understands, he tells me earnestly. 'Always remember, Kalala, *the Lord is my defence; and my God is the rock of my refuge.*'

Thy refuge, maybe.

I shake my head. I moan. I have no refuge, anywhere.

'Pray for me, if you will. And for yourself. I am done with prayer.'

Solomona sighs and shivers. Will he tell me again that God will provide? Is this injustice the work of our Lord? Oh, Solomona, can you not see what this island has laid before us? We have to help ourselves in other ways.

'Please listen to me, Kalala. It is never too late for salvation. Pray now. And if God wills it, and the worst is soon to come, then rejoice and prepare to meet thy Maker. Take comfort in this. After one short sleep, your awakening may be forever. Make yourself always ready for that blessed forever.'

I do not answer my brother. This can be no comfort.

I am not ready. I will never be ready. I want justice, here and now, not salvation.

42

LIZZIE BEGINS TO SPY. SHE LOOKS FOR CHINKS AND cracks. The first she sees is Solomona.

He comes to Mr Peacock one evening before supper. A polite cough, and then he holds out his English Bible.

'Surely not Sunday come again already, Solomona? Not more prayers?'

Pa's scorn is flustering. But slowly, carefully, Kalala's brother has come to a decision, and it is clear to Lizzie that he is determined to see it through.

'Sir, I must speak with you. It is very important.'

'Speak away.'

'My brother is innocent, sir. You must believe me.'

'I don't.' Mr Peacock – now drinking openly, all day, half an eye on the prison – raises his flask as if to toast his denial. Solomona flinches, and returns to the fray.

'You must. I swear he is. Look, sir. I come here now to swear his innocence on the Holy Book. Kalala did not kill your son and you must release him. Now. Tonight. And if not, I swear we will work for you no longer.'

Lizzie waits through a terrible silence. Release him, she thinks. Release me.

Solomona tries again.

'Believe me, sir, not one of us will lift a hand to help you if you refuse.'

There's a chance. Isn't there a chance? Solomona waits patiently, ever obedient. Until her father replies with a mocking laugh.

'Well, *Reverend* Solomona, you may swear whatever you please, and it will serve nothing. You can't blackmail me. Nor lay down the law. Because I can do without kanakas in my kingdom.'

Bent over the camp oven, stirring up smoked mutton-bird stew, listening, Mrs Peacock freezes, hardly believing what she hears. She is too ashamed to look at Solomona.

'Oh yes,' Mr Peacock continues. 'I could before and I can again. I've had enough of you natives. And your sort – with all your reading and writing and religion, you're the worst. Do you think I can't see through you? No better than n—'

'Joseph,' warns Mrs Peacock, hesitantly. But it's too late. Her husband's on his feet. He leers at Solomona. He rages at him.

'Because I know you're all the same, whatever airs you put on. Cheating, lying, jumped-up savages. Do what you like. But I'll house you no longer and I'll give you no more food.' And then he laughs, delighted with himself. 'You can eat each other, for all I care.'

Lizzie longs for Solomona to resist further, just as she always longed for Albert to fight back. But she knows it is not in his nature. *May God give him strength,* she hears her mother whisper. It seems He does. Their island minister has spoken his last words to his former master. Lips pressed tightly shut, Solomona walks away with dignity.

*

Pa's laughter quickly dies. 'How dare they?' he mutters, over and over again. The girls exchange anxious glances as they gather plates and cutlery. Something has changed, though they are not sure what. Only that the work-gang's defiance has ignited their father's anger to a new intensity. To be treated with disdain on his own land is more than he can stand. It goes against the natural order of things. It goes against God Himself. On and on and on he rants. When Ma tries to quieten him with a plate of stew, he knocks it from her hand, and takes off into the falling night. Now there's no telling what he might do.

'Follow him, Lizzie,' urges Ada. 'See where he's going.'

It's not long before she's back.

'He's up on the bluff,' Lizzie reports. 'I don't know what he's doing there. But he was dragging something huge.' A vast piece of seasoned timber.

Later, he returns for more, and also rope.

While Mr Peacock works on by starlight on the headland, ordering Billy to guard the prisoner, Queenie takes a basin of taro mash to the Islanders. But the men have abandoned their hut, she finds. Their revolt is open. Branch by branch, they are dragging green wood down to the beach, where Solomona is building a new bonfire which they plan to light in the morning, and keep smoking until the next ship passes.

43

ALONE IN MY CONFINEMENT, AND ANOTHER DAY GOES by with no word from Solomona, not even any sound nor sight of him, not since I saw him talking to Mr Peacock. And no sign of him either. But at last Lizzie's voice sounds in my ears – truly it is her voice and no imaginings of mine, as I fear – and I hear her tell her stubborn brother that he must sleep and eat while she takes her turn. Their father has ordered Billy to rest, and eat, or he will be good for nothing, or so she tells him. The family must work as one now they are alone on the island again, or good as, she preaches. All stick together. She wheedles, smooths his hair, inspects his bloodshot eyes. His will begins to falter. He releases his grip on the weapon. My hands, now bound before me, close on my bars.

She takes his place under the tree and looks at the gun. She tucks it into her shoulder, screws up one eye and slowly swings the barrel towards me. I stiffen.

She lowers it, but not entirely, and begins to talk, softly calling across the space between us.

'I am just pretending, Kalala. I am doing this for show in case Pa comes. So Billy doesn't betray us.'

I say nothing.

'How yellow the sky is today,' she tells me. My tongue unpeels from the roof of my mouth. I can see little of the sky.

'The smoke's going everywhere.' She rubs her eyes, viciously, and blinks to clear her sight. 'At the kitchen. On the beach. That's where your brothers are. You know they'll do nothing more for my father? They won't even speak to the rest of us. They work only to tend the bonfire. And they fish from the rocks. We hear them chanting. They are calling the fish. And they watch for ships from the shore.'

So Solomona has renounced his earthly master. Though my heart is thankful for this, I cannot be certain his revolt, or even a ship, will save me. I cannot yet be certain of the daughter. *Come up, come up,* I sing to myself. *Oh dark-brown fish, oh barb-headed fish, oh rough-backed fish, oh black-backed fish, oh striped-tail fish. Come up, come up, slippery fish, slippery girl fish. Come up and tell me what you mean to do with me.* What foolishness made me hope she might ever take my side against her father? They may be as slippery as each other.

'And Pineki and Luka are making something and Gus went to watch them, and when we asked her what they're making, she said stones. But that must be some nonsense. How do you make a stone?'

Nonsense that buoys my heart.

'You do understand? This is for show?' Again she says that word, holding up the gun again, then laying it beside her. She seems careless with it, which makes my breath catch. 'You know I haven't come to hurt you?'

'Why have you come?'

She looks around quickly, then shuffles closer, sideways, buttock to buttock, so that she can stop at any moment, and still be clearly guarding me.

'I'm frightened,' she says. 'Have you heard, Kalala? My father's mad for vengeance. Did Billy tell you what he is building now?'

I shake my head. She leans forward, and her voice is dry leaves.

'We believe he means to hang you.'

Unbidden, my hand rises to circle my neck; beneath my thumb I feel life throb.

'I didn't kill your brother,' I tell her.

'I know you didn't.' She does not look away.

'I never saw him alive. None of us did. None of us Rock fellows.'

'No. None of you. I know.'

Lizzie cups her hands over her eyes.

'You hoped we had,' I say. It sounds like an accusation. So I soften myself. 'I would, in your place. I would wish that too. But I will not be his scapegoat.'

'No, no. I'm sorry,' she says. 'I'm so sorry. We know who killed him. We're sure of it. All of us, except for Billy. But we will make him see.'

This will not be easy. The boy has made an idol of his father.

'When will your father be finished?'

'I don't know. It can't be long.' She looks back and up to the headland, and shakes her head. 'I think . . . I hope, he will wait for the next ship to come. He *promised* a trial. But we cannot be certain.'

'He works alone?'

'Always now. He says you fellows have all betrayed him. He

trusts nobody but me and Billy. He raves all night . . . says nobody will steal his island from him and you'll never take his family. We daren't defy him. What can we do, Kalala? How can we help you?'

Finally, we talk. And though we cannot speak for half the time that both would wish, together we shape a strategy.

44

'Joseph,' says Mrs Peacock, whose husband has not lain beside her for three nights and days. He has neither washed nor slept, and she can barely persuade him to sit to sup. Unsteady with sleeplessness as well as drink, he smells of both, and something else besides, something dank and angry and fearful.

Mr Peacock pushes his breakfast plate away and looks at her.

'Joseph,' she repeats, 'the children are sick of mutton-bird, and so am I. It turns my milk, and pains the baby. We've had no fresh meat since Joe was born. The clearing of the terraces has eaten all your time.'

'Billy will watch again today, won't you, Billy?' says Queenie, pushing him forward. She looks hard at Lizzie, who takes her father's plate and stacks it. Ada is putting on the show this morning, standing watch over the prisoner. 'Run along.'

Mr Peacock's eyes swim.

'Then who'll come a-hunting with me?' he asks, plaintively. 'If it's not my Billy. And how will we catch a goat without a gun? Where is my gun?'

'With Ada now, and soon with Billy. But I'm coming hunting with you, don't worry. It'll be like old times, won't it, Pa?' says Lizzie gently. 'Remember?'

He is remembering, slowly. The months that passed when the bullets were all spent, and all they had were hands and ropes and knives to catch and kill.

'We'll be too few,' he says. 'I'll take the gun.'

Lizzie is quick, but Queenie has become quicker still, and braver too.

'No, Pa, Billy will need it more,' she says. 'Or how can he keep us safe? I've got the knife. We'll keep the dogs here too, don't worry.'

The three big girls have agreed the part each must play. Ma knows too. Now Lizzie speaks again.

'Remember how fast I am, Pa? How strong?'

'Yes,' he says. 'You always were the strongest. You should have been—'

'Ready then?' Lizzie hands him the sack which Queenie has just passed to her, and then holds out his jacket.

'Goat hunting?' he asks, as if he has already forgotten every word they've just exchanged.

'Yes, Pa. Come on, Pa. You need to put this on.'

He forces one arm between lining and fustian, but does not hear the tearing. Ma winces. Queenie redirects his hand's backward thrust, fastens his buttons, hands him his hat.

'We're going goat hunting this morning? For milk or meat?' he asks.

'Meat, Pa. Fresh meat. The milkers are doing well. We'll have curds tonight.'

'Just us two?' Pa is plaintive, like an abandoned child.

'Ada and Queenie will come and join us later, and then we'll be four. Five with Sal.'

Lizzie puts her own hat on, and begins to steer her father out. Queenie takes Gussie's hand in hers and steps them both back a little, taking them out of the way.

Almost at the doorway, Mr Peacock turns, and the girls stare.

'Bye, baby bunting,' he sings hoarsely. 'Daddy's going a- . . . No, no. I can't leave my son, my darling boy, my Joey.' He separates himself from Lizzie and lurches over to the cradle. With pouched eyes he leans over to gaze at the waking child as if embarking on a long sea voyage, as if he'd not return for months. And then he remembers his wife, and his eyes fill up. Nobody has ever seen him so sentimental. 'Or your mother. Your excellent mother. Oh, Mrs P. What a woman you are. What a woman. How can I leave you?'

His lumbering focus switches.

'For a morning? Of course you can leave me,' says Mrs Peacock, shouldering past him to pick up the baby. She unbuttons the top of her blouse and pushes her leaning husband away. 'We've managed before, often enough. We'll manage again. And when you come back, we will cut your beard, Joseph. It's getting so long again.'

*

Arm in arm, Lizzie and her father walk away from the huts. It is like strolling – rolling – with a foremast hand, fresh in port. When they lived at the hotel, the Peacock children used to laugh behind their hands at the green young sailors, copying their gait as soon as they were out of sight. Lizzie clasps both hands together to make them stronger, and squeezes her elbow tight against her ribs, to support her father better when he swerves. Pa's hand is both familiar and strange, from its thumbnail, broad and ridged, to the back of it – liver-dappled, creeping black hairs, veins that twist like vines across a fan of bones – and that smooth, snaking scar. He will hear her heart in her throat, Lizzie frets, forcing a smile to her lips. She wonders how she will ever speak again, now her tongue has grown so swollen.

'Ah, Lizzie,' he says, and stops to look her up and down. 'My loyal Lizzie.'

'Yes, Pa,' she lies. 'Let's keep walking. Which way shall we go, Pa?'

They have to know for certain, to hear it from his own lips. That's what they all decided. And that way Kalala can never hang. You do it, Lizzie, the others said. You're the only one who can. If he'll tell anyone, he'll tell you. You need to be alone, quite alone, but we'll follow soon after. Not far behind. They promised.

'Where do you think they'll be hiding?' says Mr Peacock, considering. 'We'll look for one that's on its own. That's the way. Creep up before he smells us coming.' He pats the sheath knife tucked into his belt.

'Yes.'

They pass the powdery silver circle beneath the sturdy frame of the smoking fire, and he talks of ambushes, and pincer movements, of Taranaki, and what the wars taught him – to look for land that belongs to no one; to respect your enemy, always. She tries to listen. Down first into the gully, through the straggle of trees, but instead of heading up into the forest where the goats will be, as Lizzie expects, Pa takes the broad, grassy path that climbs up to the bluff.

It was their mother who first muttered gallows, and Queenie who went to spy, reporting something monumental in his intentions. Such grandeur was almost reassuring in that it gave them time. Pa still intended to wait. He was setting up a stage, and meant to vindicate himself in public, knowing he stood to be believed. No captain could countenance mutiny.

But Lizzie didn't want to hear what care her father was taking to make his towering structure, how deep he had dug the pit where their look out bonfire used to rage, nor how wide. Wide enough to bury the four arms of the base which would make the upright strong enough. Strong enough not to break under the weight of a man, Queenie told them. Braced by ship's knees. Lizzie won't look. She won't let him take her there.

'The other track, Pa,' she says. 'We'll be in the forest faster that way.'

She switches from his left side to his right and tries to guide him, pushing her shoulder against his side as if forcing an unwieldy cow through a gate. With her coaxing, his direction slowly alters.

'Where did you catch the other goat?' She will have to name him. 'When you were with Albert? Can you remember where they were roaming then?'

The land dips here again a little before it begins to rise once more, but they are on their way, slowed only by Mr Peacock's body's refusal to follow his feet. Again and again, despite her urging, he looks back over his shoulder, waiting for the moment when the headland becomes visible from above again. At last, satisfaction sweeps uncertainty from her father's face, and then Lizzie can't help but look herself.

All momentum gained is lost by what she sees there. Her arms drop. She pushes back her sun hat and shades her eyes, and stares again. Her vision is unbalanced by the bright sea and sky, unbalanced perhaps by the flood of relief she feels at the sight before her, an organ-shifting wave of respite. She can't believe this.

Mr Peacock stands behind her, chest rising and falling, hands weighting her shoulders, directing her gaze, as always.

'So this is what you have been making,' breathes Lizzie. She longs to run back and tell Ada and Queenie, and her mother, and Billy. And Kalala of course, and Solomona. All mistaken. Everybody must know about this, as soon as possible. If only they had all dared come before.

Rising like a mast from the headland she sees not a gallows but a cross. Majestic in its simplicity, two or three times the height of any man, it commands the ocean for miles. From the deck of an approaching vessel, you could hardly miss this rood, so straight and true, barely bowing in the strong breeze. To Lizzie, it speaks of atonement. A longing for forgiveness. This is the first step. And in the perfect place. This bluff has always seemed to her nearer to God, closer to the angels than anywhere else on the island. Her father is building the answer to Solomona's prayers.

So this must be the moment.

'Pa?' she says, preparing herself. Kalala talked of some other sort of sign, but surely her father has brought her here, in sight of the newly built cross, in order to confess and then repent? He must believe her capable of mercy. And perhaps she is. She raises her voice a little: 'Pa?'

'I trust it will be strong enough,' he says, rubbing his beard. The wind has dropped completely and Mr Peacock has also ceased to sway. Everything is still. 'It must not bend. Yes, it should be strong enough. We'll see.'

He turns his back on it, and marches towards the mountain. Lizzie fails to follow, for she stands transfixed. A ladder, also newly made, lies at the bottom of the cross. Ropes hang from the end of each horizontal arm. Bewildered, she runs to catch up with her father. All sentiment has vanished from his face.

'So what do you think, Lizzie?' he says to her. 'Will it take his weight?'

45

No food. No guard. All morning I have been alone again, voiceless, hungering, catching in my ears only rattling leaves and creaking branches. So when I see my brother far away, how can I tell what brings him, what conversations, fears, decisions? Yet I have grounds for hope: leaving the burning on the beach, they move swiftly, with great purpose. I watch them march up through the lower gardens like warriors, grim-faced Solomona in the middle, a little ahead, closely flanked by Vilipate, Likatau and Iakopo, and also Pineki, whose eyes and feet keep dancing, who throws a black stone from palm to palm, like a memory, and cannot still any part of himself. All but Solomona carry stones, I see now. More stones weigh down their clicketting pockets and drag their stride.

Rustling, unsteady, I back myself to my feet. I press my face and imploring arms against the splintering bars to hear what brings them, to call to Solomona and beg forgiveness for my too stony heart. If he brings promise of escape, I will hide nothing from him, I tell myself. Time, not proof, has given substance to my convictions. I am ready to test them against my brother's understanding, and he, I have to trust, will hear me with an open ear. So many hours of turning over thought have left me with one desire. Some hideling truths, in this world or another, may never be skewered. I accept that. I know I cannot point to where our blood father's bones may lie. I cannot thrust my hand into his wounds. But together, Solomona and I, we may resurrect him. Together we can put doubt to purpose, side by side pursue lost stories of all our stolen fathers, ask questions, put words with words, island with island, past with past. Their lives will not be buried. They have left prints in us.

At that moment I see my fellows do not come alone. From the palagi dwellings another, smaller march is leaving, this one led by Ada. As full of purpose as Solomona, the oldest Peacock girl holds her head high. Behind stalks Queenie, and little Gus. Behind them Billy, undecided still perhaps, whose footsteps weave, who looks anxiously from here to there, eyeing uneasily his former workmates across the way.

Lizzie is gone. No sign of her father either. Which means one thing. I swither again, shaken by darts of fear for Lizzie. Land or family? What's one without the other, for Mr Peacock? I remember how he looked at me at our landfall, sized up my use to him as I lay strengthless under the bluff, washed by tide, watched by the dog. He had marked me out then, perhaps, and he has watched and used me since. I cannot tell how he may be marking Lizzie out today, where he has taken her. Was I wrong to urge her on this quest alone? It was her choice.

On all faces here, both sides, suspicion simmers. They halt, slack-watered. I look from each to each, hoping for understanding. But with a vengeful grimace, the look of his forefathers all about him, Pineki stares at Ada and raises his throwing arm. At once I beat the bars with my bound fists and roar at him:

'No! No! Stop! Now!'

Like sea reflecting sun, Ada and Solomona each spread wide their arms to hold their parties back. But Solomona speaks first, a king at last.

46

Bloodless, she feels. Everything that makes her human drained away. Some demon has taken hold of Pa. Something incomprehensible. It's turned his mind utterly. And still he rants and seethes beside her. He throws his head back, and spittle flies. 'How dare they? They'll soon see what I am. I'm going to make an example of that boy . . . They'll see. I'll not stand for it. Nobody can take my land. That phoney preacher with his airs – all humbly-bumbly – sir, oh, sir. Doesn't mean a word. I know what they want. Never. Never.'

And then Pa remembers she's there, and presses her for an answer. 'So what do you think, Lizzie? Don't you think it's fine? Good and strong?'

'I don't know,' she blurts out. 'But look, Pa, look! Up there! Quick! Run!'

Somehow she has to make her stone limbs move. She's seen nothing, but Lizzie charges into the forest, certain her father will pursue her for as long as she can convince him of the urgency of this wild chase. She dashes along the track so fast he can barely keep up.

'Where?' he wheezes. 'I don't see it.'

As long as she keeps running, as long as her determination can convince him, he will follow. If she stops pretending now, he'll never drop his guard. Lizzie thunders on, closer and closer to the planned meeting point. Pa gains on her. Afraid he'll see she's chasing air, she puts on a final extra spurt to give herself some distance, then makes a sideways dash off the path, and collapses onto her knees.

'It got away . . . ' she lies, turning a face to her father, so distraught that his heart melts when he catches up with her. He kneels beside her, hoarse and burning, lurches oddly, but once he's got his breath, turns gentle. Unsuspicious. Sorrowful.

'You tried your best,' he says, with heaving lungs. 'Sharp eyes, my spadge. I never saw the beast. What would I do without you?'

Lizzie shakes her head, and delays the moment with unfeigned exhaustion. She's got him away from everyone. Now she must make him speak. Oh, but where's all her boldness gone? Where's her cunning?

'Sorry, Pa.'

'Not to worry. There'll be another. We'll not return empty-handed.'

Both still panting. Both hearts racing. They slump together against tree roots shaped into a kind of seat. He shifts his hand to cover hers, and pats it, reassuringly. She forces herself to smile.

'No. I hope not.'

And overcoming all revulsion, she compels herself to squeeze his hand, tight as she can, in both of hers. She has to make him trust her, pity her.

'What's that for, Lizzie?'

'I'm frightened,' she confesses, shivering, clinging on to him. She can't let go. 'Frightened of what you'll do to me.'

'What's this, Lizzie?'

He's slow today. Befuddled. She ploughs on.

'I mean when I tell you what I know.'

His head jerks back, and he stares at her, impenetrable, while his chest rises and falls, rises and falls, with exaggerated effort. She holds on tighter, the only way she can think to remind him that he loves her, that she's his Lizzie, and he can never hurt her.

'Because it's just you and me now, Pa. Just the two of us.'

She will drip possibilities as slowly as she dares.

'The kanakas have already turned against us. You know that. You saw them go. But it's not just them, Pa. Anger's rising everywhere. Everyone else is going to abandon us, Pa. Even Ma. Remember when she nearly left us before? But this time, oh, this time, if we go back . . . no, no, we can't. You see I've heard them talking. I've hidden, and I've heard them, Pa. I'm telling you, we can't go back . . .'

'What's happened, Lizzie? What are you saying?'

Eyes still on their clasped hands, gripping harder than ever, she fills her shuddering lungs and finally speaks.

'It's because of what you did, Pa. What you did to Albert.'

Silence. He shakes his head.

'Kalala killed Albert. He must pay.'

'No, no, Pa.' She sighs, patiently. Only kindness will work now. She actually kisses the hand she's still holding, and strokes his wrist. 'No. You know that's not true.'

And then, at last, she tells him. Though she wants to scream the words, she keeps her voice kind.

'We all know you killed him. Nobody else could have. Every-body sees that. And whatever you do now, they'll none of them ever work for you again, they say. Not Ma, not Ada, not Queenie, not even Billy. So no workers. No family. On all the island.'

'They've told you this?'

She prevaricates.

'I've heard them talking.'

Pa throws off her hand and falls to his knees in front of her, seized with sudden panic.

'And what about you, Lizzie? My Lizzie? What do you think? Will you still help me?'

She shrugs, tears quietly sliding. Still no denial, but her father becomes pitiful.

'You'll stay with me? *You* won't leave me? No, you can't. *You're* still mine.'

She can't let her hatred show. Not yet.

'Oh, Pa, I don't know. How can I know what I should do? You haven't even told me what happened.'

She stands up, loosens his hand, and begins to walk away. Slow, terrified steps, which he must follow.

'Lizzie! Stop! I'll tell you. I'll explain. I'll *make* you understand.'

She wants to run again but she waits for him, her thoughts roaring more loudly than his voice, pulling her this way and that, smashing her against cliff and coral, winding her in weed. What exactly *is* he saying? She frowns at his moving lips, flinches from the fingers whitening her arm. She *must* not show her fear.

Her father talks of the white-hot boiling turmoil that rose like lava inside him, a rage beyond his power to contain. He can barely remember what happened, he says. The details aren't import-ant, he says. He did not know what he was doing, how it happened. It was all too quick, too overwhelming. He holds her wrist now, as perhaps he gripped her brother's, and her skin burns as he speaks of his own pain. How can she know the agony of such sorrow, such betrayal, the sharp, unhealing wound carved by ingratitude? From your own son. They are shaded by tree ferns here; elegant, slender-trunked, parasolling far above their heads with effortless grace. Lizzie thinks of the neat unwinding of their central fronds, precise and promising, so like her father's fiddlehead, always more to come, and she listens bleakly to the wheedling tune he plays so insistently now: 'This was for him. It would have been Albert's, for ever and ever. But he didn't want it. He wouldn't take it.'

His pleading repels Lizzie. She reels away from the pickle smell of his breath, and shrinks from the pressure of his hands and the reeking pores of his skin. And still this is not a confession. She can't think while he is so close, surging at her, threatening to drag her downwards in his undertow. She rolls answers round her tongue, tasting them, and wonders how to spit them out. *No, Albert didn't want your paradise. He never did. And of course you never thought of me. You could have let him go, instead of hating him for being what you made him. You who gave him life could have let him live. You think we belong only to you, and we must drift in your wake, or be cast off. You are hardly better than a blackbirder.* None of this she says out loud. All pity has clabbered to loathing.

'But what happened, Pa? Tell me exactly. I need to know.'

BEFORE

'I can't see,' said Albert, and the leaves around him trembled with the dip of the branch they both straddled. 'Where are you pointing?'

'Look harder, damn you.' From behind, Mr Peacock's hand reached across to clamp the back of Albert's neck, rotating his skull forcefully to a better angle. 'There. Over there. What's wrong with you?'

Albert avoided answering questions like that. Answering never helped. He couldn't see the ship because his eyes were liquid with anticipation and relief: the day he had dreamed of, longed for, was actually here. He couldn't wipe his tears away because he needed both hands to grip the branch on which they were both balanced, having climbed up to get a better view of the ocean from the edge of the forest. Staring blindly out to sea, alarm now fizzing in every vein, Albert risked a request.

'Please, Pa, just tell me what you can see yourself.'

He waited. His father would punish him with silence now, he was sure of it. Albert was wrong.

'A ship, of course,' Mr Peacock said slowly, as if he could hardly believe it himself. 'My kanakas at last.'

He swung his leg over the branch and jumped down, leaving the tree shaking. Albert clung on with closed eyes. He and Ada

had talked about this day for ever. He had promised himself and
he had promised her. So this was it. He had no choice but to
act. He slid after his father, tumbling awkwardly from the tree
like a blanket slipping from a hammock in the night. Landing
near the limp heap of bleeding goat, he crumpled onto hands
and knees, immobile with dismay at his father's next words.

'You stay here with that animal.' Mr Peacock fumbled with
the pack, and called to Sal. 'Here . . . you'll need the rope. Hang
the carcass up in the tree – let it bleed – you can butcher it while
I'm gone.'

'Stay?' said Albert, unfolding himself.

'You heard. Get a move on. That's enough mithering.'

'Wait . . . ' He thought of Lizzie's scorn, and Ada's urgings.
He had to stand up to his father today, or he would never, ever
get away from him. Do it once and for all. Change everything,
for ever. But still there was a bleating tremor in Albert's voice as
he made his polite request. 'Please, Pa. Please can you wait for
me?'

Mr Peacock couldn't. He was already going. Now he would
play the silence game.

'Let me come with you,' Albert pleaded. Head turned from
the animal's eye, he bent to grasp the goat's forelegs, bringing a
sour burning to his throat. He hastily swallowed it back. 'Look
. . . we can carry it together. We'll soon get it back, and then we
can butcher it later.'

'Too slow,' said Pa over his shoulder. Sal had already rushed
ahead. It was useless to try to call her back. 'You're always too
slow, and I'm in a hurry. Kanakas or no kanakas, I'll not have
this vessel sailing past, and I see no smoke yet.'

Running after Mr Peacock, head thrust forward, Albert threw

himself at his back. 'No!' he screamed. 'I'm coming with you.' Mr Peacock didn't stop. His son clung on, feet dragging, words stuttering. 'I'll come back for the goat,' he lied. 'I'll help with the bonfire. I'll do anything you want me to, but I won't stay now.'

A backwards kick, a jerk of jacket hem from grasping hands – as if loosening himself from a vicious dog – and Albert fell on his back, sprawled against a mass of tree roots. He pushed himself up right away, skinned spine stinging, determined to keep going. His father continued to plunge down the mountain side, back into the damp heat of the forest, crashing through ferns and trees faster and faster. The boy tripped and stumbled after him, voice and knees jarring and jolting.

'I can't stay,' Albert shouted. Parakeets squawked away in loud, colourful protest. 'I won't stay!'

The boy could have been invisible. He gave up shouting. It slowed him down too much. No time. One limb after the other, he pursued his father, lurching, staggering, falling, getting up again no matter how often his lame leg let him down. His ankles turned and burned, a stitch needled his side, and he was winded beyond words, but at last he reached his father's heels again, all the more determined.

'Wait, Pa, wait for me . . . ' His words gurgled out, almost incomprehensible. 'Please . . . wait. Please . . . listen.'

Mr Peacock kept going. Across the widening gap, Albert launched himself again with gritted teeth. Scrabbling at fustian, he managed to force an arm around his father's neck. His wrist was instantly twisted in a smarting grip, his feet swung briefly off the ground, and in a moment the boy was on his knees in front of his father, arms raised in supplication. Albert felt the spit spray in his face, watched its droplets quiver on his father's beard, refused to turn his head away. Inches apart, their eyes bulged at each other.

'You will do as I say, or—'

'I won't.'

His father dropped him in disgust, and began to unbuckle his belt. At this point, an invisible power, quite unexpected, lifted Albert's chest like wind filling a sail, like the breaching of a whale. Courage spouted from him.

'Hit me all you like. Go on. You always do. But I'm not staying here now. I will not stay on this island.' He stood up and, as if on the point of flight, leaned forward, knees bent, clenched fists behind him, eyes fearless. 'I'm leaving on that ship. You don't own me and you can't stop me. You'll see. You'll never stop me again.'

Swerving like a hunted kid, Albert dodged past his father, and down the track ahead of him. Then he flew. The angels were carrying him, he was sure. He felt lighter than air. He thought of wind, and clouds, and sea, and he gulped at the chance they offered. He'd thrown away his terror.

But he might as well have tried to run from a landslip. The first stone his father hurled struck the back of Albert's knee, bringing him down instantly. Before he could rise, a living breathing weight on his back was flattening his lungs. Bone ground on bone. An immense blow to his head.

47

'RELEASE MY BROTHER!' ROARS SOLOMONA. 'THIS is no kind of justice. Not earth's, nor heaven's. Kalala is innocent. I'll not see him punished any longer.'

Look how he stands, an unbowed tree, strength and sap and vigour enough for all of us. How he holds his calm and dignity, I cannot say. And if Mr Peacock could see him now, even he would tremble. I think of all the times I have longed to hear Solomona speak his mind, his own mind, his own alone, and not the mouthed words of another. Hearing it speak for me, here on this earth, with no thought of the next one, I am filled with joy and pride. What glory in this moment. We are brothers again, true brothers, as we were in childhood, when he put me on his back to save my feet from the sharp rocks hiding in the water, and he showed me how thinking sideways catches crabs, when he rolled to my mat and held me fast and sang in my ear till morning while a cyclone passed.

Queenie speaks for all her family but every one of them shares her outrage.

'What do you mean?' she cries, a shower of sparks – her mother's child. 'That's what we've come for! Help us! Quickly, while Pa's gone! We've come to free Kalala too! We must destroy his prison so there is nothing left of it.'

She runs straight to my bars and pulls with all her might as if she'd wrench them free unaided. All come quickly to surround me, shaking the hut, blow by blow, no system to their fury. When Billy vanishes, suddenly, my terror shadows him. I have no reason yet to trust him. When he returns, swinging the woodpile axe, my fear shouts loudly from me.

'Solomona!'

But Billy is smiling, fiercely, crookedly.

'This will be quickest. We'll make kindling of it all!' he cries – to my vast delight. Pineki helps him, and together they fell my prison, wall by shattered wall, and we jump away from its falling, and I laugh and cry for my new freedom until I'm standing only under the sky, scratched and weary, firewood all around, Vilipate unknotting my bonds. My arms fly up, released, and Solomona is there before me. We fall together, undivided, chest to chest, head to shoulder, the world in pieces round us.

Click, click, click. Pockets are emptied of stones. No need for these, says Solomona. What can one man do now against so many united? My brother no longer speaks of prayer or patience. He whispers only of the cross that rose up on the headland while they set themselves apart on the beach below, of their growing fears and slow understanding, and the urgent knowledge that they could not stand by.

'Why did you wait so long?' I ask him quietly.

Solomona shakes his head.

'False pride? The desire to do my duty? Fear? Confusion?'

'The reasons I always jump too soon,' I whisper.

'I'm sorry, Kalala. I was too slow to act, I know, too trusting maybe. But I never doubted you. Never, never would I have let you die.'

We draw apart reluctantly. So much to say. So much lost time. I know now Solomona has faith enough for two. He will know soon enough where my qualms and questions have brought us. We are both ready, I am certain. With my brother beside me, hearts reconciled, I will be able to return to the dreadful gully, and there I will tell him all I know, all I believe, all we can remember. An end and a beginning. And then there will be choices to make. More questions too. But all in time. First there's Lizzie.

One by one, my Island brothers embrace me, and then Ada brings me water, and I gulp it down, and she waits eagerly.

'Let's go now. Quickly. We have been too long already. Lizzie will be waiting.'

I feel the agitation in Pineki run high again – guilt at his first capitulation turned to a lust for revenge – and Solomona has to settle him, and Vilipate too. I set down my pannikin, see how it quivers. I gather all my powers, test my body's strength.

'Who has the gun?' I ask.

Solomona turns me round. I see Mrs Peacock coming towards us, eyes red and swollen. Hearing my question, she steps sideways, shifts the baby laid across her shoulder, bright eyes looking, looking, and raises her chin, so that I can see the key she wears on a black ribbon round her high-collared neck. A shudder runs through her breast, the spectre of all her weeping.

'She's locked the bullets in the trunk,' says Queenie, who supports her mother.

'There'll be no more violence here, I hope.' She slips the key inside her blouse to keep it out of sight.

'Mrs Peacock . . . ' I say, bowing my head. 'Thank you. For your faith in me.'

At first she doesn't answer. She seems bewitched, as if held by a trance. All the children, all us island fellows, we all wait uncertainly, unable to act before she gives us leave.

'He never could be stopped, you know, not Joseph. And I believe he will never, ever leave this island. So, however matters fall, we may have to leave him.'

'But we need to hurry now, Ma,' says Ada, anxiously. 'I promised Lizzie. We can lose no more time.'

Every part of me is impatient to find her.

'I'll wait here with Joey,' says Mrs Peacock. I remember how she waited alone before, when we first searched for Albert. 'Gussie, you stay with me.' She notices Solomona's hesitation. 'You go too. Go with Kalala. I'll look after the little ones. But you must all go. We'll need everybody's strength today.'

48

THE PATH IS BECOMING ROCKIER, AND STEEPER TOO. Pa keeps following Lizzie, begging her to speak to him.

'Lizzie, please, have compassion. Show some mercy. Can't you see I didn't mean to kill him? Can't you persuade your mother? Ada? You know what Albert was like. You can see how easily a thing like this can happen. You must understand. You always understand.'

She can hardly tell if he is offering her a confession or a denial.

'An accident,' he is saying. 'That's what it was. A terrible, terrible accident.'

No, not that. She shakes her head. She cannot keep it still. An accident is something that slips and falls. An accident is a gust of wind plucking at a sail or flame and catching hold while your eyes are somewhere else, something unstoppable, a fragmentation of fortune. It is pressure misapplied, a blade off course, slicing into flesh. Spilled milk, falling eggs, broken shells. A moment's misjudgement. That can be counted a mistake.

It is not a rock hammering on a skull. It is not the instant blindness of anger and injustice. It is not tyranny. Nor is it the seeping away of breath from your own flesh and blood.

Do not call this an accident, she thinks.

He's as blind now as when he lifted his rock-grasping hand to kill her brother. He'll never see his mistakes. Lizzie looks at her feet. A small pale scar made long ago by a leaping ember is soil-stained and hidden. All the bones there, everything inside that skin, the blood beneath, the sinews and veins, connecting everything, all that keeps moving her, backs away now from her father's entreaties, although she has issued no orders and would like her body to halt this retreat. Better to be a tree, dripping in mist, hanging with drifting moss and shining beetles, and play no part in human life at all. Better a plunging whale. A limpet.

There seems nothing familiar about her father's feet today. Other feet of other colours splay like his. Others have big toes which strain to separate from the rest, and nails as hard and yellow as hoof or horn. These feet belong to a man who has killed his son. Lizzie watches them turn repeatedly towards her own, toes crimped in despair, all connected to the heaving body they bear, the hands that paw at her, and the voice that comes from raw, wet lips:

'Talk to me, Lizzie.' Mr Peacock rushes at her and shakes her, again and again, so that metal and salt and a taste of terror seep into her mouth. 'Talk to me. Promise me you'll help me.'

'Ah-ah-ah-ah,' she hears her throat protest. 'Pa-ah-ah-ah.' She wants to spit, and spit at him. The urge bubbles inside her mouth and guts. She wants to tell him she despises him, and he will burn in hell for what he's done, but she can say nothing while he is shaking her like this, and her head is knocking back and forth, while her clamped arms flail at her sides and her fingers reach for air. The sheathed knife in her tunic pocket thuds against her thigh. But as suddenly as he has grabbed Lizzie, he releases her. As if someone has just told him what he's doing, and until then, he did not know. The lava subsides.

She has bitten her tongue. She wipes her mouth with the back of a hand.

'Lizzie?' he whimpers.

She has to speak.

'No, Pa. No. I'll not promise anything. I won't help you. I'll never work for you again. I can't forgive you.'

Snapping twigs and swishing leaves.

Father and daughter turn at once. Ada, thinks Lizzie, with a leap of hope. Kalala? They should soon be here. They'll help her. For all she longed for it, for all she needed it, her father's cracked confession is too vast and uncontainable a thing. And she can't tell how long it's taken. If she's too early here, or late. But she knows she can no longer bear it on her own.

The noise is just a goat lolloping through the undergrowth, a real one this time. Quite alone, moaning and anxious, it's looking for its own lost companions. *Meh, meh, meh.* Lizzie sees the killing look flit into her father's eye as he reaches for his own knife – he cannot help himself – and she turns aside. Hearing the steely whisper of blade returning to sheath, she begins to breathe again.

'Don't, Lizzie. Don't,' he whispers. 'I can't bear it. Don't look at me like that.'

What does he expect?

'When have I not taken care of you? When have I ever hurt you? And it was an accident,' he says, again.

'No,' she mutters. 'You know it wasn't.'

'What?' he shouts. 'Say it louder.'

'No!' she yells into the wind. 'No. Impossible.'

Dare she walk away from him?

'I meant to stop him. I wanted him to stay.'

'But you lied.'

'I can't hear you. Don't turn your back on me! Look at me, damn you.'

She obeys, briefly, for long enough to make her accusation again.

'You killed him and you lied, I said. You lied to us.'

There's the zigzagging track. Ada will soon be there. And the others. She only needs to hold him off a little longer.

'It was to protect you,' Pa shouts. 'That's all I've ever wanted. And what could you have done with the truth? How could it have helped you to know? It would have destroyed everything we have made here. I lied for all of us. You must see that. To help us all.'

'To help yourself,' she says, ready to flinch.

Nobody has come yet but there is nowhere left to walk. On the flat rocky outcrop of Goat Point, standing between her father and the ocean, she lays her final accusation at his feet.

'And now, to save yourself, you'd sacrifice Kalala.'

And she had let herself become complicit. Out of love and misplaced pride, she allowed her father to deform her heart. Truly, she is made in his mould. If the *Esperanza* had not come, would Albert be alive? Lizzie resists this self-deceiving train of thought. She sees now that Albert always lived in danger. There would have been some other kind of accident. There would have been another day when Pa came home alone.

Lizzie bears her own guilt. Shouldn't she pay too – for her willingness to see the world through her father's eyes for far too long, as if it would make her better, stronger, wiser, as if it would make him see her more clearly, love her more, raise her higher? A kind of greediness, for which she almost longs to take her punishment. She holds on to the thought of Ada, Queenie, and little Gus, all three taking care of Ma as she's always taken care of them. There's Billy too, who will take this hardest of all. She can't betray their faith, any more than she will betray Kalala a second time. She can only play for time. The others will soon be here. She'll have to keep him talking, and for that she needs moisture in her mouth. Her tongue still sticks. She'll have to hope the wind will disguise the way she shakes and trembles.

'So what now, Pa?' asks Lizzie. Her knees are bent and loose in readiness, and her bare toes grip the rock. Where *are* they? How much longer can she hold him off alone? What if they never come? Her hand wants to slip into her pocket. She almost lets it. All her body throbs. How can she hide fear like this? She echoes Queenie. 'What are we going to do?'

Mr Peacock holds his arms out on either side of him, palms down, slightly rising, slightly falling, in small soft jerks. Like a boy walking a fence. Almost like a hovering bird. He could be readying himself to catch her or to snatch at her. They are both exposed now, to each other, and also to the wind, which has stirred itself again and buffets and nudges and pushes them from all directions. Only the faintest turning up of his mouth, barely visible – you can hardly see his face for beard – but it seems to Lizzie at this moment that his eyes have been becalmed. Sky and sea at once, clear and blue but strangely tranquil. He's found a solution, she thinks. The habit of faith returns, irrepressible, against all logic, whetting hope and shaking purpose. Of course he has. Of course. He is going to repent now. He'll say he'll change. He will show the remorse she's sought all this time, alongside the regret. And then we will put our faith in Solomona to help us find forgiveness. It's possible.

There can be a future. Nothing is the end of everything.

Pa sweeps off his hat, as if it's a hindrance to his thoughts. Flying from his fingers, it's carried away by the wind in a trice, over the cliff edge and out to sea. He looks naked and unfamiliar without it, the bleached strip across his forehead which the sun never sees suddenly exposed to glaring daylight, as if years have flown away. Emptiness, not tranquillity. His tired and crumpled eyes lack all focus. His mouth loosens and opens. And then, without speaking, with no warning at all, he rushes towards her with such violent urgency that she ducks into a crouch. Hands bound round shins, eyes screwed up, knees jammed into her face, she balls herself up like a millipede. Her father knocks into her. She's thrown off balance, stiffly, onto her side. Her bony elbow crushed against the rock, her fingers still interlocked, she braces herself. She's sure a blow is coming. In that moment her mind is somewhere else. Floating, flying, hurtling. Her body is not hers. Becoming nothing at all, she can hold everything at bay.

Only for an instant.

No blow falls. A fear sharper than any physical injury uncoils her, and the shock that freezes her now is sharper still. Pa has ceased his headlong rush. He tilts on the very edge of life, standing too far for her to reach, too rapt. He lifts his arms and stretches them out again, horizontal, and becomes a man with wings. Hadn't she always known there was nothing he couldn't or wouldn't do?

Let him be. Ma's voice in her head. Let him be. Lizzie doesn't know if she can. If he turns now . . . if he sees her . . . won't that make him stay? Is she not enough? But the begging words won't come. She's almost certain she cannot bear for him to leave, but her silence proves she's wrong.

No.

She wants him to go. She wants him to fly away from here, and let *them* be. She will keep watch. Lizzie will be his witness now. And she stares and stares and stares, and even so, it's happened before she can register the moment. There he stands still. And then he doesn't. Perhaps she hears a cry. It could have been a seabird. Perhaps she cries out herself, at the vanishing she's somehow missed.

Pa's gone.

He's left them all behind.

A passing has taken place, a crossing over, a reversal of everything and always. Lizzie stands alone on the bare promontory, inside out, flayed, and also free.

*

She cannot stay here for ever. The others will find her when she's ready, and that's not yet. She turns her back on the sea and walks away. In time, the trees engulf her, the ocean is silenced and the light softens into something green, calm and translucent. The undersong changes. It's all birds and insects here, and the gentle stridulation of leaf on leaf. The hushed hiss of life uncurls out of sight, fern fronds stretch and yawn, lichen feathers across bark. White aprons gleaming, a pair of red-eyed pigeons land in a karaka tree to peck at its orange fruit. Other fruits fall and will rot where they lie, and seedlings will soon sprout, very soon, though other seeds will sleep for years, generations, and more will grow elsewhere too, wherever they are carried away and excreted, on other slopes and even smaller islands in this little chain, and some will drop into the impossibly deep waters between and disappear or be transported further still.

She walks for some hours, no particular place or object in mind, without coherence or direction. Lizzie is not yet ready for words. They dance without rhythm, orderless in her head, coming and going, haunting and taunting her. She tries to imagine these scraps of thought turned into letters, pinned onto paper. Or syllables scratched in ash or sand, washed away by water, rewritten again and again until they cannot be forgotten. She wishes, again and again, that her father had found a better word than accident, had remembered at last the word that she'd never heard him utter. But perhaps if she uses it often enough herself, she can make up for his forgetfulness. She will stitch it into her heart and onto her sleeve. She is sorry, sorry, sorry, so sorry.

The ground rises and falls, the air moistens and cools, and her feet find their purpose, taking her towards the clifftop overhanging the tangled shore where she took her first steps here, those gritty grey sands where a shipful of stolen men never found strength to walk at all and were reburied and unburied for months and years. She is ready to look out again and comes now to honour them, and their scattered children, and also Albert.

Coming out of the forest, it's like looking out on Clapperton Bay for the first time. Wheeling birds. Infinite blue. Then she discerns the sea's horizon, a curve so vast it presents itself as straight and flat. And by the time she has reached the contorted tree where she paused with her father long ago, waiting for Ada and Albert to climb the cliff face, she can make out the movement of the ridges of the ocean.

The wind is dropping. On white-capped waters, a ship lies at anchor.

She's like no other vessel that has ever passed this way, like nothing Lizzie has seen before in all her travels. Neither a schooner nor a steamship but something crossbred, a thing in-between: clipper-bowed and schooner-rigged, she has a hull of shiny black, boot-topped with pink, and her upper works are clean and bright and white. Two masts lean slightly back, either side of a yellow-painted funnel, black-banded. A few sketchy drifts of steam emerge. A launch is being lowered.

Unsettled, Lizzie squats to watch. Dark-clothed figures descend, limbs lost against the dark-sided ship, white faces shining. She observes their efforts to unload. They balance something on their rowing boat so long and awkward that it sticks out like an over-grown bowsprit. The boat is thrown onto the beach with disdainful force, dragged back out and in again, and it is only when the sailors have safely reached shore that she sees they are in uniform. Neat and orderly; she imagines blue serge blouses, peaked caps and pigtails. She squints at their commander and his gold-braided frock coat. Brass buttons, she fancies, too far away to see, shining below a chinstrap beard. The men look up at the cliffs in awe, and then away. She is invisible to them.

The commander moves out of sight, beyond the grove of trees, and Lizzie imagines then the muffled knock at their old and battered door, and remembers the way it used to scrape the clayed floor. She cannot see them, but she knows they are breathing in the must of neglect, poking fingers through layers of dried-out palm leaves. She can wait. She will be patient. And yes . . . soon they reappear, to consult with pointing fingers and nodding heads. They look at a chart. They make decisions. Over there. Yes.

(Another nod, perhaps.) That'll be the spot. The tall pole they have brought is a flagstaff. Quite unsuspecting of their audience, the men stand around the post, and salute. They look at each other briefly, then stare straight ahead.

Outrage shakes Lizzie back to her feet. She claws at the tree trunk, and hangs on, swaying, quite unable to trust her legs to take her down the cliff, unable to trust her tongue. 'Go away!' she screams, pointlessly. 'Thieves! Leave us alone!' It is like being back inside the dreams – entirely present, watching, something dissolving between her vision and herself, never able to intervene. Where is Pa to tell her what to do?

They must be singing, for surely their mouths open and shut in time with one another. Lizzie hears only wind and surf and a kind of high-pitched ringing inside her head. Disbelief increases her uncertainty. The smallest sailor – barely taller than Lizzie, barely older perhaps than Albert – steps forward and salutes again, and he begins to haul on the rope. Up, up, up. The others sing on. *God Save the Queen*? A flag uncrumples. The Union Jack is dancing on their island.

Lizzie watches, unseen, unsure, until she can bear it no longer. She cannot run all the way home, but she knows she must hurry to have any hope of warning the others. Or even of getting back before night's steady fall. She is carrying nothing to weigh her down, and, as always, the exhilaration of speed is a release for her. She lollops back, necessarily unsteady, and also instinctively careful and determined, negotiating familiar obstacles like rocks and roots and tree trunks with little heed, saving her mind for other discoveries, pressed steadily into shape by the changing rhythm of her stride. And that's when she decides. Whether Pa meant to free his family or himself or both together from the terrible burden of what he'd done was of no account. What he wanted no longer mattered. He had brought them all an ending, and, knowing everything that could be known, together they could now work out, all of them, what was to be done next.

She needed the hours she'd spent alone, but now she finds herself longing for other voices, and all the comfort of skin on skin and living bones beneath it. Lizzie keeps following the ridge, dreading the point where she will see the cross again, but she's not halfway across the island when she hears barking. Sal and Spy rush to her together, jumping up and down like puppies, falling against each other and pawing at her tunic before racing back through the trees to report on the trophy that is her finding. Who are they running back to? The sickening sensation of trapped hummingbird wings that has plagued Lizzie all day has risen higher; she feels it just below her breastbone, a keen piercing joy that lengthens her stride and feather-cools her face. Because she can see Kalala, at the top of the next slope, and although he immediately looks round to see where the others are, to tell them she is found, they must be hanging back, out of sight and earshot, and for the moment, he is alone, and there is nothing between them.

He looks behind him one more time, and because he's standing in the shade and twilight's coming Lizzie cannot make out his expression, but he has the advantage of higher ground, so he is with her fast enough for this not to matter, and when he reaches her he smells of salt and fresh sweat. They face each other, both a little breathless, arms straight out, hands clasped, as if at the end of a wild polka. Of course they've lost the gentle ease they used to share. Of course it may never return, not exactly the same. And the morning may bring the new ship to their bay, and the ground may shift again, and worst of all, Solomona and

Kalala and the rest may choose, instead of cotton, to take their pay in the coin still locked in the trunk with the bullets, and take their chances on another ship, and leave Monday Island for ever. Or they may not. So Lizzie speaks quickly.

'I'm sorry, Kalala. So sorry.'

His eyes move over her face, reading the story of the previous hours, reassuring himself.

'He's gone?'

Lizzie nods and shudders and says yes, even as she's also shaking her head and saying no, for who knows what kind of hauntings lie ahead? Kalala doesn't move, or look away, but he quietly absorbs the little she has said.

'Come,' says Kalala, as Lizzie's words pour out. There's too much still to say, far too much to answer. It will take all night, all week, all the time they have left, however much that is. His words as well as hers. Kalala has much to decide, she knows. Solomona too. 'Everyone is waiting. Let's walk.'

He keeps listening, head slightly turned as usual, so he can watch her words as well as catch them, and they both keep walking together, and when the dogs return to tell them the others are close by, they walk somewhat faster, though it's getting harder and harder to see. Lights flicker ahead, and there's a faint smell of burning mutton-bird oil, and at last here's Ada with a smoke-blackened lantern, and Queenie is with her, tall and brave, and Solomona too, who comes to walk beside Kalala when the path widens, an arm across his shoulders, and all the other Islanders, and finally Billy. They've all come together to find Lizzie, come to bring her home, where Ma is waiting for her, and where they will have to start living all over again, and now they will know far better how that can rightly be done. Of that she is quite certain.

Author's note

This book began with a conversation: on a rare visit to London, Madeleine Brettkelly, my aunt by marriage, told me the story of her uncle, 'King' Bell, who was born at the end of the nineteenth century on Raoul Island (Rangitāhua) in the Kermadecs, a remote chain of volcanic islands about halfway between New Zealand and Tonga. Raoul was called Sunday Island when the Bell family became its only inhabitants in 1878. Monday Island is an imagined version of their home, and while the Peacocks are all entirely fictional, some of their early experiences closely echo those of the Bells – as recounted by King's sister Bessie in her old age for Elsie K. Morton's book, *Crusoes of Sunday Island* (1957). Thank you, Madeleine Brettkelly, for sharing your memories of King and his family, and even more thanks to you and Arthur and to all your children too – Tony, Jody, Sharon and Pietra – for responding so enthusiastically to the idea that I might find a novel in your family history, and for both putting me up and putting up with all my questions.

Thank you, Pietra, for introducing me to Gregory O'Brien. Thank you, Greg, for introducing me to Steven Gentry's comprehensive and beautifully illustrated history of New Zealand's northernmost islands, *Raoul and the Kermadecs* (2013), and also putting me in touch with Bronwen Golder, director of the Pew Bertarelli Ocean Legacy Project's Kermadec/Rangitāhua Ocean Sanctuary initiative in New Zealand/Aortearoa. Thank you, Bronwen, and thank you, Pew Trusts, for research support from the earliest to the latest stages of writing and thinking, and even more for finally making it possible for me to get to the Kermadecs – one of the world's most significant and unspoiled ocean environments. Hannah Prior and the Sir Peter Blake Trust welcomed me on a quite unforgettable voyage, and got me as close to Raoul as was within their powers. Hannah, I can't thank you enough. I learned a vast amount from the entire Young Blake Expeditions crew, scientists, student voyagers and educators alike – thank you all. Thank you, Commander Matt Wray and everyone on board HMNZS Canterbury for looking after us with such warmth, good humour and efficiency. Thanks to Giselle Clark and Simon Nathan for sharing your experiences and photographs of Raoul, Giselle on board, and Simon earlier in the book's journey.

Islanders from Niue worked on Raoul at various times in the two islands' histories, but, as far as I know, few of their names have been recorded. Kalala, Solomona and their companions are all entirely fictional, but I couldn't have imagined them, nor their English missionary, without Margaret Pointer's *Niue 1774-1974: 200 years of contact and change* (2015) and the archives of the London Missionary Society at SOAS. I'd like to thank all the libraries and archives I've used in writing this book, and their librarians and archivists. Sources have been many and varied. More details are on my website: www.lydiasyson.com

My Royal Literary Fund Writing Fellowship at The Courtauld

Institute of Art allowed me time, space and an income while I wrote this book: I am extremely grateful to both institutions and their very supportive staff.

So many people have been generous with encouragement, advice and reading at various crucial stages: particularly warm thanks to Ioane Aleke Fa'avae, Mark Derby, Tig Thomas, Natasha Lehrer, Antonia Byatt and Kate Summerscale. Thank you, Alexandra Allden and Naomi McCavitt for the most exquisite cover. Sarah Odedina and Naomi Colthurst were the editors who started the ball rolling long ago – thank you for believing in this book at its birth. Eleanor Dryden nurtured it into what it has become with insight, grace and boundless faith. How can I thank you enough for that? Thanks to everyone else at Bonnier Zaffre for all you've done – especially Sarah Bauer and Tara Loder. Thank you, Catherine Clarke, my indescribably kind and brilliant agent. And thanks beyond thanks to all my family, Martin most of all. Writing without my beloved sister Antonia as a reader will be much harder now, but I know that her wisdom and integrity will always be with me.

For your Reading Group

For discussion

- Did your understanding of the book's title change through the course of reading the novel? To what extent did any of the characters – or indeed anything else – really belong to Mr Peacock?

- When Lizzie finally speaks to her father alone, he says:

  'It was to protect you. That's all I've ever wanted. And what could you have done with the truth? How could it have helped you to know? It would have destroyed everything we have made here. I lied for all of us. You must see that. To help us all.'

  To what extent would this have been true had the ship not arrived at the moment it did? Would the family have had the strength and will to turn on their father without the catalyst of the ship's arrival?

- Early in the novel, Lizzie overhears the following conversation in Mr Peacock's bar:

  'You could be king of the Kermadecs,' the speaker assured him.
  'So you say.'
  'Because it's the truth.'
  'And I believe you.'
  Did Pa believe him? Lizzie wasn't certain.

  Do you think Mr Peacock ever truly believed this?

- After it has been revealed that the Peacock children can't read, Lizzie thinks the following:

   She suspects Kalala pities them. Certainly he looks at them oddly. We do not meet his expectations, she thinks, any more than he meets ours.

   To what extent do you think Kalala pities them? What is the role of expectation in the novel? In what ways did the characters conform to or diverge from your own expectations?

- When the family are discussing whether to move to the island, the following exchange takes place:

   'So that makes us the natives,' said Harriet, thoughtfully.
   'Certainly not!' her mother snapped.
   'Natives are born in a place,' explained Ada. 'We're going to this island. We don't come from it.'
   Albert frowned. There was more to it than that. There was a pause while the children separately reflected on the question, and wondered exactly where they did come from. They'd all – except Gussie – been born in different parts of New Zealand. Would they always be settlers?

   Is there an answer to Albert's question? How do you imagine the Peacock children's future after the novel ends? Will they ever feel they belong in a place, or will they simply come and go?

- When Lizzie, Ma and Queenie open *The Family Shakspeare*, the first play they read is *The Tempest*. What do you think is the significance of this?

- After Ada reveals the full extent of Mr Peacock's treatment of Albert, Lizzie begins to blame herself:

  For days she has battled with her instinct to deny what Ada has told her, and her fury at her sister's new evasions. Fathers were always fast with their fists when it came to sons. Weren't they? Lizzie is no longer certain. The family has lived so much apart from others. Hard to know what was too much or not enough of anything. In her indifference, in her failure to imagine another way of being, perhaps she had been as cruel as Pa.

  Do you agree with Lizzie's view here, that she is partly to blame and perhaps complicit? Could she have known differently, given the unusual nature of her upbringing? Could she have been expected to imagine another way of being?

- When Mr Peacock imprisons Kalala, Kalala is puzzled as to why Solomona is not defending him:

  My fury surges back, and I think to push myself against him. Instead I turn to Solomona, who stands as astonished as the rest. I am certain he will speak at least a word for me before they leave. Yet he shakes his head and makes a movement with his hands like smoothing sand.

Does Solomona betray his brother by not speaking out earlier? Does this change your view of him? Does Kalala see too much goodness in his brother?

- The author gives us direct access to Kalala's thoughts, but the passages from the point of view of the Peacocks are written in the third person. Why do you think the author decided to do this? Did it affect your reading of the novel?

Suggested further reading on related themes

Things Fall Apart by Chinua Achebe

The Coral Island by R. M. Ballantyne

The Luminaries by Eleanor Catton

Tapu by Judy Corbalis

'The Solitude of Alexander Selkirk' – by William Cowper in
    Poems, Volume II

The Life and Adventures of Robinson Crusoe by Daniel Defoe

Father and Son: A Study of Two Temperaments by Edmund Gosse

Black Narcissus by Rumer Godden

Lord of the Flies by William Golding

Seven-Tenths: The Sea and its Thresholds by James Hamilton-Paterson

'Our Sea of Islands' by Epeli Hau'ofa

The Bone People by Keri Hulme

Brave New World by Aldous Huxley

Mister Pip by Lloyd Jones

The Poisonwood Bible by Barbara Kingsolver

Rain and Other South Sea Stories by W. Somerset Maugham

Typee: A Peep at Polynesian Life by Herman Melville

Cloud Atlas by David Mitchell

Georges Baudoux's Jean M'Baraï: The Trepang Fisherman, translated
    by Karin Speedy

The Ebb-Tide and *Island Nights' Entertainments* by R.L. Stevenson

Salt Creek by Lucy Treloar

Mr Fortune's Maggot by Sylvia Townsend Warner

Little House series by Laura Ingalls Wilder

The Swiss Family Robinson by Johann David Wyss